THE QUANTUM GAMES

ROBABLY

ROBABLY.COM

Copyright © 2024 Robert Valerius

All rights reserved

The characters and events portrayed in this book are fictitious. Any similarity to real persons, living or dead, is coincidental and not intended by the author.

No part of this book may be reproduced, or stored in a retrieval system, or transmitted in any form or by any means, electronic, mechanical, photocopying, recording, or otherwise, without express written permission of the publisher.

ISBN-13 (Paperback): 979-8-9911388-0-2

Cover design by: Denver Rosario
Instagram: @Dennyver, @intothedennyverse
Website: https://www.dennyver.com

Logo design by: Jino Kopiako
Instagram: @dang.team
Website: https://linktr.ee/jinokopiako, dangteam.com

Library of Congress Registration Number: TXu 2-437-579

DEDICATION

To Linnea and Emery,

May you grow up with a love for fantasy books as deep as your Dad's. Strive to be the best you can be, but remember to embrace life's joys and cherish every moment.

To my incredible Wife, Beverly Grace,

Your support through countless long nights and hours has been nothing short of amazing. I hope this book brings us closer to that well-deserved vacation for you.

CONTENTS

The Quantum Games
Copyright
Dedication
Chapter One — 1
Chapter Two — 9
Chapter Three — 16
Chapter Four — 21
Chapter Five — 26
Chapter Six — 32
Chapter Seven — 39
Chapter Eight — 44
Chapter Nine — 53
Chapter Ten — 65
Chapter Eleven — 71
Chapter Twelve — 76
Chapter Thirteen — 84
Chapter Fourteen — 90
Chapter Fifteen — 96

Chapter Sixteen	101
INTERMISSION HERO UPDATES #1	109
Chapter Seventeen	118
Chapter Eighteen	123
Chapter Nineteen	131
Chapter Twenty	137
Chapter Twenty-One	143
Chapter Twenty-Two	148
Chapter Twenty-Three	154
Chapter Twenty-Four	160
Chapter Twenty-Five	165
Chapter Twenty-Six	176
Chapter Twenty-Seven	182
Chapter Twenty-Eight	191
Chapter Twenty-Nine	196
Chapter Thirty	203
Chapter Thirty-One	209
Chapter Thirty-Two	217
Chapter Thirty-Three	223
Chapter Thirty-Four	229
Chapter Thirty-Five	235
INTERMISSION HERO UPDATES #2	240
Chapter Thirty-Six	250
Chapter Thirty-Seven	256
Chapter Thirty-Eight	262
Chapter Thirty-Nine	268
Chapter Forty	274
Chapter Forty-One	281

Chapter Forty-Two	286
Chapter Forty-Three	294
Chapter Forty-Four	304
Chapter Forty-Five	310
Chapter Forty-Six	318
Chapter Forty-Seven	325
Chapter Forty-Eight	331
Chapter Forty-Nine	338
Chapter Fifty	343
Chapter Fifty-One	349
Chapter Fifty-Two	353
Chapter Fifty-Three	360
Chapter Fifty-Four	367
Chapter Fifty-Five	372
INTERMISSION HERO UPDATES #3	376
Chapter Fifty-Six	386
Chapter Fifty-Seven	391
Chapter Fifty-Eight	397
Chapter Fifty-Nine	402
Chapter Sixty	408
Chapter Sixty-One	414
Chapter Sixty-Two	420
Chapter Sixty-Three	427
Chapter Sixty-Four	432
Chapter Sixty-Five	439
Chapter Sixty-Six	445
Chapter Sixty-Seven	452
Chapter Sixty-Eight	459

Chapter Sixty-Nine	464
Epilogue	473
Post Author Note	479
Acknowledgement	483
About the Author	485

CHAPTER ONE

"When the world changes, you can either stay who you are or become who you were meant to be."

SYSTEM HEADQUARTERS

"In three days, the System will spring to life within the Galaxy known as the Milky Way. Reports suggest that the management is nearly, if not entirely, assembled, guaranteeing the strategic positioning of the tournament's most promising contenders," Shukar conveyed to Viggo Platard, the Head Director of this cycle's Quantum Games.

"Good," the director replied. "I am glad we finally stabilized after a few early mishaps. Do we suspect those will affect the contestants this year?"

"No, sir. Blips were managed effectively. While we did have a few more powerful ones this year compared to previous years, these are always expected. The barriers across the civilized planets are designed to shut down in waves until the go-live date."

"Shukar, thank you for your steadfast support over the past half-century. Let's ensure our fans experience a tournament they'll never forget."

∆∆∆

EARTH

Emy & James

The athletic director was livid. "She's done! She's off the team. That was unacceptable," he exclaimed.

Coach Williams defended Emy, "She went for the ball, Steve. It was a clean play."

"That's not what the referee said or, mind you, the other teams' parents. This can't keep happening. I've had more calls about your girls' club this year than all my other programs combined. Make this right, or I will."

Emy replayed the conversation she had overheard while sitting outside the athletic director's office the previous day. She knew she had made a clean play. Could they kick her off the team for that?

Anxious, nervous, and distraught, she rapidly tapped her #2 pencil on her desk. It wasn't until she felt the stares of her classmates that she looked up and saw the entire class, plus a glaring teacher, looking back at her. Her vibrant red hair had often drawn attention, but this felt unusually intense. Then, she became aware of the disruptive noise her pencil was creating.

"Sorry," Emy sighed as the class turned back around, and James nudged her slightly.

"You good?"

Emy nodded, took another deep breath, and forced herself to focus on the things she could control. Regardless of the outcome, she might as well not flunk this mid-term chemistry exam.

> When solid sodium metal reacts with chlorine gas, what compound is produced? Write the balanced chemical equation for this combination reaction.

Smiling to herself, Emy immersed herself in the question. She envisioned sodium (Na) and chlorine (Cl_2) melding together. It wasn't a conscious effort; she enjoyed it, and the answer materialized as the elements fused in her mind. Her teachers had always emphasized the Lewis Dot structure of molecules, but her brain had its way of visualizing it even before those lessons. After years of studying chemistry, her mind adopted this traditional view.

Refocusing on the test at hand, Emy confidently wrote the equation and answer of NaCl, commonly known as sodium chloride or table salt.

Emy walked to the front of the class as she finished the test, passing other students still engrossed in their questions.

"See you at practice today," Professor "Coach" Williams gestured with a smirk as Emy set down her test. Filled with newfound hope, she slung her backpack over her shoulder. The white letters spelling "Mighty Eagles" were embroidered across the back of her bag. She then stepped into the hallway of the education building's second floor. Leaning over the railing, she watched the students in the foyer below while waiting for James.

Quill Creek College wasn't her top pick for soccer programs but wasn't at the bottom of her list either. Nestled in the charming town of Quincy, California, it quietly existed along State Highway 70, a local community college with minimal fanfare—except for a few discreet signs scattered around the town.

Emy had found solace while at the junior college, but an insistent feeling tugged at her—a yearning for something more. She was a standout athlete in high school, earning the prestigious State first-team all-league title as a soccer goalkeeper. Soccer became her refuge when she first laced her cleats and slipped on her gloves during a local Reno kid's soccer program. On the field, the chaos of life settled, and Emy could immerse herself in the game—protecting the goal, leading her defense, and supporting her teammates with unwavering focus.

When the referee's whistle blew, the world shifted once more. Doctors, teachers, and even her parents attributed it to

ADHD and various other diagnoses, but Emy felt there was more to it. She could concentrate when needed and even achieve hyper-focus when she chose. However, when her mind wandered, reality would blur, shapes would dance, and people seemed less tangible. Imagine English and Math, where words and numbers perpetually swirl around you.

Despite her accolades in soccer, her grades suffered, causing her to miss out on a spot at a larger Division One (D1) college straight out of high school. D1 represents the largest and most competitive four-year college athletic programs, while Division Two (D2) is a step-down but still highly competitive. On the other hand, junior colleges are smaller two-year programs that allow athletes and students to join, showcase their talents, or improve their grades before transferring to a four-year college.

In response, Emy devised a short-term plan: start at a junior college, improve her grades, and then move on to a more extensive four-year program, all while in search of herself. Soccer was her passion, enriching her life, but it wasn't her entire existence. Now, a nagging question haunted her: What would she become without soccer?

"Dude, what's up with you today?" James's sudden appearance made Emy jump, the classroom door closing behind him.

"What? Bitter about being the runner-up once more?" she teased, making light of the situation that James had just been bumped from his starting position on the football team.

"Too soon," James murmured. "No, seriously, you've been in a different world lately. Even for you, this is strange."

"I'm sorry. My head is just… I don't know," Emy hesitated.

"I'm still waiting for the Athletic Director's verdict on my future as a Mighty Eagle," she replied, attempting to shift the conversation with a touch of sarcasm. "You're good at everything—even if you're now the backup quarterback. I can't imagine a future where you're not successful.

"You know that wound is still fresh, right?" James protested with a tinge of sadness in his voice. "I was just demoted last practice. I'm still attempting to accept that I am a second-choice junior college athlete."

Emy responded bluntly, "You could fail and drop out tomorrow, and nothing would change. Your parents can send you to any four-year school nationwide, give you the choice of any degree, and help you move on with your life. I should start calling you Dr. Gray now."

James's frustration bubbled over. "Why is that always everyone's argument? Do you think I can just get out and move on? Ahh, let's go," he added, exasperated.

Unlike Emy, James grew up in a prominent wealthy household near the base of Mount Rose. This allowed his parents to be close enough to get up to the mountain slopes while still enjoying the broader Reno community.

Emy and James, friends since elementary school, had decided to enroll at Quill Creek together. Growing up, Emy often visited James's house after school, drawn by the perks of a big house with a pool and a distinct lack of adults. Friends came and went, but their bond remained strong. Since middle school, they had an unspoken pact: stick together whenever possible. This led many to speculate about James, the handsome, slender star athlete with striking silver hair and a continuous sparkle in his eyes, and Emy, the equally captivating high school soccer standout, known for her red hair and large blue eyes. Although often seen in leggings and team-issued soccer clothing, Emy's athletic physique, a testament to her dedication at the gym, still caught many people's attention. Despite the rumors, their friendship remained constant throughout the years.

Each Tuesday, Emy and James adhered to their unwritten rule: grab lunch after Chemistry. It was the only class they shared this semester. After a 90-minute lecture, they would head to Norma's Thunder Café, nestled near downtown Quincy. The cozy spot was just a beat away from campus.

"What are you going to do?" James asked Emy, grabbing the

fresh sandwiches from Norma, the owner, and settling into a seat.

"I don't think there's anything I can do now. I just have to go and face the music. You saw the play. What did you think?"

"Yeah, me and everyone else in the stands. That play was nuts. It looked like a fifty-fifty ball in the box, but when you two collided, the girl went flying. Shoot, Emy. After that play, all the football players stood and roared at the sudden action. You were a hero."

James's recollection triggered Emy's memory to come back. It was a Sunday afternoon in the fall, the sixth soccer game of the year. Her team was playing against the Lassen "Mighty" Cougars. James and Emy joked that 50% of the junior colleges had a "Mighty" mascot. Fast forward to the game's final ten minutes: Emy was pitching a shutout as the goalie, and the score was 1-0. The game had been close, with only a few shots on goal. But a lucky steal and a long strike by a midfielder sent the soccer ball over her defense's head, landing just short of the box. Courtney Weaver, Lassen's star striker, lunged for the ball, ready to take her shot. Unbeknownst to her, Emy surged forward, intercepting the ball precisely when Courtney did. It felt like the world had shifted off balance in that fleeting moment. The next thing Emy became aware of was the unified stare of everyone around her, and their attention riveted on Courtney. She was now lying flat on her back, blood tracing a network of lines down her face along with her hair marred with grass stains.

Emy stepped back, bewildered by the feeling that just came over her and the abrupt hush that enveloped the crowd. She gazed at Courtney sprawled before her on the turf, a mix of concern and confusion in her eyes. The referee's whistle pierced the air, and he sprinted toward the scene, brandishing a red card. Emy stood frozen, too stunned to react, while the stands erupted in a cacophony of cheers and gasps from the football athletes.

"Fu-ry! Fu-ry! Fu-ry! Fu-ry!"

As for the cheer squad, their relentless "Fury" chants didn't exactly enhance Emy's image during that memorable soccer match. She glanced at James across the table.

"I appreciate the support, but could you ask the guys to ease up on the 'Fury' chants? Courtney's mom didn't seem thrilled with the yelling for the rest of the match in those tiny stands," Emy requested, feeling a bit embarrassed

James chuckled. "Sure, Fury. But getting Will to listen? Now that's a challenge. Will must have been having a party after the game, as he even managed to stir up excitement with Frank and Tuck. The three-hundred-pound pair practically ripped their shirts in two, screaming for you."

Emy laughed, picturing the scene. "Frank makes sense, but Tuck? Maybe he was just excited to divert attention from himself. I hear Tuck's been racking up penalties on the football field. Is he suspended for this weekend's game?"

"Yeah, he's a gentle giant but channels his anger on the field. Two personal fouls in the last game got him ejected, earning him a one-game suspension. At least he has a good story for not playing this weekend."

"That reminds me, who's this new guy that stole my best friend's starting spot?" Emy returned with a question.

James let out a weary breath. "His name's Trent," he said, "and he turned up this weekend. He was at Will's usual weekend bash, but I can't fault the coach. Our team is on fire, and this impressive start has caught some attention. He was at USC last year and got into some undisclosed trouble. The guy's got an arm like a cannon and might be the fastest player on the team."

James didn't voice it, but the team was more than good. Their 4-0 start was the best in the school's history. Having led his high school team to a state title, James was no stranger to winning; winning was his norm. However, junior college football presented a different dynamic. Here, individual numbers and statistical success often outshone team achievements. The more talent a school had, the better the scouts it attracted. After just two years, this led to a higher turnover to more extensive four-year programs. This turnover rate, in turn, attracted more talent, perpetuating the cycle.

"I haven't met a player on the team who doesn't love you, James. Those guys would force the coach to take a different path if you weren't so damn noble in your actions. You and I know they are better off with you, even if you don't have a great nickname to back you up." Emy smiled, attempting to take some pressure off the conversation, but something wasn't right.

The room vibrated as a short burst of energy washed into the café. Objects shook, and the table Emy held felt like it sank into itself as if its density suddenly changed. Before she knew it, the room stabilized, and the energy seemed to fade.

CHAPTER TWO

"Whether driven by life, luck, or fate, some heroes seem to be chosen by the gods themselves." – Fan.

THE PREVIOUS SATURDAY

Tuck

"GO EAGLES!" roared multiple voices as a car sped toward the street, leaving the parking lots closest to the football fields.

"We better see you at Will's place, Tuck!" the voices continued to yell as the car disappeared.

Tuck reached his '97 Bronco in the parking lot, glancing back at the dimming lights over the football fields. He knew he was gradually losing his chance at a promising future. This marked his second year in the program, and while he had garnered decent attention from several D1 schools, they all fell silent after a series of incidents this year.

What is wrong with me? Tuck wondered as he packed up his gear, tossing it into the back of the truck. His uniform landed atop several other unwashed practice jerseys. The mingling scents of body odor, grass, and blood stains forced his thoughts back to the allure of playing at the D1 level—the promise of laundry services and the potential for a brighter path.

This marked the third time within four games this year that Tuck hadn't completed a match. Throughout his life, Tuck had been known for giving his all. His dedication extended beyond the field, evident in the furious workouts that shaped his physique. He never missed a practice, and no coach or teacher had to ask him twice about anything. It was how he'd been raised by his mom in the small town of Dayton, just outside Carson City, Nevada. With his father having been incarcerated since he was just eight, Tuck's life story could easily lead one to make assumptions. Yet, his clean-cut appearance and composed demeanor would dispel any notions that his father was serving time in the local prison.

"Don't shame your family any more than your father has already done," Tuck's mom would say.

Amidst a few more honks and cheers, Tuck climbed up the side rail as the truck shifted and accepted his weight. He might as well celebrate with the team; they all knew he wouldn't have many more chances after this year.

The party was at the same place every week: Will's house. With limited bars and plenty of underage drinking, house parties became a nightly ritual for most kids in school. After the initial weeks of parties, the neighbors—though more spread out than typical suburban areas—realized they were in a losing battle this year. Mostly ranch hands and older folks, they didn't mind the parties as long as they didn't venture too far into their properties.

Tuck took the keys out of the ignition, breathing deeply as he attempted to push the night's events and subsequent thoughts to the back of his mind. Shutting the door, he stepped out onto the sidewalk.

"Damn, Tuck, we know the neighbors don't care too much about us partying, but do you have to slam your door before the party even starts?" Will, the resident home renter, and fellow Eagles football player chided.

"Oops, sorry, Will. I guess these old doors make more noise than you think."

Tuck glanced back at the old Bronco, which had a few dents in the door frame. Did he slam it without thinking?

"It's all right. It's becoming a sign that the party is about to start when Big Tuck shows up."

Tuck gave a slight smile. "Great game tonight, Brick. I'm bummed for missing your 4th down shutdown over Nick

Reese. I heard you locked him up and closed the game for us."

Unlike Tuck's large form, Will had a lean, muscular build but equally striking good looks. His presence exuded charm, and his approachable demeanor made him well-liked by everyone. On the field, Will played cornerback for the Eagles because he couldn't catch a ball even if it was tossed underhanded straight at his face. He was always assigned to guard the top wide receiver on the opposing team. Tonight, he locked onto Reese, a top Division 1 recruit in Nevada, holding him to just two catches for only 15 yards. Due to his talent as a lockdown corner, combined with the catching ability of a three-year-old, Will quickly earned the nickname "Brick." While Will took it as a reference to the wall he built in front of the wideout he was guarding, the rest of the team had different interpretations.

"Thanks, Tuck. We've got to fix that temper of yours. The team missed you out there. But none of that tonight; it looks like the start of a fun one. The usuals are inside, and our star QB decided to show up."

"James made it out?"

"Nah, Silver Hair didn't make it, but his replacement did and seems to have his eyes locked on Nadia tonight."

Will passed by Tuck, giving him a friendly shoulder bump, and grabbed the 18-pack from the back of his truck to bring inside. Ripping the top off, he tossed one over his shoulder toward Tuck with a side wink.

"Thanks, Will."

Tuck cracked open a beer, took a quick sip, and headed inside. As always, he walked into the house to blaring music and a chorus of cheers from his friends. The house had a living room—or, in this case, a dance area—in the front, with couches around it, opening up to a kitchen at the back. Not being much of a dancer, Tuck made a beeline for the kitchen.

"Yo, Tuck, right? Hell of a hit out there tonight. You messed up that kid nicely."

Tuck glanced toward the couches and saw the new replacement QB lounging lazily with a hand draped over

Nadia, who sat beside him. Both held mixed drinks in hand, and the familiar earthy scent was hanging in the air. Tuck glanced at Nadia, then looked back at Trent.

"Not my finest hour, but I'm happy the team pulled it out. How's your first weekend in Quincy?"

Trent exuded an air of superiority, his tall, tanned, muscular physique and toned arms and chest a testament to the hours spent at the gym and likely the beach or tanning bed. Dressed in a dark V-cut shirt and a large gold chain necklace, he wore his confidence like a badge. With a cocky grin, Trent smirked at Tuck, taking another long drink from his glass before glancing over at Nadia. "Just living the dream, friend."

Taking it as a sign to exit and wanting to leave the room, Tuck nodded and headed into the kitchen.

"Heyyyyyy, Tuck! The keg is ready for you!" fellow lineman Frank shouted, mouth still full of the sandwich he had been eating.

"Hey, Frank. I should have known you would be here, stuffing your face as always. Do you ever leave this house?"

"Will ought to realize by now that leaving bread out is practically an invitation for me to eat it. With the school workshop closed and football finished for the evening, the only activity left... is drinking."

Frank Arhest, with his short blond mullet and soft eyes, had a down-to-earth charm that was hard to ignore. He and Tuck had formed a solid friendship since their first day of practice last year. Both were sophomores at the school, but their paths diverged beyond that point. While Tuck dedicated himself to football, Frank pursued a different passion. He enrolled in the college's renowned welding program, playing football merely to pass the time and make some friends. Despite their contrasting pursuits, Frank's dedication, unpretentious persona, sturdy build—though a bit more round than defined—and skills on the field made him a valuable football asset for the school, much like his friend Tuck.

Laughter and banter continued as Tuck fulfilled his party

duty and caught up with the other people around the house. Say one thing about Quill Creek: there might not be much to do, but with enough alcohol and loud music, anyone could have a good time.

As the night progressed, Tuck started to feel like himself again. Regardless of the drinks, laughter, and jokes, good friends always did the trick.

With a jolt of music from the door to the living room opening again, Trent strode into the kitchen with two empty drinks. He poured generously into one of the glasses, then looked back at the guys around the room.

"You boys ready to see a real QB in action this week?"

With a few exchanged glances and an attempt to keep the fun night going, Frank, standing next to Tuck, made the first comment.

"We've been hearing some good things from Coach about you. Excited to have you on the team."

"That makes one of us," Trent said, lifting his glass. "Here's to getting out of this place."

He took a quick drink and headed back into the living room.

"Seems a little early for that type of talk," Frank commented as Trent left the kitchen.

"Let's just give him the benefit of the doubt. We all know how hard it was to come in here the first week," Tuck stated, taking another sip and walking toward the exit.

"I think I am going to get some air. I'll be back."

With that, he opened the door to the blare of music and stepped away from the crowd. It wasn't the first time he'd seen Trent pouring drinks tonight, and he had to check on a few things in the other room. Moving to the side, Tuck leaned against the wall and took another drink, his gaze drifting towards a particular figure.

Nadia and Trent had moved couches at some point, and Tuck watched as Trent gave the drink to the more petite girl. Nadia, a paradox of beauty and subtlety, was frequently present at these parties. Her stunning features were consistently downplayed by her casual attire and low-key demeanor, making her blend seamlessly into the crowd. Yet, her quiet, reserved nature and the ever-present drink or joint in her hand made her stand out to those who knew where to look. He didn't know much about her other than the half smile they always exchanged in passing, a smile that held a mysterious charm.

Holding the drink, Nadia took a whiff of it, shrugged off the arm draped over her shoulders, and made her way upstairs to the restroom. Girls were known to venture upstairs to the bathroom, as the one on the bottom floor of the place occasionally had a slug or two coming out of the floors. Having your flats get stuck on the floor was a challenging experience. Tuck didn't mind too much because, hey, what do you expect when the floor is covered with cheap beer and piss marks?

Left alone on the couch, Trent put down his drink, smiled at a few people dancing, and proceeded upstairs to follow Nadia.

Tuck sighed. Having frequented enough parties, he knew a red flag when he saw one. Frustrated that this would be the start of their relationship after tonight, he put down his drink and headed up the stairs to follow Trent.

"Hey, Trent, what are you looking for up here?" Tuck caught Trent as he headed down the hallway toward the bathroom.

"Huh?" Trent seemed caught off guard. "Oh, uh, just looking for the bathroom. Bit new here and wasn't sure where to go."

Even having seen Trent regularly use the downstairs bathroom, Tuck gave him an out.

"Ah, we usually use the downstairs one. This one is typically reserved for the girls. They called dibs once they saw the floor in the other one."

"Got it, got it. Let me head back down and look for that one then."

As Trent descended the stairs, Tuck waited and knocked on the bathroom door. With no answer and no lock, Tuck opened the door to an empty room.

Tuck proceeded to check the remaining open rooms and

once again didn't find anyone. Shaking his head, he headed back downstairs to the party.

What the heck?

CHAPTER THREE

"The best part about the Games is the players' candidness. These people are just thrust out of normal lives and into a new world. It makes them so human!" – Fan.

Nadia

This wasn't Nadia's first time making a hasty retreat from a party through a second-floor exit, but she hoped it would be her last. Dusting off her jeans and nursing a soon-to-be bruise on her thigh from the fall, she realized her descent from the gutter might have been louder than she had intended. Midway down the house, she crashed into the lawn—or, more accurately, the weeds and dirt—befitting the status of a mere college rental property.

After cleaning herself up a bit, Nadia took a deep breath, reflecting on how awkward the night had become. She attended these parties to feel something, even though she often projected a "leave me alone" vibe. Letting the music and festivities wash over her, she sought out the most inebriated individuals to avoid lengthy conversations. Nadia was aware of her own attractiveness. She had a slender, well-toned figure with curves, dark black hair, olive skin, and a button nose. However, her minimal makeup, loose jeans, covered top, and black jacket left much to the imagination. Still, it seemed Trent had a vivid imagination of his own.

To avoid confrontation, Nadia allowed the boy to sit beside her multiple times during the night. While she didn't appreciate it when he put his arm around her, leading her to shift seats to move away from him continuously, he brought her drinks and mostly chatted with the people around her instead of with her. He didn't seem to care much about what she had to say, and that was fine. When that last drink arrived, she knew where he was trying to take this. While Nadia could probably handle that much alcohol and more, Trent didn't know that and was trying to push things in his favor. Rather than deal with the drama of rejecting him, she chose the path of a hurting thigh and an Irish exit, which was a new goodbye strategy for her. Coming from a Filipino background, goodbyes were always an hour-long process at parties. When her mom led her to believe they were leaving, she knew she only then had the fun of talking to every single auntie at the party before she left.

"So quick to leave?"

Shit.

To her relief, it was just Will. He had also left the party and come around to the backyard.

"I am starting to think you may enjoy this, Nadia. You know you could just leave through the front door? You do realize you have some actual friends at the party, right? Heck, even Tuck seemed to notice your interactions with Trent, and he was in the kitchen for most of the night.

Once Will saw Nadia abruptly get up and head upstairs, he knew what she would do. He even went so far as to make sure the window out of the bathroom was unlocked for her this time. Will saw Nadia as a friend, while Nadia would probably consider him an acquaintance. Since their first class together during the first week of school and a random pairing for a homework assignment, the two had become—well, to use Nadia's perspective—comfortable with each other.

"Tuck?" she uttered, pausing briefly as she pretended not to know who Tuck was before proceeding. "You and I both know that if you didn't want the night to end on a sour note at your house, my only choice was to make that exit."

Nadia turned and started to head back to the dorms for the

night. She didn't mind Will but was unwilling to wait and see if Trent showed up.

"Let me walk with you?"

Looking out over the cow farms and the dark walk back to the dorms closer to the school, Nadia nodded. Much like Trent, Will was a good talker, but to Will's credit, you could also tell he cared about what she said. He was charismatic, and while he was usually the center of the party due to being the host, she didn't think that would change based on the location. He had a way with words, was quick with humor, and knew how to navigate a tough conversation. Due to his friendly ways and the offer to accompany her, she finally gave in.

"Not enjoying your party?"

With a quick smile, Will jogged up to join Nadia. "I host three parties a week, so I think I can allow myself to miss an hour. Did you go to the game today?"

"No, but I heard that you were the star of the show. Well done… Brick? That's what everyone calls you, right?"

Nadia secretly watched the game but didn't want to reveal that information to Will or anyone else. Surprisingly, she enjoyed sports, even though she hadn't played much while growing up. According to the Dela Cruz family tradition, she needed to prioritize education to become a nurse. Despite not participating, she often daydreamed about being on a team with others. The camaraderie, action-oriented play, and shared goal of getting a ball across some form of boundary fascinated her.

Her dorm room window faced the sports fields, providing a decent view of the games. While "studying," she particularly enjoyed watching soccer matches and football games. The flow of the players on the field conveyed the action, even if she couldn't always see the ball. Baseball, on the other hand, proved more challenging to follow, and those games were easier to ignore.

"You know, for someone who doesn't watch the games, you are always quick to ask me about them. But yes, the game ended well. It was a much closer match than any of us expected, and Tuck's departure from the game left us with a significant gap to fill, quite literally." Will and Nadia continued to walk down the dirt path, cutting through the fields. "Are you ready for the Chemistry exam on Tuesday?"

Will loved football and the camaraderie that came with being on a team. He was good, too. With his grades and talent, aside from Tuck, he was the most likely to get picked up by a D1 program after finishing his two years at the school.

As a freshman from a small high school on the outskirts of Vegas, Will was a star player. However, his school competed in a lower division, limiting his games to smaller town schools around the area. This lack of visibility made D1 colleges hesitant to offer him a scholarship despite his record-breaking performances.

Doubts from recruits about the level of talent he played against gnawed at him. But Will was determined. Weekend camps in Vegas became his proving ground, where he showcased his abilities to scouts within the junior college community.

"And you say I deflect, huh?" Nadia gently accused Will. "Yes, I think so. That is one of the few classes I enjoy right now. Professor Williams has a way of bringing life to the material. It's not hard to pay attention, even if some of the topics are pretty basic. How about you? We've studied together long enough to know you can brute force your way through those exams."

"Brute force?" Will laughed. "I guess that's one way to put it. If that's what last-minute studying and acing exams gets called, then sure. I'll take that."

With a few more chuckles and smiles, Will let the conversation slip into easy silence. One thing about Will: he knew people, and he also knew that Nadia only had so much conversation within her. He didn't mind and enjoyed the night air and stars as they continued down the path.

The walk continued until Will felt a tremor sweep through

his body. It was like a sudden jolt. As fleeting as it was abrupt, Will observed sweat forming all over his body as though a sudden shower had drenched him.

"Whoa. Did you feel something just then?"

Nadia had stopped walking as well. "I thought it was just me! I've been feeling quite a few small tremors lately. They seem to be getting worse."

Checking herself out, Nadia felt strange for a second, but the only real difference was that the nerves must have made her sober up more than she already was, like what a shot of caffeine or a cold shower would typically do.

"Let's get going. I may take an Uber home tonight," Will suggested as they resumed their walk.

Allowing for one more thought, Will wondered if the one resident Uber driver, Bill, was working tonight. Being in a small town, Uber wasn't quite as easy to use out here due to the lack of willing drivers.

CHAPTER FOUR

"It is widely acknowledged among those intimately connected to the tournament that while fate undeniably exerts influence over the Games, many individuals actively seize control of their destinies." – Tournament Director.

Emy & James

"Please don't tell me that was just me?" Emy exclaimed, rising from her chair. James stood up beside her, his expression equally puzzled.

"I felt this strange pressure, and then the table started vibrating," James said, eyes wide. "Do you think it was an earthquake?Emy shook her head. "That was the oddest earthquake I've ever experienced. It felt like my ADHD went into overdrive for a split second. I've felt a few tremors in the past weeks, but this one was the worst." Emy and James glanced over at Norma, the cafe owner, who was still sitting behind the cashier station.

"Did you feel it too, Norma?" they asked in unison.

Norma looked up, her brow furrowing. "Hmm? Yeah, those fall breezes feel nice this time of the year."

Confused and still somewhat dazed by the event and Norma's lack of reaction, Emy and James decided to play it off as nerves. They continued their lunch, attempting to move forward with their conversations.

After catching up, Emy and James gathered their things. James had another class, and Emy had a prep period before soccer practice, during which she hung out in her dorm and studied. They hugged and went their separate ways.

△△△

Emy

Struggling to convince herself that this wouldn't be her final practice, Emy gazed blankly at her chemistry book. Despite her usual enjoyment of studying, she remained fixated on the same page for half an hour until a sudden noise from her dormmate jolted her out of her trance.

Emy's dormmate was Patricia, or "Trish," as she preferred. Trish was a striking figure, her curly hair constantly adorned with colorful hair ties, and her headsets perpetually on. She was also on the soccer team, though not a star player. She held the position of backup midfielder, with a solid understanding of the game and a decent leg.

Emy soon discovered the reason behind Trish's strategic prowess on the field: her late nights spent absorbed in various fantasy games, with FIFA being her current obsession. Trish's strategic gameplay in video games honed her ability to read the field and anticipate moves, making her a more insightful and tactical player in soccer.

Trish's quirky personality shone through her gaming habits. She always wore a video game or anime shirt, adding to her unique charm. Her witty, supportive nature was constant, even if she did always leave chopsticks all over the area. Her love for nightly Doritos, mixed with cleanliness to avoid ruining her gaming console, led her to use the utensils as she gamed.

Despite their differences, Emy tried to connect with Trish by playing matches together. However, their perspectives on life were as different as night and day.

"Trish, you about ready to head to practice?" Emy asked, looking back at her dormmate.

Trish pushed aside her headset, looking up from her game.

"Oh hey, Emy! How was your test? And yep, I'm just finishing up a campaign raid with my party. This boss turned out to be way more underpowered than we expected."

Emy raised an eyebrow. Trish was now deeply immersed in a Massively Multiplayer Online Role-Playing Game or MMORPG that Emy had never quite gotten the hang of. She wondered how Trish managed to keep her grades up, but it seemed like academic success came effortlessly to her. Even with minimal study, Trish consistently earned the best grades on the team.

"Good, I think? I'm more nervous about practice than anything else. I'm still waiting for Coach's verdict after yesterday's match," Emy confessed, her hand instinctively rubbing her face in a telltale sign of her anxiety. "By the way, did you feel that earthquake this afternoon? James and I had a rather unsettling experience during lunch."

Trish nodded in agreement. "Oh, you too? Honestly, it didn't feel much like an earthquake to me. I heard a rumble and felt more like a jolt, and then my game started glitching out of nowhere. But then, as suddenly as it started, everything returned to normal. Super strange! And yeah, I figured you'd be worried about practice, but I didn't want to add to your stress. You were already overthinking it… Ready to head out? We might as well face whatever comes our way."

△△△

The practice began as expected—drills, stretching, and Coach Williams observing from a distance. The second-year players took charge, guiding the teams through the exercises when a voice called out from the sidelines.

"Ms. Fury, let's have a chat! Come on over, please."

"Good luck," Trish whispered, suddenly beside her.

Emy felt herself gulp but attempted to hold her head high and jogged over to Coach Williams. It couldn't be good if Coach were now using her nickname instead of her last name,

Brandt, which he had called her all year.

Coach Williams, a middle-aged man still in the early half of his life, embodied the image of a traditional track coach. He was always seen with a golf polo, slightly shorter-than-expected running shorts, and sneakers. His calves hinted at a former life when he might have been somewhat heavier-set, but now he had a thin, well-toned body and a defined face. A large brown mustache adorned his upper lip, always looking a touch out of place, yet Coach proudly wore it—ever since he had shown up at Emy's house during a recruitment cycle.

With multiple roles at Quill Creek, Coach Williams wore many hats. First and foremost, he considered himself a professor—and a darn good one, according to most students who took his class. Second, he served as the women's head soccer coach and the lead athlete recruiter across all sports divisions for the school. Coach Williams discovered and nurtured many of the top talents within the school. His influence seemed to extend beyond even that of the athletic director. As Emy stood there, she channeled optimism, hoping that this conversation held a glimmer of hope.

"You're out. The NJCAA has placed a mandatory two-game suspension against you. This came from the top. You must have somehow pissed off the wrong mom," Coach Williams delivered the message in a flat tone, but Emy wasn't sure if she caught a sly smile at the end.

Deflated, Emy gave the only response she could think of at the moment: "That can't be fair. We have to be able to protest in some way. What... what am I going to do? Those two games span across a full week of soccer!"

"Sorry, Emy, this one is final. With Tuck last weekend and you this week, the association is having a meltdown over this school."

The coach let the words linger, a prolonged silence underscoring their significance, before trying to embrace the saddened girl.

"You will get through this and end up stronger because of it.

You can count on that," he assured her.

"Thanks, Coach," Emy returned the gesture. But then, the man's demeanor shifted, suddenly portraying excitement over another matter.

"But... We do have an opportunity for you and several others you know. Please plan to stay after class this Thursday for a meeting with me and a few others in the school. Bring James and Trish."

Emy and Coach Williams exchanged a few more words, and the players watching the conversation saw a departing Emy with a look of confusion on her face.

"What's the verdict?" Trish blurted out as Emy joined the group.

"Bad. I'm out, everyone. Two games."

"Wait, why the look of confusion?" Trish pressed on, not sure if she was reading her dormmate accurately.

"Oh. Um. I think he wants me, err, us, to join a chemistry tournament?"

CHAPTER FIVE

"The opening questions startle even the most willing contestants—unknown risk for unknown rewards. Only the brave take that first step." – Tournament Director.

WEDNESDAY AFTERNOON

Frank, James, Tuck & Will

Tuck slammed through the football dummies as Frank and James stood on the sidelines during practice.

"I'd hate to be one of those dummies," Frank commented, munching on his energy gummies. He noted their impact on his energy for practice, but everyone knew it was because they were fruit punch flavored.

"Frank, you're a lineman. Don't you have to face that every day?" James asked, referring to Tuck, a defensive lineman, while Frank was an offensive blocker for the football team.

"Yeah, but I feel like Tuck takes it easier on friends. I like him, but the biggest benefit of our friendship is not having to face… that," Frank responded as Tuck pivoted toward the metal sled, forcefully colliding with the typically two-person training device. Perched on top, Coach Sprout was expectedly propelled back ten yards.

"There you go, Tuck!" the smaller coach yelled, catching himself from falling off the massive sled as Tuck stopped his movement. "Way to show the others how it's done."

"Shit," Will said as he walked up to Frank and James on the sidelines. "Tuck seems extra pissed today. Glad I'm on defense with him."

"Amen," Frank spoke again, earning a questionable look from both James and Will.

"Frank, aren't you…" Will started but was cut off by James.

"Frank has a different perspective on things." James smiled at Will and glanced at Frank, who was still knocking back the gummies.

"Will, did I hear you're heading to Professor Williams' class tomorrow too?" James redirected.

"Wait, you too?" Will spoke. "Williams talked to Nadia and me about a chemistry team. I told him no, thank you, but he didn't take no for an answer. He just kept talking like I didn't have a choice."

James chuckled. "Same here, but only because it was Emy who demanded it. She wrangled Trish, her dormmate, into it too."

"I wouldn't mess with Fury either," Will added, eliciting a light chuckle from James.

"You know she hates that nickname, right?"

"And that makes it even better," Will answered as Frank cut in.

"You guys were talking about Professor Williams?" Frank spoke, now catching the conversation. "He reached out to me too. He said he wanted me to be a chem champ. I told him only if we get matching uniforms."

"And he said 'yes'?" Will asked incredulously.

"Yeah, he said 'yes' almost instantly. It was like that was already going to happen. I guess chemistry contests are cool?"

"Cool enough to get all three of us to go, I guess," James responded as Coach Sprout blew his whistle, and everyone hustled back to continue the practice.

△△△

THURSDAY AFTERNOON

Full Team

Curiosity and confusion swirled in Emy's mind as chemistry class neared its end. The past two days were particularly challenging. Practice was now the only thing pushing her to survive a mental breakdown with her ADHD flaring up.

Emy immediately shared her conversation with Coach Williams with James after practice, and he later mentioned that Will and Frank had received similar feedback from the coach. While Emy genuinely enjoyed chemistry, she wondered if joining a chem club was the right move at this moment.

As the bell rang, students filed out of the classroom, as Emy and James remained in their seats, exchanging nods with friends. Waiting a little longer with Professor Williams as he gathered his things, they sensed a more significant presence entering the room behind them.

"Tuck? What are you doing here?" James exclaimed, excitement lighting up his face.

"Professor Williams pulled me aside after football practice yesterday and asked me to come here. I'm part of his second-year program on Wednesdays. He recruited me for football a few years back. I owe that man a lot," Tuck explained.

With another nod and a smile directed at her, Emy observed Tuck settling into a seat in the back as more people trickled in—this time, it was Trish and Frank. Frank exchanged a fist bump with James while Trish quietly entered the room with headphones over her ears. They both chose to sit next to Tuck in the back.

"Is this the room for the pizza party?" Will called out as he and a reserved Nadia walked in, eliciting a small chuckle from Frank in the back.

"Tough crowd," Will remarked, sitting beside James while Nadia sat beside him.

As Emy observed the newcomers, she noticed that Nadia deliberately avoided all eye contact as she made her way to her seat. They might have shared an English class, but Emy was unsure. Judging by appearances, Will and Tuck seemed the most welcoming toward Nadia. Having another girl around amidst a group of football players was always a positive sign.

"Looks like we have just about everyone here. Thank you for joining..." Professor Williams began his introduction, but the door opened again, revealing Trent, a surprise addition to the group.

"Ah, Trent. Glad to see you made it. Welcome, welcome. Please sit down with the others; I was just beginning."

Trent glided into the classroom, offering a few smirks to those present. His gaze lingered a little longer when he spotted Nadia, who remained focused on Professor Williams.

"As I was saying, thank you for joining me, everyone! It is my pleasure to assemble all my most exceptional and brilliant students in this room for the first time." Professor Williams' enthusiasm appeared slightly over the top. "While I've known many of you for years, some are mere acquaintances. But remember that familiarity is only in person. I've been observing each of you, and I can discern talent when I see it —or rather when I feel it." He winked directly at Trish in the back and gave a bright smile. While maintaining a beaming smile, he glanced at his watch as if timing something. Locking eyes with the class, he declared, "Your lives are on the cusp of a remarkable transformation. In just a few moments, we will begin training for the Quantum Games."

Emy felt a new emotion creeping in as she listened to her teacher. *Better our lives?* She wondered, glancing around the room. This situation was becoming increasingly peculiar, and she couldn't shake the feeling that something extraordinary was about to unfold.

"What the heck do you mean, Professor? I apologize. The chemistry games seem somewhat enjoyable. But... transformative?" Will looked around the room as he voiced his question, reinforcing his bewilderment.

"And that's precisely why you're going to be an excellent teammate, Mr. Weiss! Questioning the norm. Voicing your thoughts and collaborating," Professor Williams replied to Will, evading the question.

"Now, I know many of you have questions, and rest assured they will soon be answered in one way or another. Know that I will be here for you every step of the way," Professor Williams said and then paused, raising his hands with a broad smile.

"Are you ready for glory?" Professor Williams' question hung in the air, sparking a sense of anticipation and excitement among the students.

Silence followed for an unmeasurable amount of time as Williams remained still, his smile fixed. This was a side of the Coach that none in the room had seen before; it was almost as if he was attempting to oversell something to the team. As Will was about to speak again, the room started to shake violently, and a massive shockwave overtook it, knocking over chairs and books. The air vibrated with energy, and the room seemed to distort and warp.

As the surroundings shifted, Professor Williams stood still. Emy stared at her hands as the tremors continued, witnessing her bones, blood flow, and muscles change as she clenched her fists. She felt a surge of power and energy coursing through her as her senses sharpened. Gasps echoed behind her as patterns blurred and objects moved like dynamic entities rather than their typical static forms. Emy tried to stand up, unable to speak, but darkness and silence enveloped her, broken only by a voice cutting through the blackness.

> Greetings, Earthlings.
>
> From this moment forward, Earth and the broader Milky Way Galaxy are officially recognized within the Cosmos as part of the Celestial Nexus Collective (CNC). This monumental event allows all participants to engage in the 1,200th Quantum Games! The Quantum Games are a universal event that brings sentient beings from across

the Cosmos to compete in skill, strategy, and teamwork tests.

Do you have the courage to face the unknown? Will you rise above the competition to become Earth's champion? Can you achieve the legendary glory that countless predecessors have sought? Are you ready to make history and leave your mark on the Cosmos?

...The choice rests with you!

A prompt appeared against the darkness in everyone's vision:

Would you like to compete in the 1200th Quantum Games? (Y/N)

CHAPTER SIX

"Bonds make or break a Champion's success in the Quantum Games. Connections with friends, coaches, and—yes—even their AI play a pivotal role." – Tournament Director.

Emy

Emy stared at the question before her, puzzled, confused, and maybe excited? Imagining that others might find this situation eerie or unsettling, she found herself feeling… calm. This was the first time she could remember that her brain had been fully tuned out from the world around her—darkness, void, quiet, and a question that could change her life forever.

Is this just happening to me? she thought. But no, she had heard the gasps and realized that couldn't be true. *Was this just happening in the classroom?* Her second thought held more weight and settled her a tiny bit. There were strange things in the world, but this? This might just be too strange. Thinking back to the feelings and jolts she'd experienced over the last few weeks, they all felt similar to the one she felt right before everything darkened. There had to be a connection. But if it was connected, did that mean it was bigger than just a classroom?

Glancing back at the question:

Would you like to compete in the 1200th Quantum Games? (Y/N)

"What are the Quantum Games?" Emy spoke out loud.

> The Quantum Games consist of physical and mental tests, trials, and a framework designed to identify and train the next heroes of the Cosmos. If you choose 'yes,' you'll be immersed in the Games, where you can either become a future hero or support a potential hero from your world.

"Whoa," Emy spoke again as she took in the details. "Who the heck are you?"

> My name is not important at this moment. Across the Cosmos, I am known as 'The System.' I am the host of the Quantum Games. Now, please think carefully and make your decision.

The System? Emy questioned internally as she moved back to the question before her. There was only one correct answer; she knew this. She knew it immediately, but her reasonable mind told her to think first before rushing. Coach Williams was someone she trusted, or at least used to trust. Why would he go through all that effort if he thought this was not a good path for her and her classmates? Granted, he had acted like a door-to-door salesman just a moment ago, but their shared history fostered her trust. Pushing her reasonable mind to the back after giving it a touch of logic, Emy said aloud: "Yes."

Reacting to her voice or intention, the question vanished, and a new prompt appeared:

Would you like to join a team or participate in the Games by yourself? (Team / Solo)

This was not a question she was immediately expecting. Was she able to be on a team? With whom? Were there perks of either path?

The same voice as earlier spoke from the ether:

> Playing as either a team or solo comes with unique perks. Rising through the levels as a team brings about more dynamic challenges while going solo limits the experiences you will face, at least initially. Being on a team allows you to depend on one another, but running solo accelerates your chances for stardom.

Okay, freaky, thought Emy. Having not stated anything to trigger that response, simple logic says this "System thing" must be listening to her thoughts directly. Attempting to move on, her feelings went to her best friend. *Could I play in the game with James? Would James want to do this with me?*

Emy's mind wandered back to the classroom she had just left. Williams had explicitly used "teammate" while responding to Will's question. How much did the professor know? What secrets had he been concealing all this while? Emy's thoughts returned to the previous question to which she had already responded affirmatively. Her "yes" was rooted in trust, but now she felt slightly unsettled about how much her professor was withholding.

Emy drew a deep breath, once again striving to prioritize her most rational thoughts. She had already agreed to the previous question, so backing out now wasn't an option, right? Being on a Team had always been her preference over being Solo, which immediately propelled her forward. Why would she want to be alone?

As a team member, would you like to participate as a Champion or Artisan? (Champion / Artisan)

Oh wow. More choices. This sudden twist altered her perspective. *What even is an Artisan?*

Once more, the silence was shattered by the voice:

> This role resembles that of crafters, tradespeople, or even blacksmiths. Their expertise lies in supporting the

> Champions, offering indispensable services. While initial training is available at orientation, an Artisan requires a discerning eye for their chosen trade and a delicate equilibrium between skill and intuition.

Am I good at anything? Emy wondered.

Soccer and chemistry were her strong suits, but how would they serve her here? Her thoughts drifted to Trish, the night owl who loved playing in these types of role-playing games (RPGs). She was always mentioning alchemy. Her chemistry knowledge could fuel an alchemical path, but would that be fun, and was that even an option?

> The role of a crafter is unique as many assume a broader role across the Cosmos, not just as an alchemist. We provide training programs on chemicals both within your world and across the Cosmos.

New chemicals from beyond our world? No, stay focused, Emy... Emy internally questioned and promptly redirected her attention to the matter at hand. She could utilize her chemistry skills, but was that her preferred choice? Did chemistry bring her joy or just a sense of stability? The self-interrogation hit her hard. Was she genuinely choosing what would make her happy? Should she opt for a more practical choice to ensure success? Could this tournament cost her life? What role was she destined for? Would she require a weapon? The surreal nature of her situation overwhelmed her—just moments ago, she was in a classroom; now, she was eclipsed in darkness wrestling with life-or-death decisions. Emy took a deep breath, allowing her intuition to guide her again. Despite the fear accompanying each question, having fun still played a significant role in this choice. With determination, she voiced her final decision. "Champion."

You've entered the Quantum Games,

a realm of infinite potential!

......

Currently assigning teams based on proximity.

......

Cohort 13 is your new home - Grouping - Earth - United States - Quill Creek.

......

Body scans complete.

......

Talent: Generalist - Level 3.

......

Prepare to step onto the tutorial floor.

......

Emy's mind raced as the cryptic text flashed before her eyes, leaving no room for contemplation. Abruptly, she found herself in a pristine white chamber, its sterile walls enclosing two rectangular pillars resting in the center.

This is not the classroom anymore, she mused. But where was she? And what did being a Generalist entail? Emy lacked fluency in gaming or RPG-style classes, yet the term "Generalist" didn't usually bode well. Shouldn't she be a Warrior, a Mage, or perhaps even an Archer if this were a tournament involving levels? True, she knew nothing about those roles, but at least they'd come with weapons or powers from the get-go, right?

Before she could unravel her thoughts, a familiar voice resounded through the void. "Hello, Emy. I don't believe you need to worry about your soccer matches anymore."

In the room's center, a vivid projection of Coach Williams materialized. Thin air conjured him, showcasing an identical mustache, clothing, and whistle dangling from his neck—it had to be a digital image. Emy then realized she probably also needed to curb her assumptions for a while.

"Coach Williams?" she ventured. "Are you here? You look like a projection. What's happening?"

His response was matter-of-fact. "Indeed, it's me—but a digital copy. My presence here is limited, but you should still consider me your 'coach.'"

"Before you ask any more questions," Coach Williams said, "let me introduce you to your new companion. Meet your NexaBot, affectionately known as 'Nex.'"

Inside Emy's mind, A voice resonated—silent yet startling. *"Pleased to meet you, Emy! I've been waiting a long, long time for this!"*

Emy's alarm surged. "Are you inside my mind? How did you even get in there?" Panic clenched her chest.

"Oh no," Nex soothed. A gentle energy enveloped Emy, akin to the chill of ice crunching between teeth. *"That's a bit better. And yes, I've been with you since high school."*

Emy's disbelief flared, "No, that most certainly does NOT help," she retorted. "How have I not known this?"

Before Nex could respond, Coach Williams—Digital Williams—stepped in, "Nex was bestowed upon all promising young talents who shared your 'symptoms,'" he explained. "Technology beyond your world differs vastly. Something as subtle as drinking a water droplet can consume Nex's presence."

Emy's attention snagged on a peculiar choice of words: *Your World?* What did that imply?

He moved closer. "Don't perceive this as a hindrance. All members of the CNC receive an AI node like Nex. By cosmic law, Nex is you, and you are Nex. Integrated, Nex shields you from far worse AI intrusions."

"*That's right! You and I are one,*" Nex added.

Coach Williams continued as if nobody was talking, prompting Emy to wonder if Nex had spoken only to her.

"*Yes, I did,*" Nex spoke again directly to her as Coach's words reached her.

"Nex is your companion," Coach Williams continued, "and your guide, advisor, and battle communication specialist. As you grow, so will Nex. Learn to work together. They will help keep you safe."

"Shall we continue your training?" Coach Williams then asked.

CHAPTER SEVEN

"In the initial phases of the game, Champions must quickly grasp how to navigate and integrate with the user interface. Unfortunately, sluggish adoption correlates with the highest termination rates in these Games." – Games Division Data Scientist.

Emy

"Before we venture further into the depths of your training in this tutorial," Coach Williams initiated, his voice soft, "I think it's crucial to shed light on the transformations that have transpired throughout your galaxy."

"Your world and many others, much like Earth—forgive the lack of a better term—'popped.' Before this integration, new worlds such as Earth undergo gradual development and settlement. Organisms evolve, and life flourishes. The Cosmos maintains checks and balances to nurture these unique and intelligent life forms. This growth also fosters diversity and varying cultural norms, igniting inherent passion and loyalty across your world."

Professor Williams continued, taking Emy's blank stare and silence as a sign to continue. "This 'bubble' around your world, close to what you might call the Ozone layer, once held your reality in a locked state of atomic-level change and manipulation. But once it 'popped,' Earth joined the ranks of every other world beyond your galaxy—a malleable mass of quantum transformation. Earth remains stable. Yet now, you'll react to it in new and profound ways."

The connection to her previous life events triggered

newfound courage in Emy, prompting her to form words. She hesitantly asked, "Could some people feel these effects earlier?"

Digital Williams responded with conviction, "Yes, Emy. I've always known that you possess immense potential in this new world. Let's call it a talent of mine, and it's one of the many reasons I recruited you for the team. Everyone has the opportunity to shift, mold, and build within this environment, but not all can do so effectively. We call this process 'building,' akin to strengthening a muscle. As you grow, your abilities will expand."

"In developed worlds, those under the age of 13 typically struggle to grasp the subtle intricacies of the world that allow for 'building.' Even after that point, growth and development are necessary to achieve true talent. These critical growth periods shape future Champions, which is why older individuals often lack the foundational skillsets required to participate in the Games. Those aged 18 to 30 fit the archetype of typical Champions, which is precisely why I've chosen to reside near a local college teeming with talent."

Emy questioned, "But if we need time to develop these abilities, why would we be selected as potential participants?"

Coach Williams smiled as he answered, "While you may not have actively trained, your subconscious mind has been at work. The protective bubble that once enveloped your world was never infallible; it harbored gaps that gradually widened over time. Perhaps you've even noticed your symptoms worsening over the years. When the System selected you as a possible candidate, it recognized your latent potential within the vast expanse of the Cosmos."

Nex's voice then beamed positively, *"I think now is an opportune moment to show you that potential within our new interface! You just need to focus on the mental command of 'Status' to pull it up!"*

Emy followed the instructions, and pockets of text scattered around her vision. It was difficult to explain, but it was as if her vision remained the same, yet a layer of details in white text intermingled with her surroundings. Her excitement bubbled: "Holy VR, it feels like I'm playing a game!" She abruptly realized that her assessment wasn't far off. To her, it was much like augmented reality—details subtly revealed at the periphery, with text coming into focus when directly observed—everything seemed to show up based on intent.

At the top of her vision, the following information was displayed:

Location: Milky Way > Earth > United States > Quill Creek
Precise Location: Tutorial

On the left side:

Emy: Generalist, Level 3, E-Class, 100% Health, 20% Shield

On the right side:

Weapons: None
Gear: Earth Base Clothing - No Modifications

At the bottom:

Augments: None

Emy also noticed two additional items in the top right corner of her view:

Total Points: 0
Active Views: 0

Nex added, "*Nifty, huh? All the essential information is conveniently accessible in one central viewing console. Remember that you'll see a modified team-style format during battles or team formations.*"

Nex continued, "*If you want to adjust or remove any features from your field of view, simply give a mental command, and I'll make the adjustments for you.*" Emy nodded, glancing over at the silent Coach Williams. "*Oh yes, he can hear me too via his communication AI. TLDR - Too Long Didn't Read: I can interpret conversations and questions meant for the larger group or private ones with extreme precision—no need to ever worry about that!"*

Suddenly confused, Emy asked, "But... How am I a level 3 already, and what does E-Class mean?"

Coach Williams explained, "Your level correlates with your understanding of the world and your abilities. In our interconnected society, beginners usually fall within levels 1 to 3. Your Class, ranging from F to A, will be determined by your level. As you improve your 'builder' skills, your level will increase, and so will your overall Class."

"Now, let's talk about your Health and Shield. This is a bit harder to explain, so please bear with me as I try to explain. Imagine yourself surrounded by a protective energy sphere called the 'Shield.' This Shield is indicated in your Nexabot as a percentage increase to your total vitality, meaning that Health plus Shield roughly equals total vitality. The power-based modifiers will stay fairly consistent as you gain power, but the gear modifiers may fluctuate, often decreasing as your overall vitality increases. For example, you might have gloves that increase your overall vitality by 20%, but as you grow and the gloves remain the same, that modifier could reduce to 10%."

"This energy sphere is your primary defense, reinforced by your tactical gear and equipment. When your shield is depleted or hit by an overwhelming force, your physical body becomes vulnerable to harm. It's similar to a boxer wearing headgear. Even with the headgear on, a forceful blow to the head can still cause damage."

"Right... so how do I obtain new Augments or Gear?"

Nex answered this question: *"During battles, gear, weapons, and certain augments frequently drop. If fortune favors you, you might acquire something that will serve you for a lifetime! There are alternative methods to acquire new equipment through your team, although these will unfold gradually. Remember that all your status sections allow you to delve deeper for more detailed information."*

Emy interpreted this as a request and zeroed in on the word "Gear." Suddenly, new text materialized before her eyes.

Gear: Earth Base Clothing - No Modifications
  Full Body: None
  Head: None
  Upper Body: College Letterman's Jacket - No Modifications
  Lower Body: Leggings - No Modifications
  Feet: Sneakers - No Modifications
  Accessories: None

Emy nodded, absorbing the information. "That makes sense, but what about Points and Views icons? Those don't sound like typical mechanics."

Nex, eager to chime in, exclaimed, *"Ah, my favorite topic! In the Games, every action you take earns you points. The more impressive the action, the higher the points! And here's the fun part: captivating your audience leads to growing views. Active and total views contribute to your popularity and can even generate special rewards."*

Emy raised an eyebrow. "Fans? Why would I want to build a fan base?"

Nex grinned. *"Think big! Fans across the entire Cosmos! And accumulating points not only boosts your status but also reduces the chances of being dropped by—"*

Coach Williams interrupted, "Let's focus on primary details, Nex. Just know that views and points matter, so pay attention to what people and the System appreciate."

"Now, I think it's time to teach you how to build."

CHAPTER EIGHT

"It isn't until that first hit that realization settles, and you suddenly understand that you are in a new world." – The Reckoner, Former Champion.

TUTORIAL

Emy

Emy stood back in the white tutorial room as two pillars disconnected from the ceiling and smoothly lowered until they stopped, transforming into table tops. Each table cradled a substance on its flat surface—one metallic and the other a pale yellow. Across the room, Coach Williams met her gaze with a firm look.

"Let's start small," Coach began, gesturing toward the leftmost pillar. "Do you see the sodium placed there?" Emy nodded in response. "Okay, now the real question: Can you sense it?"

Emy's attention shifted to the pillar holding the silvery-white metallic shards. Trusting her instincts, she extended her hand as if to touch the object and focused her mind on one of the shards. To her surprise, the atoms responded, reaching out to her. Emy could feel the shift more than she could see the tiny particles separating themselves from the shard and floating into the air. The glimmering flows appeared as if a clear energy was encapsulating the elements. She wasn't moving the entire shard; instead, she directed individual molecules toward herself, manipulating them through the air.

"Good, good! Now, the tougher part," Coach continued.

"While focusing on the sodium particles, do the same with the second pillar substance. You wouldn't happen to remember your first question from the mid-term, would you?"

"Sodium chloride," Emy recollected after a brief pause, glancing at the second pillar. Looking closely, it held another substance—pale yellow-green crystals of solid chlorine. Emy replicated the same energy draw she had done with the sodium, channeling chlorine elements.

"Now comes the fun part. Elements naturally want to combine, which both simplifies and complicates merging. But as builders, it's our role to guide them. Imagine the creation you desire at the molecular level. What structure do you want to build?"

Emy focused on the two elemental flows on each side of her, feeling their distinct energies. With a concentrated mental effort, she envisioned pushing the flows together, guiding their interactions at the molecular level. She imagined the creation she desired, the structure she wanted to build. The sodium and chlorine elements began to merge, their formations intertwining as a white powder materialized. It fell softly to the ground, landing in the center of her connection. She had done it. She had created salt.

Her gaze held steady, her mind instantly questioning the event unfolding. In her perception, she had brought together barely visible elements and abruptly created this new compound, but how? She hadn't moved anything into a puzzle-like formation; was this just a result of force?

"A natural talent," Williams commended, his digital projection glowing with pride as if the real professor was present. "Not quite what you anticipated?"

"I suppose I was expecting it to be more challenging?" Emy thought out loud, wondering why she desired more difficulty.

"It will be, but only when you merge or force unnatural elements. In this instance, the atoms wanted to unite; you merely served as the catalyst to facilitate that union."

"So, I can do this with... anything?" Emy then questioned.

"Anything you set your mind to. As a Generalist, you can create and adapt to the needs at hand. Consider all the chemical reactions: Compression, Merges, Reactions, Acceleration, Transformation. The Cosmos is founded on atomic reactions. Understanding your energy and harnessing creativity allows for growth. Fascinating, isn't it?"

Emy felt as if she were in another lecture, but this time, her body was filled with anticipation. There were infinite possibilities, not to mention the otherworldly elements that existed. "Incredibly fascinating," was all she could utter, her mind whirling.

"What's next?" Emy directed a look of eagerness towards Williams.

Emy and the Professor spent the next hours delving deeper into her abilities. While manipulating salt was straightforward, Emy soon encountered her limitations. The more she uncovered, the more she realized she needed to learn and practice. The hammer-and-nail strategy worked for many solutions, but Emy discovered that mindset was crucial when controlling energies.

Despite this, Emy pushed on with a focus she had never been able to maintain before. Testing her newfound skills, she quickly realized that every connection or reaction required adjustments—whether it was the speed of the atoms, bond strength, concentration levels, surface area, pressure, temperature, or the presence of other sources. She soon wished she had more time.

"I'm afraid we've reached our boundaries in this tutorial," Digital Williams announced as Emy again attempted another merge scenario they had been practicing.

"Now what?" Emy questioned, realizing how quickly time had passed, yet she still had minimal knowledge about the actual Games.

"I'm afraid I cannot say. You will be taken from this tutorial and tested. To what extent, I'm never certain and not allowed to discuss the matter too much. The element of reaction is a primary training tool for the System."

Emy, uncertain of what to ask given Williams' perceived limitations, added one more question, "Professor, who are you?"

"Make it through this first level, and you'll find out," Williams said as he winked, and a white light engulfed the tutorial.

△△△

LEVEL ONE - POST TUTORIAL

Full Team

The Quantum Games have commenced— best of luck to our future Champions.

The white light shifted, and Emy again found herself in the familiar classroom. The sharp scent of ammonia tickled her nose, just as it had before. But this time, something was different. She waited for her usual perception and vision issues to return, but they remained absent.

As she glanced around, a newfound awareness enveloped her. The molecules, elements, and compounds seemed to pulse and weave within the room, similar to the elements brought into the tutorial. They fused, creating the very fabric of reality. Though still solid and stable, the tables and chairs now possessed a fluidity that beckoned her to interact with them.

Emy stood there, caught between the mundane and the extraordinary, sensing the intricate dance of matter—the unseen forces that held everything together. At this moment, the classroom was no longer just a room; it was a symphony of atoms waiting for her to play her part.

Startled and blinking, Emy noticed most of her friends were once again occupying their usual spots throughout the classroom. She then glanced at James, their eyes locked, sharing an unspoken dialogue. Meanwhile, Will and Nadia sat a row behind, their demeanor contrasting—Nadia's quiet reserve juxtaposed with Will's usual vibrancy.

As the students exchanged glances, their attention was suddenly drawn to a movement at the back of the room. Standing there was Tuck, or rather, a transformed version of him. The boy they once knew had metamorphosed into a towering figure, his muscles rippling beneath his skin. It was as if electric currents were coursing through him, animating his very being.

△△△

PRIOR TUTORIAL

Tuck

When the light of the tutorial room hit Tuck, he quickly realized he wasn't just dreaming. He had just answered the strangest questions of his life about participating in a game, yet it all felt so real. Tuck didn't question or hesitate; the answers came naturally as if he were playing a video game. Yes, he wanted to compete. Yes, he wanted to be on a team. And yes, he obviously wanted to be a Champion over building things. If this was a dream, he might as well continue with his choices. But as he progressed and didn't wake up, realization started to dawn on him.

Looking at the digital version of Coach Williams was a bit trippy, but everything was so real that it didn't much matter until his former Coach took an unusual tone.

"I didn't think you would make it to this stage," Coach Williams started with unusual disgust in his tone.

"What do you mean? What is this place?" Tuck responded, attempting to discern the intent of the comment.

"I just wasn't sure if you wanted to be a Champion. The others tend to stick it out, but you seem to take the easy way out."

"What's that supposed to mean?"

"Let's just move on. Do you want to know what this place is?" Williams' demeanor remained as he turned his back to Tuck and walked away from his former student.

"No," Tuck called out, aggression in his voice showing. "Tell me what you mean!" Tuck tried his best to hold back the rage as his former teacher and mentor, whom he trusted, turned around and started walking towards him.

"How many football games did you finish this year? Or better yet, how many games did you let your team down by getting yourself tossed out?" The professor kept his glare as he walked towards Tuck.

"That wasn't...."

"Your intent? You knew exactly what you were doing when you used extreme force against those other players."

"I didn't..." Tuck again attempted to defend himself, holding his rage to simmer at the man now striding towards him.

"You didn't what? You didn't mean to?" Williams now stood right before Tuck, looking directly into his eyes. "Bullshit."

"I didn't..."

"Save that for when you quit on your team again," Williams said as he held eye contact with Tuck, allowing his words to sink into the young man's core. Then, suddenly, two hands flashed forward towards Tuck and slammed into his chest, propelling him backward as he quickly attempted to catch himself from falling.

Looking back at his former professor, he saw the man anew, as the professor held both hands outward with a now mocking look. The simmering rage within Tuck exploded. Staring directly at the man who pushed him, who betrayed him, Tuck felt his body transform, every hair standing on end as a wave of emotion surged through him. His entire body felt weightless as he gathered his grip on the floor and stepped forward to stand straight up. It was then that he saw the face of his former professor turn again to one of happiness as Tuck questioned what was happening. Raising his hands to his face, he then noticed electric currents shifting and churning within his arms as if he were charged. He then heard his teacher's voice.

"You didn't… have control," Professor Williams said as Tuck glanced at his body. "You are an Accelerator, and your talent is triggered by emotion…"

△△△

LEVEL ONE

Full Team

"Holy shit," Will exclaimed, finally emerging from his exhilaration. "Tuck, what…what are you?" The question hung in the air, echoing the shock reverberating through the room.

Tuck: Accelerator, Level 4, 100% Health, 30% Shield

Emy examined her friend as Tuck began to explain.

"Coach Williams labeled me an Accelerator," Tuck confessed. "Given your collective expressions, I'm guessing my body chemistry shifted. I possess an affinity for electromagnetic fields, which tend to manifest with considerable force." His tone conveyed remorse as he reevaluated how this enigmatic gift had shaped his life.

Tuck's statement stood as a creaking sound came from the slowly opened classroom door, revealing a small, hairy creature. Standing half a meter tall, its brown and white fur contrasted oddly with its oversized ears, which jutted out from both sides of its head. At first glance, it almost seemed cute, mimicking that of a Gremlin.

Emy's quick scan provided a brief assessment:

Grimbletooth: Level 1

This diminutive warrior class emerged unexpectedly in the vast expanse of the Aetherium Spiral Galaxy. Initially perceived as an insignificant breach within the planetary stronghold of

Nexus, these subterranean beings carved out an underground dominion, ultimately claiming the entire planet as their own.

The group stood dazed, frozen in thought, staring at the creature. But the cuteness quickly dissipated. The Grimbletooth's face twisted into a scowl, showcasing a single sharp tooth and fangs emerging from its paws. Without hesitation, it ran and lunged at Nadia, single claw swiping at her face. The first blow landed, triggering a scream from Nadia as it poised for another attack. Yet, in a blur of motion, a mighty hand eclipsed the Grimbletooth's head, its ears sticking out comically through the gaps in Tuck's large fingers. Tuck hurtled the creature across the room with a resounding grunt, crashing into the brick classroom wall. The impact reverberated, leaving everyone wide-eyed and breathless.

SPPPPLLLLATTTTT! 3 POINTS!

Nex's exclamation reverberated as the monster disintegrated into nothing.

Emy's internal communication with her AI was immediate: "What the heck was that, Nex?"

"*Oh yeah, sorry,*" Nex replied. "*Those are all preprogrammed by the head game masters for viewers. Would you like me to turn those down a bit?*"

"Err, yea?" answered Emy.

"*At your request, Ms. Fury. Combat commentary set to 40%,*" Nex confirmed.

Glancing at her interface, Emy noticed that the "Active Viewers" count had briefly spiked to 2 and then dropped to zero. "Wait, what did you just call me?" Emy questioned, the realization of Nex's response hitting her.

Nex hesitated, his tone calm, "*Uh, Fury?*"

"Nexy, turn up combat commentary to 150%! That was awesome!" the group heard Will's enthusiastic exclamation in the background.

Unable to hold back, James addressed Will, "Firstly, there's no need to yell for Nex to hear you. And second, did you seriously nickname Nex as Nexy?"

If Will felt any embarrassment, he masked it well. He retorted to James, "Yeah, why not? It has a nice ring to it. Plus, I've even set up a sultry lady voice."

Ignoring the comments, Tuck returned to Nadia, his eyes fixed on her bloodied face, now marred by a large horizontal gash stretching from her left eye to her opposite cheekbone. The rest of the group quickly followed, realizing their teammate had been clawed during the fight.

"Thanks, Tuck," Nadia said solemnly. "I just froze."

"We all froze. Well, everyone except Tuck," Emy added, glancing at Nadia's status display.

Nadia: Cellulator, Level 2, 93% Health, 0% Shield

Will spoke quietly, "I guess we now know the answer to the question we've been avoiding."

James turned, curious. "And what is that?"

Emy responded this time on Will's behalf, her eyes tracing the blood trickling down Nadia's cheek. "That this is not just a game."

CHAPTER NINE

"Everyone possesses a unique natural gift, an innate talent that sets them apart. It's like a hidden gem waiting to be discovered. Identifying this gift is just the beginning; nurturing and honing it is where true mastery lies." – Coach Williams.

PRIOR TUTORIAL

Nadia

Amidst the opening questions, Champion candidates were suspended in stasis—in a realm beyond time, governed by the enigmatic System, time itself warped and twisted, causing all future heroes to emerge simultaneously. Within the Tutorial, there was a time limit for the future Champion to hone their talent, but this limit didn't account for the moments before their encounter with their future coach. During this initial phase, candidates had the chance to question the System. Most barely scratched the surface, asking about their choices. But not Nadia. She fired off 48 questions while suspended in darkness, challenging every answer and pushing the intel she received to the very breaking point of the System before eventually propelling her forward. Her diligence left her uniquely prepared for what lay ahead, making her subsequent conversation with Coach Williams remarkably direct.

"Nadia, do you have any idea what your talent might be?" Digital Williams asked from within the tutorial's pristine walls.

"I have a few ideas, but none of them map to that of a normal talent." Nadia countered, still questioning the reality of the situation as a projection of her Chemistry teacher stood before her.

"Good that you have ideas. Signs show up in many ways—think about your life, your tendencies, maybe your needs or wants. Think about feelings you may have encountered over the last few weeks when your world started having jolts."

"Oh…" Nadia responded, thinking about the last few months at junior college. Memories of searching for happiness, anything that could make her feel something, surfaced. She decided to voice her thoughts as the feeling in her stomach churned, urging her to let it out. "I think it has to do with my body, but that's just a guess… I sort of have a high tolerance for… things."

Williams' digital eyes shifted slightly as he heard Nadia's response. "I had my suspicions, and while that's on the mark, other signs have shown across your profile."

"Profile?"

"Disregard that. Nadia, have you ever felt your body process things or physically felt your body heal itself?"

"Sort of… Can't everyone?"

"No. Most people process and heal without giving it a second thought unless their body needs to work harder, whether from a bad meal or a deeper bruise from falling out a window." Williams winked and continued. "I have an idea, but I need you to trust me for this next part."

"Of course…" Nadia said, quickly followed by a squeak as a knife blade pierced her skin and slid from her elbow to wrist.

"Sorry… It needed to happen," Williams responded as Nadia went from recognizing pain to complete confusion about how a digital projection could physically touch her.

"Save that question for another day as well," Williams said as Nadia opened her mouth to catch up with her previous thought. "I want you to search within yourself and identify the unnatural incision on your arm. Find it and attempt to highlight it in your mind."

Choosing to hold off on more questions, Nadia followed his instructions. Looking inward, she felt... different. In the past, through meditation or boredom, she could usually let her mind wander internally, creating a mental image of herself—skin, bones, muscles, and even organs—feeling her body's natural rhythms working in harmony. Now, she could hardly describe what she was feeling. It was as if every cell within her body had its own heartbeat. Vivid details emerged from subtle shifts in her blood flow, heart palpitations, and even the air pushing through her systems. Every vein, every muscle, every nuance was identified until she found the outlier—damaged cells. Shifting her senses, she scanned her arm and felt every incision point, every blood flow stoppage, and every split cell as her body yearned to be whole again.

"Good. Stay there, Nadia, but now I want you to amplify your body's natural urges to heal. Feel what your body is trying to tell you and support those cravings."

Nadia did just that. Focusing on the cut, she felt her body's natural healing process kick in. She mentally urged the platelets to clot the wound faster, and they responded. She then sensed her immune cells cleaning the area and encouraged them to work more efficiently. Finally, she pushed her healthy cells to multiply, speeding up the healing process.

As she progressed and finished her internal recovery, she paid no heed to the now unblemished arm where a cut once existed as Coach Williams' excited eyes stared intently at hers. "Just as I suspected... the healer of the group."

△△△

LEVEL ONE

Full Team

"It's all right, I'm fine," Nadia reassured, met with a mix of stares and confusion. "Honestly, it's probably best that it happened to me."

< Skill Identified – Nadia – Vitalize >

A new prompt was shown on everyone's interface as Nex collectively announced the new skill. A collective silence remained within the group, awaiting Nadia's continued reasoning from her earlier statement. She hesitated and continued, "During the tutorial, I discovered something unexpected—I have healing powers... Coach called it a 'Cellulator' talent and showed me that my body naturally accelerates processes like healing."

Will and the team directed their Nexabots to the new prompt as a more detailed status appeared:

Skill: Vitalize

Enables the user to amplify the innate healing processes within themselves or others through touch. (T)

Will immediately questioned Nadia, "So that's how you drank so much? You were cheating this whole time?"

Nadia's head shook slowly, not quite expecting that as a first question. "It's not something I was even aware of. I honestly felt like I was cursed. But now I'm discovering it's a gift, a surprise..."

Emy's eyes widened, hearing the talent that may eventually save them. "That's... that's amazing, Nadia," she stammered. "But that said, we all have some things to share from our tutorial experiences." She looked at her team status, noticing the new talents listed after each name.

	Talent	Level	Health	Shield
Emy	Generalist	Level 3	100%	20%
Tuck	Accelerator	Level 4	100%	30%
Nadia	Cellulator	Level 2	100%	0%
Will	Condenser	Level 2	100%	10%

James	Catalyst	Level 2	100%	0%

"Wait, where are Trish, Frank, and Trent?" James was the first to notice their absence after checking the team's status. "Aren't they supposed to be with us?"

"Maybe they started in a different place?" Emy proposed, as she then recognized that they should probably better understand each other's abilities if they soon faced more Grimbletooth.

"What do we all think about sharing our…" Emy's sentence was abruptly cut off as footsteps echoed from the hallway. "Quick, shut the door!"

Tuck, once again first to react, sprang toward the door, looking out as he slammed it shut behind him. "I see five of them coming—all level 2s—and it looks like their hands are on fire!"

"Sheesh, Tuck, did you have to slam the door?" Will's voice called out as the others hastily rearranged desks to form an impromptu barrier.

BOOM! Before Tuck could respond, the door reverberated and splintered, with flickers of firelight seeping through the crevices between the frame and the door as everyone looked at each other.

The lack of movement in the team spurred James into action. "I don't think we have long. Tuck, I have a talent that can make you more powerful for a short period of time. Our best option here is to disrupt—I think we could use a fullback right about now. Blast play?"

Tuck nodded in understanding. James extended his hand, and an energy flow passed over to Tuck.

△△△

PRIOR TUTORIAL

James

Like Emy, James had limited questions directed toward the System, letting his gut guide him down the right path. Becoming a Champion and joining a team were absolute no-brainers for the athlete in him. James wondered why anyone would choose differently. When faced with Professor Williams' digital version, James quickly adjusted and adapted to the environment around him.

"You know, James, if I didn't know you well before the Games, I would be worried about your lack of reaction and questions regarding the environment you're now in. But it seems adapting may be in your blood."

The Professor was right. James had always enjoyed change; change led to growth and new learning. Yes, this was the strangest thing to ever happen to him, but he was excited to learn.

"Yes, I have questions... lots of them, but my gut is telling me to take advantage of our time and learn as much as possible. I hope the answers will come soon enough."

"I think your gut is leading you in the right direction. Let's begin. James, it's safe to say that others perform well around you. Do you happen to know why?"

James attempted to continue adapting and responded as honestly as possible. "Supporting others has always come naturally to me. Everyone has talent, and everyone has strengths. I just feel like I can get the most out of people."

"How?"

"I'm not sure. I feel like everyone has something holding them back, preventing them from being the best versions of themselves... I guess I have a knack for finding that and helping them through it."

"Ah yes, well done. In this new world, this talent is called a Catalyst. Are you familiar with the term from my class?"

"Sort of. I always thought about it as process efficiency, but just within reactants. A Catalyst can speed up the rate at which reactions happen."

"Exactly. My best description would be playing cards by first shuffling the deck. Yes, you could play cards with the deck spread out across the table, but it would create dysfunction and chaos. However, you would still be able to play. Think of your talent as shuffling; you set others up for success by having the talent to elevate the potential in others. This was done without thinking in your former life, but now, it's a bit more dynamic. With this type of talent, you can change the fate of your team. You have the power to influence everything around you. Care to give it a try?"

The professor guided James to the dual pillars in the center of the room. "Now, for this first scenario, I will use raw chemicals. Think of this as a testing ground for future potential. You may remember this example from class where I used a potato. I want you to be the potato," Williams said with a sly smile. "This is hydrogen peroxide or H_2O_2. This solution naturally wants to break down into its core elements of water and oxygen, but the process takes time. You can find and speed up these natural reactions through a catalyst."

"How?"

"Focus on the mixture before you and push your energy towards it. Feel it and let your natural willpower learn the makeup of the chemical solution."

James followed the instructions and, after some trial and error, felt his body channel a force into the substance on the pillar. As his energy covered the solution, he sensed it gradually merging with his own. He realized that as his energy understood the solution, he gained knowledge in return. He and his energy were one. Pushing further, he experienced the natural breakdown Coach had described—the minute decomposition of the solution into simpler elements. By intermingling his energy with the chemicals, he facilitated the breakdown of those elements as a Catalyst. As James's energy spread through the solution, bubbles and foam began to form.

"Excellent!" Coach Williams clapped his hands together, pulling James out of his concentration. "Now, that was the first trial! Let's see if we can get you to more living examples."

∆∆∆

LEVEL ONE

Full Team

As James placed his hand on Tuck's, their energies intertwined. James sensed a chaotic stream of energy coursing through Tuck's body, struggling to break free. Embracing the turbulent flows, James channeled the chaotic energy into focused streams, enabling Tuck to harness his talent more effectively.

< Skill Identified – James – Empower >

< Tuck is boosted by 20% >

Body boosted, Tuck glanced at the others on the team to confirm there were no other ideas before he turned and ran full blast into the door, bursting it off the hinges and sending the five beasts flying.

< Skill Identified – Tuck – Electron Surge >

Tuck stumbled to his feet, now outside the door. The nearest Grimbletooth had already gotten up and was charging towards Tuck. Just inches away from him, a chemistry book flew past and slammed into the creature's face, causing it to disintegrate on the spot.

NERDED!!! 5 POINTS!

"Tuck, get back in here!" James yelled after launching the book.

Tuck scrambled to his feet and threw a kick to the chest of the next closest Grimbletooth, sending it flying over the railing and down to the foyer below.

Rushing back inside, Tuck stood beside the others. As the remaining three creatures bolted towards the door, Tuck prepared to charge again. But James interrupted, "Wait! They're holding something!"

As if on signal, three bottles ablaze with fire were launched through the air towards the team. "Bombs! Quick, move!" urged James.

The team leaped to the sides of the room and behind their makeshift desk barriers—everyone except Will, who stood calm. He held his arms wide and swiftly brought them back together. A wave of pressure persisted, and a mist enveloped the room, extinguishing the fire and dousing the bottles before they could hit the ground.

△△△

PRIOR TUTORIAL

Will

"What do you mean I am a Condenser? Like condensed soup?" Will asked skeptically, looking at the digital Coach Williams after he had informed him of his new talent in the tutorial room.

Williams shook his head, but then his demeanor shifted. "You know what, let's go with it."

Williams gathered his thoughts, attempting to shift his originally planned explanation of what a Condenser was to Will. "Condensed soup is what? It's just soup without its full water source. The idea with this soup is to add water to make it whole again, expanding the components and mixing into an edible version."

"Professor, it was a joke. We don't have to use this as an example," Will commented, but the professor waved him off.

"Think of the final version of the soup as the room around you. Oxygen, nitrogen, water vapor, and other minute chemicals encircle the room, symbolizing the components of the soup. However, when a force like dehydration is applied to the contents, it changes into something else."

Williams continued, "Now, back to the room you are in. Will, your energy differs from others in the fact that it is spread out. You may not notice at this point in your development, but your energy is in every corner of this room surrounding us. As you develop in talent, this capacity will only expand. Yes, most of your energy is still within your core." Williams pointed to his chest. "But, you are connected with the room around you, continuously passing information back and forth. Why do you think you were so good with people in your former life?"

Will contemplated this new information as his eyes widened, attempting to consume these latest revelations. "Because I can read the room?"

"Yes, exactly! That phrase now means more than ever before. You are connected to everything and everyone in the room, continuously passing signals to your brain. Reactions, body language, heart rates, eye contact—your energy gave you insights all along."

"While this connection was one-way in the past, you should now be able to interact with the area around you. Please do me a favor and attempt to visualize your energy. Reach out to every corner of it and have it condense in on itself, bringing the surrounding chemicals with it."

Will attempted first with his mind but found that using his hands helped. As he slowly widened his hands, he felt a sensation within the room. The more he opened them, the more the sensation expanded until his hands were fully extended, and the sensation no longer seemed to grow. Now feeling the entirety of the room, he began to bring his hands back together, representing condensation in his mind. As he did, his body instinctively applied a force between his hands as if the space between them represented the area around him. The closer together they became, the greater the pressure until Will worked up a layer of water across his body.

"Ah, looks like we may have an affinity with water types. Well done, Will. Let's see if we can mix things up more now."

△△△

LEVEL ONE

Full Team

The team watched as Will stood in the middle of the room, now covered in beads of water, while glass shattered around them. Thanks to Will's new skill, the flames that had triggered the bombs were extinguished, leaving only the remnants of broken glass behind.

< Skill Identified – Will – Condense >

Confused and now angry, the Grimbletooth creatures looked ready to charge once more. "James, quick, boost on me!" Emy's voice commanded from behind Will.

< Emy is boosted by 20% >

Emy's concentration deepened as she recalled her final training session with Williams, which revealed a new, destructive combination. She intertwined her innate warmth with the surrounding air, accelerating oxygen atoms to a frantic pace. The doorway became her canvas—a focal point for devastation. With precision, she urged oxygen molecules to collide, their bonds quivering under the strain. Then, like a conductor of chaos, she infused her body heat into the mix.

The oxygen atoms now supercharged, danced with newfound energy. Bonds snapped, releasing a torrent of heat and light. A chain reaction surged through the Grimbletooth huddle, their forms disintegrating in an infernal blaze. The doorframe ignited, its wood curling and blackening.

GRIMALIZED! 15 POINTS!

< Skill Identified – Emy – Targeted Fusion >

CHAPTER TEN

"Working as a team is crucial in group competitions. Recognizing the strengths and weaknesses of your teammates can mean the distinction between life and death." – Radan, Former Champion.

LEVEL ONE

"Wow," James exclaimed, his eyes shifting between Will and Emy. "What the heck did you do?"

Emy interrupted, her voice urgent: "Wait, Nex. Can you tell us if we're safe?"

Nex responded instantly, *"According to the map, there are no active threats in this area."*

Emy squinted at her status screen. "Map? What map?"

Nex chuckled nervously. *"Oops, my bad! I get carried away sometimes. Look at the click-down location at the top of your screen."*

Emy followed Nex's instructions, and suddenly, a massive map consumed her focus. Five blue dots marked the center, labeled "chemistry classroom." Glancing around, she noticed multiple red dots moving downstairs in the foyer—nothing near them upstairs.

"I had to be sure," Emy explained, releasing a breath before she answered James's original question, "My talent is vague right now. It's labeled 'Generalist,' allowing me to modify and merge at an atomic level. But my mastered skills involve merging smaller groups of elements to create reactions."

Emy's response triggered the collective group to revisit the earlier battle skill prompts, first coming to James's new skill:

Skill: Empower

Empowers the user to enhance the capabilities of others. Utilizing this ability can augment another user's power, range, or duration of their skillset. This is a range-based ability. (R)

Next was Tuck's:

Skill: Electron Surge

Cultivates a potent transformation within the user, enabling them to project substantial outward force upon contact. (T)

Then Emy's:

Skill: Targeted Fusion

Allows user to accomplish focused elemental construction with both extended and close-range abilities. (R)

Finally, Will's:

Skill: Condense

Empowers the user to compress, concentrate, or modify vast amounts of matter, thereby granting the user the capability to directly alter the state of matter. (R)

The collective detail on the team's new skills left everyone speechless at the implications, understanding that these were only the team's known capabilities. Still, James pushed the conversation forward and attempted to gather more insight into the team. "Emy, Will, how far can you extend your skills?"

Emy and Will exchanged glances, shaking their heads in unison.

Will added, "We'll figure it out as we progress. Coach wants me to try more experiments, but I haven't had much luck with ranged skills."

Reminded of Coach, Emy voiced a question that had been bothering her, "Hey, Nex, would we be able to see other blue dots on the map if they were also on this level with us?"

Nex's response was mixed. *"Yes, but with limits. The map currently showcases an area of 500 meters in every direction, centered around your location. You might not see the full map in larger scenarios, but everything should be visible due to the school's size and mission parameters."*

Emy released another breath she hadn't realized she was holding. Trish wasn't in the school, and neither were Frank and Trent.

James caught on to Emy's line of questioning. "Nex, do you know if there are any others on our team? Or where they might be?"

"Negative," Nex replied. *"Based on previous gameplay, all core team members should be present during the first level. However, my awareness is limited to each of you. I can expand my intelligence once we reconnect with others post-level."*

Emy questioned, "Level?"

Nex's tone turned apologetic, *"Oh, this might be a good time to review the details under the map section of your status screen. I promise I'm not this spacey all the time!"*

Emy mentally commanded the map to shrink, revealing another section she hadn't noticed before:

Level One Mission: Breach Scenario
Target and remove all combatants on the primary school campus.

Emy's eyes widened, seeing the mission text for the first time, finally getting a bit more understanding of what was going on.

"So, wait, Nex, what happens after a level is completed?" James questioned.

"Expectations based on previous Quantum Games dictate that Champions will have a 48-hour break between the closure of one level and the start of the next. During this period, they can regroup, heal, train, and—if applicable—work with their coach

and teammates on strategy."

"How many levels are there?" James added to his original question.

"Ten," Nadia responded for Nex. "Did no one else ask about the actual Games?"

Caught off guard by her remark, the rest of the group turned their attention to Nadia, but Will responded, "Coach only gave me vague responses, saying he wasn't allowed to share much."

"Same," the rest said in unison, a wave of agreement sweeping through the group.

"And you didn't press him further?" Nadia's gaze swept over the group, reflecting her bewilderment at their lack of challenge.

"No," Will responded as though reprimanded by an instructor, causing Nadia to blush in response to her sudden outburst.

Nex intervened, *"Nadia is correct. There are ten levels. But let's hold off on those questions until after this first level! Remember, we have a 48-hour break without any creatures attempting to kill us."*

The group absorbed this new information as shock passed through them. As they processed the details, Will gravitated toward the door to check outside the room to see if he could get more clues about what was happening. Outside, he discovered a glowing box adorned with a thick red ribbon. "Hey, look over here," Will called out, bending over to pick up the glowing box. "It seems one of the creatures dropped this. Who wants to open it?"

Tuck grumbled, trying to conceal his excitement, "Just get on with it."

"Fine, fine," Will conceded, untying the bow and opening the box. Will smirked as he reached inside and pulled out a small **Fanny Pack**, front embroidered with an orange and yellow flame.

Upon viewing, Nadia spoke for the second time, "I think it may be for Emy. She's the only one of us with a fire-based skill. It feels like a sign, and well, her nickname is… Fury."

"Wait, how do you know about that name?" Emy questioned.

Will shrugged, ignoring the open question back to Nadia, handing over the *Fanny Pack* to Emy. Grabbing it, she then wrapped it around her waist and snapped it shut. "Huh, what do you know? Perfect fit."

New Gear Detected - Fanny Pack
Uncommon

Allows the wearer to store ten unique items within the pack. Each item resides in a small personal void space accessible only to the user at any time. Items remain locked in stasis until removed.

Emy reviewed her gear segment on the status page:

Gear: Earth Base Clothing - No Modifications

Full Body: None
Head: None
Upper Body: College Letterman's Jacket - No Modifications
Lower Body: Leggings - No Modifications
Feet: Sneakers - No Modifications
Accessories: Engraved Fanny Pack (Uncommon) **(New)**

"Wait, Nex, what does 'Uncommon' mean?" Emy asked.

"*I was saving this update for the first item drop! 'Uncommon' is this item's ranking. Rankings range from Common to Mythic, depending on the item's scarcity and the power level it represents. Here is the full list of options: Common, Uncommon, Rare, Epic, Legendary, Mythic. Typically, the better the item, the rarer it is, but there are always exceptions!*"

"*There is also one more ranking that doesn't quite fit the progression of the others, called Unique. Unique items can range from Common all the way past Mythic, as they are one of a kind. Usually, these Unique items are at least Rare, but they are always on a scale of their own.*"

"*The Fanny Pack is ranked as Uncommon, which means it is not abundant across the Cosmos, but you would still be able to find similar items if you knew where to shop!*"

Emy's eyes lit up as she spoke, "I think I know what this is for." She hurried to the backroom behind the teacher's desk, where all the unique chemicals were stored for hands-on demonstrations. Grabbing a few vials and blocks of chemicals, Emy carefully placed them into her pack. "I am now a mobile chemistry classroom!" her smile radiated excitement as she shared her discovery with the group.

With a smirk directed at Emy's excitement over the **Fanny Pack**, James raised the most crucial question: "Does anyone have any ideas for handling the rest of the level?"

CHAPTER ELEVEN

"The fans enjoy chaos." – Tournament Director.

LEVEL ONE

Blood trickled down Emy's face as she was hurled into a wall. Her protective shield had been exhausted, causing her health to drop below 40%. As the Grizzleclaw advanced to deliver the final blow, Emy's thoughts whirled, questioning what had gone wrong.

△△△

EARLIER

"I think I have a plan," James said after reviewing the map with his team. The good news was that the map showed the blueprint of the school they had been attending for the last six months.

Luckily, they had time, and the upper floor lay vacant, its sole protection being the creatures who had previously swarmed them in their chemistry class. This gave them an advantage, enabling each individual to outline their existing abilities and prospective skills and a chance to put some hypotheses into practice.

The school was a two-story structure. The upper level, in addition to classrooms, housed a round mezzanine walkway that spanned the entire building. Looking down from the railing, this walkway offered a superb view of the ground floor, which was split into two separate sections: the entrance hall and the foyer. In both areas, the team noticed a variety of Grimbletooth creatures of levels 1 and 2 vigilantly patrolling, with the majority gathered in the foyer. Moreover, each area showcased a grand staircase ascending to the second level, watched over by a monstrous creature with massive claws jutting from its paws.

Grizzleclaw: Level 4

These colossal, hairy creatures boast rounded, muscular shoulders. Initially designed for underground evacuations, their oversized, spiked claws now serve as formidable weapons, making them fierce defenders of their subterranean hives.

Fortunately for the team, four smaller stairwells were located in corners of the building, tucked back beside the classrooms.

James continued, "It's not great, but given our limited skillsets, I don't think we have many options right now. We can't press our luck much longer on time either. Those things downstairs are bound to realize something happened. Tuck literally kicked a tooth person over the edge."

"Uh, I believe the proper term would be a 'Boot Canal,'" Will said with a sly smile.

Eventually, the team agreed to the plan, silently exiting the classroom and heading towards the entry hall. James figured this was the best place to start due to the limited number of creatures surrounding the area.

Sticking with the plan, Emy stealthily descended the stairs of one of the corner hallways, moving closer to the main Entry Hall. With her vision set and the others in position, she used **Targeted Fusion**. Funneling the ammonium and hydrogen sulfide from her **Fanny Pack** toward her targeted trashcan, she merged the two chemicals into what could be called a stink bomb. Job done, Emy rushed back upstairs to the mezzanine, where a nauseating smell began to permeate the entire building.

Tears streaming down his face and gagging, Will exclaimed, "Gosh darn it, Emy. Did you really need to make one that big? This whole school is going to be hotboxed."

Wiping a tear from his eyes, Will shifted as he suddenly noticed four Grimbletooth creatures rounding the corner, investigating the disturbance.

"Do it!" Will urged over their communication channel as James channeled his skill into Will.

< *Will is boosted by 20%* >

As the creatures flocked to the trashcan and peered inside, Will gathered and used his *Condense* skill with the water vapor around him. This time, with the extra boost and a touch of cold from his body, shards of ice began to form in the air. These thick blocks took the shape of icicles, their sharp edges facing away from Will due to Will being the primary source of the cold.

Tuck stepped forward, placing his hands close to the shards. Drawing on his *Electron Surge* skill, he channeled the energy outward, accelerating it through his hand and into the shard. The jolts of energy surged into the ice, propelling the shards toward the creatures at incredible speeds.

CRACK! The first block sailed over the head of the lead Grimbletooth and embedded itself in the wall.

"Shit!" Will cursed as the first block missed. He knew what would happen next.

"Humans!" the creature yelled, looking back to where the ice had come from. But before it could react further, its torso was sliced through by a second ice shard.

CRACK! THUD! Noises resounded as the remaining ice struck the area.

Three creatures had been struck down, but one remained. Without hesitation, Tuck sprang into action, charging headlong at the final creature.

△△△

Emy & Nadia

"Oh no, no, no... SHIT. SHIT," Emy muttered to herself, watching the Grizzleclaw take off from its perch on the stairs and head toward the area with the yelling. They weren't going to be ready for him, Emy thought as she rushed to the top of the stairs. *I have to do something.*

BANG! A blast rattled off the back of the Grizzleclaw, instantly stopping it in its tracks. It turned around, its claws sparkling with a reflection of light.

< Grizzleclaw's health is at 90% >

"Uh oh."

Dropping to all fours, the creature rushed at Emy as she tried to trigger another blast.

BOOM! The strike grazed off the shoulder of the beast, its hair roasted with fire. Unstopping, the creature lunged at Emy and delivered a claw strike that tore into her chest, sending her flying into the nearest classroom wall.

< Your health is at 40% - Shield is now at 0% >

"NO!" screamed Nadia, rushing in to attempt to put a hand on Emy.

"Stay back!" Emy yelled at Nadia as the creature closed in to finish the job. Digging its front claws into the floor, the beast took a running leap, sharp fangs aimed at Emy's face. Lying on her back, Emy made one last desperate attempt. She used **Targeted Fusion**, focusing her channels into her chest and concentrating her will to hypercharge oxygen atoms into a ball of energy. As the creature struck, she forced her internal heat outward, channeling it into the ball and shoving it into the Grizzleclaw's chest.

After a brief silence, the space erupted as the ball of fire exploded outward from Emy. The initial impact obliterated the Grizzleclaw's body, but the resulting force sent Emy and the once-approaching Nadia hurtling backward, tumbling onto the mezzanine floor. Nadia reached out, grabbed Emy's hand, and poured every ounce of her willpower into her **Revive** skill.

SHAAAAZAAAMMMM! 27 POINTS!

< Level Up! Emy is now a Level 4 Generalist >

< Combatants cleared >

Nex's voice finally returned to normal, "*I'm afraid to tell you how close that was.*"

The remaining team members hurried over, joining Emy and Nadia, their breaths coming in heavy pants. Tuck effortlessly scooped up Emy, and the team made a beeline for the closest classroom to take cover.

"That didn't go quite as planned," Will added as the door closed.

CHAPTER TWELVE

"True growth comes in the heart of battle. With your life on the line and back against the wall, you tend to push yourself to the max." – Coach Williams.

LEVEL ONE

"James," Will began, his voice tinged with both gratitude and frustration, "I think we might be square after that last round."

"Huh?" James looked up, catching the attention of the rest of the group.

"Yeah," Will continued, "minus that disastrous plan, your boost helped me understand my talent better." He extended his arms, maintaining a half-meter gap between his parallel palms. With a concentrated effort, he exerted an unseen force onto the space that lay between. The air responded, condensing into a visible mist that soon coalesced into water droplets. Finally, Will channeled an icy chill from his body, compelling the water to crystalize into a delicate wall of ice that spanned the breadth of his outstretched hands.

< Level Up! Will is now a level 3 Condenser >

"That's awesome, Will," James replied. "At least my power wasn't entirely useless in that battle. But honestly, I felt like dead weight out there... Is this my story? Always the worst player on a great team?"

The team collectively turned to face James, with Will quickly backtracking, "Dude, that's not what I meant. Your plans saved our asses twice."

James sighed. "I appreciate that, but there has to be more to my power. I won't keep up with you guys if I don't figure it out."

"You will," Emy said, sitting up and holding her stomach. Her voice held no doubt. "And just because the last plan failed, doesn't mean we're not having you build the next one."

"So, wait, why didn't we get a new skill notification when Will created the ice wall?" Nadia asked.

"Oh, I think it was just because I utilized my **Condense** skill in a new way. The skill was the same, but the application was different." Will responded.

Following a moment of quiet as everyone processed the extra details on skill creation, Tuck broke the silence. "Will, did you ask your Nex to update your name on the team list?"

Everyone at once pulled up the status page:

	Talent	**Level**	**Health**	**Shield**
Emy	Generalist	Level 4	85%	30%
Tuck	Accelerator	Level 4	100%	30%
Nadia	Cellulator	Level 2	100%	0%
Brick (Will)	Condenser	Level 3	100%	20%
James	Catalyst	Level 2	100%	0%

"Firstly, it's Nexy. And second, why not? Can't I have a superhero name?" Will's voice held a mix of defiance and excitement. "Shoot, I can make a fricking ice wall now. What better name is there?" His candidness caught everyone off guard. "I also may have updated redhead over there," he glanced at Emy, "but only on my personal views. She'll have to accept that on her own when the time comes."

Emy glanced at Will but then pivoted to the rest of the team, disregarding his remark while still clutching her side. "Does this feel real to you guys?"

"What do you mean?" James was the first to respond as everyone's attention turned to Emy.

"Just a short while ago, I was on the brink, unsure if I'd pull through. Now, I'm nearly fully recovered. We're here, in the very school we once knew so well, armed with powers we could only have dreamed of, and being chased by diminutive creatures of nightmare," Emy elaborated. "Surely, I can't be the only one questioning my sanity?"

This time, Tuck responded, "I'm with you, Emy, but I keep coming back to the same conclusion."

The group waited for Tuck's response as he took his time to articulate his thoughts. "This reality, this power, feels more tangible than anything I've ever experienced."

The group collectively nodded in agreement with Tuck's insight, and then Nadia spoke softly, "I thought I was the only one… Yes, I'm confused, but if this is real, my life leading up to this point makes a lot more sense."

A solemn silence enveloped the group as they each admitted to sharing the same sentiment—the world they inhabited now felt more real than the one they had known. Acknowledging this stark truth made acceptance easier.

James cleared his throat. "All right, I think I have a new plan," he announced. The team felt hopeful as his words hung in the air.

Will smirked. "Is it better than the last one?"

△△△

This time, James crafted a new strategy, assigning Tuck the role of a high-damage tank and having Nadia on standby to provide healing as needed. Emy and Will, armed with Will's newfound shielding capabilities, maintained their positions at a greater distance.

"On my mark," James relayed through the battle comms. Stationed in the mezzanine, he found a silver lining in the chaos of the last battle—it had yielded something helpful. His eyes locked onto a cluster of Molotov cocktails, their fuses primed for ignition. Taking a deep breath, he produced a lighter and set the fuse ablaze. "Game time."

James reached back and hurled the bottle, rocketing it directly toward the stairs. **BOOM!** The glass struck the Grizzleclaw, engulfing the creature in flames. Roaring, the beast turned its gaze upward, fixing its eyes on James.

BOOM! Another fireball slammed into the Grizzleclaw's back, courtesy of Emy's *Targeted Fusion* blasts.

< Grizzleclaw's health is at 75% >

< Tuck is boosted by 20% >

As the inferno raged, so did Tuck. After receiving a pulse from James, he charged through the foyer, slamming into the unsuspecting Grimbletooth, who cried out to their overwhelmed leader.

As Tuck plowed through the diminutive creatures, Emy and James sustained their relentless attacks on the more formidable Grizzleclaw.

< Grizzleclaw's health is at 15% >

Engrossed in the battle against the Grizzleclaw, Emy was unaware of a desperate throw from below. **CRASH!** Ice splintered as Will hastily erected a wall, narrowly dodging a catastrophe.

"Thanks," Emy exhaled, her heart pounding as she stared at Will's icy barrier, recognizing her narrow escape from the explosive threat. Her eyes then darted below, taking in the sight of Tuck's unyielding assault on the remaining small Grimbletooth. His focus then locked onto the distracted boss. With sparks flying and muscles straining, Tuck charged up the stairs. His final blow—a powerful punch—landed squarely on the Grizzleclaw's chest…

OBLITERATED! 23 POINTS!

"Well, that went way better than last time," Will's voice projected over the communications as the team caught their breath, and Nadia channeled waves of healing energy to restore Tuck to total health.

"Oh, goodie! Views are growing! We just hit 700 active viewers and are still rising!" Nex exclaimed.

"Why would they spike after a battle?" Emy paused, realization dawning. "Everyone, get ready—the battle isn't over!"

James was the first to notice it. "Team, I see a new purple dot on the map. It seems to be coming from the stairs near Tuck."

"It must have been…burrowing," Emy remembered the creature descriptions from the battle. "It was underground…"

The walls trembled as a creature emerged from behind the stairs. The floor quaked, revealing the hulking form of a giant troll-like monster, its shaggy fur covered by pulsing brown armor and its fierce fangs ready for battle.

Burrow Queen: Level 6

Emerging from the abyss of a long-forgotten realm, the Queen now wields dominion over the subterranean expanse with an unyielding grasp. Her loyal subjects, architects of the underworld, construct silent empires beneath unsuspecting civilizations. With patience and cunning, the Burrow Queen orchestrates the downfall of cities below ground, ascending as their sovereign ruler.

"Oh boy," James said, hesitating, "we don't have a plan for this."

Turning around the corner, the Queen rushed at Tuck, who remained on the stairs.

BOOM! Another fireball struck the Queen, causing her to

pause mid-stride. She watched as her armor absorbed the fire attack, and her health returned to 100%. With a sly smile, she tore into Tuck, the two exchanging furious blows. The final strike ripped into his shoulder, dropping his health to 85%.

We need to do something, James thought, searching within himself for answers as the Queen's rapid armor regeneration began to shift the balance of the battle. *We need to slow her down...*

A memory from the tutorial surfaced in his mind. 'You can change the fate of your team. You have the power to influence everything around you,' Professor Williams had once stated.

I can do that... James realized. Intent shifting, James reversed his **Empower** skill. Instead of focusing on increasing energy efficiency, he scanned to discover how to create blockages and bottlenecks within the mighty creature. Once he found the vulnerabilities, he immediately targeted the Queen with a quick energy pulse.

< Queen's shield regeneration is reduced by 20% >

< Skill Identified – James – Restrict >

< Level Up! James is now a Level 3 Catalyst >

Smiling at the combat notice, Tuck and Emy retargeted with newfound confidence. Fire now consumed the boss again as Tuck delivered blow after blow to the powerful creature, dropping her health to 67%.

With a swift, brutal slash, the Queen brought the team's advance to a sudden standstill. She effortlessly caught Tuck's punch in one clawed hand while her other hand carved a swift arc through his torso.

< Tuck's health is at 45% >

BOOM! A powerful kick bashed at Tuck's newly sliced-open abdomen, sending him hurtling down the stairs.

< Tuck's health is CRITICAL at 8% >

A pulse of health rushed into Tuck, bringing him back to 20% health as Nadia stood beside him.

"You need to throw me," Nadia stated, staring intently at Tuck, who looked at her confused. "What? I can't do that. You'll be crushed."

"James, boost me. Now!" Nadia's voice held newfound confidence, "Emy, hit her with fire right before I reach her."

< Nadia is boosted by 20% >

Tuck's face bore traces of hesitation as he seized Nadia with both hands. "Do it! I need to get close," she confirmed to Tuck. Without delay, he propelled Nadia into the air, her form soaring toward the Queen.

BOOM! Emy's blast struck the beast just as the Burrow Queen reached out and caught Nadia with one clawed hand, laughing at the situation's absurdity. "What is this? Your best plan?"

< The Queen's health is at 45% >

Gripped by the mighty claws of the Queen, Nadia immediately integrated her energy with the creature, searching for the destruction that had just hit the massive being. After locating the damaged cells, she halted the natural vitalization of the Boss. Instead, she forced the inflicted cells to spread further, causing them to fester, grow, and quickly navigate through the Queen's entire body. The fire blast that had struck the Queen now spread as flames and destruction raced over her form. Quiet now, the Queen looked down at the determined Nadia, still clutched in her hand, channeling her skill.

< The Queen's health is CRITICAL at 15% >

Nadia took a moment to lock eyes with the Queen. "You lose."

An explosion of debris filled the room as Tuck rammed into

the Queen's body, disintegrating her as Nadia was tossed to the ground.

HERO MOMENT!! 67 POINTS!

< Skill Identified – Nadia – Affliction Surge >

< Level Up! Nadia is now a Level 3 Cellulator >

"You did it." Tuck's hands grasped around Nadia.

"We did it." Nadia smiled, sharing the joy of the moment with her friend.

MISSION ACCOMPLISHED!

All enemy combatants were eliminated. The breach is now being sealed.

The voice of the tutorial resounded in the air as the world faded to gray.

△△△

Cohort 13

Level One Results:

Total Team Points: **196 Points**

Total Max Active Views: **2153**

Earth Rank: **35,420,233 of 354,203,157**

90th Percentile

CHAPTER THIRTEEN

"The 48-hour window is never enough. You do what you can and train all you can, but the System will never let you feel prepared." – Codex, Former Champion.

SYSTEM HEADQUARTERS

"Status update, Shukar. How are the Games shaping so far? I've heard the rumblings of a level 6 progenitor emerging from the Earth sector. Is this true?" questioned Viggo, the Games Director.

"The Games are progressing well, Sir. There were only a few hiccups, but nothing we couldn't handle with the System. And yes, I have also noticed this outlier; they grew to level 7 by the end of the first level."

"An unprecedented anomaly. That is quite unheard of in these new frontiers and reeks of tampering. Have the Astral Dominion bypassed our security fronts?"

"While we are researching feeds, we cannot know for sure. But once integrated, the System owns full domain over the selection process."

"The inevitable path. We cannot stop the wheel from turning. Let's pray to the Cosmos that this is not the case for the future of this world."

"Already am, sir," Shukar whispered.

△△△

THE HANGAR

Congratulations on completing the first level of the Quantum Games!

You now have 48 hours of recovery before the next level of the Games begins. At the end of this period, you will be asked whether you want to proceed to the next level or remove yourself from the Games completely.

As the team reappeared in what looked like a giant, empty factory floor, Frank's voice boomed, **"YOU GUYS KICKED SOME SERIOUS ASS!"**

Without missing a beat, Will returned, "Yeah, you're telling me. Nadia stole my hero quote!"

Trish couldn't contain her excitement, "Nadia, that was the **COOLEST** thing! We had no idea you had that capability!"

Still processing what happened, Emy ran up to Trish and hugged her. "Where have you guys been? And what is this place? We thought you ended up on another team or were taken somewhere."

Trish and Frank exchanged a knowing smile, and Frank took the lead. "You see," he began, "Trish and I joined the Games as a team but discovered that our distinct abilities could be better utilized elsewhere. And as for this place..." he said, pausing, searching for words that seemed a bit planned. "We call it the Hangar—a sanctuary where eating, strategy, friendship, preparation, and rest come together."

"Interesting order of items, Frank," Trish added, but immediately continued, "We get to watch your entire broadcast while preparing for these break periods with you." She paused, noting, "Frank and I have been honing our skills as artisans. Frank continues to grow as a smith, and I've been diving deeper into cyber tech and energy sources. We've got some big ideas for you, but first, let me see those new skills, please!"

Nadia was the first to bring up her new skill to the group:

Skill: Affliction Surge

Allows the user to intensify existing ailments within themselves or others through touch, thereby escalating their effects. (T)

James then shared his:

Skill: Restrict

Enables the user to dampen the abilities of others. Using this ability, the user can decrease another's skill set in terms of power, range, or duration. (R)

"Awesome," Trish commented on the skills highlighted. "Those are what Frank and I expected to see."

James questioned, "Any ideas on what happened to Trent? We assumed he'd be with you."

Trish shook her head. "Nope. Frank and I think he may have opted for a solo game."

Tuck grunted, "That sounds about right."

The team continued to hug, catching up on each other's experiences, when a smiling Coach Williams joined them in the room, immediately breaking into applause. "Well done, Team. It seems my hunches about all of you were spot-on. I can't wait to witness your continued growth."

His smile turned sly. "Have you opened your level reward yet?"

The seven ex-students exchanged puzzled glances, unsure of what their coach was implying.

"Turn around," Williams laughed as a box resembling the one previously dropped by the Grimbletooth materialized.

"Hero Nadia, I think the privilege is yours," Will interjected while the rest of the group continued to gawk.

Nadia advanced and bent to open the sizable gift box on the floor. As she opened the box, a prompt materialized in everyone's view.

New Gear Detected - QuantumWeave (x5)
Uncommon

A body suit interwoven with subatomic threads that resonate with the wearer's natural energies. These threads form an intricate lattice, providing a 10% base shielding bonus against harm while allowing the flow of innate power. When danger approaches, the QuantumWeave responds, adapting its density and conductivity. This base layer fits underneath one's clothes, allowing for seamless integration with existing attire.

Emy and the rest of the team immediately glanced at their gear section on the status page:

Full Body: QuantumWeave (Uncommon) **(NEW)**
Head: None
Upper Body: College Letterman's Jacket - No modifications
Lower Body: Leggings - No modifications
Feet: Sneakers - No modifications
Accessories: Engraved Fanny Pack (Uncommon)

Emy couldn't help but glance down at her singed letterman's jacket and worn leggings. "Would have been nice to get this a bit sooner," she muttered.

Coach Williams nodded. "Those are remarkable items from the System. As your talents evolve, regular clothing will eventually become inadequate. Especially for those of you mastering full-body techniques."

Nex added in, *"Ah yes! There have been quite a few incidents in the history of the Games."*

Ignoring the comment, Professor Williams looked at the group. "Now that you have your new gear, I think it's time for another round of questions. Would you like more detail on what you've gotten yourselves into at this point?"

The team members exchanged glances, their minds adjusting to the unfamiliar surroundings. "Frank and Trish refer to this place as the Hangar. In reality, it's an intermission subspace equipped with various rooms designed for mental and physical training. Behind me is the main combat zone, loaded with various training software. If you can imagine it, that machine likely has it. We'll explore more later, but for now, let's proceed to the strategy room," the Professor guided.

They followed the Professor into a room that resembled a military command center. A large oval table encircled by seven chairs facing a completely digital wall instantly captured the team's attention. The faces of the five Champions were displayed on the wall, with details such as their primary talent, affinity, skillset, weapons, and gear listed beneath each image.

As everyone settled into their seats and surveyed the room, the professor initiated the discussion, "Before we delve deeper, I'd like to pose a question. Did you take in any clues about the mission from the previous level?"

James attempted to answer first, "It was a breach scenario. Based on your question, does this probably mean this may be a common scenario outside our galaxy?"

"Very good, James," Professor Williams replied. "Outside of using my question against me. Yes, within the Cosmos, this breach scenario is common. Without the support of the System holding the Quantum stabilizers or 'bubbles' together, you would have encountered these types of events all along. But your access to quantum manipulation also allows others outside your world to do the same—either by pure randomness or deliberate intent."

Emy questioned, "But who defends against these types of events in other worlds?"

Professor Williams grinned. "Champions," he replied. "Indeed, heroes beyond your world exist who can rescue the very ground we stand upon. However, they cannot be omnipresent. It falls upon each world to construct its defenses against these formidable adversaries. Guns and nuclear weapons won't suffice in countering these newfound threats. For survival, Earth must flourish, and Champions must emerge. Consider these trials as a farewell offering from the System. Either thrive and endure or falter and witness your world's demise."

The team felt the impact of those words. Until that moment, they had merely engaged in a game—a series of close calls and daring feats. Yet, despite their actions, it remained an illusion. They played roles, embodying characters, but were never truly themselves.

"Professor?" Nadia spoke up. She paused, her gaze steady. "Can we die in the Games?"

The question hung in the air, a weighty silence. Professor Williams mirrored the pause, then met her eyes. "Yes."

"You were immersed in a mixed reality," he elaborated. "Did you observe the disintegration of those creatures? Those creatures were fabricated, but you? Your death is final—there's no respawning. The risks are genuine. You can withdraw between levels, but remember that numerous young adults face the same dilemma. Can you assure that even a single competitor will rise as the Champion that your world is in dire need of?"

His words pressed on, "Now, consider this: If you hesitate even for a second when answering, is it worth sacrificing your world to quit? Continuing doesn't mean pushing your limits—it means risking everything. If you lack the conviction to lay your life on the line for your team and your world, perhaps it's time to step back... Those creatures you faced—they are real. While they might not currently inhabit your planet, there's a chance they could one day arrive. The queen of the hive you encountered was merely a dwarf version of what the creature becomes."

With a sigh, Professor Williams shifted his tone back to his version of Coach Williams. "Let's hold off on further questions. You now know the stakes. Let those sink in."

"Professor, you told me you would tell us who you are if we passed the first level," Emy commented.

"And I will, but at the appropriate time. You have 48 hours to rest and train. Every moment counts—don't waste it."

CHAPTER FOURTEEN

*"Trust in your team outweighs all doubt
and hesitation." – Coach Williams.*

THE HANGAR

James & Frank

In response to Coach Williams' feedback, the team underwent a reorganization, forming smaller groups that aligned with different roles within the larger team. From the very onset of the tournament, Coach Williams, Trish, and Frank had been meticulously preparing for this event. Frank was overly excited about collaborating with James during this intermission. So, when their names were called out as a pairing, Frank swept James into a bear hug and immediately pulled him into a room diagonally across from the strategy room.

"I cannot wait to show what we built for you!"

△△△

From an external perspective, James enjoyed a privileged childhood. James's parents had athletic backgrounds. His mother, a professional downhill skier, met his father, who worked as a trainer and agent in the downhill skiing community. Their proximity to Lake Tahoe and renowned ski resorts made them well-known, primarily due to James's mother's participation in the XIX Olympic Winter Games in Salt Lake City. His family lived in a spacious house, and their wealth allowed them to fulfill James's every desire. James benefited from top-notch private tutors, attended elite sports training camps, and dined on squarely prepared meals at home.

This upbringing and support pushed James to embrace sports from an early age. Starting with basketball and baseball, he thrived within teams and formed lasting friendships. However, it was during middle school that a friend encouraged him to try football. With his baseball arm and basketball footwork, James found his calling as a quarterback. His dedication to training and learning solidified his passion.

Judy and Mike Gray, James's parents, were steadfast supporters. Their charisma endeared them to fellow parents, fostering lasting friendships, but reflecting now, James wonders if football ever was his main passion. While he excelled and consistently played on championship-bound teams, the camaraderie within the team was the most rewarding aspect. Bus trips, out-of-town training sessions, and coaches who felt like family defined his football experience. Although he loved his parents, their hectic schedules, brimming with mountain expeditions, marketing engagements, and lengthy summer training sessions in snow-clad areas across the globe, often left them physically distant. Consequently, James sought out alternative avenues for connection, seeking friendship and a sense of family beyond the confines of his immediate household.

△△△

Rejoining Frank, James took in the expanse of the Hangar. His eyes were drawn to the main level, where the training arena was situated, surrounded by walls pulsating with electricity. The Hangar intrigued him—it was spacious enough to accommodate a mini arena or even park several charter planes yet compact enough to maintain proximity among everyone in the facility. As they progressed, James caught sight of various rooms dispersed around the perimeter—some mirrored chemistry labs, while others appeared to be advanced tech spaces.

As James and Frank walked, confusion suddenly dawned on James. He turned to Frank, questioning, "Frank, how do you even know this place so well? We were only gone for what, like, 3-4 hours?"

Frank smiled. "Yeah, I don't know the exact math, but I do know that time is dilated in this intermission… location?" Frank's voice held a hint of doubt but pressed on, "We watched you guys through our Nexs, but we only watched in bursts. It was like a TV show with really, really long commercials. After a stint in the level, it would give Trish and me time to explore, work, plan, and then watch the next segment. I think three days have passed in here? I believe it changes based on how long you are in the level, but I also think it allows everyone to stay in the same window of levels."

"Same window?" James looked at Frank, clearly confused.

"Yeah," Frank explained, "You can't have one team on the first level and five teams on the second and so on. This allows for common connection points and more time for us to support you."

Once they arrived at the other side of the facility, Frank's grin widened. "Here we are, my favorite room besides the kitchen: the Smithy!"

James entered the room, marveling at the fusion of old-world craftsmanship and futuristic technology. It was as much an arcade filled with gadgets as a traditional smithing workspace.

"I know, right?" Frank's smile was infectious. "Back in college, I thought the welding room was the pinnacle. But this place? It's a whole new level. We've got augmented reality workstations, 3D printing forges with nanotech capabilities, and AI-enabled learning models to help us create the best equipment for you."

James's eyes widened. "Can you just build anything you want?"

Frank laughed. "Not exactly. At present, my task is to steer you, but I've been gaining a wealth of knowledge from Nex and some pre-programmed software. We'll utilize commercially available technology, slightly modified to cater to your unique abilities. However, I hope to introduce my own inventions soon, which could lower the overall point expenditure and possibly offer the opportunity to re-sell to the wider Cosmos for additional points or money. I'm still trying to grasp this entire barter system. For now, let's focus on points."

James's mouth was slightly agape as he tried to digest the information Frank was sharing. "Starting with points seems sensible since I'm completely in the dark about what you're referring to."

"Ah, of course! Sorry, dude," Frank responded, "do you remember Coach Williams mentioning these Games were a parting gift? They, indeed, are genuine gifts. In addition to drops and rewards, your level points can be traded in a contribution store—for components, supplies, and anything else your creativity can envision."

Continuing, "Based on the team's total points from the last round, Trish and I made some initial assessments. That's why I've come here to show you that we will build you… this."

In the center of the room, above the square pillar with what seemed like a glass table top, a hologram appeared of a high-tech bow and arrow rotating around slowly.

Novaflight Bow and Void Quiver - 100 Points
High E-Class
The Novaflight Bow combines futuristic design with energy infusion, enabling quick draws and enhanced power for precise, devastating shots.

Stasis Alchemarrows - 20 Points
High E-Class

These arrows empower the user to infuse diverse forces into the arrowheads. The arrows remain potent while holding these mixtures in stasis until they strike their intended target. This unique ability provides a versatile array of options, from strengthening allies to disrupting and thwarting adversaries.

"Nex, could you give the newbie here a rundown on the weapon classes?" Frank asked, noticing the shock still lingering on James's face.

"Of course! Weapons are ranked slightly different from items within the broader Cosmos to classify their power level, energy consumption, durability, and, most importantly, cost. Unlike items, weapons follow the same ranking system we use for heroes but are tiered rather than level-bound. These two purchased weapons are High E-Class, meaning they should be used by heroes pushing the limits of what an E-Class user can do. Weapons should closely match the user's power level, so an E-Class hero shouldn't wield a C-Class weapon. In most cases, this mismatch would prevent the user from fully utilizing the weapon's potential. While higher-class weapons are generally better, it's more about finding the right weapon for the right hero. Weapons typically shouldn't scale more than one class jump, though exceptions exist. Additionally, each class has mid-tiers: Low, Mid, and High. As you progress in power scaling, these mid-tiers become more noticeable, especially in the upper classes, where the differences between classes grow."

Overwhelmed by the immense potential of these items, James trembled. "I... I can't accept these. It's more than half our points. It wouldn't be fair to the others."

Surprised by James's response, Frank paused to gather his thoughts, "You know," he began, "I didn't have many friends growing up. But I can say this with certainty: based on what I've witnessed in the Games so far, every single person on our team would run through a wall for you, James. Heck, Fury would ignite the wall and THEN plow through it, not just for you but for anyone else on the team. Cost be damned. Every member of this team would gladly give this to you because they know you would use it to support those around you best. Take it and own it."

A profound silence hung in the air as James accepted the gift, a quiet joy filling his heart. He felt happiness and pride, ready to take on the world for his teammates.

"We have a few ideas for arrow infusions, but first, are you ready to build and test it out?" Frank smirked.

"Hell yes, I am."

CHAPTER FIFTEEN

"Pressure, when carried in isolation, can shatter even the most unyielding determination. Hence, we distribute it among the team, forging collective resilience." – Coach Williams.

THE HANGAR

Trish & Nadia

As the group began to disperse, Trish approached Nadia, extending her hand to introduce herself formally. "Hey Nadia, I'm Trish," she said with a wide smile. "I have to say, you're a total badass. Frank and I have been evaluating the team since the integration began, and we're convinced that you have the most potential for our next level." The two engaged in conversation as they approached what appeared to be a cutting-edge laboratory.

Nadia's smile widened as she responded, "Thanks, Trish. I'm not entirely sure about all that, but I'd be lying if I said I didn't know who you were." She hesitated, then continued, "I loved watching your soccer team—er, former team—during games and practice. I, uh, sort of watched from my dorm."

Trish raised an eyebrow. "You watched practice?" she asked, noticing Nadia's immediate blush.

"Yeah," Nadia admitted, "actually, that was my favorite part. The games were fun, but I really enjoyed observing all the plays, drills, and interactions with the team—even if I couldn't hear anything. It might sound strange, but I always found great joy in pinpointing a play during a game based on what you all had been practicing during the week..."

Trish chuckled. "That's not strange at all—well, maybe a little," she teased, "I think strategy is one of the best parts of the game! Which is probably why you saw me play more during practice than in games... so wait, did you ever play soccer or any other sports?"

Nadia's expression shifted. "No," she confessed, "I wanted to, but it wasn't an option. My parents enrolled me in soccer in 3rd grade, and apparently, I just stood there in the middle of the field, staring at the other players. They told me I touched the ball once and then ran away—that was the highlight of the entire season. After that, they decided I wasn't athletic enough for sports. They always wanted me to excel at anything I did, so that was tough for them."

Nadia's eyes held a mix of nostalgia and resignation as she shared her formerly untold story with Trish.

Listening to Nadia's words, Trish grappled with the weight of this newfound connection. They had just met, yet Nadia's vulnerability had opened the door to deeper understanding. "Is that why you knew you wanted to join the Games?" Trish asked, her curiosity piqued, "did you want the chance to be part of a team?"

Nadia hesitated, her gaze distant. "I think so," she replied, "but I'm not entirely sure if I consciously decided it during those moments. The strange feelings—the anticipation, the comfort—I experienced before we met in that classroom... It was like my body was whispering to me. Urging me not to mess up another opportunity."

Trish sensed more beneath the surface, unspoken emotions and hidden motivations. She respected Nadia's boundaries, knowing some stories were meant to unfold over time. "I understand," Trish said gently, "everyone on the team is thrilled to have you. And now, it seems I have another team strategist to bounce ideas off—besides James." Her smile widened as she then completely shifted topics. "So, uh, how do you feel about becoming an assassin?"

△△△

Will & Tuck

"Tank? Hmm no. Truck? Yes, that's it. Wait. No, maybe Titan?" Will blurted out, attempting to find the right superhero name as he and Tuck walked toward the arena in the heart of the Hangar.

Tuck's response was flat and succinct: "No."

Their dynamic was a subtle game. Tuck and Will shared a deep bond, but their interactions might not reveal it at first glance. When Tuck was in Will's presence, he became terse. He relished observing Will's efforts to crack his reserved demeanor. The harder Will pushed, the more Tuck clammed up. Will understood this unspoken challenge. Tuck wasn't shy; he was articulate, friendly with friends, and genuinely caring. Yet, he found comfort in silence. And so, they continued their game—waiting for a conversation to ignite or silence to declare victory.

This time, Tuck emerged as the winner as silence enveloped them. Acknowledging his triumph, Tuck shifted the focus to their shared learning.

"Any ideas on how we should start this?" Tuck asked. "Do you have any tricks for your outward control?"

Professor Williams intentionally paired Tuck and Will, recognizing that each had mastered a talent the other needed to develop. Will could manipulate elements outside his body, condensing and shaping molecules. In contrast, Tuck's control emanated from within—he charged energy and released it with force. The challenge lay in the fact that no two individuals learned the same way. For Tuck and Will, feelings and emotions were the most potent pathways to learning, even if discussing them wasn't the most straightforward task.

Will started, "I'm not sure if this will help... but have you ever stepped into a room and immediately sensed the emotions of others? It's like that unspoken elephant in the room—everyone knows it's there, but nobody acknowledges it. With people, it's their body energy, once revealed to me through posture, conversation style, and non-verbal cues. Now, I perceive more: your blood pressure, heart rate, and even the neural connections firing in your head during contemplation. Professor Williams taught me that these triggers extend beyond humans. Now, without the 'bubbles,' the air is teeming with particles that react uniquely. I hone in on the symbolic elephant and apply as much pressure as I can force, condensing it as much as I can."

Tuck chuckled softly, his demeanor shifting. "How am I supposed to learn from that? An elephant? This isn't just a game, Will. All you do is talk, and you haven't stopped since we arrived."

Will's tone turned defensive, "So, I open up, and you shut me down? Not cool."

"No," Tuck replied, his expression stiff, "I'm trying to learn, but all you do is crack jokes. Is that your sole purpose in these Games? To be funny and famous?"

Will's response this time was flat, "No."

Tuck pressed on, "That's it? That's all you have to say? I finally uncover your true motivation for joining, and you go silent?"

Will's patience wavered. "No."

"Then speak up," Tuck challenged, "show me you care about the team."

Water dripped from Will's trembling hands, splashing onto the ground. His voice wavered, "Is this how you've always perceived me? I talk to bring joy to others. But you know what's not funny, Tuck? Real life. Family. Supporting others who depend on you. Push me on this again, and we're finished."

Tuck's tone shifted immediately, "There."

"What?" Will pressed.

Tuck gestured downward, his eyes fixed on Will's clenched fists, now encased in a thick sheen of ice. "Look at your hands.

Now we need to figure out how to release it." A half-smile played on Tuck's lips.

Still trembling from rage, Will gradually regained composure as he observed his body's reaction.

Tuck allowed Will a moment to settle, then directed the conversation. "This was the only way I could think to show you," Tuck began. "Have you ever been in a real fight? Or come close to one? My talent feels like that fight-or-flight moment —your body instinctively chooses. It's an emotional surge that transforms into energy. The split second from decision to action, charging your blood and reshaping you."

Pausing, Tuck continued, "Professor Williams triggered this for me during the tutorial. Finding that shift point has become easier since that initial 'fight' moment."

Will's realization dawned: "Your power is triggered by emotion... Those plays, your life. They were all driven by things beyond your control. I... I had no idea."

"I should have controlled it," Tuck restated.

"No," Will's voice firm now, "how can you control something no one's even aware of? That's unfair to yourself."

Tuck and Will stood in silence once more until Will chuckled softly, now with a smirk, acknowledging Tuck's second victory in their ongoing game.

Tuck caught on, grinning at his serendipitous win. "I get your elephant in the room, but can we call it a rhino instead? Rhinos are cooler."

Will's excitement surged, "Wait, is that your superhero name?"

Tuck's reply remained flat but lighthearted, "No."

CHAPTER SIXTEEN

"Intermission is critical to growth. Sometimes, I wasn't sure what was harder, the levels or the intermissions." – Beacon, Former Champion.

THE HANGAR

Emy & Williams

As the others departed, Professor Williams glanced at Emy. "Are you ready as well?" Receiving a nod in response, the professor kept her in the strategy room and modified the digital wall to display only her statistics.

Emy's attention was drawn to her image on the screen as the Professor initiated the conversation by asking, "Emy, what does being a 'Generalist' mean to you?"

As her eyes swept across the screens and returned to her name, she read:

Emy
Generalist
Level **4**
Fire Affinity

Primary Skill - Targeted Fusion - Focused elemental construction with both extended and close-range abilities

Secondary Skills - TBD

"To me, being a Generalist means having a diverse set of skills without any deep specialization. When you generalize, you're not exceptional at any one thing but decent at many."

Professor Williams smirked and responded thoughtfully, "That might be one of the widest translation gaps I've encountered in the Games." He shifted his gaze to Emy's digitized photo on the wall. "Emy, being a Generalist is an incredibly rare talent in the Cosmos. Would you like to know why?"

Emy nodded, her excitement brimming but contained. The Professor continued, "A true Generalist possesses all talents. Most individuals have talent affinities—skills that resonate with their DNA, upbringing, and personalities. These affinities make it incredibly difficult, if not impossible, to master other talents. While some appear to be Generalists due to their exceptional mastery, they are often just highly specialized in a few areas. But you, Emy, resonate with all talents. It's a challenging path but shatters your potential ceiling."

"Across the Cosmos, nobody possesses a playbook on how to train you. While some sects and societies have shared affinities and training methods, the ultimate responsibility lies with the user to discover how to wield their own talent and nurture it."

The Professor looked towards Emy, intrigued. "Emy, do you have any ideas on building up your skills?"

Emy engaged in quiet reflection, remembering her experiences during the initial level. Beyond the growth of her power under pressure, one memory did stand out: Will's timely rescue, but not because of the gratitude she shared for Will, but more the feeling when Will used his skill next to her. Then, it clicked. "During our last battle," she recounted, "Will conjured an ice wall to shield me. But it felt different —not robust or stable; rather, it was fragmented." Pausing, she gathered her thoughts, a hint of frustration coloring her words as she attempted to match words with her internal feelings. "As I observed that wall, I sensed its inner workings —elements, atoms, bonds, and the cold essence emanating from Will. His creation contained the same combinations I can manipulate through my channels. Yet, perhaps," she mused, "I felt like I could disperse it."

"Talent, intent, and willpower—these are the fundamental elements that shape the Cosmos, or in this case, dismantle it," Professor Williams declared, his gaze reflecting deep understanding. "How you described it aligns with applying willpower to Will's 'build.' As one expands their efforts in construction—be it through distance, capability, or sheer magnitude—the expression of willpower lessens in the act of creation."

"Come, let's see if we can test this willpower of yours."

△△△

Full Team

As the first day of training drew to a close, Frank, ever perceptive, caught the tantalizing scent of food before anyone else—Tuck always trailing closely behind. Both men grasped the importance of proper nutrition for maintaining and chiseling their desired physiques. Having been former linemen, they understood that bulking up required hearty consumption, and this food service consistently delivered.

The kitchen, conveniently situated close to the Smithy (much to Frank's delight), was also near a larger hallway leading to the bedrooms. The team had made it a ritual to gather during breaks for what felt like regimented meals. Given their training days—often in pairs, transitioning between rooms, refining new skills, and testing theories alongside fellow teammates—it was the least they could do as an entire team.

With syrup-drenched chicken still in his mouth, Frank declared, "I've said it before, and I'll gladly say it again: This is the finest chicken and waffles I've ever had." The cookless kitchen, precisely tuned to his cravings, served him the same delectable meal for the second time that day.

Trish, growing closer to Frank during planning sessions when the rest of the team was absent, butted in, "Perhaps we should count our blessings at the endless food options here. Our heroic friends might not have anything left, especially with you always leading the charge into the kitchen."

With a sly smile, James interjected on behalf of his friend, "Trish, Frank, you're both heroes too. I've seen the formidable equipment in the Smithy; it demands strength to wield some of those items. Frank's appetite is as essential as anyone else's at this table."

"Do you mean the buttons he presses on the monitors? Most of that stuff is automated," Trish responded with a smile.

"Hey now, mental training also necessitates a comprehensive eating regimen, and you know how much I miss my tools!" Frank defended.

Around the table, chuckles broke out as Frank snorted appreciatively. After that, the team fell into joyous conversations and banter over new learnings from the day. Nadia, primarily quiet but enjoying the team's company, added, "I feel like we could train on this stuff forever and still not understand everything. Today was intense. Are you all ready for round two tomorrow?"

Coach Williams made his appearance at the door, capitalizing on the moment. "Well, thank you for the smooth transition, Nadia. How very considerate of you," the Coach remarked, a sarcastic smile playing on his mustache-ridden lips. "Wrap up your meal, and let's gather in the strategy room. It's about time I shed light on some matters you've all been curious about."

△△△

Full Team

Frank methodically picked at his teeth, determined to extract the last morsel of chicken. Across the strategy room, the team settled into their seats, their collective exhaustion tangible.

Suddenly, a voice shattered the quiet, *"Hello, everyone!"* Nex materialized at the center of the table, catching everyone off guard. "What do you think of my human form?"

Will scrutinized Nex, his features etched with skepticism. "You don't strike me as a Nexy." The AI stood approximately half a meter tall, enveloped in a digital blue glow. They had a perfectly styled haircut neatly parted to the side, a letterman's jacket, tennis shoes, a whistle hanging from their neck, and a comically oversized mustache on their upper lip.

Nex chuckled. "Oh, Will, my apologies! I take the form preferred by the collective group."

"Looking good, Nex," Professor Williams said as he moved into the room.

Will leaned toward James, whispering, "Strange. I wonder why he thinks that."

Professor Williams cleared his throat, capturing everyone's attention. "All right, team, it's time for more information about the Games—and a little about myself. As you're aware, the Quantum Games are orchestrated by the System. However, what might be news is that a company called the Celestial Nexus Collective, or CNC, also backs the Games. Despite this being the 1200th game, the CNC has progressively established itself as the producer, while the System continues to be both the scriptwriter and the performer."

James butted in, "You keep talking about the System. Someone must have made it, right?"

Professor Williams explained, "The System predates the CNC. This event marks only the 1200th in *recorded* history. The System continually expands its AI web, integrating all life forms across the Cosmos. Many believe ancient civilizations established the System to safeguard newly created galaxies, but certainty eludes us. The System nurtures talent to protect civilizations while the CNC markets it to the wider Cosmos. For instance, points and views were initially absent from the early broadcasted Games, but the System always utilized a scoring mechanism behind the scenes. The CNC gradually learned how the System calculated 'heroism' and integrated it into their own AI."

Emy interjected, "So, Nex hasn't always been around?"

"No," Coach Williams replied, "while some suspect the CNC has only monetary motives behind the Quantum Games, positive outcomes have emerged. Nex and I are prime examples of the CNC enhancing Champion success rates."

Tuck's curiosity reached its limit as he blurted out, "Okay, so who are you?" The table responded with a collective nod, acknowledging the question.

Coach Williams grinned. "I wear multiple hats: Coach, Professor, and... game guide."

The team sat up straight, urging him to continue. "I'm also part of the CNC Games Division. Millions of Coaches integrate into new worlds 3-5 years before full immersion. Our mission? To identify and merge talent, empowering strong individuals and groups; however, some coaches excel more than others," he added with a wink, "but all share good intentions—or at least motivation—for our teams' success. We thrive when the Champions thrive."

"What about our parents and families? Do you have any information about them?" James asked, now understanding that Williams might possess more information than he initially believed.

"For non-integrated civilians, safety is generally assured during the early stages of the Games. However, I don't have any insights about your parents' whereabouts, so I cannot provide concrete details. At this moment, your parents may not even be aware of any changes. Unless you actively participate in the Games, your memory of the decision not to play is lost, and weak 'builders' typically experience only a subtle shift in the world due to integration. Unfortunately, I can't dig further into this topic, but information will be revealed gradually. It's important to understand that immediate intel isn't necessary. I request your trust in my intentions to prioritize your best interests, and at this point, we need to focus on discussing the levels."

The team edged on the brink of pushing their former professor further. Still, he continued, "You've successfully cleared the first level, which essentially served as a second tutorial, but you all need to prepare yourselves—the upcoming levels won't be as forgiving. There are ten levels within Earth's domain."

This time, it was Will who spoke up, "Earth? Does that mean —"

Williams interrupted him, "Yes. Levels beyond Earth exist, but they're not our current concern. Only the top Champions from each world advance to the next Games. You'll first need to be in the top five of three hundred and fifty-four million."

"Have you ever taken a course in athlete communication, Will?" Williams asked, shifting the conversation.

"No?" Will replied hesitantly.

"One of the first lessons is never underestimating your next opponent. This isn't just good advice for sports but for life and survival. In our training, we'll always focus on preparing you for the immediate threats within the next level," Williams explained before he moved on with topics once more.

"The Games follow a natural progression, with recurring events during each integration. However, we can't precisely predict what challenges you'll face. Our task is twofold: prepare you for anything while maximizing our intermission time effectively. Tomorrow, day two, will focus on combat training. No matter how potent your talent, someone can always match it. You must know how to defend yourself in hand-to-hand combat. And remember, proper rest and recovery are crucial for maximizing our time.

Coach Williams now grinned. "Now, get some rest in your dorms. Tomorrow awaits. Oh, and feel free to blame Trish and Frank—they've spent the remainder of your points on combat insights for your Nexabots."

Will groaned, and Emy exchanged a grim look with Trish. "Dorms?" Emy asked.

Nex spoke enthusiastically, *"Yes! I thought maintaining some normalcy would be beneficial. Separate areas for girls and boys, down the hallway by the kitchen!"*

INTERMISSION HERO UPDATES #1

"This chapter delves into our hero's advancements, paralleling the contents displayed on the strategy room wall. It's fascinating, but feel free to skip it!" – Nex.

Cohort 13

Total Team Points: **196 Points**

Total Points Spent: **190 Points**

Total Points Remaining: **6 Points**

Total Max Active Views: **2153**

Earth Rank: **35,420,233 of 354,203,157**

90th Percentile

△△△

Emy
Generalist
Level **4**
E-Class

Fire Affinity

Primary Skill: Targeted Fusion (R) (**Level 3**)

Secondary Skills: Disintegration (T & R) (**Emerging**)

Health: 100% Health + Natural Recovery Rate 3% each minute

Shield: 40%: 30% Power based + 10% Gear based

Weapons: None

Augments: Level 5 Combat Training Module

Gear:

    Full Body: QuantumWeave (Uncommon) - 10% Shield Coverage

    Head: None

    Upper Body: College Letterman's Jacket - No Modifications

    Lower Body: Leggings - No Modifications

Feet: Sneakers - No Modifications

Accessories: Engraved Fanny Pack (Uncommon)

△△△

Tuck
Accelerator
Level **4**
E-Class
Electron Affinity

Primary Skill: Electron Surge (T) (**Level 4**)

Secondary Skills: Ion Storm (AOE) (**Emerging**)

Health: 100% Health + Natural Recovery Rate 2% each minute

Shield: 40%: 30% Power based + 10% Gear based

Weapons: None

Augments: Level 5 Combat Training Module

Gear:

Full Body: QuantumWeave (Uncommon) - 10% Shield Coverage

Head: None

Upper Body: Football Jersey - No Modifications

Lower Body: Jeans - No Modifications

Feet: Sneakers - No Modifications

Accessories: None

△△△

James
Catalyst
Level **3**
E-Class
No Affinity

Primary Skill: Empower (R) **(Level 3)**

Secondary Skills: Restrict (R) **(Level 3)**

Health: 100% Health + Natural Recovery Rate 2% each minute

Shield: 10%: 0% Power based + 10% Gear based

Weapons:

    Bow: Novaflight (E-Class, High)

    Arrows: Back Quiver with Statis Alchemarrows (E-Class, High) (∞) (Fireball, Neurofluxine, Crimson Cascade, Piercing, Ice, Fire)

Augments: Level 5 Combat Training Module

Gear:

    Full Body: QuantumWeave (Uncommon) - 10% Shield Coverage

Head: None

Upper Body: Letterman's Jacket - No Modifications

Lower Body: Jeans - No Modifications

Feet: Sneakers - No Modifications

Accessories: None

△△△

Nadia
Cellulator
Level **3**
E-Class
Physiology Affinity

Primary Skill: Vitalize (T) (**Level 3**) 15% Recovery Rate per minute

Secondary Skills: Affliction Surge (T) (**Level 3**)

Health: 98% Health + Natural Recovery Rate 15% each minute.

    Minor Inflictions: Neurofluxine (1%); Crimson Cascade (1%)

Shield: 10%: 0% Power based + 10% Gear based

Weapons: None

Augments: Level 5 Combat Training Module

Gear:

    Full Body: QuantumWeave (Uncommon) - 10% Shield Coverage

    Head: None

    Upper Body: Black Leather Jacket - No Modifications

    Lower Body: Jeans - No Modifications

    Feet: Sneakers - No Modifications

    Accessories: Phantom Veil (Rare)

△△△

Brick (Will)
Condenser
Level **3**
E-Class
Water Affinity

Primary Skill: Condense (R) (**Level 3**)

Secondary Skills: Cryostrike (R) (**Emerging**); Flow Perception (T) (**Emerging**)

Health: 100% Health + Natural Recovery Rate 2% each minute

Shield: 30%: 20% Power based + 10% Gear based

Weapons: None

Augments: Level 5 Combat Training Module

Gear:

    Full Body: QuantumWeave (Uncommon) - 10% Shield Coverage

    Head: None

    Upper Body: Brown Jacket - No Modifications

    Lower Body: Jeans - No Modifications

Feet: Sneakers - No Modifications

Accessories: None

Legend:
(T) = Touching, (R) = Ranged, (AOE) = Area of Effect

CHAPTER SEVENTEEN

"The Games will test your abilities in various ways. While combat and control remain crucial, the System also ensures you possess diverse skill sets." – Prowler, Former Champion.

LEVEL TWO

Full Team

Would you like to proceed to Level Two of the Quantum Games?

"Yes"

The radiant glow of white light gradually faded. Just moments ago, the team had been huddled together in the Hangar. Now, they were stepping into a familiar scene—the lively foyer of the campus education building. Lockers slammed shut, footsteps echoed, and the noise of chattering students filled the air.

Will was the first to react. Surrounded by students, he stood there, questioning reality. "Did we just wake up from a dream?" he wondered aloud. Everything around them looked like any other weekday before their unexpected journey started. The group was stunned, their gazes fixed on their former classmates. Some of the faces were familiar, yet everything felt so surreal.

"Nope, we're not dreaming," James responded slowly to Will, breaking the silence. "Check your status. We're still in the

Games."

"Oh, thank goodness you're still here, Nexy," Will jokingly said when his attention shifted to a girl walking by.

"I think that's Mary. She is in one of my classes. She looks so real!" Will pointed out as all five turned to look at her. Mary, hearing Will's voice and seeing the group collectively stare at her, stumbled away, quickly trying to avoid their gaze.

Will caught up to her, tapping her arm. "Mary... hi. What day, uh, what class are you going to?" Will adjusted mid-question, realizing that asking about the day might be odd. However, he instantly realized that this question wasn't much better.

"What... What are you talking about?" Mary looked taken aback by the strange question. "I'm heading to the same Calc class we have every Friday. Well, at least one of us attends the same class every Friday. Late night last night? I guess it was a Thursday night."

"Oh, right, my bad... Well, I guess I'll see you in there," Will stammered, letting her continue walking.

Returning to the group, he announced, "It's... Friday? And I guess I have class?"

James chuckled. "Wasn't quite expecting this. Can you brief us on the mission, Nex?"

"*On it!*" Nex said diligently.

Level Two Group Mission: Infiltration Scenario

An unknown entity has infiltrated the school. The objective is to remove this insurgent group from the school premises, determine their intentions, and protect all civilians.

Civilians Killed: 0

Tuck started, "Whoa. This one feels a bit more loaded than our previous mission. And why the 'Group Mission' label this time?"

James, standing in the middle of the school with his

Novaflight Bow in hand and arrows strapped to his back, had a sudden realization.

"*Don't worry about attire and weapons,*" Nex quickly explained to the group, reading James's alarm, "*unless you actively use them, the System will restrict their visibility during this type of mission.*"

"Does that apply to all weapons and skills?" Emy asked.

Nex confirmed. "*Any gear or weapons you carry won't be visible to others on this map. However, if you actively use them, that cover will be blown if someone sees you. This is also applicable to Tuck's… form. He is the same size as he was before the Games.*"

Emy turned to the team. "So, what's our next move?"

"It's obvious," Nadia spoke as all eyes turned to her, quickly adding, "The System wants us to go to class."

△△△

Will

DING, DING, DING. The bell rang as Will closed the door, entering the Calculus class.

"Mr. Weiss, so nice to see you on this Friday. If we hadn't had a test today, I wouldn't have expected your presence," commented Will's calculus professor, Mrs. Wallen, as Will took his seat next to a blushing Mary. Mrs. Wallen, with her frizzy brown hair and a polka dot dress that reached down to her ankles, had a plump face but was full of energy and life. Despite her appearance, she was known as one of the more relatable and exciting teachers, always managing to engage her students with enthusiasm.

Not entirely learning from his previous questions, Will leaned sideways and whispered to Mary, "We have a test today?"

"Mid-Terms… What's with you today?" Mary responded, inching her chair away from Will.

Mid-Terms? For calculus? On a Friday? What kind of sick game is the System playing here? Will questioned internally, glancing up at the empty ceiling tiles in the classroom.

"It's odd to see so many students absent on test day," Mrs. Wallen remarked hesitantly, noticing the surplus of tests in her hand after distribution. "They must have attended Mr. Weiss' party last night." The students chuckled in response; it was a small school, and Will's nightly gatherings were well-known.

Will received his test with a slight grunt from the professor. Flipping it over to begin, he silently asked his companion, "Are you ready for this, Nexy?"

Nexy answered in her sultry tone, *"Born ready, hot shot."*

△△△

Emy & Nadia

"I truly don't get this class, English," Nex commented to Emy and Nadia, *"we live in a time with translation services and AI—who still needs grammar lessons?"*

Emy and Nadia exchanged brief chuckles as they sat in their Friday class. Emy was thankful she had remembered correctly that Nadia was in the same class. Once settled, both girls quietly searched for clues or anomalies within the room.

"Guys, we have a problem," Will's voice came over the communications channel a few minutes after Professor Hartman started his lecture. Nadia and Emy exchanged glances.

"What is it, Will?" James asked. "Tuck and I don't have class for an hour. We can be there soon."

"Yeah, big problem... Nexy and I are absolutely acing this exam," Will dryly remarked.

"Will, get off the comms," James retorted.

"Roger that, James," Will confirmed sarcastically.

The lecture topic on "Modernism in Literature" proceeded without incident. The room was sparsely populated, as was customary for a Friday. A handful of students even attended briefly before excusing themselves due to illness. Professor Hartman promptly directed them to the nurse's office, a routine occurrence at Quill Creek on Fridays.

As the bell rang to mark the end of class, Emy shrugged at Nadia as they began packing their books and headed for the door.

SLAM! A noise shook the room, and Emy felt a surge of energy beside her. Quickly turning, she noticed a girl from the volleyball team had accidentally dropped her book bag, triggering two girls to run over to help her.

Surveying the room, nothing seemed out of the ordinary, and the energy was gone. *Where did that come from?*

"Guys, I think we have an actual problem," Emy communicated.

"You have a mid-term, too?" Will's voice once again came over comms.

"No, I think we just found another builder in our classroom," Emy replied, receiving a confirming look from Nadia.

CHAPTER EIGHTEEN

"Every new level of the Games brings different challenges. Adapting and utilizing your strengths no matter the task is the only way through." – Quist, Former Champion.

LEVEL TWO

Emy & Nadia

"What's the plan?" James questioned, his voice tinged with concern.

"I think we should follow the three girls," Emy responded, her expression serious. "There were only a few of them close enough to create the energy, but we don't know what to expect with this level yet. We can't make any assumptions at this point." She exchanged a knowing glance with Nadia as their training kicked in. Professor Williams had been right—you couldn't prepare for every scenario, but this was one they had trained for.

Nadia packed her bags and backpack, moving with practiced efficiency. She slipped out the door, avoiding any unnecessary attention. Once outside, she doubled back, moving into a nearby empty classroom to activate her new accessory.

△△△

TWO DAYS PRIOR

Trish & Nadia

When Trish asked Nadia how she felt about being an assassin, Nadia's reaction was peculiar. She didn't flinch, which unsettled her in a way. Yet, excitement bubbled within her—the prospect of playing this role for the team intrigued her. Nadia cherished her newfound friendships but also found joy in her solitary moments. During these times of separation, she recognized her talent for observing and responding to others' interactions.

"Assassin?" Nadia spoke, her gaze searching for more context before revealing too much interest.

"Yes! But we don't necessarily have to categorize it that way. Have you ever dabbled in video games?" Trish glanced at Nadia's vacant expression, who was, in turn, wondering if her experience of observing her cousins play Xbox from afar counted. "All right, I gather that's a no. Let me try and explain. In adventure-themed video games, a key skill often revolves around embodying an assassin, but it's more complex than eliminating NPCs—Non-Player Characters. It's about mastering stealth, adapting to situations, and utilizing your environment and sharp observational skills without getting detected. Sure, there's an element of killing, but you can also neutralize enemies or partake in a bit of thievery!" Trish's passion for gaming was evident. Sensing enthusiasm might be waning in Nadia, she adjusted her approach. "Anyway, under the Professor's guidance, Frank and I have developed some fascinating ideas in our new workshop. Here's the first one!"

Phantom Veil - 20 Points

Rare

Manipulates molecules and atoms for near invisibility— The Veil allows its users to blend seamlessly into their surroundings but can also reflect light so that it bends around them, rendering them virtually imperceptible.

"How is that even real?" Nadia asked, her voice filled with amazement.

"I know, right?" Trish responded, her smile widening. "The items in the System store are mind-boggling. But when you consider the capabilities of users beyond our galaxy, it's no wonder they can achieve incredible feats with the right tools. Imagine what the A-Class can build!"

As she walked over to a workbench in the tech lab, Nadia stood there, puzzled. "Wait, what's an A-Class?" she asked.

Trish glanced over, "Oh, that's right! Professor Williams introduced us to the class structure while you were all in the level. It's Nex's way of tracking significant milestones in our leveling journey. Nex, do you mind?"

"*Certainly!*" Nex responded, projecting the criteria onto Nadia's status display:

F-Class: Levels 0-1
E-Class: Levels 2-9
D-Class: Levels 10-19
C-Class: Levels 20-29
B-Class: Levels 30-39
A-Class: Levels 40-49

Nex concluded, *"Each Class grouping ultimately requires a skill-based test related to command, control, or power."*

Trish added, "Professor Williams didn't delve into the intricacies of the classes just yet. He believes that Class is a marker, and understanding one's skills and talents should be the primary focus."

"And that's precisely why I think we can harness your talent in more imaginative ways," Trish said, guiding them back to the present course. "In addition to stealth, now enhanced by the **Phantom Veil**, we've considered another addition to your toolkit." Her smile broadened. "Are you up for trying something new?"

Nadia hesitated before answering, "Um, sure?"

"Sweet," Trish pressed on with continued excitement. "So, after discussing with Frank, we think you have the potential to hide or store things within your body."

"What?" Nadia commented, a bit confused by the weird change in topic.

"That was a bad way to put it, sorry," Trish said with a blush. "What I mean is that your body can naturally heal extremely quickly. If we can enable your body to reach a state of equilibrium, healing itself while holding some foreign chemical, we believe you can open up many more doors in your powers."

Trish held out a small scalpel. "I am going to make a small cut on your finger, and I want you to try and fight your body's natural reaction to heal it."

Nadia extended her hand in agreement as Trish made a small slice on her index finger. As her finger started to bleed, she could instantly feel her body's regeneration kick into overdrive, healing the wound. Closing her eyes, she focused on the area, attempting to halt the rapid healing, sealing away the cut from her natural energies.

"It worked!" Trish said with enthusiasm while still monitoring the wound.

"Now, I know this is strange, but I want you to see if you can increase the wound with your **Affliction Surge** skill," Trish prompted.

"Let me try. I haven't done that on myself yet," Nadia said, realizing where this was going. She refocused on her finger, activating her skill within her body, pushing the inflicted wound to fester and grow. As the wound expanded, she reactivated her **Vitalize** skill to re-heal the wound again.

"I think I've got it," Nadia said with a smile.

"Yes! I thought that would work. Ready to try with a bit more potency?" Trish's excitement was evident.

△△△

LEVEL TWO

Emy & Nadia

Activating her **Phantom Veil**, Nadia vanished from view. She checked her surroundings, assessing her form by dashing in front of two kids loitering near the mezzanine. Their uninterrupted stride signaled success.

As Nadia faded from sight, Emy was tasked with the more painful, direct approach. After the energy surge materialized, three girls from the volleyball team congregated.

"Man, that just scared the crap out of me. I feel like I've been on edge since yesterday," Emy confessed, her gaze fixed on the girls assisting with the fallen books.

All three glanced her way, but the one closest to Emy responded hesitantly, "Er, uh. Yeah." The trio resumed gathering their belongings and headed for the exit.

"Your name is Tabitha, right? I've seen a few of your games. You girls are impressive this year," Emy said, trying to break the icy silence. The girl, nearly as tall as Emy, had shoulder-length curly blonde hair and was now giving her a wicked side-eye. In truth, the girls' volleyball team was far from stellar. Both matches Emy had watched with James had been disastrous—no sets won, and they lost both games 0-3.

Tabitha smiled. "Oh, thanks. Yeah, I'm Tabitha, and these two are Darya and Michele. And you're the Fury girl, right? Emy?"

"Yeah, Emy is good. Fury is my not-so-liked nickname, I guess," Emy responded.

"Ha, yeah. Michele over there spiked a ball right into a girl's face during a match and earned herself a lovely nickname." Tabitha glanced at Michele, a taller girl with light brown hair, pretty green eyes, and a look of absolute disgust on her face. "What was it again, Michele?" she snickered as she finished the question.

Rolling her eyes, Michele looked at Tabitha and then back at Emy. "Chel-ter," she said and then paused, softening her tone, "Apparently, they think the other team should run for 'Chel-ter' when I go up for a spike."

Nex must have informed everyone on the comms about the story, as Will's voice popped into Emy's head, "Ha. One of my best ones yet."

Tuck agreed, "I'll admit, that was one of your better ones."

"Those guys need to get a life," Emy retorted, ensuring Nex passed that message to the team.

"Harsh," Will commented but remained quiet afterward.

"You guys doing anything fun this Friday?" Emy continued to insert herself into the conversation, now very much out of her comfort zone, clearly overstaying her welcome. The other girls hesitated in their responses after exchanging a few glances.

"I think we'll head to the café, but…" Tabitha started, only to be cut off by Emy, "Oh, awesome. Mind if I come along?" Emy tried not to show her internal cringe at her perceived lack of social awareness.

"Don't you normally hang out with some soccer girls around this time?" Tabitha asked.

"Sometimes, but lunch sounds better." In reality, Emy only pretended to hang out with the team. She typically went to the dorms to study or relax by herself during this time.

Lacking other real options, the three volleyball girls shrugged and headed toward the door. The café was in another building close by and offered limited choices. They had the standard grill fare—hotdogs, burgers, and French fries—but also featured a few local sandwich vendors bringing in outside options for a bit of diversity. Regardless, this was usually why James and Emy ventured off-campus for food.

Brushing off the clear, cold shoulders the girls were throwing her way, Emy followed the group as they made their way through the education building and out to the less busy corner exit by the stairs. Outside now, as a single food delivery truck pulled off, the girls continued alongside the path for a few steps and then abruptly turned around.

"What's the play here, Emy?" Tabitha demanded, her energy

pulsing off her hands. "We know that you felt our powers in the room. So, what is this? Are you part of the insurgency?" Her eyes held a hint of rage as Michele and Darya formed a half-circle facing Emy.

A whisper suddenly found its way into Tabitha's ear, accompanied by a sharp prick at her neck. "Release your energy, and I'll release mine," Nadia voiced, her words punctuated by the spreading sensation of a new concoction - Trish's ***Crimson Cascade***. It seeped wider, igniting a flush of itchiness across Tabitha's neck.

This innovative serum by Trish was crafted to empower Nadia to embed a potent virus seamlessly into an adversary's circulatory system. This affliction, programmed to seek and annihilate, erodes the internal cellular structure. Its residence in Nadia's bloodstream ensured swift access and precise application, combined with ease of access to Nadia's ***Affliction Surge*** skill, and it was a deadly combination.

Solution Detected – Crimson Cascade

This potent virus is genetically coded to target and annihilate the internal cellular structure of a living organism. It triggers a rapid degradation of cells upon contact. Its cascading effect on cellular structures results in a quick and devastating impact on the host organism.

Emy's voice remained steady as she spoke, "I believe it's now my turn to ask the same question." She displayed a calming demeanor without using any skills, unwilling to reveal more cards than necessary.

The girls' faces registered shock; they hadn't anticipated being put in this situation. A few nods from Darya and Michele prompted Tabitha to step forward and speak.

"We are... Cohort 8."

Emy relayed instructions over Nex, "James, Tuck, hold. We're good here. Go to your class. We'll keep you posted. There are other teams present."

"Roger," James replied, his breath slightly labored from halting his pursuit.

< Level Up! Nadia is now a Level 4 Cellulator >

CHAPTER NINETEEN

"Despite Mr. Weiss's arrogant or flippant demeanor, I've always known that he possesses a heart of gold." – Former Professor.

LEVEL TWO

Will

The most challenging aspect of Will's Calculus test was estimating the time he needed to complete each question before submitting his answers. Despite consistently earning excellent grades, Will could have aced the test without studying extensively. However, why bother when you have the Cosmos's most incredible AI discreetly guiding you? Mary, seated beside him, probably suspected him of cheating, given how he observed her subtly extending her elbow over her exam. Little did she know that he was merely trying to figure out which question she was working on to keep an unsuspecting pace.

Will gathered his things and walked his exam up to Mrs. Wallen, turning it in with a smile. "You make one heck of a professor, Mrs. Wallen. Consider this the first 'A' you will be grading," Will said, returning the joking that had fallen in his direction earlier. Catching the eye of his professor as he said it, something seemed off. Worry? Hesitation? Another emotion?

"It will be my pleasure to grade it, Mr. Weiss," she stated, then hesitated as if deciding. "Do you mind if we chatted outside the room for a second? I have a bit of a favor to ask of you."

"Of course," Will stated, a bit taken aback, considering he had never talked with Mrs. Wallen outside the four walls of the classroom before.

Positioned at the front of the classroom door, a wave of déjà vu struck Will, the location eerily reminiscent of their recent battle with the Grimbletooth. He pushed to suppress these memories, shifting his focus to meet the professor's gaze. "What's up, Professor?"

"This is a bit hard, Will, and goes against my better judgment, but I am a bit worried about Penny."

Will racked his brain, trying to think about the kids in the class. Usually good at names and faces, Will couldn't think who that could be... Will cursed himself for not going to this class very often.

"I'm sorry, Mrs. Wallen. I'm not sure if I know of a Penny. Is she in class?" Will returned, chastising himself.

"She normally is, and that's the problem. Missing a class, let alone a mid-term exam, without at least an email or a phone call to the school is out of character," the Professor stated. Will was correct in sensing the genuine concern and worry from her earlier.

The Professor hesitated, her voice lowering, "Things have felt peculiar lately, especially since yesterday afternoon. I can't quite pinpoint it, but... well, never mind," she trailed off, reluctant to share further details.

Will decided to probe, "I've noticed it too. It's not just you."

She nodded. "Perhaps others are experiencing it as well. Several professors have been acting strangely, and the classrooms are emptier as the day progresses. Will, you're well-connected here. Keep an eye out, would you?"

"Absolutely."

"And Will," she spoke again, "if you uncover or need anything, don't hesitate to reach out."

"Thank you," Will acknowledged, then turned toward the stairs.

"Hey, Team?" Will's voice sounded over the comms.

"This better be important," James replied, sounding out of breath.

"I've got a lead. I'll keep you posted. I am going to ask around about a missing girl named Penny. If you hear anything about her, let me know."

"Keep us posted," James confirmed for the team.

△△△

Tuck & James

For James and Tuck, Fridays were a unique ordeal, setting them apart from their teammates. Their entire day was consumed by one demanding class: Weight Training, held in the school's gymnasium. This class was a melting pot of athletes, with football players forming the majority, peppered with representatives from various other sports. The intensity of the class schedule was amplified since football players were usually restricted to light workouts on the eve of their Saturday games. Consequently, this current Friday class centered on calisthenics and stretching exercises.

Coach Sprout's voice resounded through the gym: "Tuck! Since you're out this weekend, you'll be participating in the full workout. The rest of the football players, take it easy." Coach Sprout, the head football coach and part-time teacher, also taught weightlifting and other athletic classes, including pick-up basketball and a random half-marathon training class. "Oh, and Tuck, being that you're the only football player participating today in the full workout, what do you have to say about giving the class a bit of a show? It is leg day, after all."

Tuck gave a nod to the coach, trying to hide the rush of panic flowing through him as the coach's gaze moved to the front of the class when the door swung open, and another student walked in.

"Ah, Mr. Blackwood," Coach Sprout addressed the new arrival. "I wondered if you'd be joining us today. Settle in with

James over there; he'll show you the ropes of the class."

The boy walked directly over to James with a sickly grin plastered on his face. "I was hoping I'd see you here, James. We have lots to talk about."

"Good to see you too, Trent."

△△△

Emy & Nadia

"Cohort 8? Well, say hello to Cohort 13," Emy announced, her calm demeanor transforming into an open smile, still attempting to navigate the unknown. "How was your first level?"

The question triggered Nadia to quickly heal Tabitha's neck while taking off her **Phantom Veil**. "Sorry about that. We needed to make sure," Nadia commented, proceeding to go and stand next to Emy.

Tabitha, rubbing her neck, was momentarily startled by Nadia's sudden appearance. However, to her credit, she accepted the situation. "I would have done the same. Well, actually, we tried the same, but you girls did it better."

Tabitha recounted their experience: "The first level kept us in the volleyball gymnasium, battling a rabid rabbit population followed by some rather unusual, larger bunnies. It was the strangest thing I've ever seen in my life—aside from that question asking if I wanted to play a game."

Darya, the third and shortest girl with a highly athletic build, short brown hair, and a side shave, had been silent until now. With a cheerful yet quiet demeanor, she interjected, "Those rabbits were relentless. Our survival was thanks to Tabitha and Michele's impressive offensive skills."

Michele chimed in, giving credit where it was due, "Don't sell yourself short," she told Darya with a wink. "We couldn't have done it without your speed. You distracted those furry guys long enough for Tabitha and me to have a chance."

Curious, Michele turned her attention to Nadia and Emy. "What about you two, tough fight?"

Emy revealed just enough, "Nadia is a healer, and I specialize in fire manipulation. We also have three other team members scattered around the school." She glanced at Nadia and continued, "Our level featured gremlin things instead of rabbits. It's funny how it seems fur was a common theme for the first-level monsters. Nadia and I formed a solid hit-and-retreat strategy, while our other three excelled at a punch-and-block skillset. Very technical stuff," she finished with a smirk.

"We were all a bit surprised that this is a group mission. Do you all have any leads yet?" Emy questioned.

"No, unfortunately," Tabitha added, her expression thoughtful, "our lack of a better idea led us to attend class, but it proved useless—except for meeting you two. Initially, we assumed that other Champions might be excluded from the mission, which would explain the sparsely populated classes. But then again, here you are, so it must mean there is something else to these empty classes."

Emy thought about that comment. If this group was present and currently here, the missing individuals were probably absent for a reason—perhaps they hadn't survived the initial level. A pang of sorrow gripped her as she considered this possibility.

"Yeah, that's sort of what we thought," Emy continued. "Our teammate Will is looking into the absence of a girl named Penny. He mentioned that while she could be a part of the Games, her personality doesn't quite fit the mold," Emy said, wondering if that were true and if there was a personality type within the Games.

"Would you like to connect with us and stay in touch as we gather more information?" Emy gestured.

"That sounds like a plan; we will keep you posted if we find anything. Oh, and one more thing," Tabitha replied on behalf of the team.

"Is the fanny pack a trend? Or some sort of accessory? I

can't tell if I find it stylish or not…" Tabitha said with a joking demeanor.

Glancing down at her **Fanny Pack** with the embroidered flame, Emy smiled and replied, "You don't think it goes well with my burnt letterman's jacket?"

< Alliance Established - Cohort 8 – Limited communications are now available >

△△△

"That's super cool. Did you know Nex could make groups?" Nadia said as they departed from Cohort 8.

"Nope, but Nex is pretty amazing," Emy remarked. Internally, she expressed silent gratitude toward Nex and felt a gentle surge of energy in response.

As the energy subsided, James's firm voice came through the communications.

"Guys, we've located another team."

Emy's anticipation grew. "Oh, that's great. We just allied with 8. Who is it, James?"

"It's Trent," James stated firmly. "He's in weights with Tuck and me. I'll keep everyone posted."

"Got it," Emy replied, her tone hollow as she glanced at Nadia, having heard the story of Will's party. But James had more to share.

"That's not the only challenge we have," James continued. "Tuck is currently participating in max leg day."

"Huh?" Emy's confusion was evident before James abruptly ended the transmission. "What the heck is max leg day?" Emy said, looking at an equally puzzled Nadia.

CHAPTER TWENTY

"Trust becomes evident when you grasp an individual's underlying motivations and aspirations." – E.B.

LEVEL TWO

Tuck and James

The weight room reverberated with a symphony of encouragement as Tuck, fueled by adrenaline and determination, faced the colossal challenge. With seven plates on each side of the bar, nearly 320 kilos, Tuck pushed to increase his pre-tournament max squat as the air thickened with testosterone, the scent of effort, and the collective energy of onlookers.

Tuck's secret talent teetered on the edge of exposure. James, his silent cheerleader, urged him inwardly. *Hold it, Tuck. You've got this.* But instinct loomed, threatening to reveal their concealed abilities.

The crowd's howls swelled into a primal chorus, "**DRIVE, TUCK!**" "**GO, GO, GO!**" The bar ascended, each inch a testament to Tuck's agonizing effort. His legs quivered under the strain, his resolve wavering. With a grimace, he marshaled every last ounce of strength, acutely aware that he couldn't afford to stall. A mental countdown propelled him, a reminder that he needed to control his energy or risk exposure. One final push was all it would take. *1… 2… 3…*

Then, a sudden pulse—a surge of energy—engulfed the room. Once struggling to contain its energy, Tuck's body exploded with power, sending surges of electricity across the room. The lights shattered, and darkness swallowed the room. Panic overwhelmed James as he sprinted to Tuck's aid. The bar slammed into its stand as Tuck emerged victorious. James helped him up as the bar still glowed with an electrified warmth.

JUICED! 7 POINTS!

< Skill Identified – Tuck – Ion Storm >

< Level Up! Tuck is now a level 5 Accelerator >

Cheers erupted as the lights flickered back on, "**YEAH, TUCK!**" "You blasted the lights off!" "**SCHOOL RECORD!**" Mr. Sprout, bewildered, scanned the room. His gaze settled on Trent, who stood next to the light switch. Trent's apologetic expression spoke volumes. The celebration continued, slaps on Tuck's back punctuating the awe and confusion as James read into Tuck's new skill:

Skill: Ion Storm

Allows the user to harness the electrons in their environment, causing them to surge and ignite, similar to a lightning storm. (AOE)

△△△

Will

The ongoing investigation had Will combing the campus, searching for any trace of Penny's whereabouts. Some students suggested she might have attended a class earlier in the day, but their certainty was shaky, and Will wasn't even sure they knew who Penny was—they simply wanted to be helpful. Trapped in his thoughts, Will had no options left except one.

Drawing a deep breath, Will convinced himself this was merely augmented reality—albeit remarkably lifelike. With determination, he knocked on the door. "Um, Steve—I mean, Mr. Reynold," he stammered, "I was wondering if you could help me with something."

"Oh, Will! Yes, yes. Come on in!" Mr. Reynold, the school's Athletic Director, responded with enthusiasm.

As Will entered, he saw Mr. Reynold, dressed in a collared shirt and loosened tie, looking worn down by time and stress. His once athletic build had been overtaken by a desk job, with a few stretched-out bottom buttons and a pair of glasses perched on top of his gut. Mr. Reynold jostled the glasses as he cleared his desk, his eyes brightening as he prepared to talk to Will. He was just hanging up the phone. "Never mind that. I might lose my mind if I get another call from the district or another concerned parent complaining about the girls' soccer team." He took a deep breath, slowly regained his composure, and smiled. "What do you need, Will? Are you ready for tomorrow's big game?"

The question brought back a flood of memories for Will. Mr. Reynold, also known as Steve, had been Will's father's best man at their wedding. Steve and Will's dad used to have drinks and talk about their high school football days as teammates. However, as the evening progressed, Steve would disappear, leaving Will's dad in a drunken stupor. Will didn't blame Steve, but the memories of those disruptive nights often left someone in their family with a bruised face or a black eye.

As time passed, Steve found an escape route from the small-town life, landing a job at the junior college. This left Will's father alone, his only companion being the bottle. His singular obsession became molding Will into a football prodigy he would soon become. Will treasured these father-son moments, but as he matured, his father's condition deteriorated. The line between weekends and weekdays blurred, and late-night trips to the gas station and returning with a brown bag had become a grim routine.

Finally, a tipping point arrived. On a night that would forever be remembered, Will bravely decided to confront his father, protecting his mother and brother, ultimately expelling his father from their lives—never to return.

Whether Mr. Reynold ever learned the whole story remained uncertain. However, when the D1 schools failed to call, Mr. Williams and Mr. Reynold stepped in. Will appreciated their support, even if shaking hands with the man who reminded him of his father was challenging.

"I believe I'm nearly prepared for the game, Sir," Will said, glancing down and meeting Mr. Reynold's eyes. "However, I'm struggling in English class, and I have a test on Monday after the game. I was hoping to contact a girl named Penny today—perhaps she could tutor me."

"You need a tutor?" Mr. Reynold raised an eyebrow.

"Yeah," Will lied, "football practices and games have set me back. Anyway, I'd like to check her schedule and arrange a meeting. Could you look that up for me?"

△△△

James & Tuck

"Thanks for the save back there," James said to Trent as the two boys walked out the door and headed toward the track.

With the lights malfunctioning, Coach Sprout sent the team to the track for light conditioning.

"Don't worry about it. The way I look at it is that we need each other. How would it help me if you two get caught showing off your skills?" Trent continued, glancing at Tuck, who was headed in their direction. "I imagine the big guy over there has some electric talent, so I made the call, and it worked out."

"Either way, you didn't have to, and we appreciate it," James commented.

As Tuck reached them, he nodded to Trent and asked, "Did

you go solo?"

Trent grinned. "Right into it, huh? Yeah, I did. If I'm going to be in some game with my life on the line, it'll just be me that I trust."

He continued, "I didn't realize we would be set up in group missions like this."

James pressed further, "Do you have any leads so far?" He recognized that, like Tuck and himself, Trent would have had time before class to explore or research a bit—plus, Trent was late to class doing something.

"I'll share if you do," Trent replied, getting a nod back from James. "My answer is maybe. I started at the football fields, and due to the emptiness, I didn't realize it was a different type of mission until I returned to the campus and saw all the students roaming around. Once I got the details from my Nexabot, I explored the campus more and looked for anything suspicious."

"Any luck?" Tuck asked.

"I am not sure. I am fairly new to this campus, so I don't quite get the dynamics of this school, but people seemed to be in pairs all over, and no, not just coupled up. I know that doesn't sound like much, but in the normal world, you see that, but people are more so grouped up in cliques or larger parties. It was more of an oddity."

Tuck and James glanced at each other. Both recognized the depth with which Trent was analyzing the situation. They would have been entirely absent-minded about gathering that point of view. Attempting to hide this thought, James shared the details the team understood: information about the other cohorts, missing students, and the alarmed teacher. None of it came as a shock to Trent.

James told Trent about Will's search and then asked him about his plans.

"I am going to follow one of the more awkward pairings and see where it leads. I'll keep in contact via communication."

< Alliance Established - Cohort 1 – Limited communications are now available >

As Tuck and James separated from Trent, they exchanged a puzzled look. They had no idea what to anticipate during the session, but it certainly wasn't what they encountered. Instead of the arrogant, overconfident, and brash demeanor they had braced themselves for, they were met with a confident, intuitive, and calculating persona.

Walking back, attempting to meet with Emy and Nadia, their vision lit up with text:

Civilians Killed: 1

-5 Points

CHAPTER TWENTY-ONE

"During missions, you'll encounter situations beyond your control. Focus on understanding your team and the enemy. When you do that, everything else will naturally fall into place." – Coach Williams.

LEVEL TWO

Will

Looking down at Penny's schedule, Will was immediately blown away at how many classes this girl took this year. The typical schedule for a first-year college student was 15 credits representing five classes, typically one of those being a filler easy class, such as weights. On the other hand, Penny was taking 24 credits, representing eight classes, with the only filler class being History of Dance, clearly a mandatory elective based on the other choices of classes.

The schedule read:

Friday, 8:30 A.M.: Biology with Mr. Shade
Friday, 11:30 A.M.: Calculus with Mrs. Wallen
Friday, 2:00 P.M.: History of Dance with Mr. Shultz

"8:30 A.M. Biology? On a Friday? This girl is crazy," Will muttered to Nexy as he strode toward the west wing of the education building.

Approaching Mr. Shade's classroom, Will was immediately assaulted by a sharp tang lingering in the air. Formaldehyde, ethanol, and disinfectants blended, almost driving him away. As a business major needing only one science elective, Will hadn't entered a biology room since high school. Still, the scent catapulted him back to the day he dissected a frog with his classmates—an experience that had nudged him away from pursuing a biology-related major.

The biology room door was slightly open, and Will cautiously peeked inside. The room was adorned with anatomy diagrams on the walls and six workstations, each equipped with its own sink and faucet, strategically placed throughout. At the back of the room, a man gathered instruments from a previous class. He had a tall, lanky frame and wore a lab coat that seemed a size too big. His eyes, sharp and observant behind thick glasses, scanned the room with a sense of authority.

"Professor Shade?" Will called out.

The man turned, adjusting his glasses with a steady hand. "That's me. How can I help you? I don't think you're one of my students, are you?" he replied with calm assurance.

"No, sir. I'm looking for someone. Her name is Penny," Will paused, trying to gauge the professor's limited reaction. "You see, I need a tutor for calculus, and I thought she would be in class, but she never showed up," he continued to fabricate. "She had mentioned having biology in the morning, so I wondered if there was a lab today or something."

Reacting to the questions, Will strangely thought he sensed a bit of intrigue and maybe interest from the professor.

Mr. Shade's expression then shifted. "Ah, Penny, one of my best students. It is wise of you to want her as a tutor. Yes, she was in class this morning." A wave of worry and sadness washed over Will.

"Wait, is she okay?" Will's concern grew.

"She might have just needed some fresh air. Dissections tend to make some people queasy, but this hadn't happened before to her. She mentioned feeling dizzy since yesterday."

"Oh. Okay, good," Will's voice wavered, still recovering from the mixed emotions surging within his body as he suddenly felt lightheaded. "Do you think she's still around campus?"

"Maybe. She does a bit of extracurricular activities around the site, and I know she likes to visit our equestrian center out on the grounds. She may have ventured there."

The professor continued, "You seem like a bright kid, Will. Why didn't you sign up for biology? I would have loved to have you in class this year. Someone with your talent for investigation and passion for success would surely have succeeded here."

The professor's words sparked envious and eager desires within Will as he stumbled into a worktable, emotions overloading him.

"You think so? I wasn't ever much of a biology…" A wave of nausea hit Will as he stopped mid-sentence, clutching the table near him.

"Are you feeling all right? You look like you could use some help." Professor Shade reached out, placing a hand on Will's back.

"Come on, let's get some air. Maybe we can go check on Penny together." The professor hooked his arm with Will's, leading him toward the exit. Relief and reassurance washed away any of Will's lingering concerns.

△△△

Emy, James, Nadia & Tuck

< Communications with Brick have been severed >

Emy's vision caught the blinking message. As she reread it, she paused, standing on campus grounds alongside James, Nadia, and Tuck.

"Nex, how can this happen?" Emy questioned, worry in her voice.

"Okay, I can still get his bio reading, and he is still okay. It seems an AI blocker of some sort may have hit him. His Nex, er, Nexy is still with him, but the device has severed the connection to his

mind," Nex communicated to the group.

"We need to do something," Nadia commented, stress evident across the group.

"Okay, let's go by what we know," Emy attempted to calm herself and looked at the team. "His last known location based on Nexy was that he was headed towards the biology room."

"He can't be far from there," Emy said, then paused, suddenly remembering Darya's speedy talent. "Wait."

"Tabitha, you there?" Emy directed over communication.

"Here. What's up?" Tabitha immediately responded.

"We are missing a team member. He was last seen in the west wing of the building. He is probably with a teacher, and most likely, it's just the pair of them," she revised. "Any chance you could get…"

"On it," Darya spoke into the communications, understanding the intent.

"We will know soon enough if she sees anyone," Tabitha interjected once Darya took off.

"Thank you. Keep us posted."

Observing the conversation's conclusion, James voiced over comms, "Trent, any leads on your tail?"

"Well, hello, James, and friends… I do. It appears that several groups are headed into the architectural fields. I don't quite understand the situation, but there seem to be a handful of kids and students congregating in the vicinity."

"We'll be there shortly," James replied.

"I advise Tuck to maintain control this time. My instincts tell me there's more to this than meets the eye. We can't afford any more lost points."

Tuck audibly groaned at the mention but refrained from speaking, acknowledging the truthfulness of the statement.

"I've got eyes on him," Darya interrupted.

"What do you see, Darya?" Tabitha questioned.

"They appear to be heading toward the outer fields. If I didn't know better, it would seem like nothing unusual is happening. No restraints, blindfolds, or anything of the sort.

He and the professor are engaged in a lively conversation?" Darya's expression reflected her perplexity. "The only sign I have noticed is that he's stumbling a bit, but nothing too extreme."

"Let's move," Emy urged the team. "James, we need a plan."

CHAPTER TWENTY-TWO

"Courage can come from anyone, not just heroes." – Local news reporter.

LEVEL TWO

Emy, James, Nadia & Tuck

Quill Creek was renowned for pioneering the first-ever bachelor's degree in Equine and Ranch Management. This pilot program attracted children from ranching families, offering them a unique blend of education and exposure to cutting-edge farming techniques. These techniques were not confined to the classrooms but were actively implemented across the vast expanse of Quill Creek's campus.

From their vantage point atop a dirt mound, the team of now just four surveyed the outer fields. The landscape sprawled before them, a patchwork of livestock centers, open plains, and farming biodomes. Among these features were a few equestrian tracks, each adorned with larger barns and horse stalls.

James, lying prone in the dirt, shifted slightly and glanced down at Nadia beside him. "Nadia, I think you're up first—if you're willing."

Nadia nodded in agreement.

Tuck interjected, "So you want her to make contact with Will?"

James nodded. "Yes. But first, we need to proceed cautiously. We're still uncovering the limits of her **Phantom Veil**. Let's start small, exploring the outskirts around the main barn."

The impressive barn facing the campus was the focal point of activity across the plot of land. A longstanding fixture of the school, this barn was situated near the horse tracks, providing ample space for horses to move about. Although its door remained closed, the team had noticed individuals entering and exiting. Beyond the barn, up to six students and teachers acted as lookouts, strategically positioned away from the building yet within earshot of one another.

Tuck rolled his body toward James. "But why not take out one of the lookouts first?"

Upon catching on to James's plan, Nadia answered on James's behalf, "We can, but we don't know exactly what we're up against. Based on Darya's observations, the infiltrators could be invisible, telekinetic, or even some sort of changeling. The worst-case scenario is that it's a student, and we'd end up holding them hostage out here."

Darya's voice came through the communications channel, "Will is coming."

Emy's gaze followed the path leading to the school. She spotted Will walking side by side with the biology professor. The team observed as he headed toward the barn. The professor nodded to one of the lookouts as he and Will continued down the trail. Oddly, there was no aggression toward Will, nor did he exhibit any defensive maneuvers. *What is going on?* The team thought as frustration simmered.

Outside the barn now, Will shook hands with a few students who stood near the entrance. His gestures seemed friendly—greetings and thank-yous—before he stepped inside, and the door closed behind him.

James's voice sounded over the comms, "Cohort 8, Trent. We're sending someone in. Hold if you can and avoid disruptions until we get her out of there."

"Copy," Tabitha confirmed.

Trent's divisive tone cut in, "Sending in Nadia, huh?" He paused, then added, "Copy that." His words ignited a pulse of anger in Tuck. Sensing this, Nadia, standing beside him, gently touched his arm, sending a stream of *Vitalization* to steady him. She then activated her *Phantom Veil* and disappeared from view.

△△△

Will

As the door shut behind him, Will's gaze swept across the dimly lit barn. The crowd inside buzzed with a frenzy of emotions—anticipation, happiness, fear, appreciation, curiosity—all swirling together like leaves caught in a storm.

A burly boy, unfamiliar to Will, stepped forward with an amiable grin. "Welcome. You're Will, right?" his voice filled the room with warmth. "I'm Greg. It's great to have you here. Please help yourself to some…" his sentence hung unfinished in the air, abruptly interrupted by a sudden movement at the back of the room.

"**Will?**" The tone was one of horror, a desperate plea. "**Oh no, no, no. Will. Not you.**" Mrs. Wallen suddenly appeared before him, her urgency showing across her face. "Will, you must leave—**now. Go!**"

Greg lunged, trying to restrain Mrs. Wallen, but she wrenched her arm away. "Will, don't listen to them! You need to get out of here!"

Four pairs of hands encircled the frantic professor, forcefully guiding her aside. "Mrs. Wallen," their voices were soothing, "we have discussed this. We kindly request that you depart. We all have the freedom to leave whenever we decide," the voice echoed as trusting energy enveloped the room, filling the space.

As they escorted Mrs. Wallen toward the back door, Will grappled with conflicting forces, sensing something was profoundly amiss. He'd always known, deep down, but now he needed answers. Focusing, he searched internally for clues and found them almost immediately. An invading energy stream had penetrated the emotional core of his brain. Now found, he rushed his energy through the invading streams as a river might break through a weak dam. What was once haze and confusion turned into calculated rage. Will was back, and the scene unfolding before him made him react anew. Will quickly targeted the two men, taking Mrs. Wallen and raising his hands, ready to channel energy, when a firm grip seized his wrist.

"*Don't*," the whisper clung to him. "*Not now*." He glanced down to find a girl standing beside him, eyes fixed ahead, persistent—the hushed message passing between them.

Will lowered his hands, surveying the room anew. The girl was right; he had no idea what was happening here. He had to put faith in his team's ability to find Mrs. Wallen. He had to let them go for now.

After the two imposing figures reentered, the back door was sealed shut.

"Everything is okay," Greg reassured the crowd in the barn, his voice a soothing balm. Another wave of calmness washed over Will.

Approaching Will again, Greg picked up where he had left off. "Sorry about that interruption. As I was saying, there's some food over in the corner, and you're welcome to mingle with everyone here. We're a friendly community, and we're in the process of starting our club."

Will let his excitement flair up, "Yeah, this place sounds fantastic. Mr. Shade filled me in during our walk down. Looking forward to meeting everyone here!" Greg seemed pleased with the response, retreating to the door and settling into a seat.

Will's gaze shifted to the food spread at the back. He grabbed a burger, noting that it had likely been transported from the campus cafeteria. Scanning the room, he spotted an empty seat next to the girl who had grabbed him earlier.

Taking a bite of the burger, Will observed the people around him, his focus settling on Greg first. Something felt different

—like his brain had the same connections but rearranged, scattered across unfamiliar territories. Digging deeper, he sensed no internal thoughts but more projections outward, directed at the group.

Perplexed, Will turned his attention to a girl near the food. Her smile radiated as she chatted with a friend. Delving into her energies, he felt a whirlwind within her brain—pleasure, comfort, happiness, trust—all looping endlessly.

Suddenly, a voice jolted him from his trance, "So, what made you decide to join the club?" Realizing the abruptness of her question, the speaker added, "Sorry… my name is Penny."

"Penny," Will repeated, emotions surging through him.

"Yes, Penny. Have we met?" The girl, with long brunette hair cascading down to her mid-back, dressed in a dark skirt and stylish round glasses, looked puzzled. "I know you're in my calculus class, but that reaction was unexpected."

"Oh, it's just…" Will hesitated, deciding to change topics, then continued, "Mr. Shade told me about the club after I visited him in class. He mentioned it's a place for friendship and fun. Beyond that, I don't know much."

"What more is there to know?" Penny half-blurted, forcing Will to suppress a grin. "The people here are awesome. Greg is great, and so is the other guy who helped Mrs. Wallen out. There are other fun folks mixed in, too."

Comprehending the cryptic hints woven into her words, Will nodded in response.

Glancing at Penny's energy, he glimpsed swirls of conflicting forces. Her natural energy seemed to be battling against the foreign energies.

"Yeah, these friends do seem nice," Will agreed. "Does the club have other activities for key members?" He glanced toward the girl engrossed in conversation with her friend.

"Oh, yes. Key members take on important roles—setting up camps, supporting recruiting," Penny explained with euphoria but quieted down as Greg and his friend shot her a curious look.

"Anyways, it was great meeting you, Will. Let's chat again soon." With that, Penny stood and joined another group near the center of the room.

As Penny departed, Will sat alone. *Nexy, are you with me yet?* He thought, hoping for a response.

Silence returned, leaving Will to sigh and reevaluate his situation. The barn harbored multiple infiltrators, subtly manipulating students and teachers using targeted mental energies. His strategy of following Mr. Shade had led him here, but it seemed he was a little too successful in getting himself caught. Losing Nexy was a significant blow to his working plans.

Determined, Will knew he had to find a way forward.

CHAPTER TWENTY-THREE

"Everyone has their breaking point." – E.B.

LEVEL TWO

Nadia

Nadia slipped away from her team, activating her **Phantom Veil** to move silently through the area. She tested the device by gliding past one of the guards patrolling the perimeter before approaching the barn.

"Guys, heads up," Nadia's voice sounded over the comm channel, "several of these people have what look like knives strapped to their belts."

"Got it, Nadia," James replied. "Anything else?"

"No, but I think I just heard a noise on the other side of the barn. Let me go investigate."

Sweeping around the central structure, Nadia observed more figures patrolling the area. Her gaze shifted to the opposite side of the barn, where two burly men handed off a woman—likely a professor—to two others. Once the exchange was complete, the two men retreated into the barn while the others guided the professor down the road toward a pair of massive farming biodomes.

Nadia fell in step behind the trio, her senses alert. But a comm interrupted her focus.

"Nadia, we have company," James's urgent voice cut through. "A car is headed toward the barn. We need eyes on it."

Turning, Nadia retraced her steps back to the barn. "Cohort 8, can you keep an eye on the three moving away from the rear of the barn toward the east? I believe they're heading to the biodomes."

"On it," Darya acknowledged.

As Nadia neared the barn again, her eyes caught sight of a parked car and a man emerging from it—the very same man who had been walking with Will before he was led into the main barn. As she closed the gap, she deftly evaded the familiar patrollers as an unforeseen tremor shook the barn.

BOOM! The building swayed, its large structure protesting.

"WILL!" Emy's panicked voice resounded through the communication channel as Nadia hurried toward the front of the barn.

ΔΔΔ

MOMENTS EARLIER

Will

Will savored another bite of his burger, his eyes methodically scanning the two dozen figures huddled in the shadowy barn. *How can I do this?* He wondered. His swift appraisal identified the crowd: A group of seven covert operatives, including Greg and his companion at the forefront, their motives concealed, and a half dozen students—each lost in their emotional turmoil, making them pliable to the leaders' will. Apart from these individuals, four more were on the verge of succumbing, their innate feelings dwindling into oblivion as their inner energy struggled to maintain dominance. Will cautiously evaluated the predicament; these students could inadvertently bolster the infiltrators in a revolt. He couldn't bear to gamble with any more lives.

As his eyes shifted to Penny, a flicker of inspiration ignited in his mind. He had successfully purged the unnatural emotions from his consciousness. Perhaps he could extend that gift to the others?

Taking a calculated risk, Will approached Penny. She met his gaze and then glanced toward the door, where the infiltrators conversed with another student. For now, they were safe.

"Will, this is my friend, Shelby," Penny introduced, her voice steady. "She's been part of the club longer than I have."

Shelby beamed, "Oh, it's nice to meet you, Will! Isn't this club great?" Her wave exuded enthusiasm, though Will detected a subtle cringe on Penny's face—a fleeting expression replaced by an exaggerated smile.

"Nice to meet you too, Shelby," Will returned the gesture. "Penny, do you mind if I sit next to you?"

"Of course," Penny replied, with a hint of confusion.

"And may I see your hand?" Will leaned in, whispering. Penny's nod conveyed understanding.

As he clasped her hand, Will allowed his energy to flow. Reaching out, his energy soon found another source willing and eager to merge with his. Looking inward, his energy surged through Penny, seeking the tangled threads within her mind. The draft of energies swirled, lighter than the chaotic turmoil in the other minds. Will seized the opportunity, constructing a miniature barrier within Penny's consciousness—a defense against the rampaging external forces threatening to consume her.

Will's gaze lifted to Penny, and he saw her eyes widen as her natural emotions returned to life. "Will," she whispered, her voice a mix of joy from escaping the mental fog and fear from their current predicament.

It was as if Will saw Penny anew momentarily—her thoughts vibrant, her essence bare. He leaned in, his voice low, "There you are…" he murmured, a smirk tugging at his lips as he locked eyes again through her large glasses, noticing how beautiful this girl truly was.

Penny's attention shifted again to the door, then back to Will. "Are you willing to give it another try?" she asked, her gaze flickering to her friend.

With a nod from Will, Penny turned to Shelby. "Shelby, Will

has a unique talent related to our club. Can he hold your hand for a moment?" Penny clasped Shelby's hand, motioning for Will to sit on the other side. Will took Shelby's other hand in his.

As he initiated the same process, Will sensed a familiar energy—Penny was attuned to it, too. Wrapping their energies together, he guided Penny through Shelby's channels, ascending toward her consciousness. This time, a torrent of energy hit Will like a hammer. He concentrated, gathering more power and erecting the protective barrier he had used before.

"Who... What? Where am I?" Shelby's voice wavered with confusion and hesitation as if she were seeing the room for the first time.

"It's okay, Shelby," Penny reassured softly, her emotions flaring. "You're with us. Everything will be fine."

"No, what's going on? Why are we here?" Shelby's tone grew louder, echoing her inner unrest.

"Shelby, I need you to calm..." Penny's urgent plea hung in the air as a hand abruptly seized hers from behind.

"I think it's time for you to leave," Greg addressed Penny, his tone firm. Will froze, his attention moving towards the two men now gripping Penny.

Penny's eyes locked with Will's: *Don't.* Her emotions pleaded silently, a desperate understanding passing between them. She knew the consequences if he intervened.

Hand in arms with the guards, Penny allowed herself to be led toward the door as those within the captured, still fighting against their emotions, attempted to hide their despair as they watched another get taken away.

Greg's hand hesitated above the latch, but as he glanced downward, he detected a layer of ice forming. The frost began to creep onto his skin, chilling his fingers.

"***No***," Will's voice eclipsed the room from behind, his figure near the trio.

"Will. **No!**" Penny screamed as Greg and the other infiltrator turned.

"I think Will may also want to leave," Greg addressed the room, his gaze sweeping over everyone. His eyes called for support against the threat.

"Come on, Will, let's go," Greg's words punctuated Will with a tidal wave of emotions—no longer for implanting thoughts but for crippling internal awareness.

Will staggered, overwhelmed by invading mind energies from several places around the room. His knees hit the barn floor, desperation driving him to find a path through it.

With aggression, Greg smashed the icy barrier, unlatching the door. He yanked Penny toward the opening, but a cold mist enveloped them both.

"*I... SAID... NO,*" Will's voice quivered as he shattered the binding emotions that had once sought to imprison him.

Frost slowly gathered across Will's body as the cold mist in the air crystallized, encasing the barn in a shimmering sheet of ice.

The remaining students trembled, their emotions still raw from the assault. Only five of them remained standing. The now-identified infiltrators cautiously approached Will, who stood in the center of the icy chamber.

Will looked down and noticed the ice coating that now covered his arms and upper back. At the same time, he felt a familiar sensation returning to his mind. Despite this, he focused on the task at hand and slowly raised his hands. He used his **Condense** skill to create thick chunks of frozen air around him, forming jagged shards that hung suspended around the room.

"*Drop,*" Will mentally urged Penny, who responded by slipping from Greg's grasp and tossing herself to the icy floor.

SLAM! The airborne ice projectiles streaked around the room, striking the walls and the seven infiltrators still standing. The frozen blades pierced their bodies, slicing through their forms and dropping them on the spot. Will, now devoid of emotion, crumpled beside them. The abrupt dissipation of the cold left the room trembling and groaning from the impact.

"Will!" Penny's voice caught as she sprinted toward his falling form.

"Will, stay with me," urged Nexy, who had returned. *"You've endured a massive mental assault. Stay conscious—I'll do what I can to help."*

ICE BRIGADE! 63 POINTS!

< Skill Identified – Will – Flow Perception >

< Skill Identified – Will – Cryostrike >

< Double Level Up! Will is now a level 5 Condenser >

"Two levels, huh?" Will's internal voice addressed Nexy as he attempted to gather himself. "Welcome back, Nexy. I missed you in here."

But Nexy's warning cut through the moment, *"Will, we may need to expedite your recovery. Trouble awaits outside."*

CHAPTER TWENTY-FOUR

"When you're out there, at times you're acutely aware that rage has ensnared you, yet you chose to cling to it stubbornly." – Titan, Former Champion.

LEVEL TWO

Full Team

< Communications with Brick have been re-established >

"I'm okay," Will confirmed over the comms. "What's happening out there?"

"Hold tight, Will. Mr. Shade is outside the barn now. The eruption has everyone on edge," James replied calmly. "Nadia is coming."

"What was that!?" Mr. Shade yelled at the crowd of onlookers as he approached the barn. Two teachers and a student stood with him by the barn door as the lookouts cautiously returned around the area.

A firm knock landed on the barn door, and Mr. Shade's voice emerged—quiet yet commanding, "You'd best step out now. No other options."

"Trouble-makers," he continued, eliciting laughter and smiles from the assembled group, "receive the finest punishments."

But then, the man turned, and the team could see his face shift as if noticing something amiss.

"And who stands before us?" he mused, turning unnaturally.

SNAP! His hand lunged, gripping Nadia's throat. Waves of emotion overwhelmed her as the ***Phantom Veil*** fell off, leaving Nadia visibly dangling.

< Nadia is UNCONSCIOUS >

< Nadia's health is at 68% >

The air hummed with tension as Mr. Shade spoke, averting his eyes across the broader area, "Did you think a mere device could hide you? You, humans, are walking strobe lights of emotion to us, Weavers."

Status updates flooded the team, and a new yellow glaze veiled the former professor's eyes.

Baron Mindweaver: Level 7

Emerging from cosmic obscurity, the Mindweavers defy biological norms. They flow like forgotten tides, not flesh and bone, sculpting their essence to mysterious ends. Emotions—mere threads—bend to their will, twisted, amplified, or dulled as they desire.

"Team, we need to strike together—," Emy's voice started over the communications.

"Detect this, bitch," James muttered. An ***Alchemarrow*** already streaked from his bow, unerring, slicing through the air with precision, and lodged itself into the Weaver's skull. The ***Alchemarrow***, infused with Emy's ***Targeted Fusion*** blast creation, remained dormant until impact.

BOOM!

Moments after the incision, a powerful blast was unleashed, obliterating the Weaver and propelling Nadia sideways.

< Nadia's health is at 19% >

Leaving the remaining weavers no time to react, an enraged Tuck charged into battle, roaring like an elemental force. Sparks flew from his colossal figure as he unleashed an ***Ion Storm***—a disruption of electrifying energy that swept through the remaining fighters. The air vibrated, and tendrils of electricity struck out, causing bodies to convulse and the remaining combatants to collapse into the ground.

< All known combatants are UNCONSCIOUS >

DON'T TOUCH MY GIRLFRIEND! 37 POINTS!

< Level Up! Tuck is now a Level 6 Accelerator >

Nex's excitement surged, "*Woah, boy! Active views just hit 8740!*"

"Wait! Don't kill them!" Will urgently called out as he pushed open the barn doors with Penny beside him.

"Some of them are under Weaver-based mind control," Will continued as he reached Nadia, who still lay unconscious. He cradled her head off the ground and sent a stream of energy inside her using his **Flow Perception** skill, immediately disrupting the hold the Weaver had placed on her. Nadia's eyes jolted open, allowing her **Vitalize** skill to activate through her body.

"What happened?" Nadia asked the team, her gaze following Penny's hurried approach toward the other brainwashed humans amidst the Weavers. As a swift learner, Penny deftly applied the **Flow Perception** skill that Will had previously shown.

James and Tuck exchanged guilty glances. Nadia's question hung in the air, unanswered. Thankfully, she hadn't overheard the combat commentary.

The answer came from an unexpected source. Emerging from the fields, Trent's voice dripped with disdain as he strode toward the group. A black blade hovered before him, and fragmented pieces of blackened armor shifted and coalesced, forming armor and shields. His gaze bore into the still-unconscious Weavers, their bodies sprawled on the ground.

"You," Trent pointed at Tuck, "were fortunate. That reckless fool's pulse could have wiped out everyone nearby."

Without hesitation, the blackened armor dispersed, shards erupting from its formation. They sliced through the Weavers' necks, ending their lives instantly, only to promptly reappear within Trent's suit.

James couldn't control himself. "You're killing our only sources of information," he confronted Trent as the area filled with distaste, the aftermath of Trent's lethal efficiency hanging heavy in the air.

"Do you think I'd trust all of you with that?" Trent retorted. "Did you even consider that they might have communication devices themselves?"

One remaining Weaver stirred from consciousness, still prone, and began laughing. "She's already coming. You're all done for." Trent spun and, this time, sent his black blade slicing into the creature's chest.

Trent sighed, "Is that what you wanted? These creatures are nothing more than insult-spewing nuisances." He continued without waiting for an answer, "Let's just finish this mission."

Undeterred by Trent's dismissive words, Will urgently addressed the group, "They've taken Mrs. Wallen." His gaze moved on to James. "We need to hurry."

"Look," he added, "these might be helpful. There was a box drop in the barn." Will then openly shared the new device with the group.

New Devices Detected – NeuraBlocker(x25)
Uncommon
These devices attach just beneath the first layer of the user's skin, strategically positioned near neural pathways. Its primary purpose is to interfere with signals exchanged between the user's brain and the AI system.

"I was able to fry the one I had implanted in my back with my ice," Will assured, "but these will effectively remove any

Weaver from their communication channels." He then turned his gaze toward the stunned Penny, who was now hovering over a recovering student. "Can you take the others back to the campus?" he asked. "They'll need to be with someone we trust."

CHAPTER TWENTY-FIVE

"Adapt and Endure." – Coach Williams.

THE HANGAR (LEVEL TWO)

Frank & Trish

"What the heck was that? We've seen Tuck's **Ion Storm** in the weight room, but Will's pulse on those shards and that crystal ice covering his upper body was intense," Trish exclaimed as she sat next to Frank and Coach Williams in the strategy room.

It was the middle of the second level, and the three had just watched Will rescue Penny, followed by the intense field battle with Mr. Shade. After each broadcast, there was time for reflection and strategic planning, allowing the team to refine their strategies, build, and prepare for the next intermission.

The broadcast was available on everyone's Nexabot interface, but it had become a tradition to watch together in the strategy room. The supporting team watched both scenes from multiple angles, with replays and deeper analysis done after the primary broadcast.

"I believe Mr. Weiss was on the verge of a full-body technique. It is a very challenging move, especially with ice as the primary substance. Those shards that shot toward the infiltrators were just a combination of a few skills he had already mastered, with the primary one being **Cryostrike**. It also seems like that ice may have disrupted the signal on his Nexabot device, allowing him to regain access to his AI."

"Those last mind-blasts were no joke," Frank added. "Even

with Will's new skill to disperse them, he still had to shake off that last blast from the Weavers."

"Do we know if Tuck knew his **Ion Storm** would work so well against that large group? That seemed to be a bit risky," Trish asked.

"I don't think he did. Instinct and rage can often progress one's capabilities beyond one's understanding. Tuck may have had a hunch that it would work, but ultimately, that was untested," the Professor confirmed.

The three continued to delve into other aspects of the battle, discussing James's proficiency with the bow, Nadia's cloaking limitations, Will's *Flow Perception*, and finally, Trent's skill with his armor and blades.

"Professor, any ideas what Trent's primary talent is? Seems like some affinity with metal?" Trish asked as they wrapped up their discussions.

"I believe so. His talent and energy showed up similar to Emy's when I was first recruiting the team in that it wasn't grounded in one area. Trent possesses both internal and external flows, making him an excellent talent for recruitment."

"Does he need to carry around metal to enable his skill? Similar to Emy's talent?" Trish followed up her original question.

"I don't think he has to do that. Some users have an affinity for elements and materials, which, in this case, is metal. Metal is abundant in this world, and it looks like Trent can sense and interact with it. On the other hand, Emy lacks a direct affinity to anything outside of fire. She is a Generalist, and her sensations can grow, but ultimately, she needs to feel in order to interact. This is why the *Fanny Pack* is necessary; it allows easy access to known reaction types during the early stages of her growth."

"Now then, I don't think this most recent broadcast changes anything with what we want to achieve for this cycle. We have more ideas for future rounds, but ultimately, we should push those to the back of our minds and continue our current endeavors."

Like the others, Trish and Frank were deeply committed to maximizing growth within the team and themselves. When they weren't watching the events, they spent their cycles honing their crafts and studying their squad. Frank's talent was unsurprisingly labeled as a "Creator," fitting his background in smithing. Williams noted that creation takes many shapes and forms, but a person's affinity ultimately guides them to specialization. For Frank, this was metallurgy.

In contrast, Trish's talent was identified as a "Manipulator," a more versatile ability. Her early skills allowed her to match affinities with the items they were building, manipulating the genetic makeup of objects and attuning them to specific affinities for better hero alignment. Despite her ability to align affinities with objects, she had not yet been paired with a specific affinity herself. The Professor reassured her that this sometimes happens later as one delved deeper into their talents. Due to their skill sets, both were tasked with developing a new weapon for one of the team members.

Through their learning with Williams and online tutorials, the two had been directed to a rare metal called Celestium. Most heroes across the Cosmos were known to possess a weapon or armor made of this material. The only challenge was that it was costly. A weapon made of Celestium started at a minimum value of two thousand points and could go upwards of two million points, with those just being the available weapons. Because of this, Williams had challenged the two with a task that was a bit out of their depth, knowing it would be a test. Eager to take on the challenge, they invested 400 credits, which would later convert to points, in a block of raw Celestium and materials to attune the metal to their chosen affinity. Although the team didn't have the points at the time of purchase, the System allowed for a credit application based on the expected point totals by the end of the current round. This common practice supported the Artisan roles, providing them with the necessary materials and time for crafting, ensuring the team could avoid delays in completing the level.

"I think it's starting to take shape. What do you think?" Frank posed to Trish as the two looked at the metal sitting in the center of the room.

"You clearly are an artist because that looks like a block of metal on top of a stick," Trish said, grinning.

"Ha, maybe, but using these big AI-driven machines doesn't make me feel much like an artist. I just wish I could use my old tools. These new devices are cool and all, but it just doesn't feel the same without being able to throw my weight into molding the metal. At least you get to use your hands. I'm stuck behind this computer, telling it where to put pressure and where to strike."

The metal "block" was in the center of the table, and with each meticulous strike of the automated machine, Trish needed to rebuild the connection established to maintain the affinity. A single gap in affinity in the metal would lead to a gap in the energy transference and limit the overall potential of the object. The binding process was similar to weaving, taking the source element—in this case, Celestium—and weaving a string of affinity energy through it, cutting through the inner bonds of the compact metals. The denser the object, the more complex the weave.

"That's true," Trish commented. "I am learning a ton, but this all feels too meticulous. Don't get me wrong, I love it, but it just feels like there is a better way. I wonder if this is some Mr. Miyagi training."

"I've found nothing in our guidebooks that says different. Maybe it will just take time to get faster. I keep thinking how awesome it will be to see this thing in action!"

ΔΔΔ

LEVEL TWO

Full Team

James assembled the entire team, except for Darya, who remained on surveillance duty around the biodome.

"First," James began, "we're in the dark about these Weavers. These 'people' may appear human, but their true forms and abilities remain a mystery beyond mind control. Second, they're holed up in a massive biodome, limiting our visibility. Civilians, including Mrs. Wallen, are potentially caught in the crossfire, ruling out a direct assault. Lastly, the Weavers' numbers and distribution across campus remain unknown. We need a strategic approach."

Tuck responded, "That's quite a list of challenges."

James nodded in agreement. "True, but we're not defenseless. Darya's biodome observations reveal no signs of unrest or unusual behavior among those entering or leaving. Which means we still have the element of surprise."

"But before we get too far into the planning," James continued, "We need to dig deeper into the broader team's capabilities. Will, do you mind sharing your new skills with the broader team to kick things off?"

Will shared both new skills learned in the barn:

Skill: Flow Perception
Enables the user to perceive the internal energy flows of intelligent life, granting them the unique ability to alter or adjust the emotions of others. (T)

Skill: Cryostrike
Grants the user the capability to release a pulse that can accelerate matter. Once activated, this pulse exhibits heightened effectiveness with substances that have a pre-existing connection with the user, such as water or ice. (R)

Once the team had enough time to understand Will's new skills, James looked at his new allies. "Mind giving us a run-down of your talents? I believe you have now seen most of ours."

Tabitha and Michele exchanged glances, reaching the same conclusion. Despite their initial interactions, Cohorts 8 and 13 had proven to be strong allies, always ready to support one another. While everyone understood Darya's fundamental skills, the team only knew that Tabitha and Michele leaned toward the offensive side of the talent spectrum, as indicated by their level-one feedback to Emy earlier that day.

Tabitha, usually the team's conversational leader, deferred to Michele. "It may be easier to show you," Michele said. She glanced up at Tuck, the team's resident strongman, who towered over the group. "Tuck, mind helping with a demonstration?"

Nodding with a hint of hesitation, Tuck stepped forward as the group circled the two. "Okay, nothing too complex of a show—just a high five," Michele said, smirking. "Oh, and add just a little zing to it. Not too much, though."

Now more confused, Tuck agreed and stood facing Michele, who counted down, "Okay, 3...2...1..." At the mark, both flung their hands toward each other at an accelerated pace. Tuck's hand pulsed with a small amount of energy as the two palms collided.

WHAM! A mini shockwave pushed the group back, and neither hand budged an inch. Tuck was the first to move, flexing and clenching his hand, trying to regain normal sensation.

"Dang, Chel-Ter! That nickname is a gift that keeps on giving!" Will exclaimed, eyeing the two. "What the heck just happened?"

"It felt like I was hitting a hammer at every point of contact," Tuck said, still looking at Michele in amazement.

Michele explained, "I have a talent that allows me to increase the density in my body. Right now, I can only target specific areas, but I suspect I'll be able to influence my whole body with practice."

Smiles spread as they considered their new ally's remarkable skillset. Then, all eyes turned to Tabitha.

"I think I'll save my demonstration for combat," Tabitha began, exchanging a look with Michele, "but our success in the first round was due to a team effort. I am a Vibration user—or at least that's what my talent is called. I can focus on a small area and hold things in place through vibrations."

"Darya distracted, I immobilized the creatures, and Michele punched the living crap out of them," Tabitha continued. "It worked well, but we need to develop our talents further to maintain our effectiveness."

"I think we may have a good use for that one..." James commented as a plan took shape in his mind.

"Trent," James said, turning to their last new ally, "last up... Do you mind sharing a bit about your skillset?" Despite their previous differences, both parties recognized their mutual need.

To everyone's surprise, Trent willingly obliged, offering just enough relevant information to support the current situation: "I am what they call a Morphist. I can create, manipulate, and shape matter at my discretion, with a particular focus on metals."

James arched an eyebrow. The plan was now fully taking form. "Impressive. Would you be able to reconstruct the biodome wall if we were to... dismantle it?"

△△△

Team One

"All clear, Will. Rejoining Team Two. Good luck," Nadia confirmed, deftly implanting the second human-formed Weaver with a **Neurablocker** as it crumpled to the dirt. Her **Phantom Veil** and a delicate application of **Neurofluxine** to the necks of the patrolling groups allowed Nadia to dispatch them swiftly, ensuring that Will and the team could explore deeper into the base. This chemical was Trish's second concoction for Nadia to hold within her bloodstream—giving a knockout punch when combined with Nadia's touch of *Affliction Surge*.

Solution Detected - Neurofluxine
This solution is a potent concoction, a distinctive mix of chemicals that flawlessly melds with the cellular framework of living beings. It imparts a formidable impact, rendering the target powerless. Whether the goal is to neutralize a danger or induce slumber in a creature, this solution stands as your premier selection.

"Thanks, Nadia," Will acknowledged, silently encircling the dome. His newfound **Flow Perception** skill revealed that the larger group of Weavers occupied the northside of the structure. This finding matched what their maps had showcased, but they weren't willing to take any chances. Will then signaled Team One forward for entry.

"All right, Emy, I think you're up. This is likely our best target spot," Will said as he looked towards the other three members of Team One gathered near the biodome. Will, Tabitha, Trent, and Emy had been tasked with taking down the main base, while the others focused on handling the watch parties and Weavers surrounding the school.

Emy approached the biodome before her and placed her hand against the wall. Feeling a Teflon-like material, the wall was solid, but Emy searched for more. Elements and molecules bound up together, interacting with each other and constructing this object. It comprised carbon, hydrogen, and fluorine—bonded, mixed, and compacted. Letting her energy interact with these elements, she started to break them apart. Her hand bent into the once firm material, pushing further until there was nothing but a hole in the wall, revealing a lush flourish of greenery beyond.

< Skill Identified – Emy – Disintegration >

< Level Up! Emy is now a Level 5 Generalist >

"Couldn't let me stay ahead for even 30 minutes?" Will whispered, his tone a mix of amazement and playful grumpiness as he looked at Emy's new skill:

Skill: Disintegration

Allows the user the power to dismantle the chemistry of an entity, scattering its atoms until the entity ceases to exist. (T & R)

"Let's go," Trent grunted with annoyance at the two, Tabitha following closely.

Once inside, Trent turned around to the hole and, like Emy, placed his hand against the wall next to the gap. As if trying to find the right mixture, Trent channeled his energy, and the edge closest to his hand started to fill with material. It was as if someone was knitting a wall together right before their eyes.

"Done," Trent's tone was no-nonsense, as if what he had done was child's play. "Split up. Stay quiet. Stick with the plan."

Emy and Will moved in tandem, hugging the western wall as they advanced northward toward the larger Weaver cluster that had caught Will's attention earlier. Meanwhile, Trent and Tabitha stealthily navigated the brush, veering toward the east side.

Trent's hovering black blade danced through the shrubbery as he mentally relayed a terse message through the comms: "One patrolling infiltrator down, and communication jammed. Stay alert." Tension remained as the team pressed forward, their senses attuned to the unseen threats lurking in the room.

"Copy," Will acknowledged, allowing Emy to lead their team quietly toward the main pack of Weavers. Suddenly pausing, Emy raised a hand to Will as she spotted another level 5 Weaver. "Additional patrol spotted and looking in our direction. Going to proceed with the next stage."

"Ready," Tabitha confirmed.

Upon acknowledgment, Emy channeled a blend of gases from her **Fanny Pack**, merging them with the surrounding air. Nitrogen, hydrogen, and chlorine intermingled with the ambient moisture, resulting in a concoction one would never expect within a biodome. The air thickened, veiled in pure white smoke, rapidly expanding as Emy exerted her willpower throughout the larger room.

< Level Up! Emy is now a Level 6 Generalist >

Thick plumes of smoke enveloped the dome, creating an opaque cloud that allowed Will and Emy to advance along the path stealthily. Will's internal sigh showed as the level-up notification flashed before their eyes.

Shifting into motion, Will erected an emotional shield with his **Flow Perception** skill to conceal any trace of visibility as they stalked the bewildered Weaver. Ice crystallized around Will's hands, forming lethal spikes. With precision, Will's spiked fist struck the side of the humanoid creature's neck, sending it sprawling and collapsing to the ground.

As the smoke continued to billow, the duo cautiously emerged into clearer visibility, revealing a scene at the back of the dome that sent fear coursing through their veins. Ten humanoid Weavers intermingled with an additional ten entities—Weavers in their raw, primal form. These beings bore no resemblance to flesh and bone; instead, they resembled constantly shifting clay, composed of ethereal energy, poised for transformation.

Yet, the true terror lay in Mrs. Wallen's prone form on the ground. A colossal Weaver hovered over her, channeling essence across both figures. As they looked toward the scene, a message flickered before their eyes.

Civilians Killed: 2

-10 Points

"**No!**" Will's mouth blurted out before his brain could catch up. Emy's hand immediately covered Will's mouth as the group in front of them pivoted toward the sound, their eyes widening at the massive white smoke plume.

"We have an incident. All parties, return now!" shouted a Weaver voice through the dome.

"*We're too late,*" Will declared over the comms, his eyes welling with tears as an internal rage surged.

CHAPTER TWENTY-SIX

"Courage comes from embracing risks."
– The Reckoner, Former Champion.

LEVEL TWO

Team Two

"Team One should have been our name," Michele remarked as she and Tuck stood near the main entrance of the biodome. "When have front-line enforcers ever played a secondary role?"

Michele and Tuck occupied this position for two distinct reasons: first, as a reliable fallback for Team One in case they had to retreat from within the dome's confines, and second, due to the regrettable absence of effective long-range or stealth capabilities in the two of them.

"At this point, I'm feeling more like Team Three," Tuck grumbled, sensing that his team was moving forward without him. "We're just standing here while the others play critical roles."

"Push those thoughts aside. You know your role is crucial to the team," James interjected as he loaded a **Neurofluxine Alchemarrow**, aiming at a Weaver 100 yards away. Unlike the other arrows in his quill, a single strike from Nadia and Trish's creation could completely incapacitate an unaware Weaver, no matter where it hit.

"Target down, Darya," James relayed over comms. The **Alchemarrow** had found its mark, allowing Darya to investigate whether the fallen figure was a Weaver or a mind-controlled human before using her blade. Since their formation, Will had taught the team a simple scan technique to assess the mental state of humanoid targets. The only challenge was that the subject needed to be unconscious.

"Weaver eliminated. Nice shot, James. I count five more targets within sight," Darya reported.

Beyond the technologically advanced bow and arrows, the team remained unaware of how ideally this weapon suited James. Perhaps Coach Williams or even Nex had dropped subtle hints, but beyond his parents, only a select few knew of James's passion for archery. Growing up amidst the Olympic Games, his parents seized upon any interest James showed in sports that could qualify him in the future. While archery was typically associated with summer, the moment his parents detected even a hint of curiosity, they promptly enrolled him in local coaching sessions with experts in the field. Over time, football and team-based sports consumed much of his attention, but his love for precision-based skills remained steadfast.

"Slow and steady, team. Keep up the good work," James urged as Nadia, a one-woman wrecking crew, dispatched Weaver after Weaver with her assassin-like stealth and fingertip energy control. James couldn't help but shiver at the transformation he witnessed in Nadia. He felt grateful to have her on his team.

"Two left, then we proceed to stage two," James announced as Nadia closed in on her next Weaver.

Civilians Killed: 2

-10 Points

"Shit," James muttered, the message flashing across their vision. But he responded firmly, "This doesn't change our plan. Push forward, Nadia."

With the *Phantom Veil* activated, Nadia moved stealthily toward her target. The Weaver, its humanoid frame standing and looking over the horizon, seemed oblivious—until it shifted, a ripple of panic coursing through its veins. Instantly, it bolted toward the biodome, driven by some unseen urgency.

"Tuck, Michele, heads up! Weavers are headed your way. I suspect they received a recall via communications," Nadia blamed herself for not reacting fast enough.

"On it," Tuck acknowledged, excitement bubbling as he prepared to leap into the action.

Michele's hands shifted density while Tuck's body instinctively triggered its "fight" response, activating energy currents to spike all over his body.

"Darya, maintain your patrol. We still need your eyes on the field. Nadia, you and I need to head back to the dome for backup," James directed the team.

Near the biodome's main entry, Tuck and Michele observed two Weavers emerging into view. Tuck, ready to unleash his **Ion Storm**, hesitated—Michele stood beside him, and Nadia remained nearby. Fearing accidental harm to their allies, Tuck confronted the Weavers directly.

An older teacher-based humanoid Weaver approached, accompanied by a younger student-based Weaver. The older Weaver cackled, declaring, "Well, it seems we've found the problem."

Before the Weaver could finish speaking, Tuck and Michele took off. Fueled by rage, they charged toward the approaching adversaries. However, their bravado dissipated when they locked eyes with the Weaver. Fear seemed nonexistent in the eyes of these new foes. Within three strides, both Weaver unleashed a massive outpouring of energy, overpowering Tuck and Michele's minds and sending them hurtling to the ground.

The situation escalated further. "Everyone, we've got incoming. This is bad," Darya voiced over the comms. "The communication must have reached the entire Weaver population in the school. I count at least 20, and five are dangerously close to you." Horror struck her face as she observed Tuck and Michele's dire situation.

"Hold on, I'm almost there. We need to extract you," Nadia said firmly as Tuck and Michele now knelt, their bodies trembling, caught in a vortex of overwhelming emotions.

"No, Nadia, stay back!" James's desperate plea resounded through the comms.

But it was too late. Nadia extended her hand, attempting to trigger her ***Crimson Cascade*** on both Weavers. The toxin surged into them, yet her willpower faltered. She couldn't muster a potent ***Affliction Surge*** for both, resulting in the toxin slowing down before it could reach a lethal dose.

"Enough!" the larger Weaver bellowed, unleashing another burst of energy at Nadia. She crumpled at Tuck and Michele's feet, her mind tormented by the crippling force for the second time.

"***No. No. No. No.***" James paced from a distance, watching his team fall and slowly become surrounded by incoming Weavers converging toward the dome. Using arrows would send them running his way, and a fireball bolt would put the team at risk. James's mind raced for more options.

"I need to get in there," James flatly stated to his now sole ally, Darya, as if having no other choice.

"What? No, James! We can't lose you too! We should hold our ground and inform the others," Darya exclaimed.

"We risk everything if that group gets inside. I have to do this," James insisted, leaving no room for debate. "Come here and grab an ***Alchemarrow***. I need a distraction."

With a fireball ***Alchemarrow*** in hand, Darya moved away from James. Using her momentum, she flung the arrow toward the opposite side of the Dome while James shot a second arrow to the nearest side.

BOOM!... BOOM! Dual explosions surrounded the Weaver pack as fire and energy exploded from the ***Alchemarrows***, scattering the Weavers as James sprinted toward the group. A few Weavers still targeted his team, but he didn't care. He was their only option. James triggered his power.

< James's is boosted by 20% >

James reached the team but was immediately assaulted by waves of mind-blasting energy as the Weavers soon noticed him. James fought the energy churn and attempted to channel more power, becoming encircled with force. Pushing inward, he held on with everything he had.

< James's is boosted by 30% >

"What kind of plan is this?" Now regrouping around the four, the Weavers began to laugh at the foolish sight before them.

As they pushed, he held, and as the mental energy washed over him, he slowly began to understand it—the flow, signature, and wavelengths that created this force. As his energy's intelligence grew, so did James. A surge of new life propelled James further. His fists clenched, he stared down his foes as they closed in, unimpressed by the latest wave of power.

"It's..." James forced his lips to move, "called a distraction." With that, he slammed his fist toward the ground as an energy dome enveloped the team.

< Skill Identified – James – Energy Blocking Field >

James felt he could expand his *Empower* skill to those around him, but he didn't expect this... Surprised by the resulting barrier, James glanced at the notification as his energy expanded within the dome:

Skill: Energy Blocking Field

Allows the user to construct a field that restricts and limits energy sources. The shield can protect against all external forces, but its effectiveness is subject to the user's control. (T)

As the barrier sparked to life, Michele seized the nearest Weaver by the neck, slamming her head into its face. Not far behind, Tuck unleashed furious energy punches at the nearest Weavers, sending them flying in every direction. With space now opening up, James drew his bow, sending piercing arrow after arrow toward their foes. Meanwhile, Darya incapacitated the stunned onlookers with precise knife strikes.

The team stormed through the cluster of Weavers like bulls seeing red. Enraged and efficient, they struck down the last of the combatants.

WEAVERDOME! 115 POINTS!

< Combatants cleared >

< Double Level Up! James is now a Level 5 Catalyst >

"Active v*iews peaked over 15,000 and are still climbing*!" Nex exclaimed.

As the adrenaline subsided, a weary Nadia pushed herself off the ground. The team rushed back to her, all catching their breath.

"You. You saved us," Michele expressed her gratitude, gazing not at James but toward Nadia. Despite being hit with brain-blasting energy, Nadia had managed to grab both Tuck and Michele, breaking the torrent in their minds.

"And you," Michele turned her attention to James, "did you know what she had done?" The group suddenly looked back at James, and a blush tinged his cheeks.

"Yes. Of course," James replied hesitantly. But their focus shifted as a cry from inside the door drew their attention back to the dome.

CHAPTER TWENTY-SEVEN

"You don't truly know someone until you see them in their most desperate moments." – E.B.

LEVEL TWO

Team One

Emy's heart raced as she pressed her hand firmly against Will's mouth, muffling any remaining sounds. From her **Fanny Pack**, she channeled the same mixture from earlier. With her willpower, she merged the solvent into the air, continuing to create a billowing white fog that stretched across the dome, obscuring everything in its path. Emy stole one last glance at Mrs. Wallen's lifeless form, confirming the dreadful truth: She was gone. Her pale face lay on the ground as Emy saw her body twitch and a purple dot emerge on her map. Unease entered Emy as she forced herself to scan Mrs. Wallen once more. "Oh no."

Marchioness "Alarice" Mindweaver: Level 8

Second in command, Alarice treads the fragile boundary between existence and oblivion. To some, she is a beacon of salvation, unraveling mysteries and stitching fractured realities. To others, she embodies chaos, pulling at the threads of fate until they fray. But all who encounter her agree: when Alarice, the Mindweaver, plies her craft, the universe shivers, caught in the delicate dance of creation and dissolution.

"Will, I know this is tough. But we need you... I need you right now," Emy pushed her friend out of his mental haze.

"It's all real, Emy," Will spoke in a hushed tone. "*All of it.*"

"What do you mean?" Emy pressed.

"This. All of this. The Weavers, our classmates, Mrs. Wallen. This mission is real," Will's voice was shallow as Emy guided them back into the brush of the dome. "Thinking back to our first mission, I couldn't feel the creatures' minds. They 'existed' but lacked the connectedness to the world. Here, in this mission, everyone has a soul. Everyone has a mind shaping their thoughts, past, present, and future. I can do what I am doing because these 'things'... they're real." Will's eyes widened, staring off toward Mrs. Wallen's form.

Emy grappled with the weight of Will's revelation. Yes, they knew they could be killed in these Games, real or not, but she hadn't considered the people she was attempting to protect. Real or fake, these individuals needed help, and she was thrust into a situation to provide it. She wouldn't have altered her path, regardless of the truth. But what did it mean for her? Will thrives on interaction, friendship, and connection. Emy? She thrived on doing the right thing and protecting those closest to her.

"Will," Emy hesitated, gathering her words, "if this is real, then I stand by our actions. We did everything in our power to get to this point. Yes, we could have done better, but we are here. Look around—it's us. This would have existed regardless, but we can stop it from growing. The school needs you, and our team needs you." Emy's tone was firm, even as an inner voice challenged her. *Why?* Something was responsible for this, and nobody else was stepping up. She pushed that thought to the back of her mind as Will looked to gather himself.

"Let's go." Will's face lacked its normal emotion as resolve took over.

"Trent, Tabitha. You're up," Will communicated while Emy

shifted her status to combat mode.

	Level	Health	Shield
Emy	Level 6	100%	60%
Will	Level 5	100%	50%

"On my mark," Trent spoke, gathering the chemical imbalance from the room and creating shards of thin metal stretching across the smoke.

"**Now.**" In an instant, the shards of metal pierced through the air toward the gathered party, now facing in the direction of the billowing smoke. Voices howled in pain as the metal cut through the Weavers.

Tabitha channeled her talent as the metal struck. She was searching for those same metals; once found, she pushed them to vibrate, accelerating their movement and creating a chorus of high-pitched noise, debilitating the Weavers' mental energy as they attempted to channel toward the brush.

Emy and Will surged ahead, seizing the moment. Using *Targeted Fusion* fireballs and *Cryostrikes*, the two ignited the area, unleashing a storm of destruction upon the space as a dozen Weavers fell to the ground.

< Three humanoid and five base form Weavers remain >

"**Enough!**" exploded a female voice, ripe with venom. The former metals used by Trent surged back toward the heroes. Having limited visibility on both sides, the metals tore into the group. Only Trent emerged unscathed, his body's metal affinity catching the return before striking him.

Glancing at the impact, Emy had taken multiple slices through her legs and torso while Will received glancing blows to his arms.

< Emy's shield is at 0% >

< Will's shield is at 21% >

Hearing the updates from Nex, Emy looked at her status field.

	Level	Health	Shield
Emy	Level 6	93%	0%
Will	Level 5	100%	21%

"Team, those shards got me pretty good," Tabitha's voice was low as she clutched her stomach, attempting to slow blood flow. "My health is starting to stabilize, but I'm now down to 43%."

The menacing voice returned, "Still wanting to fight from the dark?... Let's change that."

As if channeling a windstorm, the Marchioness triggered a blast of wind, sweeping the white smoke to the back of the biodome. The four-person team was now visible, only partially concealed in the greenery.

"Ah, now there you are," the creature's voice softened, "and it seems I may have hurt one of you. I am terribly sorry about that," the now sultry voice coming from Mrs. Wallen's former body addressed Tabitha directly. "Why don't you come over here, and we can heal you right up."

Stepping forward, Tabitha emerged fully from the brush, taking a few steps toward Alarice.

"**NO. Don't!**" Emy beckoned.

"**QUIET!**" growled the voice of Alarice, now coming from Mrs. Wallen's transformed body. A mental wave eclipsed Emy, her hands hitting the ground. Will steadied her from behind, and using his *Flow Perception* skill, he freed her mind from the energy bombardment.

"*COME*," the voice commanded again as Tabitha continued toward the Weavers, holding her side in agony.

Emy resumed channeling as the Marchioness tossed a glowing dark object to the ground. It projected a light beam, forming a translucent barrier between the two sides as Tabitha crossed the divide.

Testing the new barrier, Trent channeled a shard of metal toward the translucent wall. The metal struck the barrier, its momentum halted, and it dropped to the floor.

"That will be enough of that. Leave us the girl and go. This is your only warning," Alarice commanded in a low voice as she saw the metal drop to the ground.

"It appears to be an energy barrier. Our castings won't get through," Trent stated firmly over communications.

Seeing an opening for information, Emy spoke with conviction as she rose from the ground and approached the boss, "No deal. *She's with us.* Go back to the hole you came from."

"Ah, now you see where we have a problem," Alarice tsked. "This is OUR home now. Once the Duchess arrives, this planet belongs to us."

Emy moved to communications as her body burst with energy. Fire kindled her fingertips, spreading down her arms, now blazing with a blueish hue. There was no question in her eyes about what she needed to do.

"Ready?" Emy noted to her teammate, not sparing a moment to glance back as Will pulled his external energy inside himself and ignited his body with rage, activating his primal fight response. In that moment, it was easy; this was now personal. As energy burst outward from within Will's body, ice began to form across his entire form, his internal energy merging with his external **Condense** skill. Behind Emy, he now stood, his body completely covered in crystal ice.

< Skill Identified –Will – Permafrost >

"Ready," Will spat, staring at his former teacher's new form.

"On me," Emy addressed Trent, who was also prepared for battle. Dark metal shards circled Trent's body, and a black dagger was held firmly in his hand.

Emy walked forward slowly, flames dancing in her hands. Her eyes remained fixed on the still-glaring Marchioness as she mentally searched for the source of the barrier between them.

"You see," Emy began, pausing as if in thought, "we may not understand what has become of our world, but whatever it is, it's still ours, and **NOBODY** is taking it from us." In moments, Emy's mind latched onto the translucent force blocking the two sides. Targeting a small area, she pushed her willpower into the essence, discovering unfamiliar elements, possibly from another galaxy. She paid no mind to it; atoms formed bonds, and those bonds could break. Emy dispersed the connections into nothingness using her *Disintegration* skill. Seeing the weave break, she shifted forces and funneled a fireball through the opening.

"GO... **NOW**!" Emy commanded the team as the fireball tore through the gap. It struck the Marchioness squarely in the chest, hurling her backward. She landed with a resounding thud, sprawled flat on the cold floor.

Channeling her energy again, Emy widened the breach, allowing Trent and Will to charge through. Will led the way, unleashing waves of *Cryostrikes* that shattered the base form Weavers, their fluid forms splintering into fragments. Trent followed closely, his metal shards slicing through the remaining humanoids with chilling precision.

< Base form Weavers are resisting piercing attacks >

Hearing the news, Will searched for other means to destroy the creatures.

"Emy, we need your fire... On my mark," Will called out as he shifted his energy, applying his *Condense* skill and freezing the water vapor around the five base Weavers. Their bodies immediately collected the water, turning frosty white as they fought to break the restriction. Now realizing their dire situation, they started sending waves of mental commands at the charging heroes.

Will pushed forward, blocking their feeble metal attacks with his *Flow Perception*. "Now," Will urged as the bodies of the Weavers froze, halting their movements with constricting ice.

On command, Emy sent two fireballs at the creatures while Trent flung his knife. The two blasts hit among four grouped Weavers, bursting and dispersing their bodies like ice hitting the ground. Trent's knife separated the head of the last Weaver with a crack, snapping it off and shattering it on the ground.

HUMAN POWER! 73 POINTS!

< Level Up! Emy is now a Level 7 Generalist >

< Level Up! Will is now a Level 6 Condenser >

Silence enveloped the dome as a yell echoed through the air. "**No! NOOO!**" Tabitha shouted. The team turned their gaze toward the voice and saw that the Marchioness had recovered. She held Tabitha frozen, hovering in the air, a knife poised at her neck.

"This ends now. Surrender and leave, or the girl dies," Alarice spoke with quiet rage, positioned directly behind Tabitha's suspended form.

< Marchioness's health is at 38% >

The words of the Marchioness hung in the team's ears, unease building.

"And then what?" Trent was now challenging, with violence and indifference in his eyes.

"You think **SHE** matters?" Trent continued, pointing firmly at Tabitha as shards of metal spun violently around him, forming shadow-like patterns across his body.

"Trent, what are you doing?" Emy reached out over comms, confusion evident at the sudden change of events.

Ignoring his team, Trent continued, "You don't know what true leadership looks like." Darkness consumed the space as tiny bits of metal filled the room, vibrating with energy.

"You know nothing about the Cosmos, child," Alarice asserted, but Trent continued.

"Nothing, huh?" Trent smirked. "I know this galaxy is mine, and no pathetic infiltrator like yourself will ever stop me."

Emy and Will moved forward, attempting to halt Trent's actions as darkness ensnared Alarice and the floating Tabitha.

"I am the future of this planet…. And **YOUR** path ends today."

Shadows of metal enveloped the two figures. The tiny particles were violently shot into Alarice and Tabitha's bodies as if all the surrounding metal were sucked into a vortex. The metal imploded into a small sphere and dispersed to the ground, leaving Alarice and Tabitha prone, covered in a fine dust of metal, blood flowing on the floor.

BETRAYAL! 35 POINTS!

MISSION ACCOMPLISHED!

The insurgent group has been identified and eliminated.

Emy and Will stared at the shadowy figure before them as the world turned gray.

"Why?" Will spoke quietly, sadness evoking his voice. Trent looked back toward the two with a slight sly smile and vanished from view.

△△△

Cohort 13

Level Two Results:

Total Team Points: **540 Points (-10 Point Penalty)**

Total Max Active Views: **37,978**

Earth Rank: **2,124 of 106,260**

98th Percentile

CHAPTER TWENTY-EIGHT

"Grief, guilt, and sadness are the true dangers of the Games." – Noble, Former Champion.

EARTH - WHITE HOUSE

"Mr. President, we have a problem," the National Security Advisor said, closing the door to the Oval Office.

The National Security Advisor, Chief of Staff, Secretary of State, and Vice President stood in the center of the office, their expressions grim, facing the President of the United States.

"Have out with it. What is it?" The President urged, his face now hostile. He expected grim news, especially considering all four individuals approached him together.

"Sir, you may want to sit down for this," the Chief of Staff addressed the now stern-faced President.

"I said out with it, now!"

Looking at one another, the Vice President took on the burden of delivering the news after aligning with all parties before entering the Oval Office. "We have reports, sir. Multiple reports from all over the world," she said, glancing toward the nodding Secretary of State. "There have been attacks."

"Terrorists?" the President questioned.

"Well, yes and no," she said hesitantly, unsure how to phrase the next part. She decided to rip off the band-aid, knowing that global unrest was inevitable. "Sir, we have reason to believe that multiple monsters, uh, alien groups, have made their way to Earth and are currently hostile toward numerous local regions."

She continued, "These alien races have been flagged globally, and no insurgency or lifeform has shown to be similar. They possess, uh… different powers."

Lost for words, the President searched for questions, but ultimately, he could only come up with one. "How many are dead?"

"We don't have a count, sir. We believe it to be… numerous. We have received thousands of missing person reports over the past 24 hours, and we cannot differentiate the two at this point."

The National Security advisor stepped in now. "Local police are either actively engaging or inundated with calls." He paused. "What should we do?"

Eyes wide, the President answered, "*What can we do?*"

△△△

THE HANGAR

Emerging from the grey, the scene dramatically shifted from the previous level's conclusion. Tuck, James, and Nadia emerged, their exhilaration palpable. Their broad smiles signaled their readiness to celebrate the prospect of advancing to the next level. However, as their eyes fell upon Will and Emy, their expressions wavered, clouded by confusion.

Breaking the stillness, Trish rushed forward, enveloping Will in a tight hug. Will's body seemed to sag in her arms. Frank followed suit, providing additional support and joining the embrace.

"Emy?" James's gaze bore into his best friend, who stood motionless, eyes hollow. "What happened?"

Will pushed away from Trish's shoulder, eyes red and tears hovering across his eyes. "She's dead… Tabitha is dead."

Shock registered on the faces of the three as they absorbed the news. Emy's solemn voice broke the silence, "It was Trent…

He killed her."

"Tabitha, Mrs. Wallen, all those other people... dead." Emy's gaze drifted.

"But why?" James's voice trembled, his expression wild. "Why would Trent do that?"

Silence hung heavy until Frank stepped forward. "We watched the feeds," he said, glancing at Emy and then Will, who was still locked in Trish's embrace. "Trent sacrificed Tabitha to defeat the boss. Tabitha was held hostage by the final boss when Trent's power transformed."

Trish reflected further, "His skill—well, it grew in control and power at the end. We're unsure if he concealed it from you or gained the skill during the act." She then turned her gaze to Will's pallid face. "And... those events were real. Everything was real."

"Wait, what?" Tuck interjected.

Trish continued, "Our school was under attack. It wasn't a simulation. You saved everyone."

"She's right." Coach Williams walked toward the group, his expression somber. "We didn't know."

"Bullshit. 1200 Games, and this has never happened? Not even once? You knew. Everyone knew. Except us. Except Earth," Emy retorted to her coach, her voice brimming with rage. Her team members looked on as she spoke, recognizing the truth in Emy's words.

Coach Williams took a breath. "Yes, Emy. This does happen in the Games, but the timing is unpredictable. Please let me explain."

He continued, "This scenario occurs, but normally not this early in the Games. We were all only in the Games for 24 hours before these events unfolded in your world. Not every 2nd mission was on Earth. Only those residing in areas of influence were thrust into real-life scenarios. The System allowed it because these events matched the tests it tried to train you for. Earth needed its best defenders."

Pausing, Coach added, "You... All of you... Saved your

school."

James found his words, "You could have told us. We could have prepared."

Coach's voice carried sadness, "No. Nothing I say would prepare you for losing those you love. Trust me, I've tried everything. In these early levels, my role is to train you to the best of my abilities, and I'll continue to do so."

His tone grew firmer: "We plan, we train, we adapt."

Softer now, he concluded, "Take the next hour to regroup. You're a team. Share this burden. Meet me in the strategy room in an hour. We'll need to debrief there." Coach Williams departed from the group.

James was the first to speak, sober in his tone. "Emy, Will, I'm so sorry. We should have been there."

Emy's response was firm: "No. It's not anyone's fault. Our plan worked because everyone played a key role."

Nadia, a silent observer during the conversation, stepped forward. Her voice was quiet but determined, "But we can still feel sorry for you." She placed her hands on Will and Emy's, allowing her *Vitalize* skill to flow between them. As the rest of the team gathered around, they joined the circle, connecting with their teammates. At a hunch, Nadia let her talent surge, absorbing the collective emotions—anger, pain, and sadness—across everyone. "We can share the burden with you," she said. The feelings didn't lessen, but they surged and flowed across everyone. Now, they were felt by all, unspoken yet deeply shared.

It could have been seconds or minutes when Will finally spoke, "Thank you…"

The circle slowly dissolved as the team looked around, embracing the shared feeling that they had not only survived but succeeded, allowing the loss of a friend to bring them together.

Trish was the first to speak, attempting to shift Will's somber mood to one of success: "Will, did we see it right? You triggered a full-body technique in the dome?"

With a shrug, Will shared his new skill:

Skill: Permafrost

Empowers the user to manifest a full-bodied ice form, with differing states of matter at critical joints, enabling similar movement to their normal physical state. (SELF)

"If it's okay, I'd like to know how you guys did outside the dome?" Will questioned as Tuck and Nadia glanced at James with a smirk, and the tone of the moment shifted.

"Uh, well..." James started.

"I think that superhero story should be told over dinner!" Frank urged the team, giving James a brief save as the large man took off toward the new scent of dinner being served.

CHAPTER TWENTY-NINE

"Hero-inspired fashion has taken center stage, becoming the pinnacle of style. While donning full battle suits might not be the trendiest choice, there are ways to streamline the look and infuse it with flair." – Chief Marketing Officer at the CNC.

THE HANGAR

The team huddled around the cafeteria-style dining table, its white surfaces and bench seating creating an inviting atmosphere. The informal arrangement lent a charming quality to these shared moments with friends, which the team deeply appreciated.

Now scooping a generous portion of clam chowder into his mouth, Frank began, "You know, meals aren't quite as satisfying when it's just me and Trish."

"What? Am I not good enough company?" Trish shot back, earning a wide-eyed look from Frank as he mentally scrambled for a way to backtrack.

"No, uh, that's not what I meant," he stammered. It's just that when you guys aren't here, I feel like I'm stress-eating. You wouldn't believe the culinary disaster the kitchen churns out when we're left here, watching you all. My emotions keep triggering the need for a pint of ice cream and a bag of nacho chips."

Nadia couldn't contain her emotions. "A pint of ice cream?" she exclaimed. "Frank, we may need to schedule an ice cream date sometime."

Frank shifted uncomfortably, glancing at Tuck, who seemed confused by the sudden attention. "Oh, uh, yeah," Frank agreed. "We can do that anytime! Maybe we'll have a *team* ice cream outing later." The group exchanged puzzled glances, wondering what had just transpired.

Trish shifted her gaze, giving Frank a sidelong look. "Okay, that was weird. Moving on... spill it, everyone. Both groups got a box drop during the final fights, right? And surely there's a Level Two mission award?"

Emy nodded. "There was! Will and I grabbed this before we were escorted off the grounds." She presented a small box neatly tied with a bow. Its contents remained a mystery until she unwrapped it, revealing two glowing microchip-like devices. "Nex, can you bring up the details?"

New Devices Detected - Soulpulse (x2)
Rare
These remarkable tracking devices resonate with up to two distinct energy signatures within a 3-meter radius. Once attuned, they weave an intricate energy web, enabling the user to track targets up to 20 kilometers away. **Note:** *Power draws from an internal energy battery, demanding a recharge after each spectral pursuit.*

James grinned. "Well, that should come in handy," he said. "I felt bad relying on Darya for support during that last mission. *But* we may have you beat. Nadia, care to do the honors?"

Nadia's smile widened as she lifted her foot and slammed a boot against the table, earning wide stares from everyone. "Oops, sorry. I guess they're a little heavier than I'm used to," she chuckled. "Nex?"

New Gear Detected – Ghostwalkers
Rare
These mysterious boots, crafted using energy-based engineering, embody stealth and graceful motion. When activated,

*they defy gravity, propelling the wearer 20 feet skyward—
a fleeting waltz with the heavens for 2 minutes. However,
due to limitations in the current engineering, these boots can
only be used up to three times a day.* **(UPGRADEABLE)**

"Yep, that takes the win," Will ogled at the description on the screen. "So, can these change size?"

Nadia began to speak, but Will cut her off. "Joking. I can see no better option than a flying assassin," he pressed with a smile. "But, I expect to be flown off like a bride on my wedding night at some point."

Emy observed that Will had to push himself a little, and he still wasn't his usual self. However, witnessing him joking around with the team was heartening—a positive step in the right direction.

"Upgradeable, huh? Does that mean these boots can improve?" Will questioned, glancing over at Trish and Frank.

"Absolutely," Trish responded enthusiastically, her eyes shining. "Frank and I can tweak the design or upgrade the internal components. We'll explore the possibilities. I think these might win the best prize!"

Suddenly, Nex's holographic projection materialized in the center of the cafeteria. Clad in their signature attire—slicked-back hair, letterman's jacket, tennis shoes, and a whistle—their voice resonated with anticipation as they addressed the team: *"Hold on a moment regarding the prize selection, Trish. You all need to witness the next-level prize!"*

New Gear Detected - Mighty Eagles Letterman's Jacket (x7)

Unique

Crafted from enchanted wool and adorned with intricate embroidery, these jackets seamlessly blend style with practicality. Their 10% base shield protection ensures wearers can withstand formidable blows, while subtle runes woven into the fabric grant a reduction in piercing *damage—a boon for any hero team facing dangerous foes. As the team dons their matching jackets, they become more than mere individuals; they become a cohesive force, their fates interwoven like the fabric itself.*

"Mighty?" Emy questioned, casting a side glance at James.

Frank's enthusiasm overflowed. "Oh boy! Did that say seven?" he exclaimed. "Does that mean what I think it means, Nex?"

"You better believe it, bucko! You are a large part of the team!" Nex beamed, delivering the news.

"Wait, Unique ranking?" Trish asked Nex before the team could diverge further.

"Yes! Unique means one of a kind. Most teams receive these types of items as a prize for this level, but these jackets have never been made before, which makes them Unique."

"Okay, I'll admit it—I secretly hoped for a skin-tight suit, a giant 'B' on my chest, and a cape. But I guess that's asking too much from the System," Will confessed.

Tuck glared at him. "This just proves we need to be careful what we say out loud..." He silently prayed that the System didn't have a comical side.

Will raised an eyebrow. "What? Weren't you the one who mentioned wanting a bedazzled leotard with yellow lightning embroidered all over your body earlier?"

Will's joke sparked lively debates among the team about the best and worst hero costumes. As they savored their first meal together, the conversations gradually tapered off. After finishing their last bites, they donned their new jackets and headed to the strategy room.

Nex's low whistle reflected through the strategy room as the team filed in, their eyes drawn to the holographic display shimmering at the center of the table. *"Now that,"* they declared, their attempt at a sly grin resembling someone who had wedged an acorn into their upper lip, *"is a team! Feels like the System has been reading my mind."*

Emy raised an eyebrow. "You haven't…," she retorted. "What made you think we'd want to be called the 'Mighty Eagles'?"

Nex proudly responded, *"Well, I've been rummaging around your thoughts for years. And when I sensed the System reviewing level rewards based on team dynamics, I may have slipped in some of your and James's conversations about how much you adore the 'Mighty' moniker!"* Their satisfaction radiated like a charged circuit.

Despite their similar design, each jacket had its unique style. Tuck's jacket stood out because it didn't have sleeves and looked more like a basketball uniform tailored to fit his muscular arms. Despite the differences, each jacket had a unique base color, a bold white "E" emblem on the front, "Mighty Eagles" written across the back, and a giant eagle underneath. Except for Tuck's jersey, all jackets had white leather sleeves draping down their shoulders, reflecting their unity.

Emy's jacket was a vibrant combination of deep crimson and blue, evoking the presence of fire. Will's jacket was a cold, light blue, reminiscent of a winter morning. James sported a sleek silver-gray jacket, giving him a polished and modern look. Nadia's jacket exuded intense blackness, almost absorbing the light around her. Tuck's dark blue jersey seemed to capture glimmers of light as he moved, creating a mesmerizing effect. Together, their jackets formed a vivid tapestry of colors and styles tailored to their skill sets.

Nadia chuckled, examining her black **Letterman Jacket**. "I never thought I'd wear one of these in my life," she admitted, "but I've got to say, I'm digging it."

"Heck yeah, these are sweet!" Frank added as he and Trish also donned similar stylish jackets—Frank's colored in a steely grey, and Trish's in a deep purple.

Coach Williams stepped into the room, nodding approvingly. "You're shaping up into a true team. Nice vision, Nex."

"I'll get into it in a bit, but know that these 'uniforms'

THE QUANTUM GAMES

are a common Level Two reward," Coach continued. "They showcase who you are and what you represent in the next level." He paused, his gaze sweeping over the team. "But first, we need to debrief from that last mission. Your heroism out there was as inspiring as reckless and impulsive." He knew this conversation would be tough after the earlier confrontation.

"I won't go through every detail; instead, I want each of you to reflect on your actions. Who'd like to go first?" Coach's question hung in the air as he awaited the team's responses.

"I think I'd like to go first," Will started, standing up from his chair. "I'm sorry, everyone. I put you all at risk by improvising a plan on my own. I got in over my head and should have ensured I had backup." He paused, his voice softening. "My actions led to premature engagement and, ultimately, more lives lost..."

James immediately defended Will, "No," he said, his remorse evident. "Great plans allow for improvisation based on the team's instincts. I failed when we didn't adjust quickly enough to your audible. You saw a better path, and I didn't adapt fast enough. We should have sent someone sooner. I won't let that happen again." James looked around. "Don't hesitate to deviate from my plan or anyone else's. Follow it as best you can, but if you see a better way, take it."

Tuck shifted in his seat. "I didn't see a better path. Once again, I let my emotions take over. Trent was right about me. I didn't understand the impact my talent would have across the field and lacked the willpower to control it." He paused, looking down as he continued, "I can't promise it won't happen again. I will always fight for us, especially if anyone needs help. I just can't let my rage put us at greater risk."

The room lapsed into silence after the three men had spoken. Each statement held significance, weighing their impact on the team against their individual choices. Nadia and Emy exchanged glances, aware that their final perspectives would diverge.

Coach Williams urged them to continue, "Nadia, Emy, final

thoughts?"

"I was dumb," Nadia said bluntly. "You all had reasons for your actions. I would have been tempted to do the same in your spots. Me? I put faith in a tool without understanding its capabilities. We all recognize that the Cosmos harbors extremely powerful heroes with capabilities beyond our imagination. But I thought I was invincible because my body was invisible. It was reckless, and I'll do everything possible to improve. Our failure to reach Will was my responsibility."

Emy spoke up, "We all need to grow stronger. Will and I could have tested your device if we had known our capabilities. It's on all of us to train ourselves and each other."

"Agreed," Coach Williams continued, his gaze fixed on Emy. "Last words, Emy?"

The room held its breath, waiting for Emy's response. Amidst the flood of thoughts, only one surfaced as she spoke quietly.

"Trust only those closest to you."

CHAPTER THIRTY

"The Cosmos is boundless—imagine discovering that your world is merely the most recent chapter in an eternal cycle of chaos." – E.B.

SYSTEM HEADQUARTERS

"Director, how are preparations shaping up for the upcoming Trials?" questioned Bekek, The President of the Interstellar Mergence Strategies (IMS) department.

Within the CNC monopoly, the IMS was one of the largest divisions of the corporation. Its core mission revolved around assimilating recently unearthed galaxies into the established cosmic collectives. This multifaceted endeavor included activities like integrating indigenous populations from frontier worlds, managing diplomatic ties, facilitating commercial transactions via AI storefronts, and nurturing the emergence of fresh heroes. Although the Interstellar and Void Travel divisions lay outside the group's direct purview, they maintained a crucial alliance due to the proliferation of these newfound cosmic realms.

"Promising talent, sir," replied Viggo, the Games Director. "I foresee thrilling events in this year's Trials. Fans should be buzzing with excitement. And, as I mentioned earlier, one particular talent is demonstrating unprecedented capabilities —far quicker than any previous cycles. Our initial assessment seems accurate. While tampering is likely, it shouldn't overshadow the Trials' success or our bottom line."

"Glad to hear," the President acknowledged, "is this

connected to your recent report on the Astral Dominion? The Champion's progress surpasses the typical limits for external interference." The President paused. "People are talking, Viggo."

"Indeed," agreed the Games Director. Dialogue is crucial in our line of work. Our top priority remains to generate buzz. Speaking of which, we're nearly set for this year's initial round of merchandise. The System provided specs for the traditional Level Three apparel, and our AI seamlessly integrated that into our marketing databases. We'll soon deliver fan gear across the Cosmos enhanced with our AI tracking feeds and fan forums."

"Excellent," said the Director. "I expect nothing less from the Games branch and eagerly await the final roster of the Stellar Ascendancy. Perhaps we'll discover contenders who can rival Echo or Boost someday."

△△△

THE HANGAR

"Firstly, let me express my sincere appreciation for your openness and self-reflection," Coach Williams began as he addressed his team. "In my view, the essence of a true hero lies in their consistent and persistent internal feedback, but let there be no doubt that your recent performance was nothing short of remarkable."

"In moments that might appear reckless, I witnessed acts of courage, and during times of adversity, I observed dynamic problem-solving." Williams paused, locking eyes with Will. "Will, in the heat of battle, when you faced the loss of someone dear, you didn't hesitate to step back and follow Nex's tactical guidance when your ice strikes fell short. The ability to reason amidst intense emotions is no small achievement." His gaze shifted. "Nadia and James, despite limited options, you both threw yourselves into an improvised plan without full certainty of its success. Yes, it was daring, but your individualistic decision-making ultimately saved your team." Coach's smile widened. "Nadia, please just ensure you share your plans with James before he dives headfirst into another 'situation.'"

"Tuck, despite your limited experience with the *Ion Storm*, you skillfully executed an area-of-effect attack while safeguarding your injured colleague, Nadia. Much like Will's 'intelligent rage,' I'd describe your approach as 'controlled chaos.' Excellent work." Finally, Coach Williams turned to Emy. "Emy, I'll be candid. Your powers' versatility both impresses and unnerves me. Shifting seamlessly between two talents—bridging the gap between intent and skill—usually requires D-Class abilities. Your instantaneous adaptation against the barrier left me in awe."

"Having said that, our preparation must continue. The upcoming level will test both your abilities and your teamwork. To what extent? Well, that remains uncertain," Williams declared, his eyes sweeping across the room, hesitating on Emy. "This next level is the one we're most familiar with before entry. During each third level, the System hosts something known in the Cosmos as 'The Trials'—A level where Champions compete for a coveted spot in the Steller Ascendency."

"But aren't we already being ranked each level?" James pushed his question before Williams could continue.

"Yes, that is true, but the Trials test more than just points and 'flair.' These Trials normally encompass various missions: timed trials, power evaluations, skill assessments, and wave-based scenarios. We've borne witness to them all."

Anticipating more inquiries, Williams succinctly explained, "Whether you're a solo contender or part of a team, these events manifest as individual or collaborative challenges based on the mission set forth. If team-based, a weighting system will ensure fairness, allowing solo players to play by themselves and teams to maintain the current structure. The

System initiates the event with either just you or your entire team with you."

James raised an eyebrow at this unexpected detail. "How do you know all of this? You've given us nothing to go off of in the past two levels."

"These Trials have long been a way for heroes to compete against each other." Williams sighed. "The System deems it a natural way to bring out the best in individuals—to push for greatness or reveal the strength of their competition. The difference in today's Games is that fans become part of the experience. Imagine sold-out stadium events—like the Super Bowl or iconic musician concerts—where fans witness every move."

"Wait," Will interjected, wrestling with a mix of guilt due to his excitement. "The System creates these Games. So, how does the CNC fit into all this?"

"Great question," Williams responded. "These repetitive occurrences, surfacing every third level, captured the CNC's attention. It clung to them, seeking integration. Like Nex and myself, the System transcends finiteness; it welcomes 'updates' that align with its purpose. Observe how the System interfaces with your internal NexaBot, tailoring personalized rewards. Yet, the intriguing revelation lies in perception—the System's willingness to collaborate with the CNC, especially in matters of 'fandom.' Showcasing these Trials as central events holds significance for our new planet's future."

Emy's skepticism flared. Her unrest battled the voice in her head. "But what does this mean for us?" she demanded. "Monsters are wreaking havoc on our planet. Friends have died, and we know nothing about our families. How can any of this be good for us?"

Williams fixed his gaze on Emy, a touch of sorrow in his eyes, before countering with a searching question, "Who would take notice if your planet confronted an extinction-level catastrophe? And what if Earth's heroes faltered in safeguarding your world during a cataclysmic monster invasion?"

Emy waited, not taking the bait of the open-ended question. Coach Williams sighed but answered, "Your fans will care, and more significantly, larger-than-life heroes that view those fans as opportunities to expand their influence."

"So, you're marketing us to prove Earth's worth in the eyes of this Collective?" Emy's skepticism was palpable.

"Exactly," Coach Williams affirmed, "you must demonstrate your value as defenders worth protecting or become heroes capable of self-defense. This is a fundamental law across the Cosmos." His words hung heavily in the room, the weight of reality settling in.

"Is that the fate of every planet that integrates?" Nadia spoke up. "To raise Champions capable of defense or witness your planet's downfall?"

"No..." Coach Williams faltered as emotion threatened to overwhelm him. Regaining his composure, he re-started, "Yes, it's crucial to anticipate that Earth needs Champions, or else face the risk of devastation. However, numerous outcomes exist across the Cosmos. Unknown discrepancies in energy, combined with the size of the energy pool, create and dictate the magnitude of the void breaks. Worlds with potential like Earth are at the greatest risk of incursions."

The System's assessment is based on the stabilization of planets on a galactic scale, but it's important to note that many planets are still sparsely populated with life. Tournaments and integrations occur, and life can continue to thrive, even without a clear victor, albeit under somewhat unusual conditions. Imagine a primitive society abruptly gaining access to drop boxes from a system crafted by technology that's billions, if not trillions, of years more advanced. The basic structure of that society would transform, and you can observe diverse versions of this scenario across the known Cosmos. These worlds often need Champions acting as their guardians."

After a lengthy silence, Williams redirected the

conversation to the primary topic, "The 'Steller Ascendency' is the outcome of these Trials. The top 100 rankers from your world will be displayed on a board shared across the Cosmos. And the top 25 rankers from your galaxy will follow that listing below. Once you're on that board, views and support surge."

"These rankings are so renowned that even beyond the Tournaments, the CNC hosts a 'professional' hero circuit termed the 'Celestial Ascendency.' Break into that listing, and you shape your destiny. You become the architects of your world. You shape the direction of your galaxy."

Emy's voice resonated through the room, "So, these fans don't care that monsters are tearing apart our galaxy. What they care about is a silly list and the celebrity status of the resistant beings living on the planets?"

Williams hesitated, collecting his thoughts, but James responded first. "Is that really any different than Earth? Wars and death happen every day, yet a celebrity's bad haircut can dominate the news." James pointedly looked at Emy, "Minus a few more deaths, are we much better?"

Williams then added, "Your world has changed. The galaxy has changed. As much as I don't like it, you either adapt to survive or grow strong and change the game."

Emy nodded. Earth might not be better, but that didn't mean people couldn't be. An idea took root in her mind after this realization. They would do more—but first, they would rise to the top of the Stellar Ascendancy.

CHAPTER THIRTY-ONE

"You can't truly understand someone's journey until you ask about it." – Codex, Former Champion.

THE HANGAR

Nadia & Williams

Much like the previous intermission, the team split into smaller groups, each targeting specific growth areas across their diverse team. Frank and Trish, unsurprisingly, had been immersed in ceaseless analysis since Level Two officially commenced. Fortunately, the pace of the intermission sessions wasn't tied to real-time, granting Trish, Frank, and Williams ample opportunity to prepare.

"Tell me, Nadia," Williams questioned, now adjourning his professor hat as he paired himself with Nadia for the initial grouping, "when you envision your future self—the Champion of Earth, defender of the Galaxy—what do you see?"

Nadia's expression shifted to one of confusion. "You mean my talent?" she asked.

The professor nodded. "Not just your talent, but your skillsets and your presence within the team. Take it all into account."

Nadia took a moment to collect her thoughts. "Well," she began, "I find fulfillment in my role as a healer, offering support when the team needs it… But I think it may go beyond that—I have a passion for assisting the team in any way they need… Don't get me wrong—I want to prove my capabilities and grow, but fundamentally, I've always admired the role of someone who can... help."

Williams encouraged her with a smile. "Go on."

"Emy wields formidable powers, Tuck is an unstoppable force, Will specializes in his own way, and James provides crucial support and strategy," Nadia continued. "I want to fill in the gaps. I aim to be adaptable and ready to assume any role as needed. Having been on my own, I know the vulnerability of feeling inadequate. I've experienced the weight of failure without anyone to rely on. I won't let my team face that same struggle."

"There," Professor Williams spoke empathetically, sensing the underlying currents in Nadia's words. "Now consider your talent. How do you envision it fulfilling that role?"

Nadia reflected, her thoughts weaving together. "Healing and affliction skills have come very naturally to me. I understand there's much more to learn, but those paths are well-defined... Being a stealth-based user was merely a necessary role to fill. While I enjoyed it, I believe I can contribute even more."

"You can, and you will," the Professor assured her softly. "Now, delve deeper into what your power truly represents."

Nadia's words flowed deliberately as she continued to think through her unique ability: "I manipulate the body's domain—both my own and others'. I can enhance or alter natural and unnatural body chemistry, whether to strengthen physical attributes or facilitate internal transformations."

"Transformation," Nadia mused, eyes widening at the realization. "I possess the capability to transform myself!"

The professor's smile widened. "Nadia, your gift extends beyond mere change. Enhancing existing conditions—whether for healing or affliction—is just the beginning. You've demonstrated the ability to modify and change every aspect of your body. Everything within *here*," he emphasized, tapping her shoulder, "is under your control."

Nadia turned her gaze back to the professor. "What should I do? Or, I mean, what can I do?"

Professor Williams smirked, but his expression was thoughtful. "That's where my guidance reaches its limit. A talent like yours can transcend boundaries—both within your body and externally. That's why I spoke to you early on this time. It may sound cliché, but you must look inward to grasp your full capabilities. Meditate, reflect, stretch, or even delve into a biology book. Find what resonates best with your unique gift, then explore and test."

"I can do that," Nadia replied, her eyes betraying a hint of unease at the revelations churning in her head. "Thanks, Professor," she added, her voice firm. Abruptly, the room boomed with the sounds of colliding boulders, causing the door to shudder. Nadia cast a glance back at Williams.

"Yes, yes," Williams urged, hearing the loud noise. "Go see what Tuck is up to. But remember this: Work closely with Will and Emy to shield your mind. We can't accept another weak mental pulse catching you off guard," his words shifting into coaching mode as Nadia grinned and dashed out the door.

△△△

Trish & James

"Did you know that they cut to a 'commercial break' right as you jumped in front of the Weavers?" Trish pressed James as they walked toward Trish's favorite lab room. "I had to wait a **FULL** day to see if you'd survive, and this was after witnessing Nadia's apparent failure. James, I'm not sure I can handle that again."

"Sorry, Trish. I thought I was completely out of options," James said solemnly.

"Do you know what I went through during those 24 hours?" Trish continued, not waiting for James to respond further. "I cried, James. I cried, then I came in here to think, and then I cried some more. It was agonizing. But do you know what?"

Still reeling from Trish's barrage of words, James managed

to ask, "What?"

"I analyzed everything I could to make sense of what I believe your **Energy Blocking Field** can do with time," Trish said, her determination steadfast.

"Wait, my blocking field?" James muttered, trying to process Trish's revelations.

"Yes! Do you realize what happened when you boosted yourself before creating the **Energy Blocking Field** skill?" Trish asked, now giving James a moment to think.

James hesitated, realizing that Trish was now looking for a two-way conversation. "Well," he stammered, "I thought it might be because I've gradually adapted to the energy. It's as if my body learned to resist and fight its effects over time."

"Yes, well, mostly. Based on everything I've read and with Williams' assistance, we observed that you essentially resonated with the mental energy. The more you were immersed in the attack, the more your barriers learned and could separate you from harm. Expanding that bubble allowed you to project what your natural resistance had become, sharing it with others."

James listened, absorbing this revelation. "Do you know what this means?" she asked, her wicked smile sending a shiver down James's spine.

"That I won't like whatever you have in mind..." James ventured.

Trish's grin widened. "We need to do some resistance training," she declared. "Let's start small."

A loud, crushing noise reverberated through the room as Trish moved to retrieve a few items. "Well, maybe we should wait. Do you want to check that out before we begin?"

"I think I'd prefer that," James said with a nervous smile, walking toward the source of the disturbance.

△△△

Will & Emy

"I know you tend to be more of the silent, brooding type, but I am here if you want to talk," Will remarked as he and Emy made their way toward one of the larger training rooms. The space was intentionally sparse to prevent any unnecessary damage to their equipment. Emy and Will were paired to challenge each other's current power sets and explore more diverse use cases.

Emy raised an eyebrow, caught off guard by Will's observation. "Brooding? What makes you think I brood?"

Will smirked, attempting to lighten the mood. "Trust only those closest to you?" he added. "That's about the broodiest statement a brooder could say." His smile widened. "Come on. I know I'm not James, but know you can trust me. I do owe you several times over."

Emy considered his words. Will had a disarming charm, and she had grown close to him over the past week. She trusted him, just as she did everyone on their team. Their backgrounds were different, but trust was a two-way street. "You owe me? Maybe I was returning the favor for the first level when you saved my ass," she replied.

Emy's voice softened, "James has been with me since we were kids. That's not fair. You know I trust you guys as well."

Will chuckled. "Okay, then give me something. Tell me something that only James would know about you."

The question caught her off guard again, but it felt like she should give in. "On a scale from sad to pathetic, what kind of answer do you want, Mr. Weiss?" she teased.

Will's surprise at her playful yet open response was evident. "How about an 8, Ms. Fury... Wait, I don't think I know your actual last name?"

"Brandt. Emery Brandt," Emy replied, "but my red hair and anger usually found a way of getting me more unique nicknames growing up." She sighed, gazing at Will. "8, huh?" she scrutinized him, ensuring his curiosity and empathy were genuine. Emy made a mental note to inquire whether he subconsciously pushed those feelings or learned about them through his Weaver experiences.

Emy continued, her tone measured, "I've been on anti-depression and ADHD medication since I was four years old." She observed the lack of reaction on Will's face as she spoke.

Her voice wavered slightly, "When I was a child, I had trouble learning. I still do... or at least did before these Games started?" Emy questioned herself aloud. "On top of being behind others on the learning curve, my parents told me that once I started putting words to what I was doing and seeing, they came off as... uh, very strange."

"What do you mean?" Will questioned, urging her to continue.

Emy hesitated, then pressed on, "I don't think they ever shared the full stories, but I believe it was more about witnessing things—unnatural things." She shuddered, consumed by memories. "It's creepy. They always said I talked about seeing my dolls move or objects shifting. At first, they dismissed it as a phase, but as I continued bringing it up, they took it as a sign of just seeking more attention."

As Emy reflected more, a heavy silence hung in the air, "As I got older, I started seeing more specialists. I picked up on the recurring questions they would ask. The more honest I was, the larger my prescriptions became, and the dullness of the world enveloped me." She sighed. "Eventually, I began to lie. It was the only way to break free from the cycles. Yes, the 'movements' slowly subsided, but so did my energy and, well, my personality to some extent. Although I didn't fully grasp it then, James played an essential part in that, at the very least."

Will pushed just a tiny bit, "What does James have to do with it?"

Emy's gaze shifted. "We were either incredibly foolish or brave—I'm not sure which anymore. One day, he asked why I took my medications, and I couldn't give him a satisfactory answer. So, we decided to toss them in the toilet and see what would happen, knowing that he would look out for me. It was reckless, but for a while, I felt happier. I cracked jokes and felt more alive. But soon, my ADHD spiraled out of control, and my grades plummeted. Conversations became overwhelming, so I reluctantly went back on the medications and gradually worked my way back to maintaining my *'superior'* C averages."

She continued, her voice tinged with complexity, "Don't get me wrong. I've been around doctors who prescribed medications to many kids, and it helped them. But it always felt like I was trading one part of myself to suppress another."

Will's question hung in the air: "So that's why you don't trust anyone?"

Emy's response was measured, "I trust everyone has their motivations. My therapists were trying to help me, yes, but I think they were trying to help my parents more. I learned that everything I said would make its way back to my parents one way or another, no matter how eloquent the doctor's speeches on trust were. James was the only person in my life whom I knew would listen without repercussions."

Will sensed more beneath the surface, especially regarding her parents, but he chose not to pry further. "I'm sorry, Emy," he offered, letting the words settle as he gathered his thoughts.

He continued, attempting to connect to a bit of his past, "I may not know what that's like, but I do understand how trust can be shattered in an instant." His smile returned. "I'll keep this between us, but I hope we can continue these conversations. And hey, I'm more than willing to share my 'level 8' stories, although they might operate on a different scaling system."

"I would like that," Emy commented and then took a deep breath, shifting her focus away from the past. "So, what were we supposed to be doing…" Her question was abruptly interrupted by a loud rumble from the central area of the Hangar.

Both exchanged knowing glances, smiles tugging at their lips. Will spoke first, "I say we check that out first, and then we can get back to training." The excitement of the unexpected interruption fueled their curiosity. They headed toward the source of the disturbance.

CHAPTER THIRTY-TWO

*"Some weapons are destiny." –
Trident, Former Champion.*

THE HANGAR

Frank & Tuck

"Dude," Frank prodded, "are you going to confess your feelings or what?"

While Frank and Trish were meticulous in their preparations, Frank's first question to Tuck veered away from tactical readiness.

Tuck blinked, caught off guard. "Wait, is this what the whole awkward dinner was about? What makes you think I have a thing for Nadia?"

Frank grinned. "There! You knew exactly who I meant."

Tuck squirmed uncomfortably. "Well," he began, "you were pretty obvious about not wanting that ice cream date with Nadia. But come on, you know she was just being playful, right?"

Frank's expression flickered. "True," he conceded, "but what about that last battle? You charged in like a man possessed. Friendship alone doesn't explain that level of fury. And every time you see Nadia in person, it's like your heart takes a nosedive. I might be a 'dumb welder,' but I see things."

Caught off guard, Tuck's cheeks flushed as he shifted to the offensive, "Should I ask you the same thing about Trish?"

This time, it was Frank's turn to redden, and a hush settled over them until they finally reached the Smithy, where Frank surged ahead with his customary enthusiasm.

"Are you ready to feast your eyes on what I've been crafting?" Frank gushed to Tuck, then corrected himself, "Well, what Trish and I have been working on."

He paused dramatically. "We had to allocate some team points for raw materials and energy absorption merging to get the right affinity, but trust me, it was worth it."

Tuck's eyes pleaded. "Frank, please don't tell me you spent too many points on me."

Frank waved off the concern. "Don't worry about it. **This**—this is worth it." His hand rested on the Smithy door.

With a flourish, Frank closed his eyes and then popped them open. "Behold," he declared, "**BERTHA**!"

Tuck began to say something but caught himself as the door swung open, revealing a massive weapon. It pulsed with electromagnetic hues, dominating the center table.

"I believe it's closest to a Spiked Warhammer," Frank explained, "but this one has a bit more... *style*."

Tuck stood frozen, staring at the awe-inspiring creation.

The weapon, stretching two and a half meters in length, emanated an otherworldly aura. Its metallic axle thrummed with energy, connecting the broad handle to its dual-sided pinnacle. On one facet, a half-meter-diameter hammer stood resolute, poised to deliver bone-crushing blows. Its counterpart featured a lengthy spike, its curve leading to a menacing tip. At the base of the handle, threads of blue-hued energy wound along the long weapon, converging toward the dual-sided hammer. Sparks danced along its edges with each passing moment, hinting at the raw power within.

Celestium Spiked Warhammer
Low D-Class

Emerges from the cosmic forge, its birthplace nestled within distant stars. Its pulsing metal is enveloped with energy akin to veins of azure lightning. Along its edges, sparks ignite, fueled by the very essence of the Cosmos.

Forged from one of the rarest alloys known to existence — Celestium, whispered of in cosmic legends—this Warhammer transcends mere weaponry; it becomes a conduit for the universe's raw power. **(UPGRADEABLE)**

"It's incredible, D-Class even?" Tuck exclaimed, the words pushed out in shock.

"I know, right?" Frank beamed, his eyes fixed solely on Tuck, eager to absorb every nuance of Tuck's reaction to the weapon. "We initially considered spreading our points across various items for the team, but once you all hit the point thresholds necessary to create this weapon, we decided to go all in. Trust me, the team needs a hammer. Your bare-knuckle approach has been effective so far, but there will come a day when it won't suffice. Imagine facing a C or B-Class user like Michele. We'd require Nadia right behind you, healing you up after each strike."

"Trish and I were thrilled about the weapon's Class," Frank said, smirking. "Not to brag… well, actually, I am totally going to brag. Coach Williams mentioned it was remarkable that two E-Class users could build a weapon beyond their current Class range. Additionally, there shouldn't be any side effects before you reach D-Class. With your power and affinity for it, we believe you'll be able to wield it to its full potential immediately. Plus, the upgradeable marker means we can keep enhancing and improving it!"

Tuck sighed, defeated, ultimately accepting the amount of points spent. "I won't be naming it Bertha," he declared, ending the statement with a slight smile directed at Frank. "Can I test it out?"

"I've been waiting nine days for you to say that," Frank responded with unbridled excitement.

"Nine days? That long?" Tuck countered, raising an eyebrow.

"Yeah, this time dilation over here hits differently. Mentally, I'm already preparing for the length of the upper levels. But don't worry, boredom won't be an issue for us. We have plenty to do," Frank assured him.

The pair stepped out of the Smithy, the weapon securely in Tuck's grip. As he held it, sparks flared to life, the handle reacting to his touch. "Let me program a scenario for the arena," Frank suggested, leaning over a console near one of the outer windows. Meanwhile, Tuck positioned himself at the center of the enclosure, feeling out his new weapon.

"All right, there we go. Just some simple rock dummies—don't be afraid to swing hard," Frank called out from outside. The walls closed in, and translucent barriers shot toward the ceiling, signaling that the combat arena was ready for action.

Tuck swung the **Warhammer** a few times, testing its weight and balance. As he did, four colossal rock creatures emerged from the floor, each standing three meters tall. They settled into the room's corners, their stony forms frozen. These creatures resembled earth elementals, with massive boulders forming their heads, chests, arms, and legs. Fractured rocks joined these components, allowing the creatures to move if needed.

"Here goes nothing," Tuck declared as he charged at the first rock creature, which suddenly sprang to life. Its arms started to separate from its body as a gigantic spike tore through its chest. Tuck hadn't even given it a chance to activate entirely. With a final step upon the creature, he spun around in a 180-degree arc, hurling the **Warhammer** like an Olympic hammer thrower. The spike pierced the creature's chest, but it didn't stop there—the half-meter base of the hammer followed, obliterating the rock across the room.

Applause erupted, and a laughing Frank exclaimed, "You certainly didn't hold back!" Within seconds, the rest of the team gathered, watching through the arena's transparent walls. They seemed to be there to witness the new weapon in action, although their initial curiosity was likely sparked by the loud noise that had just emerged from the center of the space. "Now, let's see some different moves!" Frank clamored again.

Twirling the handle in one hand, Tuck felt the weight of the shaft in the other. He turned toward the next creature, now awakening. He allowed it to activate this time and walked toward it with glee.

Facing the creature, the rock golem hurled a massive stone fist at Tuck. He blocked the punch with the **Warhammer**, holding the weapon vertically. The hook struck the metal just below the spike. Using the momentum of the blow to his shaft, Tuck swung the **Warhammer** in a reverse sweeping motion, landing a counter at the knees of the rock monster. The creature was sent off its feet, its chest slamming into the ground. Without hesitation, Tuck swung the weapon like an axe, slicing down the creature now at his feet, rock-spraying the arena floor once again.

Whirling around and charging towards the third golem, Tuck gripped the ends of his unique weapon, positioning it horizontally across his chest. With a surge of strength and the **Warhammer** pulsing beneath his hold, he rammed into the golem's chest. The impact force sent the golem reeling backward with a thunderous growl, hurtling towards the nearest wall. Upon collision, the wall shuddered as stone fragments peeled away from the creature's form.

Instantly, Tuck clasped both hands around the weapon, swinging it around in a wide arc before hurling it across the space. The weapon twirled through the air, reminiscent of a tomahawk spinning end over end. It flew straight towards the stone figure, its spiked end making contact with the creature's upper torso, decapitating it with a force that separated the heavy stone head from its body.

"Holy shit!" Frank yelled from the viewing windows. "THAT. WAS. **AWESOME**!"

Tuck inhaled deeply, absorbing the scene before him. He mused about how Frank had somehow unearthed his high school track experience as a hammer thrower. "I suppose all that practice wasn't in vain," Tuck reflected aloud. He strode over, retrieved his newfound weapon, and joined his jubilant team.

CHAPTER THIRTY-THREE

"Champions emerge from their inner fire, stoked by determination, and perhaps fueled by a touch of healthy rivalry." – Coach Williams.

THE HANGAR

Full Team

Frank's triumphant shout resounded through the battlefield as he watched Tuck obliterate the final stone golem. The rest of the team gathered around their colossal teammate, their eyes wide with awe as he effortlessly wielded the pulsing **Warhammer**. The weapon seemed to defy its weight, even though it was probably half the size of Tuck himself. His body had undergone a remarkable transformation after the tutorial, and now he stood at an impressive two-and-a-half meters tall, swinging the **Warhammer** with ease.

Will couldn't contain his curiosity. "What the heck is that thing made out of?" he blurted out, staring at Tuck in disbelief.

Frank grinned, clearly enjoying the attention. "That, my friend, is made of Celestium metal—the strongest material we could purchase with our hard-earned team points." He gestured toward Trish, who was equally pleased. "Trish, care to fill in the details? I might have already stolen some of the thunder with Tuck in the Smithy. I think it's your honor."

Trish stepped forward, her smile matching Frank's. "From the beginning of this round, Frank and I knew Tuck needed a weapon that matched his incredible strength—something that could share his love for ... bashing. But buying a weapon of this caliber directly with points wasn't feasible. So, Frank acquired the raw cut metal and honed his smithing skills using our new tools. While that was being done, I took on the task of aligning the weapon with Tuck's known affinity for electrons." She paused dramatically. "The result? Well…"

"Freaking **AMAZING**!" This time, the quiet Nadia came out of her shell, causing smiles to spread around the room, especially on Tuck's face as he stood beside the crew.

"Yes, we both agree," Trish said, looking at Frank. "Williams was our greatest asset in guiding us to the right training and tools we needed to learn. But we should be able to replicate this process in the future and continue to build."

"Yeah! Coach Williams even mentioned a potential future tournament for us Artisan crew members. So, please, keep bringing in those points so we can keep working on cool stuff!" Frank declared.

Feeling bashful at the attention, Tuck attempted to break up the party. He cleared his throat and addressed the group, "Thank you for the cheering squad, gang, but shouldn't you all probably get back to work? I'll try not to be as disruptive. But no promises."

"Actually," James started, glancing at Trish and then the rest of the team, "I think I may need the team's help."

△△△

"I thought you wanted to start small?" Trish's voice carried concern as she leaned in close to James.

"After seeing Tuck's performance, you want me to go small?" James replied, a half-smile playing on his lips, accompanied by a wink.

"Hey, now, I am all for it. As long as you aren't in danger of dying," Trish said while pointing at herself, "I approve." With that, she walked out of the enclosure and joined Frank, leaving James in the same position Tuck had once occupied in the center of the mini-arena.

"Should we take bets?" Will's enthusiasm filled the arena. "Loser has to sit in the splash zone directly across from Frank during his next meal."

"Hey! I heard that!" Frank yelled from behind the wall, now standing next to Trish. Meanwhile, Will, Emy, and Tuck huddled near the wall, with Nadia positioning herself as close to James as possible while still staying out of range, ready for instant healing if necessary.

"James, you sure you want to do this?" Emy shouted over as James silently nodded his confirmation. Earning the approval, Emy turned back to Will. "Nah, that's too easy. Loser has to map out James's next plan in a mission?"

"Brutal... I'm in," Will declared, and Tuck gave an accepting shrug. "But I get to go first. Let's say the longest to make him tap out loses?"

"Deal," Emy agreed. She and Tuck left the floor, leaving the stage to Will.

"All right, Will. Let me first create the barrier. Then, could you start small and attempt to ramp up every ten seconds until failure?"

"Nex, can you put a thermometer on my display for this first run?" James commented to Nex as a temperature display appeared on his interface. Once ready, James knelt, pressed his hand against the ground, and closed his eyes as he activated his **Energy Blocking Field**. *Let's see what you got, Will.*

< James is boosted by 30% >

△△△

Will stepped confidently in front of James, a smile on his lips. "Ain't no way I'm losing to Tuck."

"Nexy," he addressed his internal AI aloud, ensuring others could hear, "make sure those other Nex's judge fair and square."

Nexy's reply bore an accent so thick that it practically smirked across the AI's face, "*Oh, darling. That contradicts our primary coding. You know Mama always has your back.*"

Will arched an eyebrow. The term "Mama" had mysteriously entered his interactions with Nexy lately. He couldn't quite place its origin, but he had to admit he enjoyed it. With a nod, he settled onto the ground, positioning himself three meters before James's **Energy Blocking Field**.

His hands, palms facing inward, rose slowly. Will focused on feeling the room around him, attempting to recreate the sensations he'd experienced in the barn. His willpower stretched across the entire arena, condensing gradually.

Droplets of water formed across Will's body, clinging to the field that enveloped James. As before, the water droplets crystallized, their icy lattice growing more intricate. Will pushed his internal cold outward, amplifying the source, and felt the frost expand.

22°F/-11.1°C

Will pressed his hands closer together, allowing his spread-out willpower to compress bit by bit into the space in front of him. James's eyes remained closed as the temperature continued to drop.

-20°F/-28.9°C

Ice chunks now formed across the energy barrier, overwhelming the shield. Cracks split across the surface as the ice continued to grow and shift, and Will's hands now moved inches away from each other.

-80°F/-62°C

Trish was first to act, sending a note to the broader team—excluding the two currently locked in the battle of willpower, "Nex is reporting that James's vitals remain strong, but body temperature is gradually dropping, resulting in shortness of breath. Let's monitor and continue on."

Will had surpassed the point of control. His team would

stop the process if any doubts arose about James's health. So, Will persisted, now channeling all his willpower into the area. His trembling hands strained to move closer. As he exerted force, the ice transformed, assuming an unusual shape—irregular crystals spreading across the structure.

-125°F/-87.2°C

Will's body trembled as the temperature fluctuated, rising and falling. "Enough!" Trish called out. "We've got what we need. Stop them."

On command, James was directed to maintain his barrier while Will released his condensing, allowing the cold air to dissipate slowly. Emy strategically deployed a few fireballs in the larger area to infuse warmth.

"James," Trish said firmly, "lower the shield. We need Nadia to reach you now."

The last remainders of ice clinging to the shield splintered and crumbled, exposing a pale and shivering James. "Oh, goodness. This was for sure not starting small, James!" Trish stepped forward, wrapping him in a blanket, while Nadia focused her *Vitalize* skill on his core. Emy, now standing behind him, pressed her warm palms directly against his back, coaxing forth his innate warmth.

James let out a cough. "I'm fine. I promise," he rasped, managing a small smile as his body gradually recovered. "I... have been cold all my life."

Will, positioned beside Frank, who was providing support, interjected, "Hold on a second. Why do you get all three girls touching all over you, and I'm stuck with Frank? Was this the grand plan all along?"

But then Will's curiosity changed, "Wait, cold all your life? What does that even mean? That can't be fair."

Emy answered with a dry smirk, "Didn't remember that James grew up in the mountains, did you?"

"The mountains?" Will spoke, now more confused and looking towards Frank.

"Dude, James's parents are legends in Tahoe. Olympic champs... remember?" Frank's voice was softer, given their shared proximity.

"Bet's a bet. I'm sure our Nex's can confirm," Tuck addressed Will, and the group settled into light laughter as the two continued their recovery.

James glanced at Trish. "Well," he said softly, "I think it worked."

CHAPTER THIRTY-FOUR

"Train as if you're competing." – Mike Gray.

THE HANGAR

Full Team

"Tuck, you ready?" James asked, determination evident in his voice as the rest of the group hesitated. Noticing everyone's stares, James added, "Why wait? I feel better than ever with these three healing me up." He shot a wry smile at Will. "Besides, don't we need to determine a winner? I sense a grand battle plan looming in my near future."

Tuck remained skeptical despite James's apparent enthusiasm. "Are you sure? We still have some time."

"Time is one thing we don't have," James replied. "I promise I'm ready. But instead of starting with your lightning, how about we give that…" James glanced at the **Warhammer**, "thing a try?"

"Bertha?" Frank questioned.

"No, definitely not Bertha," Tuck clarified. "But it does need a name soon. You want me to swing this at you?" Tuck waved the sharp edge in front of James.

"Absolutely," James said thoughtfully. "Same process— just start slow and maybe use the hammer side first?"

Frank leaned in to whisper to Will, "I'm not sure that side is any better…" as Will huffed in agreement.

Trish caught Frank's comment. "Frank, hush."

"What? Can't a guy be proud of his work?" Frank retorted.

"Our work," Trish corrected with a wink as they watched

Tuck and James move to the center of the ring. "Maybe we should, uh, step back a bit."

"Can't argue with that," Frank agreed. He, along with Will and Emy, stepped out while Nadia remained close again in case of any mishaps.

△△△

Tuck observed as James's protective shield rippled around him. Lowering the head of his **Warhammer**, Tuck adjusted his grip, wielding the weapon once more like a baseball bat.

"Hope you're ready, James," Tuck muttered as he slowly advanced toward his friend.

"*Rest assured; James is safe...ish,*" Nex addressed Tuck directly, attempting to instill confidence. Instead of immediately striking with the hammer side, Tuck positioned himself next to the dome enveloping James and gave it a slight tap. The dome yielded slightly but rebounded like a firm windowpane reacting to a knock. Satisfied that the hammer wouldn't penetrate it immediately, Tuck decided to take a swing.

Putting in just 20% of his effort, enough to set the **Warhammer** in motion, Tuck spun and drove the weapon toward the **Energy Blocking Field**.

BONG! The **Warhammer** struck the side of the dome, sending vibrations rippling across its surface and producing a distinct sound reminiscent of wobbling glass.

< Shield integrity maintained >

Tuck smiled, observing the now calm dome that held James. At that moment, he could have sworn he saw a slight smile from James, who remained facedown with his eyes closed.

"Well, it looks like we're in for some fun," Tuck declared, joy surging through him as a pulse of energy overwhelmed his body.

"Uh oh," the collective group watching murmured in unison as Tuck's form began to glow. Without further hesitation, Tuck hurled the weapon's weight directly into the air, bringing it down with 60% force upon the shield.

BONG! The shield exploded with noise, vibration waves pulsing through the room while Tuck's hands tingled from the vibrations running through his fingers.

< Shield integrity maintained >

Tuck's smile faded as he gazed at the unscathed dome enveloping James. "Looks like ramp-up is now over. Let's do this," Tuck muttered, stepping back and surging toward the energy field. Like against the rock creatures, Tuck executed a 180-degree twist, channeling all his force into the next strike like a hammer throw. **BOOM!** The *Warhammer* struck, and the momentum of the blow reverberated away from the shield, akin to a flexed metal spring forcefully expelled back. Tuck and his weapon were thrown 4 meters backward, landing on the floor.

As Tuck hit the ground, a lightning pulse crackled through the air. He pushed himself up, eyes fuming with energy as his irises pulsed white. Taking two giant steps, he leaped into the air, driving the hammer side back and slamming the spike of the *Warhammer* into the dome. **CRACK!**

< Shield compromised >

The group watched as Tuck stepped back from the dome, the white glow in his eyes suddenly dispersing as he realized what he had done. "**JAMES!**" Trish yelled, sprinting into the area with the others following.

"Oh no," Tuck gasped, looking toward his weapon, now piercing through the shield. The shaft pointed outward, directly where James had been sitting. "Oh no."

The silence overwhelmed Tuck, amplifying the gravity of his actions. Muffled footsteps and urgent cries echoed from his friends behind him. "What had he done?" he wondered aloud, then urgently called out, "James!" as the voices behind him closed in.

......

"Tuck?" the voice came from inside the cracked dome.
"James! You there?"
"I am, but do you mind pulling this thing out? I'm afraid that if I disperse this shield fully, the stabby part will drop, and I think it weighs more than me."

Tuck immediately wrenched the **Warhammer** from the shield as the energy dispersed, revealing a smiling James.

"It looks like my shield may be better with blunt damage than piercing," James remarked, surveying the crowd rushing toward him. Relief was evident on everyone's faces.

"Guys, I'm perfectly fine." James raised his hands, halting the group. Will trailed behind, realization dawning on him.

"Nexy, I'll assume Tuck outscored me on this one?" Will said to Nexy, not bothering to lower his voice.

"Oh, honey, yes. But don't worry; we still have one more to go," Nexy replied, offering hope. But somehow, those words didn't quite settle Will, as he knew who was up next...

△△△

"James is quite the determined one, isn't he?" Trish's voice carried to the group gathered outside the area, peering in at the final pairing of Emy and James.

Tuck and Will exchanged knowing glances, but this time, Tuck expressed their mutual perception. "James is very committed. He's never missed a practice, even on the scorching double days. Even beyond those scheduled sessions, he's always there, tossing the ball to anyone willing to stay longer. We're sure he's maintained straight A's this semester and even earned the All-State Academic Award in High School. But this?

This demonstrates a whole new level of dedication."

Emy ignited her hands and addressed James with finality, "Last chance, James."

James smirked. "And miss out on a chance to face you?" His eyes sparkled. "I need to challenge the best to understand my limits." With now practiced ease, he dropped to one knee, and the energy field returned to life.

Emy allowed the energy field to merge, giving it a few extra seconds for safety. Then, without much fanfare, she sent a fireball hurtling directly at the shield.

BOOM! The shield pulsed briefly but held its structure.

< Shield integrity maintained >

Emboldened, Emy unleashed a rapid succession of fireball blasts, each striking the shield with precision. The energy field flickered, wavering with each hit.

< Shield integrity maintained >

Will winced from behind the outer barrier, recognizing the shield's vulnerability and his potential lost bet. Emy's relentless assault overpowered the shield's stability.

Yet, Emy shifted her focus as the team prepared for the onslaught of additional fireball blasts. She extended her hands and closed her eyes with a serene composure, immersing herself deeply into the ambient energy permeating the room. Time seemed to elongate as the air around her grew warmer, a testament to the intense focus Emy was channeling. Her heightened senses allowed her to perceive her surroundings not as mere physical structures but as variables in a complex equation she was unraveling in real-time. The very makeup of the arena, with its assortment of elements, mixtures, and compounds, was effortlessly cataloged, analyzed, and manipulated in her mind.

Fully committed and unwavering in her resolve, Emy shifted her willpower towards the environment. She wasn't merely interacting with the material world but reshaping its essence, straddling the line between destruction and creation. Commanding the elements around her, she employed fire as a volatile catalyst at the epicenter of her focus, with smoke emerging as an inevitable byproduct. This wasn't just a display of chemical prowess; it was an intimate dance with the forces of nature, a testament to Emy's ability to conjure and deconstruct the very fabric of reality. What would become in a world without substance, a realm where the laws of physics and chemistry cease to exist?

With her eyes still veiled behind closed lids, the aftermath of her intervention became tangible. Gray smoke billowed through the air, swirling from pockets throughout the room and, more notably, around James's enclosure.

The team watched in awe as the mini-fusion spheres gathered across the arena. Unlike the fireball blasts she typically unleashed, these appeared as fiery manifestations, scorching the open air. As the holes in the room grew larger, within their flaming edges, an eerie blackness emerged—a void created by the very fire that it now consumed.

Having achieved what she set out to do, Emy opened her eyes and strolled casually toward the now-fuming shield, its burning holes expanding. She selected the most significant breach and opened it with flaming hands. The once tiny hole tore apart, dissipating the energy around it. Emy then playfully stuck her head through the gaping hole in the dome.

"Gotcha," she declared her tone light.

James's eyes fluttered open. "You do realize you'll have to do that a few more times, right?" he quipped, amused by the red-headed intruder poking into his protective sphere.

"Well," Emy replied, a hint of greed and playfulness in her eyes, "I still need the practice… just don't tell Will I learned all that from him?"

CHAPTER THIRTY-FIVE

"As a team, we cherished every moment together during intermissions, making them feel longer than they were. We trained, conversed, and got to know each other intimately. We became a close-knit family in no time." – Quist, Former Champion.

THE HANGAR

Full Team

Following the initial group exercise with James, the team split into their respective groups for the remainder of the intermission. James and Trish maintained their collaboration, testing various shield resistance techniques. They simulated scenarios involving chemical attacks and a wide array of piercing assaults, which seemed to exploit the shield's primary vulnerability. While Trish took the lead in most of the tests, she also leveraged the team's expertise to expand the range of experimentation. Will contributed with his **Cryostrikes**, Tuck commanded **Ion Storm**, and Emy relentlessly attacked the shield using her **Targeted Fusion** and **Disintegration** skills to challenge James's willpower. Additionally, they evaluated the shield's limits—how long James could sustain it and the time required for resummoning. On average, the shield held for around two minutes, and James could reactivate it after five-minute intervals once he regained his composure.

Like James, Tuck maintained a rigorous schedule, teaming up with Frank to familiarize himself with his new weapon. Together, they engaged in numerous battle scenarios, facing different opponents to understand the strengths and weaknesses of the **Warhammer**. Beyond using it as a hammer or spike, they attempted to channel Tuck's **Ion Storm** through the weapon, although success remained elusive. The resulting area-of-effect attack tended to scatter across the arena but enhanced the electric damage dealt to opponents.

During this break, Will and Emy took a more theoretical approach and delved into the complex world of energy manipulation. Will focused on refining his control over ice, aiming for greater precision. Meanwhile, Emy worked on enhancing the size and strength of her area-of-effect (AOE) attack, which seemed to scorch the air. In addition to their long-range and targeted techniques, they both dedicated themselves to improving their full-body techniques, aiming to unlock more combinations for future battles.

Lastly, Nadia charted a different course amidst the team's bustling activities. She was seated cross-legged in a secluded corner, her eyes often closed, and a wall of mirrors surrounding her. Her teammates occasionally stole glances in her direction—concerned yet respectful of her introspective process. Unlike the others, Nadia wasn't practicing combat maneuvers or poring over energy diagrams. Instead, she embarked on a self-understanding journey, delving into the intricacies of her anatomy and the untapped capabilities within her body.

As always, the teams broke away from training, drawn by Frank's rampaging sounds toward the kitchen area. But soon, they faced their last meal before the team expected to be thrust toward their next level.

"What do you guys think the Trials will be like?" James asked as the team sat around the cafeteria table.

"I honestly can't imagine them being anything too extraordinary. Who wants to watch junior college kids from Quincy?" Emy spoke with indifference.

"What? No way! You guys are bound to be superstars soon!" Frank objected. "I just hope Trish and I get to witness everything."

"Ha. Let's focus on surviving these Trials before we think about stardom," James responded. "Do you think anyone we know will be watching?" He paused, trying to remember. "Nex, can 'Earthians' even watch?"

"I'm sorry, James. This one is always tricky to answer, as it has differed over the Games. I can tell you that they will have the ability to watch in the future, but we never know at what level they'll obtain access. It depends on the agencies of the IMS —oops, sorry, I mean the Interstellar Mergence Strategies. They're in charge of integrating Earth into the larger Cosmos, and with that comes access to their services, like the Quantum Games broadcasting."

"How does that even work, Nex? Do they show up and hack into our existing networks?" Trish interjected.

"Well, once again, it depends. Different paths emerge depending on the planets' success in defending themselves during the early attacks. Either a representative from the IMS will attempt to contact a leadership official on Earth, or if that's not available, they may provide access through local means. For Earth, that would probably involve injection into internet forums or local networks."

"I'm not sure if anyone close to me would want to watch, even if it were broadcast here," Emy mused, and a series of unexpected nods of agreement rippled around the table.

"Wait," Emy continued, directing her attention to Will after observing everyone's reactions, "you all have lots of family who would be thrilled to watch you. Will, you must have tons of friends who'd tune in."

"I am not sure if that is true. To be honest, you all are my only true friends. Most everyone else is an acquaintance, outside of maybe now Penny," Will said with a slight smile, reflecting on his newfound friend. "I suppose my mom and brother might want to watch, but I'm unsure if I'd want them to see me like this."

Tuck responded with a simple, "Same." Though his mind

briefly wandered to his mother's lectures about his behavior, all the while, he tried to steer his thoughts away from the reality of what his father's incarceration now looked like.

"I guess my parents would want to watch me, but honestly, I think I would feel better knowing that they weren't watching to avoid any more pressure on the situation," James stated quietly.

Emy didn't want to push any of them further, but she couldn't help but look at Nadia. "How about you, Nadia?"

"Oh. I don't know. I think my family would mostly like to know where I am and if I was alive, but I don't think they would believe that I was training to 'save humanity,'" Nadia spoke, forcing a bit of a smile.

The responses of his friends blew away Frank. "You all are the future heroes of Earth. I can't imagine anyone not wanting to watch you all, especially your families. My dad, while he may be a bit lost at what is going on, would be screaming at the top of his lungs for you all with even a slight mention that you all were close to me." Joy filled Frank at the thought of his dad, but it quickly sank as he considered the loneliness of his father, now without Frank or his late mom, who had passed away a few years ago.

Trish continued Frank's sentiment, "Both of my moms would be thrilled that I have found real-life friends like all of you. Yes, they may be out of their comfort zone, as they didn't quite understand my gaming, but they treated all my friends like their own family, even if most of them were only online."

"We will have to watch for them," James said with a soft smile. "Knowing you two and Coach are waiting for us is all I need, plus, well, all of you in there with me, of course." This earned a collective round of nods from the others at the table as Coach Williams walked in. He usually allowed the team to enjoy their time together and seldom interrupted.

"Coach?" James acknowledged his appearance.

"James... Team. Time is trending down, and I wanted to discuss key feedback points with all of you before the next round."

"Should we go to the strategy room?" James suggested.

"No. No. I'll keep this informal. Enjoy your last moments together before the next event." Coach Williams grabbed a chair and sat down near the head of the table.

"Let me just begin… I don't know what to expect from this round, but I want you to know that you can and should consider stopping if you have the option between segments. The System will usually give you a choice to move on or drop out if you face any wave challenge. You can still stay in the tournament if you drop before the end. Remember, this is a ranking level. Don't risk your lives for fame, but know that tournament success pushes you and Earth down a better path. Make the call that works best for everyone."

"Second and last comment, which may be tough for some of you," Coach Williams said before he turned to look at Emy and Nadia. "Be memorable." He paused before continuing, "Show off. Act a role. Build your character." He then looked at Will with a smile. "Be Brick."

"As I have said before, fans matter. Celebrities are made regardless of your ranking at the end of these Trials. Heroes are remembered. Play into that."

Williams proceeded to stand up from the chair. "And good luck."

INTERMISSION HERO UPDATES #2

"Repeating the previous break in the story, this segment explores our heroes' progress, mirroring the information showcased on the strategy room's wall." – Nex.

Mighty Eagles (Cohort 13)

Total Team Points: **736 Points**

Total Points Spent: **710 Points**

Total Points Remaining: **26 Points**

Total Max Active Views: **37,978**

Earth Rank: **2,124 of 106,260**

98th Percentile

△△△

Emy
Generalist
Level **7**
E-Class
Fire & Void Affinity

Primary Skill: Targeted Fusion (R) **(Level 5)**

Secondary Skills: Disintegration (T & R) **(Level 3)**; Pyroform (SELF) **(Emerging)**; Umbral Void Blaze (AOE) **(Emerging)**

Health: 100% Health + Natural Recovery Rate 7% each minute

Shield: 80%: 60% Power based + 20% Gear based

Weapons: None

Augments: Level 5 Combat Training Module; Map Extension (Rare)

Gear:

   Full Body: QuantumWeave (Uncommon) - 10% Shield Coverage

   Head: None

   Upper Body: Mighty Eagles Letterman's Jacket (Unique) - 10% Shield Coverage

Lower Body: Leggings - No Modifications

Feet: Sneakers - No Modifications

Accessories: Engraved Fanny Pack (Uncommon); Soulpulse (x2) (Rare)

△△△

Tuck
Accelerator
Level **6**
E-Class
Electron Affinity

Primary Skill: Electron Surge (T) **(Level 5)**

Secondary Skills: Ion Storm (AOE) **(Level 4)**

Health: 100% Health + Natural Recovery Rate 5% each minute

Shield: 70%: 50% Power based + 20% Gear based

Weapons:

> **Two-Handed Weapon:** Celestium Spiked Warhammer (D-Class, Low) (Upgradeable)

Augments: Level 5 Combat Training Module; Level 5 Combat Weapons Training; Map Extension (Rare)

Gear:

> **Full Body:** QuantumWeave (Uncommon) - 10% Shield Coverage
>
> **Head:** None
>
> **Upper Body:** Mighty Eagles Letterman's Jersey (Unique) - 10% Shield Coverage
>
> **Lower Body:** Jeans - No Modifications
>
> **Feet:** Sneakers - No Modifications
>
> **Accessories:** None

△△△

James
Catalyst
Level **5**
E-Class
No Affinity

Primary Skill: Empower (R) **(Level 5)**

Secondary Skills: Restrict (R) **(Level 4)**; Energy Blocking Field (T) **(Level 5)**

>(Resistance - Cold (**M**), Heat (**M**), Electric (**M**), Blunt (**M**), Piercing (**L**), Toxic (**L**)
>Duration - 2 Mins, Reactivation - 5 Mins)

Health: 100% Health + Natural Recovery Rate 4% each minute

Shield: 40%: 20% Power based + 20% Gear based

Weapons:

>**Bow:** Novaflight (E-Class, High)
>
>**Arrows:** Back Quiver with Statis Alchemarrows (E-Class, High) (∞) (Fireball, Neurofluxine, Crimson Cascade, Piercing, Ice, Fire)

Augments: Level 5 Combat Training Module; Map Extension

(Rare)

Gear:

Full Body: QuantumWeave (Uncommon) - 10% Shield Coverage

Head: None

Upper Body: Mighty Eagles Letterman's Jacket (Unique) - 10% Shield Coverage

Lower Body: Jeans - No Modifications

Feet: Sneakers - No Modifications

Accessories: Neurablocker (21) (Uncommon)

△△△

Nadia
Cellulator
Level **4**
E-Class
Physiology Affinity

Primary Skill: Vitalize (T) **(Level 5)** 15% Recovery Rate per minute

Secondary Skills: Affliction Surge (T) **(Level 4);** Body Manipulation (SELF) **(Emerging)**

Health: 98% Health + Natural Recovery Rate 15% each minute

Minor Inflictions: Neurofluxine (1%); Crimson Cascade (1%)

Shield: 30%: 10% Power based + 20% Gear based

Weapons: None

Augments: Level 5 Combat Training Module; Map Extension (Rare)

Gear:

Full Body: QuantumWeave (Uncommon) - 10% Shield Coverage

Head: None

Upper Body: Mighty Eagles Letterman's Jacket (Unique) - 10% Shield Coverage

Lower Body: Jeans - No Modifications

Feet: Ghostwalkers (Rare) - Flight (20 ft.), Duration 2 mins, 3x per day

Accessories: Phantom Veil (Rare)

△△△

Brick (Will)
Condenser
Level **6**
E-Class
Water Affinity

Primary Skill: Condense (R) **(Level 5)**

Secondary Skills: Cryostrike (R) **(Level 4)**; Flow Perception (T) **(Level 5)**; Permafrost (SELF) **(Level 4)**

Health: 100% Health + Natural Recovery Rate 2% each minute

Shield: 70%: 50% Power based + 20% Gear based

Weapons: None

Augments: Level 5 Combat Training Module; Map Extension (Rare)

Gear:

    Full Body: QuantumWeave (Uncommon) - 10% Shield Coverage

    Head: None

    Upper Body: Mighty Eagles Letterman's Jacket (Unique) - 10% Shield Coverage

    Lower Body: Jeans - No Modifications

    Feet: Sneakers - No Modifications

    Accessories: None

△△△

Trish
Manipulator
Level **4**
E-Class
No Affinity

△△△

Frank
Creator
Level **5**
E-Class
Metallurgy Affinity

Legend:
(T) = Touching, (R) = Ranged, (AOE) = Area of Effect
(L) = Low Skill, (M) = Moderate Skill, (H) = High Skill

CHAPTER THIRTY-SIX

"You would think the Trials led to the fewest deaths among all the missions. But actually, the Trials bring out competition and foolishness, enabling the largest death toll over any other level." – Games Division Data Scientist.

LEVEL THREE

Would you like to continue to Level Three of the Quantum Games?

"Yes"

......

Welcome to the Trials!

In this team-based event, you and your team will embark on a thrilling journey through a 7-stage mission. After each stage, you will have a decision to make as a team: Continue or Leave. Opting out before the end of the third stage means elimination from the Quantum Games. However, if you pass the first three stages, you can exit the Trials and maintain your spot in the Games.

Rankings will be determined by:

1. Stages completed

2. Mission successfulness

3. Total time to finish the last completed stage

The **top 100** from each planet will top the Stellar Ascendancy.

The **top 25** in the Galaxy will be shared across the Cosmos.

In cases of a tie, rankings will compare to the next level of success. For example, if two teams complete stage 5 and exit, the ranking will be determined based on mission success.

Now, prepare yourselves! You're about to be transported to your trial locations.

Best of luck!

......

Emy stood in a gray mist, her mind racing to comprehend the details provided by the System announcement. A surge of exhilaration coursed through her when the notice confirmed she'd be with her team, yet she braced herself for whatever lay ahead.

"Fu-ry! Fu-ry! Fu-ry! Fu-ry!" the room—no, not a room, but an entire stadium—rumbled with noise as the gray dissolved, revealing an unfolding scene. Emy stood back-to-back with her four other teammates, their faces filled with awe. Before them stretched a sea of hundreds of thousands of fans, shrieking their names, jumping, and brandishing signs and banners.

"What the...?" Emy exclaimed, her gaze fixed on the

spectators, who appeared startlingly real. A cacophony of voices surrounded them—life forms of all kinds, filling the space with their cheers. "Are they all speaking English?"

"*Oh, that's just me translating for you!*" Nex explained. "*Isn't this something? I knew you'd become famous.*"

"Nex," James interjected, "our peak active views were only around 37 thousand. Why are there so many people... I mean... spectators here?"

"*Silly you,*" Nex replied, "*those are just active views! You must have made some headlines during the after-hours. Fans can always revisit and rewatch if they hear about amazing feats by the team.*"

"Emy," Will said, surprised, "I think I've found your doppelgänger." He pointed to what seemed like a female humanoid in the stands. This lookalike had bright red, curly hair and unmistakably wore a red letterman's jacket, just like Emy's. The girl in the stands jumped up when she noticed the five heroes looking her way. "Yep," Will added, "and there's the matching fanny pack."

Emy's eyes widened as she stared at the fan and surveyed the stands. "This is beyond anything I could have imagined," she marveled, her attention drawn to the vibrant tapestry of skin tones that painted the crowd. The diversity was not limited to just colors; it also extended to physical forms. Among the spectators, figures with three or even four arms were a common sight, each unique in their own way. "How many different life forms are here?"

"Thousands," Nadia answered with amazement. "Each group looks completely distinct... And look—I even spot some that look like us. Think they could be from Earth?"

"*Ah, I don't think so, but we can hope!*" Nex's words burst forth. "*Most likely, those are just humanoid-based life forms. Even in the Cosmos, dominant traits favor two-legged, two-armed forms. But your human heads—so round! That's an anomaly. Why put your women through that type of pain in childbirth? Your genetics surprise me sometimes!*"

The team settled into a contemplative silence, each member wrestling with the ramifications of their newfound fame and the possibility of friends and family eventually joining the fans in the stands. Shattering the stillness, Nadia asked the group, "So, what's our next move?"

Will grinned at the question and replied, "Remember what Williams mentioned?" He paused dramatically and added, "We've got to put on a show."

On cue, Will activated his **Permafrost** skill, his body shimmering as it became encased in ice. The crowd exploded, swept up in the spectacle.

"Brick!" the fans howled in unison, their voices a low rumble.

Tuck allowed his **Warhammer** to fall, the impact resonating through the ground. He then lifted the handle, slamming the top with force, sending electric pulses rippling outward.

James joined, kneeling as he pressed his hand to the ground, creating an **Energy Blocking Field** around him. His bow was now drawn, ready for action.

Nadia followed suit, her form flickering as she vanished from her original spot. In the blink of an eye, she reappeared two meters before the crew, her movements seamless. She disappeared again, rejoining the team with a sense of purpose.

But Emy remained still, her gaze fixed on the unfolding scene. The crowd's enthusiasm intensified, their voices merging into a single, thunderous chant: "Fu-ry! Fu-ry! Fu-ry! Fu-ry! Fu-ry!" They hungered for more, their excitement palpable.

Will, encased in ice, urged her forward. "Come on, Emy," he implored, "listen to them."

Emy hesitated, torn between confusion and anger. Finally, she nodded at Will and raised her palms to the air. Fire enveloped her, igniting from her hands and growing with each passing second. Her entire body glowed blue, with orange and red embers shooting forth.

And in that moment, the crowd reached an absolute peak of

noise. Their sounds transformed into vibrations, enveloping the entire area.

< Skill Identified – Emy – Pyroform >

Will smiled as he glanced at Emy, wondering if she knew what she was doing as the crowd continued to erupt. Will took a closer glance at the skill similar to his **Permafrost** skill:

Skill: Pyroform

Grants the user the ability to transform into a complete form of fire, creating a heat shield and gaining additional offensive power. The flames cover the entire body while maintaining movement similar to their normal physical state. (SELF)

Trials will begin in 30 seconds.

As the notice appeared in their view, the stadium floor began to shift. The dirt on the arena vibrated as the area within the stadium took form.

Behind them, a stone lighthouse emerged from the ground, rising to what appeared to be two stories. The stone masonry structure featured a single door and a winding staircase leading to the top deck. The top deck was a circular overlook with walls that enclosed the room and a single door connected back to the stairs.

"What is that?" Emy questioned, her gaze locked on the unfolding scene. The five of them found themselves standing in a courtyard before the lighthouse. The stadium floors, which had extended toward the arena walls, are now dissolved and replaced by three expansive walkways spanning an abyss. These walkways led to massive entryways shrouded in absolute darkness.

Further changes occurred at the intersection of the three walkways. Large gates materialized, connecting the three entrances and forming another circular enclosure around the courtyard. Finally, a 1.5-meter-high stone wall emerged between the outer walls and the lighthouse, creating a sub-wall with openings on each side, allowing entry into the lighthouse's single doorway.

Trials will begin in 15 seconds.

Emy visited the status screen, which displayed the new mission:

Level Three Mission: Wave Trials

1. *Survive the seven waves of attack.*
2. *Prevent the destruction of your Castle.*

Your Castle is currently at 0% damage.

"Castle?" Emy spoke aloud, suddenly realizing it referred to what she believed to be a lighthouse. "I guess 'Castle' does sound cooler," she murmured, her thoughts racing. But before she could dwell on it further, James's battle communications snapped her out of her daze.

"Emy, Will, Tuck—take positions at the doors leading into the courtyard. Nadia, run safety—no, I mean—"

"On it," Nadia interrupted, understanding her role as James continued, "I'll head up the stairs and provide guidance and air coverage from the balcony. Communicate, adapt, and shift as needed!"

Trials begin in 3... 2... 1...

The noise in the arena suddenly went deathly quiet. The counter ticked to zero, and a loud rumble resounded from the darkness encompassing the three doorways...

CHAPTER THIRTY-SEVEN

"In the Trials, strategy prevails over pure power. Quick adaptation to your enemy and the surrounding landscape is often the key to success." – Coach Williams.

EARTH - SECRET BUNKER

"Mr. President," the National Security Advisor's voice was tense, "the White House has been breached."

The small council convened in an undisclosed location 100 miles outside of Washington, DC, held their breath upon receiving the alarming news.

"Has the Secret Service made any progress in impeding their advance?" The President's concern was now showing.

"Sir," the advisor responded, "our attempts to circumvent these alien intruders have been futile. Our weaponry and tactical advances have failed to hinder their advance. With limited options, should we reconsider using large-scale weapons as a viable solution?"

The President hesitated, fully aware of the dire situation. The disturbing details of these intruders made him want nothing more than to obliterate them from the face of the Earth. "No," he finally said, "leave large-scale options off the table. A destroyed White House would only fuel more unrest in our great nation. We must look for an alternative."

"There has to be a way," the Vice President interjected, her voice hopeful. "Other regions have reportedly stopped similar attacks worldwide. Can we not just seek advice from our allies?"

The Secretary of State responded, "At this point, Madam Vice President, we only have rumors and speculation. Sources speak of unknown forces quelling the invaders, but the methods remain a mystery."

As he spoke, the Secretary of State received a call on the secured line. "One moment," he said, answering the direct line to the United Nations.

Hope spread among the group as the Secretary of State joined the call. But that hope quickly faded as they watched his eyes widen in concern upon hearing the news.

"Mr. Secretary," the President urged, "what's the situation?"

"Mr. President," the Secretary of State said, confusion forming, "it appears that a collective group of aliens wishes to speak with us directly. The United Nations reports that they seem to be non-hostile."

"What?" the President's voice now held anger. "I currently have a hostile alien race invading my home. My family and I have been uprooted from our lives, and now you're telling me these aliens are friendly?"

"Um… Yes," the Secretary of State replied, still with his ear on the phone. "They claim to be from an organization called the CNC."

△△△

LEVEL THREE - STAGE ONE

The abrupt shift from cacophonous roars to deafening silence overwhelmed the senses. Just moments ago, chaotic and ear-pounding noise had filled the air. Now, the fans remained, their wide-mouthed expressions devoid of sound. In the absence of the former noise, rumbles emanated from the ground—a constant vibration causing the floor to shake, and the solid sandy ground pulsated up and down with each tremor.

"Call out if you see anything," James bellowed from the top of the Castle balcony, his footsteps echoing as he paced around. His eyes scanned each of the three walkways leading toward the ether gates at the far end.

Emy, Will, and Tuck stood at their courtyard gates, peering through narrow windows. Each gate, about 4 meters tall, boasted a sturdy 1-meter metal latch, allowing for exit from within.

"I see something!" Will's voice rang out as a diminutive creature, roughly half a meter tall, darted onto the path before him. The beast appeared rat-like yet lacked any discernible threat. It paused, nibbling its paws as similar critters emerged along Tuck and Emy's walkways.

"Any ideas here?" Will called out, the team perplexed by the sudden appearance of these creatures. As more materialized, James remembered he could scan them.

Ratkin: Level 3

These horde creatures, meticulously bred in clandestine laboratories, are renowned for their ferocity and overwhelming numbers. When these elusive Ratkin emerge from their subterranean lairs, they unleash a vicious, inhuman, lightning-fast onslaught, swarming like a chaotic tide of verminous rat warriors.

"Team, listen up!" James's prompted. "Check the description. These creatures are..." His words trailed off as lightning struck nearby, illuminating the lifeless gnawing rat at Tuck's gate.

The rats, once scattered, looked on at their dead companion as their beady eyes turned from friendly to fury, revealing sharp fangs and menacing claws. The once timid rodents transformed into a relentless horde, now swarming the walkways. James cursed under his breath, realizing the gravity of their predicament. He swiftly drew his bow, fireball **Alchemarrows** ready to fly.

Will, Tuck, and Emy fought back, their attacks resounding

through the arena. But the challenge lay in their limited vantage points—skills strained to reach the encroaching vermin.

Will's instincts kicked in as he assessed the situation. The Ratkin were relentlessly tearing at the gates, threatening to breach the courtyard's defenses. He turned to James, urgency in his eyes.

"James, cover me," Will commanded. "I'm opening my gate."

Without waiting for objections, he added, "I can't get a clear shot. We're on the brink of being overrun. James, on my mark, send your arrows towards the base of my door. Emy, provide cover fire if you have an opening from your viewpoint."

James and Emy acknowledged together, snapping to the new plan as Nadia shifted to support Will's side, ready for the impending battle.

"Now!" Will's voice called out as he released the latch on the door. Fireball blasts from James's **Alchemarrows** and Emy's **Targeted Fusion** soon exploded behind the gate. Next, the gate opened, and a biting coldness permeated the surroundings. With his **Condense** skill, Will pressed both hands on the pathway, channeling moisture into a concentrated force. A sheet of ice spread across the floor, creating a slippery path similar to an ice rink.

The short lull and gate opening still allowed several Ratkin to cross the divide, scampering into the courtyard. But they were met with swift strikes, their spines severed.

< Level Up! Nadia is now a Level 5 Cellulator >

James's eyes widened in shock. One moment, the Ratkin hurled themselves into the courtyard, and the next, they writhed on the ground. Nadia materialized behind Will, her hands dripping blood—or rather, blades protruding from her knuckles dripped blood. James's breath caught.

< Skill Identified – Nadia – Body Manipulation >

"Well, those are new," he muttered, his voice barely audible.

He shook off the surprise and resumed his position at the overlook. The fights below demanded his attention.

Will wasted no time. As the ice settled on the pathway, he seized control of the horde. The Ratkin's frantic scurrying transformed into desperate slides on the newly created ice. Waves of **Cryostrikes** flew down the walkway, flinging some into the abyss below. Those who clung to the edge met a swift end—skewered and silenced.

< Level Up! Will is now a Level 7 Condenser >

"My turn," Emy's voice rang out, determination fueling her next move. James positioned himself above her third of the arena. On cue, James recreated their previous success, unleashing a barrage of fireball blast strikes in front of Emy's gateway. Meanwhile, standing at the midpoint of his pathway, Will also pivoted to deliver multiple **Cryostrikes** to the Ratkin closest to Emy's gate.

As the gate swung open, Emy wasted no time. She conjured a blazing wall of fire as the creatures frantically searched for cover. The air burst with flames, engulfing the entire bridge as the Ratkin met their fiery demise.

< Level Up! Emy is now a Level 8 Generalist >

"The Ratkin are breaking through!" Tuck's urgent voice called out as Nadia, already positioned next to him, thrust her blades through the fresh holes in the gate, piercing the Ratkin as they clawed and gnashed in a frenzy of terror.

On cue, Will and Emy pivoted again toward the final walkway, where crazed rats surged. Ice and fire clashed, encircling the bridge. Tuck stepped through his gate, anger pulsing on his face.

"That's enough. Save some for me," Tuck quipped, adopting a mock-heroic tone. He hefted his **Warhammer** and triggered his **Electron Surge** skill within his body as he pulsed toward the center of the pathway. Rats flew, their fur electrified. The **Warhammer** whirled in Tuck's hands as he danced across the walkway. The remaining horde faltered, then froze as Tuck spun and brought the hammer side down on the last remaining creatures.

As the *Warhammer* struck, the arena noise vibrated anew across the surroundings.

RAT ON! 78 POINTS!

< Double level up! Tuck is now a level 8 Accelerator >

The crowd echoed in unison, their voices echoing with a low, thunderous boom: "**SURRRRRRGE!... SURGE!... SURGE!**"

Will couldn't help but grin. "Now, *THAT* is a superhero name!" he exclaimed, excitement on his face.

STAGE ONE is now COMPLETE!

......

You have one hour to regroup and prepare for the next stage.

CHAPTER THIRTY-EIGHT

"No matter where you are or what you are doing, enjoy the little time you have with your team. Those precious moments can mean more to the team than any training exercise." – Coach Williams.

LEVEL THREE

As if a switch was flipped, the raging noise of the crowd once again subsided. But this time, the screaming fans were not only silenced; they were no longer there. Hundreds of thousands of seats now sat empty.

"What the heck?" Will was the first to react. "All those people, suddenly gone?"

"I mean, we knew they weren't with us," James responded to the larger group, "but I didn't expect them to just vanish like that."

"Oh, maybe I can help here!" Nex added with a short laugh. "The CNC is equal parts supportive and greedy. In the earlier Games, fans would buy seats for the whole Trials, but as soon as the CNC realized they could earn more by selling tickets by stage. The higher the stage the team moves into, the higher the ticket price!"

"And fans just agree to that?" Emy's face twisted in disgust.

"Why wouldn't they? You should watch your team in action!" Nex continued. "But to help you out a little more, the CNC—or IMS in this case—avoids the greed moniker by stating that these breaks allow Champions a chance to breathe between stages, away from prying eyes."

"Couldn't they just send us to intermission, like during our levels?" Nadia suggested.

"They could," Nex replied, "but that would require more negotiations with the System, and the System agrees that breaks within the venue help Champions and provide moments of candidness that wouldn't exist with all those fans watching. Only your teammates and coaches have access to these feeds."

The group shifted, accepting Nex's answers. They had experienced stranger things, so sometimes it was easier to accept the unchangeable, at least for now.

"Well, at least they're rewarding us for each round," James spoke after a brief silence. "This showed up at the top of the tower after Tuck smashed that last rat." James held out another drop box prize. "Who wants the honors?"

Tuck, as usual, wasn't having any of it, "Can we just agree that whoever gets it opens it?"

"Yes, *Surge!*" Will's eyes lit up with enjoyment as he repeated the nickname. "But can you let the rest of us have some fun before you go all commando?"

Tuck knew when he was on a losing path, so he shut his mouth and waited for James to open the box. James seemed to prolong the moment, letting the comment sink in, and Tuck definitely felt it.

New Devices Detected - Energy Signature Implants (x5)

Rare

These cutting-edge eye modifications seamlessly integrate with your Nexabot. Once equipped, they grant you the ability to perceive the energy signatures of those around you. The closer the energy source, the more finely tuned the signature appears. Additionally, these implants can detect surges in signatures, potentially alerting you to impending attacks. Apply a single drop of liquid from the provided bottle into your eye to activate this extraordinary enhancement.

"Oh my!" the Nexs collectively gasped in everyone's heads.

"Explain, Nex," Emy said with playful irritation, knowing Nex wanted to elaborate further on the item.

"Of course! These are amazing!" Nex exclaimed with enthusiasm as the team passed around the eye drops. *"I haven't heard of any early prize drops provided by the System to give items like this. Based on my integrations with Trish and Frank's Nexabots, these items ran very high on their 'must-haves' for future points purchases, but they were much too high of cost for one for each of you!"*

Will squirmed as James attempted to hold him steady with the bottle hovering over Will's eyes. "This is worse than rat attacks!"

"Didn't you ever need contacts?" James asked, forcefully pulling Will's eyelids back.

"Yes, but the doctor's assistant couldn't manage to get them in," Will replied while wincing.

"I guess it now makes sense that you were a cornerback and not a wide receiver," Tuck jabbed.

"It also explains why I can now see quite a bit better since the start of the Games. Nexy, you must be doing something in there," Will remarked, suddenly realizing.

"Of course, honey! It was silly of me, but I was implanted after your vision went bad, so I couldn't help much without drawing notice. Now, I just align the images for you," Nexy explained.

"Almost there... Got it!" James confirmed as he backed away from a blinking Will. "Awesome, right?"

"Oh man... It's like the mod gives sight to what I can feel. This should come in handy," Will exclaimed, looking at the differing energy signatures now exposed around each team member. The translucent, clear energy wove through their bodies, manifesting as a natural and captivating force in unique interactions. It flowed seamlessly, moving fluidly with each teammate, highlighting the dynamic power connections within each individual and the world around them.

Observing closely, he discerned Nadia's energy flowing in thick, radical patterns throughout her body, akin to a singular flow.

Tuck's energy differed; it formed a strong core yet radiated through large pulses across his body. Continuing around the team, he noticed that James also had a unique energy field—it expanded both inside and outside his body, forming a web of connections, attempting to merge with other energies around it.

But finally, when he looked at Emy's energy, it was equally distinct, modeling different pieces he noticed in the others, combining a large, bright core with radical internal patterns and expanding out externally simultaneously.

"Wait, what does my energy look like to all of you?" Will asked after analyzing the team's signatures.

"It's almost like a large cloud with a powerful energy core within it," Nadia attempted to describe it. "The cloud isn't as dense, but it reaches further than any of ours."

"Wicked..." Will smiled.

"All right, this is cool, but we do have another conversation topic," James interjected, trying to get back on track as the clock ticked. "Nadia, what the heck was coming out of your hand?"

"Oh," Nadia said, blushing as the team turned to her, realizing the significance of the previous events. Tuck and James had seen it, but Will and Emy were in the dark. "You mean these?" Nadia clenched her fists, and bonelike blades pierced through her skin, widening eyes across the group as they all collectively looked up her new skill:

Skill: Body Manipulation

Endows the user with the ability to transform or adjust internal structures, such as pathways, muscles, and bones. It opens up the possibility for significant modifications and improvements to the user's own body or that of others. (T)

"I-uh, well... I can modify my body. I've tried several things during intermission, but these are some of the easiest and most useful to manifest."

"Those aren't creepy at all," Will said, smirking as Nadia pulled back her hands. "No, no. Don't you dare hide those from us. Can we flash them at the next monster and scare them off?" Will gestured, earning a small smile and chuckle from Nadia.

"What else can you do?" Emy spoke, ignoring Will.

"This is it, for now at least," Nadia replied, "but I've attempted other... things with little success. Williams believes harnessing my talents and energy control will take more time and practice."

"Sorry to put you on the spot, Nadia, but I figured everyone needed to know," James said, taking the pressure back off Nadia and looking around with a wry smile. "Now, after that first stage is done and we know our map, I think it's time we build a battle plan."

Collective laughter consumed the group, accompanied by a single groan from Will. "Now?"

"Why, yes," James replied, "we have an hour to map out every possible scenario." He paused, gesturing with a stick he'd picked up. "First, let's plan on leaving the gates open until we know what we're facing." James handed the writing stick over to Will.

△△△

"Well, I think that just about does it. All potential items mapped out," James said, looking at the large diagram now displayed across the dirt and sand mixture in front of them.

"It's too bad we probably won't be able to use any of this," James concluded. Another round of laughter ensued, and a moaning Will sprawled on the ground, stick still in hand as another prompt filled the team's vision.

Would you like to continue to Stage Two of the Trials?

"Yes"

......

Stage Two of the Trials will begin in 60 seconds.

......

Activating Arena in 3... 2... 1...

Within moments, the pounding noise and applause struck the team once again. Will was already up, activating his *Permafrost* moments after being sprawled across the dirt.

"Let's do this," James declared as the team rushed to their former positions. They all agreed to maintain what had worked before shifting again.

Stage Two Begins in 3... 2... 1...

Screams and screeches immediately echoed through the air as giant black hawk-sized creatures flocked into the room from all three entrances.

"**EVERYONE, BACK ON ME!**" James commanded as the birds soared over the courtyard walls, heading straight toward the Castle tower.

BOOM! The Castle rocked as multiple birds dive-bombed the tower from the air.

< Castle currently at 2% damage >

CHAPTER THIRTY-NINE

"True Champions can make any mission look effortless." – Tournament Director.

LEVEL THREE - STAGE TWO

Arrows, ice, fire, and electricity filled the air as the team attempted to halt the birds from taking down more of the Castle, but the large birds were just too agile. They could dodge with ease as the torrent of energy streams flew past them.

"They are too fast! Everyone to the top of the stairs. We need to protect the Castle!" James called out as the team scrambled to send off more long-range attacks while backtracking to the stairs.

The birds were falling to the strikes, but not at a fast enough rate as hundreds of birds now circled the tower, honing in on the tall structure.

James did a quick scan of the birds in flight.

Siegebeak: Level 4

Renowned for its blistering speed, this formidable avian species stands an impressive half-meter tall and is a blur in flight. They can reach velocities that challenge the eye's ability to follow. Their most distinctive feature, however, is their robust, pointed beak, evolved specifically for impact. Siegebeaks use their beaks like battering rams, slamming into structures with astonishing force.

BOOM! BOOM! Two more birds struck the tower, sending crumbling stone debris to the ground.

< Castle currently at 5% damage >

"James, we need your shields. Hold your fire until we have a plan," Nadia commanded, taking in the scene as she ascended the stairs, now standing shoulder-to-shoulder with James.

Nadia addressed the others, "Will, prioritize defense alongside James." As the remaining trio crested the stairs and joined them on the balcony, she continued, "Emy, Tuck, stay on the offensive."

On the command, Emy and Tuck continued their assault on the sky, a frenzy of lightning and flames swirling together.

Emy pushed inward as she once again attempted to combine her **Disintegration** and **Targeted Fusion** skills across the area, much like when she faced James's **Energy Blocking Field**. Just like in the arena, mini-voids appeared, shaped by fire. These voids scattered across the arena as darkness and fire consumed the area.

< Skill Identified – Emy – Umbral Void Blaze >

The glowing fire infernos tore through the atmosphere, creating vacuums that devoured any energy in their path. Countless birds plummeted, victims of the aerial onslaught's indiscriminate fury.

< Level Up! Emy is now a level 9 Generalist >

James took a brief glance at the notification as black swirls surrounded the area.

Skill: Umbral Void Blaze
Grants the user the power to use fire as a catalyst for the destruction of matter, creating miniature void holes of annihilation. (AOE)

"So that's what she used on me in the training arena..." James muttered in disbelief at the skillsets Emy had started developing. He then refocused on the battle at hand.

The Siegebeak ranks dwindled, yet their relentless assault on the tower persisted. Three more birds broke away from the flock, their beady eyes fixed on the tower.

SLAM! This time, James was ready, no longer relying on his usual dome-shaped shield. Instead, he channeled his energy, creating a focused *Energy Blocking Field* against the tower, absorbing the birds' blows on contact.

< Level Up! James is now a level 6 Catalyst >

Beside him, Nadia sprang into action. As the downed birds plummeted, she sliced through them with precision, ensuring they wouldn't rise again.

Emy observed the dwindling number of birds attacking in isolated groups and attempted to adjust her tactics. Her area-of-effect attacks shifted to more *Targeted Fusion* blasts, but the agile birds proved elusive.

"James," Emy said, "we need to switch it up again. Work with Tuck; he might be able to electrify your arrows." She retreated to the Castle's diminishing wall, her gaze fixed on the circling bird threat, and immediately used *Disintegration* as a shield against a striking bird.

Tuck spoke as James neared him, "My *Ion Storm* is too scattered to do significant damage. If you can get your arrows close enough, I can expand their impact."

"Worth a shot," James replied, adjusting his bow, suddenly realizing the unintended pun in his words.

"*Literally!*" Will shouted, still focused on the descending birds. He erected ice walls one after another, disrupting their flight path.

"On my mark," James moved on. "I'll target the largest remaining packs first."

With a nod from Tuck, James released his first metal-piercing arrow at a trio of circling birds. Lightning followed its trajectory, striking next to the flock and igniting the birds, sending them tumbling.

< Skill Identified – Tuck – Lightning Bolt >

James brought up Tuck's new skill:

Skill: Lightning Bolt
Equips the user with the ability to guide electrons within the atmosphere towards a specific point. This is particularly effective with metal-based objects, but the flow of electrons can be further enhanced when interacting with items that share similar power characteristics. (R + Metal)

Tuck and James grinned as they continued electrifying arrows, thinning the pack until only one bird remained.

"Wait!" Will interjected, a mini-ice shard forming in his hand. "Never waste a practice opportunity, right?"

"Care to bet on it?" Tuck turned to watch Will aim at the bird.

"I have confidence, but not enough to chance another note-taking session… No offense, James." Will smirked.

Will took a deep breath, tracking the bird's frantic flight with an index finger. With focused willpower, he propelled the mini-ice shard toward the final airborne foe.

POP! The bird was caught and tumbled to the ground.

< Level up! Will is now a Level 8 Condenser >

Will swiveled toward Tuck, his finger still extended. "Now that is what I call a finger gun," he quipped, smirking. He playfully blew on his index finger, then mimicked holstering his hand in the nearest pocket.

Tuck responded with a grunt, grumbling, "You should have taken the bet."

HAWKWARD! 87 POINTS!

······

STAGE TWO is now COMPLETE!

......

You have one hour to regroup and prepare for the next stage.

"**MIGHTY-EAGLES, MIGHTY-EAGLES!**" the crowd yelled in unison, shouting at the group of five. Suddenly, they were acutely aware of the audience's presence once more. They allowed themselves to soak in the moment before the screams once again abruptly cut off.

"Yeehaw! Now, that was some fun," Will exclaimed, maintaining his cowboy persona a tad longer. His words shattered the silence that had enveloped the air as the crowd dispersed. The group's reactions ranged from amusement to sheer exhaustion.

His voice tinged with nostalgia, James said, "You know what? I felt like a 7-year-old playing bird hunter all over again." James glanced at Will with a smirk. "But I *reckon* this stage might be our last hurrah for experiencing some fun." He turned abruptly, drawn by the familiar sound of a box being unwrapped.

Tuck wasted no time tearing into this stage's drop box, evoking Will to interject in his best cowboy drawl, "Hold your horses there, partner!"

Nadia, quick-witted, joked, "Looks like he caught a sudden *surge* of excitement to unwrap that present!" Will stared at her, eyes wide with both amusement and pride.

"Hot diggity dog! Nadia scores 2 points!" Will beamed while Tuck sighed, unable to navigate a prize opening without some ribbing from the team.

New Device Detected - Skyward Whistle

Rare

A wooden whistle surface inscribed with ancient symbols. When activated, it emits a piercing, high-pitched noise that reverberates through the air. In response, a frenzied horde of ranged animals and monsters converges upon the whistle's location, their eyes wild and their claws ready for battle. Those who wield this whistle must brace themselves for an immediate onslaught, for its call is both a beacon and a warning.

"Sounds like it does the same thing as fresh food does to Frank in the kitchen back at the Hangar," Will jested and then looked up at the vast expanse of sky. "Sorry, Frank, not as funny without you here. Hopefully, you can re-play this joke later."

CHAPTER FORTY

"There is always something or someone out there that can counter your skills. Work harder." – Coach Williams.

LEVEL THREE

"Sorry, Team. I wasn't much help on that one," Nadia began, her gaze sweeping across the faces of her fellow team members. "It looks like I need to figure out something for ranged attacks."

Everyone shifted, ready to voice their thoughts, but Tuck was the first to comment, "We all signed up for this event as a team. You've got nothing to apologize for. Teams share weaknesses and strengths. And while we might need something different down the line, we just proved we have plenty of ranged prowess for now."

The words hung in the air, unspoken implications echoing silently. They all knew what lay ahead—the inevitable need for a healer. And that talent, they recognized, would save them more than any long-range attack ever could.

"We never discussed this, but now may be the opportune time. Let's talk about team name dynamics. Should we create a dance or a battle cry?" Will continued, his eyes alight with enthusiasm, attempting to break the sober conversation. "Like, do I need to squawk like those birds?"

The team sat in stunned silence, caught off guard by Will's sudden change of topic. "You know, Mighty Eagles?" Will grinned. "How the heck do we capture the essence of what it means to be team bird?"

Nex couldn't contain their excitement any longer, "*Oh. Oh. Oh! I've been waiting for you to bring this up! Permission to give guidance?*"

Emy's matter-of-fact tone was clear, "Nex, you never need permission to speak. You are one of us—heck, you are ALL of us."

Nex's energy bubbled over, "*Okay, hear me out—I've got LOTS of ideas. First one! No more of those dumb human knuckle bumps. Next time, stick out your thumbs and interlock them like an eagle would!*"

Silence settled over the team, but Nex interpreted it as encouragement to continue, "*And before battles, we need to start interlocking arms—symbolize nest building among the group! Showcasing our combined efforts.*"

Emy hesitated. "Hey, uh, Nex? When I said you have permission always to speak, I may have to take that back."

Nex sounded confused, "*Wait, what?*"

Emy's smile returned. "Oh, nothing, Nex. I think those are great ideas. I nominate Will to put them into action." She resisted the urge to deflate her new companion.

Would you like to continue to Stage Three of the Trials?

"Yes"

......

Stage Three of the Trials will begin in 60 seconds.

......

Activating Arena in 3... 2... 1...

"There's no time like the present," Will declared, his voice filling the area. "Huddle up, everyone." The fans materialized as if summoned by his words, and their new voices rang out from the stands. The arena was once again filled to the brim with life.

"Arms in," Will continued, the team gathering around him. "Now, grab the arm of the person next to you."

"Will, we need to move into formation," James interjected, but Will held up a hand. Undeterred, everyone followed suit, creating a weave of hands that formed a pentagon-like circle in the middle.

"Fly as one," Will spoke with unusual candor, his eyes locking onto each teammate. "Succeed as one."

"You've got to be kidding me," Tuck muttered as the clock ticked. Adrenaline once again surged as everyone rushed to their places. The three gates, this time, were held open, anticipation hanging thick in the air.

Stage Three Begins in 3... 2... 1...

As the arena fell silent again, a new sound emerged. Faint taps reverberated across the vast expanse, drawing the team's attention to the walkways. The taps intensified, rapid and insistent, until they crescendoed into a cacophony. Emerging from the void within Will's segment, a meter-tall black spider materialized, its eight legs moving with eerie precision. The creature was as dark as night, with a crimson marking adorning its belly.

"This is my worst nightmare," Will's voice quivered as frost encased his body.

"Scanning now," James called out. The group assumed defensive stances, ready for any sudden movements.

Widow's Blast: Level 5

It prowls in the shadowed veil of night—a creature with a body as dark as the abyss. Its spindly legs, reminiscent of earthly spiders, propel it silently through the darkness.

A sinister red emblem graces its belly, mirroring the markings of a local arachnid. But beware, for when this beast strikes, it unleashes a devastating blast with a two-meter radius, leaving naught but chaos in its wake.

"Team, these new energy signatures scare the heck out of me. It's like the energy within them is bubbling," James yelled out from above. "Keep your distance. Will, the first strike is on your mark. Everyone be ready to adapt."

As more creatures emerged from the voids, Will fostered a medium-sized ice shard from his forearm, focusing on a solitary target. *"Here we go again,"* he murmured, propelling the shard directly at the abdomen of the first spider. The ice sliced through the spider without a sound, killing it instantly. The lifeless arachnid lay prone on the pathway, yet its residual energy continued to churn. "Well, this may be easier than we..." Will's words were cut short by an explosion that rocked his pathway—**BOOM!**

The sudden blast stemming from the dead creature's body reverberated across the area, sending spiders scurrying in every direction along the path.

"They're going under the walkways!" Tuck exclaimed, unleashing an ***Ion Storm*** along his path.

"Close the gates!" James's voice screamed over the noise. "Target anything you can see. Hit them before they breach the gates!"

BOOM! BOOM! BOOM! Noise and light seemed to pulse, engulfing the entire arena with a symphony of luminescence and sound as spiders relentlessly swarmed toward the gates.

"Will! Focus on the ones heading under the walkways!" Emy's voice carried desperation as she lost sight of numerous Widows.

Another explosion—Tuck's gate shattered as a spider reached the barrier, detonating upon contact with the massive wooden and metal gate.

A shiver ran down James's spine as he soon witnessed a

spider scaling the outer wall. It must have scaled the wall from underneath.

"They're breaching! Fall back to the middle walls!" James commanded with urgency. Spiders had now vaulted over the outer wall and infiltrated the courtyard.

"Will! Behind you!" Nadia's scream cut through the chaos as a Widow lunged toward him. Encased in ice, Will unleashed a flurry of **Cryostrikes** at the advancing spiders on the walkway but didn't see the approaching spider behind him. Reacting swiftly, James sent a piercing arrow, striking the creature down before it struck Will.

"Move, Will!" James's voice echoed urgently as the residual energy churned within the lifeless spider.

BOOM! Will flung himself away from the downed arachnid, but the explosion caught him a split second too soon.

< Will's health is at 38% >

Though Will's energy shield absorbed most of the blast, the explosion still tore through his body. His left arm hung limp from the shoulder, and his face bore multiple lacerations.

"Cover me!" Nadia's cry rang out as a fresh wave of arrows found their mark, dispatching the remaining nearby spiders.

Nadia tapped into her **Vitalize** skill as she moved amidst the exploding forms of spiders, reaching Will as James activated an additional **Empower** skill on her.

< Nadia is boosted by 30% >

With a burst of healing energy, Nadia created an aura field around them, building up her current **Vitalize** skill to expand into an AOE skill.

< Will's regeneration is now operating at 20% per minute >

< Level Up! Nadia is now a level 6 Cellulator >

"Nadia, get Will back to the inner wall. Everyone, fall back! Prioritize your safety over the Castle," James commanded, sprinting down the stairs to join the team at the inner wall.

BOOM! BOOM! The surrounding walls breached from all sides as spiders flooded in. The lower walls crumbled, revealing gaping holes at their base as rock flew from the explosions.

< *Castle currently at 23% damage* >

Tuck gripped his *Warhammer* and stepped away from his gate. His swings calculated the trajectory of the spiders, sending the arachnids flying away from the courtyard.

Emy, too, retreated from her gate. She unleashed fireball blasts at the spiders while maintaining a *Disintegration* shield to absorb the energy and shrapnel from the explosions.

Now backed into the side of the Castle, the five heroes united, working together to shield each other from the cacophony of erupting blasts as Nadia's aura soon covered them all.

< *Full team regeneration is now operating at 10% per minute* >

James, positioning himself next to Will and Nadia, erected a protective field around the team. At the same time, Emy and Tuck stood just outside, maintaining their rhythm of damage dealt to the incoming horde.

< *Level Up! James is now a level 7 Catalyst* >

< *Castle currently at 47% damage* >

Tuck and Emy shouted out warnings, their voices urgent amidst the bedlam. They skillfully used James's shield as a refuge when danger drew near. Meanwhile, Will held his ground within the protective barrier, maintaining a barrage of *Cryostrikes* upon the walls using his remaining arm. The spider ranks dwindled, many sacrificing themselves to dismantle their surroundings.

With one final heave of Tuck's *Warhammer* and an explosion resonating from the Castle wall behind them, the scurrying of spider legs ceased, and the crowd's voices reemerged.

EIGHT LEGGED DYNOMITE! 95 POINTS!

STAGE THREE is now COMPLETE!

......

You have one hour to regroup and prepare for the next stage.

"You know, I thought an hour was almost too long of a break," Will forced a chuckle after his words, his left arm still hanging at his side. The pain had vanished, and his body had healed, but the limb hadn't reattached.

"I think I can help there," Nadia said, smiling and rushing to Will. "It will just take more time. I'm sorry I couldn't assist more during battle."

As Nadia assessed Will's limp arm, the others surveyed the scene, weighing the stage's final damage.

< Castle currently at 54% damage >

"Well, that went from good to shit fast," James's candidly remarked, taking in the gravity of the situation at hand.

CHAPTER FORTY-ONE

"The future can be daunting. Every path to success comes with steps. Focus on what's next and stay present." – Beacon, Former Champion.

LEVEL THREE

Nadia & Will

Will and Nadia now sat next to each other on the crumbling Castle stairs as Nadia clasped Will's shoulder and left hand with both of hers. Gently, she channeled energy from a single focal point near his neck, directing it toward the natural energies within his arm. As her focus intensified, she pinpointed the damaged areas, using a touch of her own ***Vitalize*** skill to purge the dead cells and initiate a fresh start. Once the remaining arm was fully restored, she tapped into her ***Body Manipulation*** skill, meticulously reconstructing the missing cells. Drawing from her intimate knowledge of her body and connecting with Will's intact arm, she replicated and rebuilt what had once existed. It wasn't a creation from scratch but a response to the body's innate yearning for wholeness, guided by an intuitive force.

< Level Up! Nadia is now a level 7 Cellulator >

"Wow," Will stated, his gaze fixed on his arm as it reformed itself, "that is incredible."

Still immersed in deep concentration while reconstructing Will's arm, Nadia spoke softly, "You know, I never imagined myself taking care of anyone again."

"What do you mean?" Will encouraged Nadia to continue. "You've never told me much about your background."

"You know it's not one that I really want to share," Nadia replied with a hint of remorse.

"Try," Will urged, his tone supportive. He understood that Nadia needed to confide in someone, even if it did come with him nearly getting his arm blown off.

".... My family—well, all Filipino families—push their kids to work in the medical fields, primarily in nursing. I'm unsure if it's the saving people part or simply the stability of a job where hard work pays off and you're helping others as a side benefit."

Nadia continued, her voice carrying the weight of her experiences, "My family values diligence, putting your head down, and excelling at what you do. If you fail, you're not on the right path. I told Trish this earlier, but I didn't mention that my family never really supported my sports endeavors, but they absolutely loved that I was studying to become a nurse. Every party, every interaction with a Tito, Tita, Lola, Lolo—before even saying hello—it was always about me pursuing nursing."

Will remained silent, understanding Nadia's struggle. He trusted that she would share what she needed to, and he kept his focus on her.

"I poured everything into nursing. Did you know you need close to a 4.0 GPA at the University of Nevada to enroll in their nursing program? If you get a B and want to enter the nursing program, you must retake the class—even if it has nothing to do with medicine." Nadia sighed. "I only had to retake one class, and when I applied and got accepted, my family threw the biggest celebration. Their daughter was joining the prestigious program."

"So, what happened?" Will questioned, hoping to encourage Nadia to share the next part of her story, though her apprehension was visible.

"During the program, nursing students participate in clinicals at local hospitals. Each student is assigned to a registered nurse who acts as a preceptor, guiding them through nurse duties," Nadia began, her voice tinged with sadness and a hint of anger—which surprised Will. "It was my second day of clinicals, and my preceptor and I were dealing with a challenging patient. She had been attending to this man for five days, so my preceptor pushed me to take on more responsibility with him, hoping to avoid direct interaction herself."

"That's not right," Will interjected, sensing the source of Nadia's anger.

"No, it wasn't," Nadia concurred, "but I didn't mind. Difficult patients were part of the job, and I was willing to assist. When it was time for the patient's medication, my preceptor handed me the pills, and I carried them to his bedside. Before I could inspect them, he snatched the medication and swallowed it. I didn't think much of it until the bedside alarm blared, and the man convulsed on the ground."

Nadia continued, her words rapid, "We'd administered the wrong medication—a simple antibiotic—and he had an anaphylactic reaction. The entire medical team rushed in, and I was pushed aside as they intubated him. Fortunately, he survived, but he sued the hospital."

"That shouldn't be on you, right?" Will urged.

"The preceptor never admitted any wrongdoing. Instead, she blamed me for grabbing the wrong medication. Since I was the only one in the room, I bore the blame, with the primary nurse receiving only a slap on the wrist. After a day in court, the hospital settled, but I was removed from the program and had to leave the school."

"That's awful, Nadia." Will looked on with remorse as Nadia finished on his arm and pulled back her hands.

"The worst part is that my parents stopped talking to me. Once proud, they now look at me with shame. I haven't talked to them since the start of the school year." Nadia sighed. "It may sound dumb, but knowing they supported me gave me purpose, and when that went away, I struggled."

Nadia then looked at Will for the first time. "But these Games have given me a new hope. A reason to push myself again."

"I think it sounds like fate," Will said, looking down at his arm and triggering his frost to cover himself, ensuring it still worked the same. "And I don't know what we would do without you."

△△△

Full Team

"You're looking better than ever!" James exclaimed as Will and Nadia stepped out from the Castle staircase.

Will grinned. "Feeling good as new with Nurse Nadia here," he said, winking towards Nadia.

Nadia noticed the Stage Three drop box in Tuck's hands. "Did we miss the gift unwrapping?" she asked.

This time, Emy replied, "No." A smile spread across her face. "Tuck here has been a real surge protector for that thing."

Tuck's arms, which had been holding the box aloft, dropped to his sides in mock disgust as he heard Emy's playful comment.

"Really? Have you been thinking about that this whole time?" Tuck questioned Emy.

She grinned, and a chorus of chuckles resounded around the group. "Maybe?" Emy said. "Come on, Tuck, just open it already!" Another small laugh escaped her after the response.

New Devices Detected - Energy Trigger (20)
Rare
The device allows users to set up predefined energy events and hold them in stasis until specific triggering conditions occur. These conditions can include set timers, proximity detection, or similar events. Once triggered, the stored energy promptly springs into action.

"Well, that introduces another element for us to incorporate into our plans," James remarked after reviewing the description. "But I believe we need to address one more thing before we continue planning."

James took a moment to survey everyone. "Should we continue?"

Emy started, considering her friend, "Will, you've just had your arm blasted off. I think you should go first…"

Will's tone was resolute. "Whatever decision we make must be unanimous," he asserted. "Yes, I took a hit last stage, but it could have been any of us. And you all heard what Williams said. Do we even have a choice?"

James responded in a non-argumentative manner, "We always have options."

Will paused. "No. I don't think we do—at least not in the upcoming rounds." His gaze swept the group. "Sure, there might be another team out there better than us. But I refuse to believe that. We can't afford to. If we don't give everything to strengthen ourselves, we risk losing everything… and everyone."

Emy softly repeated Williams' statement: "Show that you're worth protecting or become heroes capable of self-defense."

"Exactly," Will concluded, meeting the team's nods of agreement. "We can't quit."

CHAPTER FORTY-TWO

"Innovation and creativity are the cornerstones of success. The System is designed to cultivate these essential traits in our future heroes." – Coach Williams.

SYSTEM GAMES HEADQUARTERS

"Shukar, how are the Trials progressing? Anything we need to report up the chain?" Viggo, the Games Director, addressed his top employee.

"Would you like the good news or bad news first?" Shukar spoke hesitantly.

"Let's get the good news going; your tone scares me," Viggo replied.

"The initial three stages have been completed, sir. The Games have seen a 9% increase in attendance compared to previous tournaments. We are preparing to broadcast the Games to local viewers in major hubs across the galaxy, such as Valerian and the Ring of Radiance, and on numerous smaller planets. However, at this stage, we are using more direct methods."

"That's excellent. Every planet has to begin its integration journey somewhere."

Shukar continued, "We're witnessing some incredibly gifted individuals from these clusters and beyond. The talent pool grows stronger with each tournament, and this year is no different. Our expanded coaching programs deserve some credit; our team-based Champions are thriving under pressure."

"Good to know our incentive programs in recent years have enhanced our pool of hero applicants," Viggo said, shifting his posture slightly, preparing for what was to come. "All right, Shukar, let's get to it. Bad news, please."

Shukar redirected his tone, "We foresee some challenges in our fan dynamics. This last stage may have been the deadliest in game history."

"Go on," Viggo pressed.

"Well, Sir, the combination of an early elimination stage with certain hero groups lacking proper shielding capabilities made this one, uh, explosive," Shukar continued. "Our early-stage fans aren't typically prepared for eliminations as much as the later-stage fans. The stage three fans got more than they bargained for in some of the viewings."

"I see. That's a bit unlike the System, especially this early in the Trials," Viggo observed with certainty.

"Agreed, sir. It was significant enough to prompt a reevaluation of our system integration points for dynamic event changes, leading us to more news..."

"Shukar, you already have my attention. Out with it, please."

"We now have insights into the later rounds," Shukar sighed. "Reports indicate a medium to high-level D-Class beast set for the final stage, based on team size weighting."

"High D-Class possibility? Do we even have Champions within the D-Class yet?"

"Yes, sir. Our top remaining 0.01% is now within the D-Class. This aligns with my earlier statement that our heroes this round appear more gifted, and it seems the System is adjusting accordingly."

"Let's get ready to inform our audiences and mitigate the situation. At the very least, we should be transparent with our fans about their involvement. I'll personally notify the board about these missteps," Viggo affirmed.

△△△

LEVEL THREE - STAGE FOUR

The team assumed their familiar formation, bracing themselves for the next challenge the Trials would hurl their way. Unlike previous rounds, they found themselves within a crumbling domain. The battered and worn tower teetered precariously at 54% damage—a structure on the brink of collapse.

James, perched on the top balcony, confronted a formidable challenge. Though partially intact, the stairs leading to the balcony granted him access to the strategic vantage point. However, the once-sturdy scaffolding now revealed gaping chasms, remnants opposite where their last stand had taken place. These gaps bore witness to the damage inflicted upon the least protected areas. Undeterred, James leaped across these treacherous gaps, diligently fulfilling his role as the primary lookout.

In the courtyard, Tuck stood sentinel by the sole remaining gate. The team had repositioned themselves, with Tuck now guarding the gate Emy had once defended. The other two gates lay shattered, their remnants strewn across the ground—a testament to the explosions that had targeted them in the previous round. Considering Tuck's modest shielding capabilities and the diminished necessity for visibility in his ranged attacks, the unanimous decision was for him to secure the only intact gateway. Meanwhile, Will and Emy stood ready to deploy their shielding skills.

Stage Four Begins in 3... 2... 1...

As soon as the time clicked down, the team immediately heard a humming noise coming from the entrances. The noise blossomed into that of a small engine as the humming grew.

A small flying creature popped out of the void nearest to Emy, mini bow and arrow in hand, as its wings beat and hovered in the air.

Sprite Archer: Level 3

Resembling hummingbirds in size, Sprites display iridescent hues that glisten as their delicate wings flit in harmony with a melodious hum. These diminutive creatures wield various talents, but their unyielding resolve to face any adversary sets them apart. Despite their small stature, their power is formidable.

Like the preceding stages, the Sprites multiplied, now swirling and encircling the tower in all directions. Although the initial scan revealed an Archer Sprite, their abilities ranged from fire, ice, and air wielders to those skilled with blades and weaponry.

"I don't think we can wait any longer," James declared, directing the team into action. The sky ignited with brilliance as Tuck summoned his **Ion storm**, ensnaring the entire arena. Lightning crackled and popped, electricity tearing through the ranks of creatures. However, instead of plummeting to the ground, the targeted Sprites vanished, only to reappear in different areas.

Perplexed, James, Emy, and Will launched their strikes to the skies. **Alchemarrows**, fireballs, and **Cryostrikes** struck the Sprites, resulting in more disappearances with reemergence. It was then, as if choreographed, that all Sprites raised their weapons or hands, and within moments, a destructive wall of ranged attacks descended upon the dismantled Castle from all directions.

"Oh no," James murmured, contemplating the challenging path ahead. Emy and Will scrambled to support, erecting **Disintegration** shields and ice walls to protect the upper balcony. Unfortunately, their efforts were too late and too distant from the direction of the Sprite offensive.

James, positioned closest to the target, erected a massive

energy barrier, shielding himself and his side of the tower from the onslaught of fire, ice, and arrows, which were now moments away from striking.

TING, TING, TING! The expected chorus of explosions and metal strikes against the wall never materialized. Instead, only a few arrow strikes caused further destruction to the already beleaguered tower.

< Castle currently at 55% damage >

"1%?" James checked his mission status immediately.

"There's something amiss here, team," James directed his companions. They all seemed to share the same realization.

Will, about to respond, was interrupted as a Sprite wielding a dagger hurtled toward him from the skies. Will deftly dodged the initial strike, then retaliated with an ice-bladed hand. The creature vanished upon impact.

"They're illusions," Will coughed, catching his breath after the sudden attack.

"But they can't all be illusions," James countered. The Sprites surrounding them prepared for another assault wave toward the Castle.

Nadia's voice rang out urgently: "Look for disparate energy signals!" She circled the courtyard, eyes scanning as many Sprites as possible. "I've found a few anomalies, but they keep shifting!"

TING. TING. BOOM! Another wave tore through the sky as James desperately attempted another shield wall to block the relentless rampage.

< Castle currently at 56% damage >

"I see it too!" Emy's voice rang out, confirming Nadia's sentiment. "Some signatures have stronger cores. But every time I target one with a fireball, they shift. We need a distraction."

"Nadia, can you call them out somehow?" James's voice called out over comms, an idea sparking to life as another wave threatened to breach the Castle walls.

"On it," Nadia said as she moved into action. She scanned the battlefield, her eyes locking onto a rogue energy signature. "Will, right above you. Moving into position."

Will, Tuck, and Emy mirrored James's movements, launching attacks in all directions except directly above Will. As the next fiery wave surged, the rogue energy signal Sprite locked onto the Castle again. But this time, a floating bone dagger swooped in, intercepting its path.

"Got it!" Nadia's voice came through the comms from her now hovering position. She'd activated her **Ghostwalkers** for the first time while simultaneously engaging her **Phantom Veil** to remain unseen. The leader Sprite plummeted to the ground, defeated—a third of the total Sprites disappearing.

Phantom Sprite: Level 8

An enigmatic being exists on the cusp between reality and illusion. With the ability to conjure potent illusions, it weaves intricate mirages that deceive the senses. But its true mastery lies in its unique power: the ability to seamlessly transfer its consciousness into the illusions it creates. In battle, it dances across the shifting veils of its own making, a phantom figure that sows chaos and confusion among its foes.

"Looks like we still have a few more," James warned. "Nadia, we go on you."

The illusions seemed to shift as the first real Sprite met its demise, realizing one of them was caught. Energy signatures danced; the remaining Phantom Sprites were desperate to remain hidden within their illusions.

"I've got only two minutes left in these boots before a recharge," Nadia announced. "Everyone, call out when you spot one. But keep your find discreet."

A minute ticked by before the team identified the next stagnant source. Nadia thrust her bone blades at the distracted creature—a fire welder this time. Once again, the field of illusion split in half. "One more!" Nadia's voice carried urgency as she lost altitude, slowly descending to the ground. "Energy is depleted. My boots need time to recharge," Nadia spoke with concern as the Sprites continued their circling dance, now spreading out like startled fireflies.

"We need to drive them closer together!" Emy's voice carried urgency. "Tuck, focus your Storm across the walkway, and I'll do the same. Will and James, get ready."

Lightning and fire clashed once more, cleaving the arena into segments. The Sprites, undeterred, reconstituted themselves within the sole safe segment available. Yet this time, a frigid frost surged forth, encasing the final segment in ice upon contact. Wings flapped frantically as the Sprites struggled to escape their frozen prison. Amidst the chaotic tempest, a solitary arrow streaked through the air, finding its mark with impressive precision. The struck Sprite plunged into the abyss, its demise dispersing the remaining winged illusions.

PIXILATED! 93 POINTS!

STAGE FOUR is now COMPLETE!

......

You have one hour to regroup and prepare for the next stage.

"Nice shot, James!" Emy's voice rang out amidst the deafening crowd, their joy evident in the intensity of their cheers. Catching their breath, the team looked to assess the aftermath of the relentless attacks.

< Castle currently at 63% damage >

James, still catching his breath, managed a wry smile. "I'm just relieved the plan worked," he admitted, wiping sweat from his brow. "But I'm not sure how much more punishment this Castle can take." The ground trembled beneath him as a large section of the walkway crumbled, sending James tumbling from his perch. He plummeted a story down, landing hard on his back.

< Castle currently at 68% damage >

Emy and Nadia rushed to his side. "James! Are you okay?" they both said in unison, concern showing on their faces. James pushed himself up, wincing. "I'm fine," he assured them, feeling a healing surge course through his body from Nadia.

"Dude," Will spoke, a playful glint in his eye, "are you trying to destroy our Castle yourself?" James grimaced, dusting off his clothes. "If you think I did that intentionally, you're out of your mind." He surveyed the half-ruined overlook, the remnants of their once-advantageous position.

"At least," Will started smiling, "the fans got a front-row seat to your fall before they dispersed." James's expression shifted from relief to horror.

"What? No..." he stammered, fear creeping into his eyes. Will pressed, a mischievous grin playing on his lips. "I'd hate to think they'd come up with a nickname for something like that..."

CHAPTER FORTY-THREE

"The mightiest trees often crumble with the greatest force." – Titan, Former Champion.

TRIARA CLUSTER - PLANET BETA
LEVEL THREE - STAGE FOUR

Nea always sensed that her life was anything but ordinary. Growing up on the second habitable planet within the Triara cluster, she marveled at the diversity of life across the Cosmos. Her civilization stretched across 20 planets, united under the Ring of Radiance, also known as the Halo. Yet, Nea couldn't shake the feeling that there was more beyond their known boundaries.

Light had a peculiar affinity for Nea. No matter the occasion or setting, it would shift toward her, creating dazzling refractions and reflections. Others noticed, but no one could explain the phenomenon. Nea was said to have been "kissed by the sun" as a baby, always having a golden skin glow, freckles, and darker hair that seemed to sparkle. Her light brown eyes could ignite a room, despite having to wear eye coverings indoors to shield herself from its persistent glow, much to the amusement of her heckling classmates. Just as her peers found humor in her predicament, attempting to explain this unusual condition to a doctor during a routine check-up proved to be an exercise in futility.

Everything changed with the System event. Nea impulsively chose "Yes" to participate in a tournament spanning the galaxy. Her unique ability? Manipulating light, a talent aptly named Prismatic. Suddenly, everything in her life made sense.

A mentor at her preparatory academy had taken her and two other students with similar experiences under their guidance. Her former classmates, once considered outcasts, were now her teammates, each with intriguing abilities. Cass, with her striking blue hair and a reputation for incidents with sharp objects, now brandished dual reflective blades that could generate an energy vortex. Kip, the school's renowned musclebound brawler with a jagged scar running from his left cheek to his jawline, could absorb and strategically release energy. Nea took pride in their combined strength as they eased their way through two system-based levels.

Fast forward to the present. Nea and her team stood as the epitome of warriors—beauty, bronze, and talent unseen for thousands of years. Shoulder to shoulder with her comrades, Nea stared down a horde of Sprites (or were they fairies?). Amidst the uproar, she experienced a moment of clarity, recognizing that her life had taken a turn for the better despite the looming threat in a coliseum with millions of fans cheering for her death or glory. Without uttering a word, the trio acted in harmony. Nea cast blinding, concentrated rays of light toward the levitating Sprites. Her teammates noted that the light waves passed through most of them, leaving light burns on a few phantoms who were the puppeteers of this illusion. In the blink of an eye, those marked by the burns were struck by reflective blade projectiles or blasted with concentrated energy. The spectacle concluded before the audience could fully comprehend the unfolding events.

△△△

EARTH - UNDISCLOSED
LEVEL THREE - STAGE FIVE

"Who's taking bets on James's new nickname?" Will joked as the team approached the drop box from the previous round.

"I'm starting to think that naming yourself early was one of your better ideas," James replied, a hint of worry in his voice.

"You're just now realizing that?" Will scoffed. "In a championship galaxy-wide game, and you thought you'd get away with just 'James?' How basic can you be?" Will added, a mischievous smile playing on his lips.

"Very basic," Emy joked, happily supporting James. She glanced around the team and noticed that Tuck seemed a bit off.

"Tuck, what's going on? Are you okay?" Emy asked with genuine concern.

Tuck remained silent, his gaze fixed on the drop box at their feet—the result of their successful previous stage.

"Wait, are you afraid to say something right now?" Emy chuckled, observing Will's face brimming with meddlesome satisfaction.

"Come on, Tuck!" Will reassured his friend, who maintained a deadpan expression. "We wouldn't dare make fun of you again. How many 'surge' jokes can there even be?"

James then spoke, his tone dripping with sarcasm, "Guys, this isn't brain surge-ry." He reached into the center of their now circle with a look of fake disgust and opened the box.

"Welp, congrats to you, Tuck; James has officially killed the joke," Will retorted as the group looked at the new item.

New Items Detected - Rootbound Seedlings (20)
Uncommon
A peculiar botanical creation that defies the ordinary. When these seeds are dropped or placed at the base of your feet, they sprout into a tangled weave of vines that attach to your body. This natural embrace lasts 30 minutes unless you decide to free yourself by cutting through the verdant bonds.

"These are unique," Nadia spoke, unsure of the award they had just received. "Nex, what do you think?"

"I think these are great! But yes, those are a bit unique. Think of these as items that will hold you in place, anywhere. My guess is that these may come in handy later," Nex stated.

"I am not one to turn down a gift," James said. "Nex is right; we probably will use them at some point. Come on, let's get ready for the next round." The team looked on at James with concern at his unusually unenthusiastic demeanor.

"You're nervous about the fans next round, huh?" Will spoke with a glimmer, understanding James's tone.

"Very much so."

△△△

Would you like to continue to Stage Five of the Trials?

"Yes"

......

Stage Five of the Trials will begin in 60 seconds.

......

Activating Arena in 3... 2... 1...

The arena ignited with life once more as the five heroes reconvened, forming a tight circle. New lights and beams danced around the arena, encircling the team while triumphant trumpets filled the room—a regal melody akin to what one might hear at a coronation.

"What the heck?" the team exclaimed, bewildered by the

unexpected light show. They strained to comprehend the spectacle as a voice boomed from the stands, and the lights converged directly on James.

Ladies and Gentlemen, may we introduce your Grace.

The crowd moved into a cacophony of shouting, their voices overpowering the announcement. The chaotic energy filled the arena, drowning out any other sound.

"Your Grace?" James murmured to himself, glancing at his teammates. Tuck and Nadia struggled to maintain their composure, their shoulders shaking with suppressed laughter. James avoided eye contact with Will and Emy, fearing their probable reactions.

"On me!" Will's face flushed crimson as he fought to regain his composure. "You know the drill."

The team linked arms, once again mimicking that of a nest. Will surveyed their faces, finally able to control his expression. His voice took on a theatrical tone.

"He is Beauty," Will declared, and the team's expressions merged into smiles. "He is Grace."

"Dude," James managed to utter, his teammates teetering on the brink of tears.

"Kidding. Sort of," Will shifted gears, adopting a more serious demeanor. "Okay, while that was **VERY** entertaining, we all know the System is about to throw something significant our way. Get ready." He paused, allowing everyone to refocus. "Fly as One."

"Succeed as One," the team spoke as one.

Stage Five Begins in 3... 2... 1...

The lights and noise abruptly ceased, replaced by a thunderous, guttural roar reverberating through the arena. Without warning, a giant foot descended upon the walkway closest to Tuck. The massive creature bent its head, emerging fully from the 3-meter void entrance. Its eyes were fixated, and saliva dripped from its lips as it stood towering over 4 meters tall. In its grasp, a massive stone club awaited its next move. Meanwhile, two more similar forms materialized, now positioned to face Emy and Will on their respective walkways.

Boulderbane Titan: Level 10

A colossal and hulking behemoth emerges—a living fusion of flab and knotted muscles. Its rough and mottled skin resembles ancient tree bark, and its eyes gleam with primal intelligence. Despite its brutish appearance, it moves with surprising agility, each step sending tremors through the earth. Its weapon of choice is a massive stone maul, worn smooth by countless battles.

The spectators in the stands gaped in astonishment as the three D-Class monsters unexpectedly burst onto the scene during the fifth stage of the Trials. But Tuck, oblivious to the crowd's reaction, focused solely on his new adversary with glee in his eyes at the seemingly straightforward battle. Determined to halt the troll-like creature's advance toward their crumbling Castle, Tuck vaulted to the center of the walkway. There, he slammed the base of his **Warhammer** into the ground, the weapon now humming with energy.

However, unbeknownst to Tuck, he wasn't the only hero facing this challenge head-on. On the opposing walkways, Will and Emy stood their ground, now positioned in the middle. From their outstretched hands, fire and ice ignited their bodies as they summoned their challengers for battle.

"Do they have a bet on this or something?" James spoke out, glancing over at Nadia. The two of them stood side by side in the courtyard, poised to offer immediate assistance to their teammates.

△△△

Tuck

Undeterred by the colossal creature before him, Tuck gripped his **Warhammer** with resolve. Closing the remaining gap between himself and the Titan, he stepped into the hulking beast's path.

The Titan shifted, its massive maul swinging in a horizontal arc—a test of Tuck's newfound weapon. Tuck intercepted the stone maul with precision, absorbing its energy without flinching. A smile tugged at his lips; he knew this battle might have taken a darker turn without the aid of Frank and Trish.

Before the Titan could strike again, Tuck twisted, driving his weapon into the creature's side. The tough skin yielded, but not enough to halt the beast entirely. Tuck wrenched the spike free, surging backward as the Titan launched a massive downward strike with its stone weapon.

As the creature's maul crashed into the ground, shaking the entire arena, Tuck seized the opportunity. He stepped onto the Titan's weapon, vaulting into the air with his own **Warhammer** drawn back. The spike gleamed as Tuck descended, aiming straight for the monster's head.

The giant shifted, narrowly avoiding a direct hit. Instead, Tuck's blade sank into the creature's shoulder blade. The Titan retaliated, flinging Tuck to the ground, his weapon still in its flesh.

Tuck seemed undisturbed by losing his weapon as he called out to his team, "Anyone need help?"

△△△

Emy

Emy stood, fire blazing from her hands, awaiting the creature's first move. The colossal Titan fixed its gaze upon her. To the beast, Emy appeared as nothing more than a weak obstacle—a mere annoyance in its inexorable path.

With a mighty grunt, the Titan launched itself at Emy. However, its eyes were not on her; they were fixed on the distant tower, a beacon of some unknown purpose. The ground trembled beneath its colossal weight as it closed the gap.

Now, steps from Emy, the creature's massive foot descended, but the earth seemed to yield beneath its weight, a hole forming as if the ground rebelled against the Titan's advance. The creature jerked, its momentum disrupted, and it tumbled forward.

Face-first, the colossal beast crashed into the ground, mere feet from Emy's position. The impact sent shockwaves through the arena, dust and debris swirling.

"Miss a step?" Emy asked, looking at the downed creature. Without hesitation, she unleashed fireballs upon the creature's head, eliminating it from the stage.

△△△

Will

Like Emy and Tuck, Will stood in the center of the walkway, **Permafrost** enveloping his body as he locked eyes with the colossal Titan.

"Your move," Will spoke in a low tone, observing the creature's calculated movements. The Monster began its deliberate advance, its massive club held casually to the side—a silent dare to Will.

Will held his ground, channeling his energy to create an icy walkway between himself and the approaching behemoth. The ice caused the creature to shift, momentarily unsteady as it tried to find purchase, digging its large toenails into the frozen surface and gaining immediate traction. The Titan's smirk seemed to mock Will's failed attempt.

"That's disgusting," Will muttered as the creature strutted toward him, poised to strike. Will focused, condensing the air around him. A wave of ***Cryostrikes*** shot toward the colossal face, but the Titan deflected them with its remaining hand and massive maul.

As the creature raised its weapon for a downward blow after blocking the ice, Will vanished. But in that fleeting moment, the colossal beast felt an ice blade slicing through its underbelly—a swift strike from an icy blur that slid through its legs.

Now positioned behind the creature, Will unleashed another wave of **Cryostrikes**, driving them into its resilient hide. The air reverberated with a growl of agony, but as the beast pivoted to confront him, its eyes soon rolled back as it collapsed towards Will. An **Alchemarrow** protruded from the back of its skull, and veins, pronounced with black from Nadia's **Affliction Surge** skill, pulsed ominously across its massive form.

"I totally had it," Will declared, catching his breath as Nadia materialized behind the downed Titan. "Yeah, but we couldn't let you guys have all the fun."

△△△

Tuck

"Waiting on you," the team responded abruptly to Tuck's open question directed at the broader group.

Tuck's smile waned as he heard his team's answer. Unwilling to accept that he was the last to bring down his Titan, he watched as the creature raged, Tuck's weapon still protruding from between its shoulder and neck.

Without hesitation, Tuck reached toward the sky. The atmosphere transformed with energy as a massive storm ignited overhead. Gathering his power, he channeled it into a devastating **Lightning Bolt** aimed directly at his **Warhammer**. The Titan remained rooted as the electric strike rushed through the weapon and into its body, detonating its internal organs. The last monster crumpled backward, defeated.

ASSWHOOP'N! 134 POINTS!

STAGE FIVE is now COMPLETE!

……

You have one hour to regroup and prepare for the next stage.

CHAPTER FORTY-FOUR

"The System's target success rate of those who pass the 6th stage of the Trials is set to 0.001%." – Games Division Data Scientist.

LEVEL THREE

Full Team

Tuck stood there, bewildered. The colossal Titan lay defeated at his feet, its once-mighty form now reduced to mist as the creature disappeared. "How the heck did everyone finish before me? I took it down in seconds."

"**GRACE! GRACE! WE LOVE YOU!**" the words chanted from a particularly vocal fan, their voice resounding with excitement. Tuck watched as James blushed, once again caught off guard by the realization of his new nickname.

Will sidled up to Tuck. "Firstly, Surge," he joked, "maybe spend less time on showboating and more on smashing." Will winked, then shifted his attention to James. "And second, who wants to address our Royal Highness here?"

James scoffed. "His Highness would like to speak first. Seriously, how did they even come up with that name? Am I really that bossy?"

A collective silence settled over the group. James clearly missed the references to his newfound moniker. Emy couldn't resist. "All right, James," she said, her laughter barely contained. "What's your last name?"

"Gray," James replied, still uncertain where this was headed.

Emy drew out the syllables, "GRAY...CE." She paused, letting it sink in. "And how would you describe the way your **Energy Blocking Field** affects others?"

James hesitated, then muttered, "I protect others from harm."

Emy leaned in. "Exactly. You might say others are 'saved by Grace.'"

Will, never one to miss a beat, took over, "Now, James, what would you NOT call someone who fell from the top of a balcony in front of millions of fans?"

"Graceful," James whispered. The realization dawned as a smile tugged at his lips. "It's perfect."

"No, James," Will said, his grin sly. "You're perfect. And the fans? Well, they outdid themselves this time."

On that note, the fans vanished again, and the room fell silent. With a smile, Nadia broke the silence, "Can I now comment on how amped up Frank will be after watching that round? Heck, my blood is pumping after seeing all of you, and my blood is always moving quickly."

James let the former conversation wash over him as he recognized Nadia's statements. "Agreed. You guys were all incredible."

Emy, speaking on behalf of Will and Tuck, nodded along: "It was just nice to have a straightforward battle for once. I think that gave me more courage than anything—that, and knowing you both were behind me."

Tuck's eyes suddenly went wide as he addressed the group. "Why don't we just 'reign' it in over here and let royalty open his coronation gift?"

"Now that's the spirit, Tuck!" Will laughed and then picked up the drop box. He knelt and bowed deeply toward James, offering the gift in his outstretched hands.

James, without option, accepted the box and opened it for the team.

New Gear Detected - Stonebreaker Gloves
Epic

Coveted by builders and artisans alike, these gloves are a remarkable prize. This construction-type item modifies object densities, enabling the user to lift and move heavier objects, granting the unique ability to alter any given location. With these gloves, a builder can reshape landscapes and erect structures with unparalleled efficiency, making them an indispensable tool for those who want to shape the world around them.

"Wow... Epic ranking," James exclaimed as he read the description. "Nex?"

"*I am speechless—well, actually, I am always speechless. Whoops! I am lacking words to merge into our neural connection! Ah, that's better. Okay, so these **Stonebreaker Gloves** will come in handy—outside of Tuck, lifting huge objects will be tough for any of you. These gloves essentially grant you a new skill without learning anything!*"

Emy then questioned Nex, hoping for a straightforward answer, "Based on your work with Trish and Frank, who do you think would most likely wear these?"

Nex replied, "*As the description states, these gloves are more for non-combat interactions. I would put them in the same realm as strategy and innovative battle design. The best logical choice would be James or Nadia.*"

"James can have them," Nadia rushed to speak, while James's mouth opened and closed, also wanting to give them to someone else.

"Let's see it then, James," Will stated. "Think we can rebuild the Castle?"

The group exchanged curious glances, wondering if Will was onto something. "I guess it couldn't hurt to find out?" James said as he threw on the gloves.

James then looked at his **Stonebreaker Gloves**, unsure what to do, so Nex offered him guidance, "*Think about the gloves as you would your talent. Direct your willpower through the gloves, and it will impact the density of the object you are trying to touch.*"

"*Start small—touch the object you want to interact with—and then push your willpower into guiding it where you want to go."*

James placed his hands on one of the large stone blocks that once formed the circular Castle wall. The blocks were about the size of a large refrigerator. While this was small compared to the other objects scattered across the area, this brick probably weighed close to 800 kilos.

As James interacted with the stone, he directed his willpower and energy to surge into it, shifting its unique makeup. With a slight push, the stone glided through the air as if it were lighter than a feather. "What do I do now?" James looked back at his team.

"Try putting it in one of the gaping holes in the side of the Castle," Will jested.

"How about adding it back to a wall that still has some structure? It might decrease our damage rate," Nadia stated logically, and the team nodded without any better ideas.

Walking toward the Castle, James pushed the boulder into place. It hovered over a more intact wall, with stones still intermingled about. "How do I drop it?" James called out to Nex as the boulder suddenly plummeted from its once-hovering position. It slammed down on the assembled blocks below, jarring them out of place. The remaining wall soon tumbled to the ground.

< Castle currently at 74% damage >

"Holy shit, James, leave some tower for the monsters to destroy," Will immediately rumbled.

△△△

Would you like to continue to Stage Six of the Trials?

"Yes"

......

Stage Six of the Trials will begin in 60 seconds.

......

Activating Arena in 3... 2... 1...

The team reached a consensus, and given the extent of damage to their Castle and the relative ease of their success in the previous round, they should advance to the next level. Any alternative decision would leave them questioning whether their choice was correct.

Once again, the team gathered around Will. His words carried weight as he addressed them: "From this point forward, remember to protect each other above all else, even if it means sacrificing some crumbling stone. A complete loss of the Castle does not equate to elimination from the tournament; it simply signifies our exit from the Trials. Let our bond be our shield and safeguard one another at all costs."

"Wow, Williams Jr., these are getting good!" James joked, a mix of jest and genuine pride in Will's complete ownership of the role.

Stage Six Begins in 3... 2... 1...

Unlike the previous stages, the arena stayed silent as the crowd noise dissipated. There was no distant rumbling, no tremors—not a speck of movement—as to what might emerge from the void tunnels. Instead, as time stretched out, the black void started to expand. Traces of darkness and shadows spread across each walkway, and three formerly hidden figures emerged from the dark, all shrouded in black gowns. A glint of silver shone from their waists.

Mistblade Warrior: Level 11

Shrouded in darkness, this enigmatic figure moves with the shadows, shifting seamlessly with the wind. When they strike, they use a blade that cuts through defenses like piercing steel—swift, precise, and deadly.

"I have a bad feeling about this," James whispered to Nadia, who stood beside him.

CHAPTER FORTY-FIVE

"At times, you simply need to confront talent with talent." – Titan, Former Champion.

LEVEL THREE - STAGE SIX

Will

Will's gaze bore into the shifting Warrior before him, mist funneling around the creature. The humanoid figure seemed to taunt him, gliding along the corridor—a dance of illusion: two steps forward, a retreat, then a lateral shift. Will resisted the urge to fixate on the mesmerizing movements. Instead, he timed the creature's leaps, observing its agility.

His mind raced, strategizing. This encounter demanded precision. Will transmitted a silent message to his teammates via Nexy: "The mist looks to be a decoy. All shifting patterns maintain a 3-meter maximum jump radius."

Intel mattered. The creature closed in, now within 5 meters. Will triggered his ***Permafrost*** ability and assessed the team's battle status, acutely aware that this clash would be anything but quick.

	Level	**Health**	**Shield**
Fury (Emy)	Level 9	100%	100%
Brick (Will)	Level 8	100%	90%
Surge (Tuck)	Level 8	100%	90%
Grace (James)	Level 7	100%	60%

| Nadia | Level 7 | 98% | 60% |

Will wanted to give Nadia a hero's name. However, he quickly dismissed the idea as there was no time for that now. The approaching warrior drew its blade, a glint of danger in its darkened eyes. Will's focus snapped back to the imminent threat.

"Let thissss be the end of you," hissed the creature, its form undulating. It flowed backward, then advanced toward the threshold, vanishing once more. Will's ice patterns tightened across his chest and arms, but the creature reappeared at his side. A metal blade pierced the ice, striking just above his left hip. The blow sunk into Will's shielding as the creature swiftly retreated.

"SSSurrender now," the elongated voice spoke.

Will's response was short: "Strike a little harder next time, and I might." He regrouped, fear absent from his tone as the warrior pulsed with anger.

Once more, it disappeared as black mist engulfed the vicinity. Energy buzzed next to Will as he twirled, raising an ice wall. However, the beast had relocated again, this time directly behind him as a blade thrust into his lower back—bypassing both frost wall and shielding.

< Will's health is at 80% >

He swiveled, contorting laterally to capture the blade with his ice shield, but it disintegrated as the Mistblade materialized again, its weapon gradually reassembling in its grasp.

△△△

Emy

Emy heard Will's feedback as her gaze locked on the creature. Its mocking grin showed on its half-hidden face; she made a decisive choice: offense.

Her hands lifted, a forward strike feigned, then spread

outward. Emy targeted areas of opportunity, each blast honing in on locations two meters to each side. **BOOM! BOOM!** The creature staggered, a glancing hit to its shoulder. It pulsed, retreating once more.

< Mistblade's health is at 90% >

"Attempt to restrict their movement and target areas of likelihood," Emy transmitted to the team, seizing on their small success.

The creature adapted. No more grinning. It leaped erratically, and Emy's fireballs cascaded across the walkway—none close to the Warrior's new positions. But chaos reigned, and suddenly, it was behind her, blade aimed low. Her energy shield yielded as blood flowed from her calf as the creature withdrew.

"Blood for blood," the sinuous voice spoke, the streaked knife tracing its open mouth.

△△△

Tuck

Tuck recognized a dire mismatch when he saw one. The diminutive creature lacked raw power, yet its speed and finesse outstripped Tuck's abilities. Aware of this, Tuck bided his time, invoking a *Lightning Bolt* to the skies. His aim focused on the solo blade wielded by the warrior. But as electron energy targeted the small object, the creature's rapid shifts confounded the lightning, leading it astray.

As Tuck now listened in on Will's and Emy's guidance through Nex, he braced himself for the inevitable strikes. The creature had caught on to his stalling tactics and shifted into a strike as Tuck attempted a sweeping motion with his *Warhammer* across the walkway, hoping to predict its elusive movements. Instead, observing Tuck's maneuver, the creature cut its shift short and slid underneath. The blade sliced through Tuck's energy shield, gouging a large chunk of skin.

With success, the Warrior pressed forward, striking at Tuck. It feigned surges, waiting for Tuck's large form to shift before engaging. As the battle wore on, Tuck's body transformed into a sliced husk, each blow taking its toll.

< Tuck's health is at 51% >

In that moment, Tuck understood that endurance was his only path. He continued anticipating future attacks, launching quicker strikes and channeling energy through his body, but it wasn't enough. In a moment of weakness and doubt, Tuck realized he needed to harness his energy more effectively. As he adjusted his willpower, the Mistblade shifted once more. Tuck pushed his energy to expand across his body, driving it to expand and interact with the elements around him to generate force. As the next blade came, Tuck acted, and a pulse burst out from his body. His energy merged with the environment surrounding him, creating a powerful wind gust reaction, repulsing the weapon mid-air. The fleeting victory was short-lived. The creature pivoted, stabbing again, but Tuck's defensive shift had triggered a change.

< Skill Identified – Tuck – Repulse >

< Level up! Tuck is now a Level 9 Accelerator >

Skill: Repulse

Endows the user with the ability to initiate targeted mini bursts of energy across their body, akin to a magnetic repulsion field. This unique capability provides the user a defensive shield against physical attacks, creating a force field that repels incoming threats. (SELF)

Despite the newfound defense, the blades still relentlessly pierced Tuck's form, threatening to shatter his resolve. Thoughts of failure crept in as another strike aimed at his vulnerable back. Tuck winced as he awaited the next blow, but the blade met bone, and a wave of ***Vitalization*** coursed through Tuck's aching body.

< Tuck's regeneration is now operating at 20% per minute >

Relief flooded Tuck as Nadia positioned herself between him and the relentless assailant. "Read the energy," Nadia commanded to the team through Nex. "Its signature reveals the direction of the phase shift."

△△△

James

In the heart of battle, James pushed forward, his ***Empower*** skill triggering toward Emy as he raced to support Will.

< Emy is boosted by 30% >

As James reached Will's position, he conjured a remote shield—a protective barrier that deftly caught a surprise strike from behind. Will seized the support, his ice-clad fists striking the creature's abdomen.

< The Mistblade's health is at 72% >

The battle was far from over. The creature vanished, only to reappear next to James. Its blade poised high, driving the sharp dagger into a quickly activated ***Energy Blocking Field.*** The shield held firm, its integrity unyielding.

< Level Up! James is now a level 8 Catalyst >

Caught off guard by the sudden shift in momentum, the three Warriors surrounded their areas with darkness as they shifted forward, bypassing the heroes. Their sights were set on the Castle—their ultimate goal.

BOOM!

< Energy trigger activated >

Amidst the push to relocate to the Castle, a single warrior—previously locked in combat with Tuck—made a fateful shift. It landed squarely on a pre-set *Energy Trigger* placed by the team. The arena shook as a fire bomb ignited, its scorching energy propelling the warrior backward, momentum carrying it over the precipice into the abyss.

Realizing its fate, the warrior attempted to pulse to the next walkway. But it fell short by mere meters, its form disappearing into the yawning darkness, leaving two remaining warriors.

James did a quick check on everyone's status.

	Level	Health	Shield
Emy	Level 9	73%	20%
Will	Level 8	65%	14%
Tuck	Level 9	47%+	5%
James	Level 8	100%	60%
Nadia	Level 7	98%	60%

△△△

Will

WHOOSH! An enormous gust of wind swept through the air, directed at the beleaguered Castle. The two Mistblades, their forms ethereal and fierce, lined up and focused on the Castle walls. Once used for Mist channeling, their secondary talents now served a different purpose.

< Castle currently at 89% damage >

Will glanced over at his team, noting the varied expressions of bravery, fury, and resolve on their faces. They observed the two remaining elusive mist users, their frustration growing as they came to terms with their unsuccessful efforts to pin them down. The two adversaries, slippery and defiant, continued their relentless attacks on the Castle. Recognizing their limitations and the futility of their pursuit, Will and his team understood that the mist users would keep evading them until the Castle finally fell to their assaults.

"Hey, losers!" Will's voice resounded across the arena. His tone dripped with mockery as he attempted to use his *Flow Perception* to evoke the creature's emotions. "Do you honestly think we give a damn about that Castle?"

With a flick of his wrist, Will conjured a *Cryostrike* and shot toward the remaining structure, adding to its demise.

< Castle currently at 96% damage >

Everyone now gathered around him, sharing his determination. Will's hands glowed with power as ice crystallized, forming pristine blades that reflected the light. His voice rang out, confident and challenging: "Why not test your steel against ice?"

< Level up! Will is now a level 9 Condenser >

△△△

Full Team

Will's provocation had the desired effect. The two remaining Mistblades abruptly halted their relentless assault on the Castle and redirected their fury toward the team. Their half-hidden faces radiated a potent mix of contempt and anger.

Positioned at the forefront, Will brandished ice blades on both hands, his skin now encased in frosty armor. Lined up behind him was the rest of the squad: Tuck and Emy, their figures vibrating with sparks and flames, while James and Nadia held their ground at the back; soon, a calming rush of aura enveloped them all.

< Full team regeneration now operating at 10% per minute >

Without hesitation, the Mistblades shifted to opposing sides of the group. Their movements were swift, their blades ready. Simultaneously, a second aura spread across the space, being James's **Restrict** skill.

< Mistblade's shift talent has been restricted by 50% >

< Level up! James is now a level 9 Catalyst >

The warriors' expressions morphed from disdain to sheer surprise as their primary movement ability was halved, leaving them momentarily disoriented.

Emy and Tuck seized the opportunity, maximizing their talents in the only direction the Warriors could retreat—backward.

With a mighty swing of his **Warhammer** and a pair of fireballs, the strikes dispatched the two Mistblades, leaving them sprawled face-down on the ground.

"Silly Misters, maybe next time I'll actually get to use these," Will challenged the disappearing figures, his ice blades still out, as the crowd noise assaulted their ears again.

COLD AS ICE! 147 POINTS!

STAGE SIX is now COMPLETE!

······

You have one hour to regroup and prepare for the next stage.

CHAPTER FORTY-SIX

"To ascend to the status of a Champion, one must embrace risks—risks that have the potential to alter the very essence of one's being." – Codex, Former Champion.

EARTH - SYDNEY, AUSTRALIA
LEVEL THREE - STAGE SIX

Lee & Isla

As the two Mistblades bore down on the sibling Champions, Lee and Isla exchanged a knowing look. Lee, once a humble cattle hand, still wore his weathered cowboy hat. Now, he brandished an energy whip powered by meticulously harnessing photon interactions. His broad shoulders and muscular build were complemented by a distinctive tattoo of a coiled snake wrapping around his left arm, shimmering with energy. Opposite him stood Isla, a Wind user capable of accelerating matter. Her fringed leather jacket fluttered like a breeze, and her piercing blue eyes were framed by a unique crescent moon-shaped birthmark on her right cheek. Her long, braided hair, adorned with small feathers that danced in the wind, added to her striking presence as she prepared to confront the elusive creatures.

Lee let his whip fall toward the ground as the Mistblade advanced. Within meters, he struck with ferocity, igniting his energy weapon and extending it across the pathway. This level's setup catered perfectly to Lee's weapon of choice, allowing him to cover the entire walkway with a deadly slice. As the creature shifted to black mist, Lee flicked his wrist, snapping it out of the air. It fell before him, a cauterized hole through its abdomen where the laser-like whip had sliced cleanly through. Without giving it a chance for a second move, Lee finished the job with a downward strike, the enhanced whip crack echoing across the arena.

On the far side of the Castle, Isla stood in the heart of a dust and wind hurricane, its velocity escalating relentlessly. With its lethal speed, the second mist creature darted straight toward the girl. Yet, amid its shift, a potent gust swept through, bearing minute particles that ripped the attacker off its course, propelling it against the Castle's reinforced gates.

Bewildered, the mist creature was trapped by another cyclone of debris, its sight veiled from all directions. A dirt vortex formed a confining circular barrier around it. Suddenly, hefty stone objects breached the vortex, colliding with the defenseless form of the last warrior. The creature met its demise as it was slammed off the walkway and into the abyss, triggering another wave of cheers from the crowd.

Emerging together, Lee and Isla smiled, realizing they faced a favored grounded battle, unlike the several aerial encounters they'd previously endured. And much to their delight, this battle lacked the overpowering might of a colossal troll. The chants around them continued:

"Saviors, Saviors, Saviors!"

Just one more stage and they could get back to training—back to their city and families, already devastated by hordes of creatures.

△△△

EARTH - UNDISCLOSED
LEVEL THREE - STAGE SEVEN

With minimal ceremony, the team unveiled the drop reward from the previous level, aware there were other matters to address.

New Devices Detected - Map Extension (x5)
Rare
Enhancement for the existing Nexabot mapping system. This expands the map's coverage to a 1-kilometer area and enriches the current details. Notably, it expands the color-coded system for lifeform indicators: blue signifies allies, grey denotes neutrality, yellow indicates adversity, red signifies an imminent attack upon sighting, and purple showcases a potential leadership role based on energy signals.

After reading the description, Tuck remarked, "It seems like we're gathering materials for upcoming missions. Didn't we already have these map capabilities?"

"*Only some of them!*" Nex replied eagerly. "*The map has expanded its coverage, now spanning a 1-kilometer area. But that's not all—I can now determine intent and track energy surges. This will synergize perfectly with your* **Soulpulse** *tracking item!*"

Emy assessed the situation: "Considering this arena falls well within our former limits and everything here is hostile, let's table this chat about the upgrade for now."

James interjected, looking towards Will, "After all that bravado, did you seriously demolish half of our remaining Castle?"

In a playfully regal manner, Will declared, "Worry not, my noble King! I merely followed the path of my esteemed leader!"

Nadia stepped in, her expression a mix of concern and curiosity, "We all know those two would have evaded us had we not provoked them. But that level of damage? Will, you may need to explain yourself."

Will reverted to his normal tone and addressed Nadia, "It's based on more of a hunch."

Silence from the team prompted him to continue, "Look, we don't know what we are facing in this next round, should we even decide to proceed forward… the real question is if the System would passively choose for us to continue a battle if we already failed the stage?"

"You mean if we have no more Castle?" Tuck questioned.

"Right. Regardless of whether my jest worked against those two, our Castle is close to ruin. Maybe we could have forced them to come over with only a taunt, but why risk it when I see that remaining Castle as our primary failsafe," Will finished.

"Eliminate ourselves from the Trials," Emy spoke, understanding Will's direction.

"Williams told us to play it smart. This is only a ranking level, and we are well outside those first three stages. Should we choose to, we need to give ourselves an easy exit. The higher the stage, the higher the ranking, regardless of secondary achievements."

"Will, that is brilliant," James spoke once again. "When did you think of this?"

"The idea struck me when I realized the spider bombs might be doing us a favor," Will spoke in a sober tone.

James paused again, caught between Will's candid realization and something else. "Wait, so you had these plans in your head before I contributed to damaging the Castle by accident?"

"Absolutely," Will said with a smirk.

Nadia returned to their impending decision: "Knowledge suggests that this final level will be the most dangerous. In a trial, spanning galaxies, they intend to push us to our limits."

Emy's gaze fell upon the remnants of the Castle—a single half-demolished wall still standing. "What are the odds that Will's correct?" she wondered aloud.

"Honestly, I'd say it's a coin toss," Will responded as Emy approached the remnants of the Castle wall. Without warning, Emy ignited with energy and threw a fiery punch at the wall's summit.

< Castle currently at 97% damage >

"I'm in," Emy declared back at the team, faces mixed with reactions as dust clung to her shoes.

Amused, Nadia was the first to approach Emy. She chose a section already half-broken and delivered a powerful kick.

< Castle currently at 98% damage >

"Me too."

Tuck let out a grunt. "Well, since you two already had your say with the wall, I guess that leaves me," He commented with a slight smile. He walked over to Emy and Nadia, where the final four stone blocks stood in their original spot.

"Wait," Will interrupted before Tuck could take his swing. "Come on, James."

Will and James approached the last blocks as Will generated an ice shield behind the lower two blocks. "James, use those **Stonebreaker Gloves**. Let's ensure we don't accidentally disqualify ourselves with this behemoth."

Now in position, Tuck grinned and reared back his fist. He struck the top two stone blocks, breaking them off from the remaining two.

< Castle currently at 99% damage >

△△△

Would you like to continue to the Final Stage of the Trials?

"Yes"

……

Stage Seven of the Trials will begin in 60 seconds.

Activating Arena in 3... 2... 1...

For the final time, the lights flared up, and the team formed a circle, facing outwards towards an entranced audience. But in just a few moments, the stadium's seating configuration transformed. What had previously been hundreds of thousands of spectators had now become... millions. It almost seemed like an illusion. Everywhere Emy turned her gaze, she saw onlookers. Farther back, higher up, in every direction she looked, there were cheering fans.

How can they even see from there? Emy wondered, feeling as though she was reliving the introduction of the first stage all over again, her eyes wide, bewildered, and invigorated.

"Huddle!" Will shouted, trying to draw the team's focus amidst the shifting surroundings. "Nothing has changed. James is still stationed by our Castle's remains, ready for any outcome. I'd imagine we need to maintain our defenses for a while before the System can extract us in an emergency... Fight until the very end."

"Hands in," Will commanded. "No one dies here. We win, or we get out. No other options."

"Fly as One."

"Succeed as One."

At that moment, a resounding voice emanated from the arena:

> And now, we at the CNC Games Division present to you the Mighty Eagles!
>
> Will the fan-favorite Eagles survive the final round? Wait until you see what the System has in store for them!
>
> Last chance merchandise on sale now! Items are going

fast!

Here we go!

Stage Seven Begins in 3... 2... 1...

CHAPTER FORTY-SEVEN

"Do not presume to understand the System's actions or inactions in any given scenario. The System has a singular objective, and ruthlessness is a means to this endeavor." – E.B.

LEVEL THREE - STAGE SEVEN

The atmosphere grew stiff as the surrounding noise dissipated, leaving the team in silence. It felt as though the room's energy was being siphoned away. James, glancing at his teammates, noticed their energies pulsating as if struggling to break free from their grasp.

James stood ready in the middle of the courtyard to safeguard the last remnants of the structure while having his **Stonebreaker Gloves** prepared for their secondary purpose: swift stone extraction.

Suddenly, a static sound emerged, followed by an abrupt silence, creating an unsettling absence of sound. Then, a movement caught the team's eyes at the western entrance. The void, spanning three meters in height and width, seemed to stretch outward and... forward. As if aided by a fourth dimension, the creature navigating the entrance caused the once flat void to bulge. The emptiness expanded, consuming more space as the bubble grew.

As the portal neared its breaking point, a large, crimson-forked tongue slithered out, followed by a pair of luminescent yellow eyes and a head that grazed the edges of the void, struggling to extricate itself from its previous confines. As the colossal serpent's head emerged from the void, the team stared at its enormous jaws and razor-sharp teeth, visible beneath the closed mouth. The snake continued to glide into the arena, its elongated form unfolding over what felt like minutes. The serpent, a deep black with hints of purple enveloping it, eventually stretched to just over 50 meters, equivalent to the height of a 15-story building.

Singularity Serpent: Level 19

Born in the voids of space, an adolescent serpent embarks on a celestial journey. This spectral being voyages through the emptiness, seeking energies from all corners of the Cosmos, both known and unknown. Its levitating motion, almost ghost-like, testifies to its unique ability to morph and navigate through matter. With an insatiable hunger, it consumes life and energy in its path, fueling its growth and reinforcing its formidable presence in the Cosmos.

James instinctively edged closer to the remaining two stone blocks, his team watching the beast in horror. "A late D-Class beast?" Nadia's voice caught. "I didn't think that was possible at this early level."

As if choreographed, the giant snake shifted its course, heading straight for the center of the arena. Its menacing form undulated with raw power. As the snake drew nearer, it activated a skill, causing a void to appear. The snake smoothly slid into the void, its body disappearing as if being swallowed by the emptiness, resulting in an empty arena once more.

"Did we just lose a 50-meter snake?" Tuck's disbelief spread through the team.

"I'm afraid so. Any ideas on this thing?" Will's gaze shifted from James, who stood near the remaining blocks.

After tense moments, a new void materialized in the distance, and the gigantic snake reappeared. The electric hum once again enveloped the room.

"What options do we have?" Nadia's eyes darted. "Should Tuck try his *Ion Storm*?"

"That might just enrage it further," Will replied. "We're left with an all-in move or our backup plan. My ice probably won't dent that monstrosity, and this arena is starting to feel a little too confining."

As if eavesdropping, the snake slithered through another void, recognizing it wasn't alone. It rapidly reappeared, now directly aligning with the team's position.

"Move! James, do it now!" Will's urgent command shouted as Emy stepped forward.

"No. Wait."

"Emy, what are you doing?" the team's voices questioned together, their concern evident as Emy distanced herself from the group. Her gaze fixed on the creature, moving relentlessly toward her.

Drawing upon her previous experience with the biodome wall, Emy sensed the snake's existence, the void, and the pressure of the surrounding room converging.

She reached for the ambient forces, merging her willpower across the entire space as the snake emitted a static-like squeal as if ensnared.

Emy's hands moved in a deliberate closure.

"This is my domain…" she whispered as the void constricted around the snake's body.

Emy pressed on, the void slicing deeper into the creature's neck. The snake convulsed, locked in a desperate struggle for survival as the void flickered uncertainly, probing the true force that steered it. Emy stood resolute, detaching herself from everything and everyone surrounding her. It was just her and the void, locked in a silent confrontation. With a surge of willpower and the feeling that something within the void had accepted her as its leader, she firmly closed the gap within her hands. The void vanished as if it had never been, severing the monstrous snake's head from its body in one swift, decisive stroke.

The colossal head crashed onto a pathway, only to be redirected into the abyss below.

< Skill Identified – Emy – Void Control >

< Level up! Emy is now a Level 10 Generalist >

< Emy has Ascended to D Class >

The sound barrier that had previously shielded the crowd shattered again, yet the arena remained eerily silent. Millions of fans stared in disbelief.

"What?" Emy's voice quivered with intense emotion.

Then, her emotions surged, and she found herself screaming at the surrounding fans, challenging them: "Did you want more? Did you not get your money's worth?"

Fury consumed Emy, her rage igniting her arms with flames and smoke. The fiery display showcasing an image visible to all in the arena.

A phantom eagle, sculpted from the swirling smoke, took flight towards the spectators. Its expansive wings of smoke unfurled, casting a shadow over the multitudes present.

WHERE SNAKES SLITHER, EAGLES SOAR! 205 POINTS!

The stadium reverberated with thunderous applause as the team's vision turned to the familiar grey as they were pulled away from the arena.

STAGE SEVEN is now COMPLETE!

······

MISSION ACCOMPLISHED!

You have completed all seven waves of the Trials.

······

Final Stage Complete: **7**

Destruction of Castle: **99%**

Time to Finish Final Stage: **53 Seconds**

······

Mighty Eagles (Cohort 13)

Level Three Results:

Total Team Points: **839**

Total Max Active Views: **1.3B**

Earth Rank: **113 of 37,191**

99.7th Percentile

······

Stellar Ascendancy - Earth

1. **Morgrax - AD** - 7 / 37% / 4:34
2. **Kann - AD** - 7 / 78% / 5:37
3. **S6** - 7 / 88% / 5:03
4. **Saviors of Sydney** - 7 / 93% / 6:34
5. **Zephyr - AD** - 7 / 95% / 5:15
6. **Hydro** - 7 / 97% / 8:13
7. **Mighty Eagles** - 7 / 99% / 0:53
8. **Templars** - 6 / 34% / 4:53
9. **Vorg - AD** - 6 / 43% / 4:05
10. **Ionic** - 6 / 49% / 3:59

  -

100. **Bravados** - 5 / 53% / 2:54

Stellar Ascendancy - Galaxy

1. **Halo** - 7 / 7% / 1:57

2. **Constellation** - 7 / 20% / 2:15
3. **Empty** - 7 / 34% / 1:43
4. **Morgrax - AD** - 7 / 37% / 4:34
5. **Nova** - 7 / 45% / 7:45
6. **Cohort 34** - 7 / 49% / 11:43
7. **Celestials - VV** - 7 / 53% / 6:32
8. **(Blank)** - 7 / 54% / 8:39
9. **Flare** - 7 / 59% / 2:58
10. **Illusion** - 7 / 60% / 8:32

    -

24. **Kann - AD** - 7 / 78% / 5:37
25. **Finite** - 7 / 79% / 4:38

CHAPTER FORTY-EIGHT

"Before long, you'll gaze at the stars and planets in the sky and identify places you've visited." – IMS Integration Specialist.

EARTH – RENO, NEVADA

When the Brandts were alerted by an unfamiliar message on their mobile devices inviting them to witness their daughter's participation in the Quantum Games, they were clueless about what would come. They were naturally curious about their daughter's well-being but wholly unprepared for what unfolded.

What initially seemed like a possible hoax or fraudulent message had catapulted them into a full-blown virtual reality setting, leaving them utterly stunned. The news had been awash with reports of global catastrophic events. Events that took place even in their hometown of Reno, just a few miles from their residence, yet their lives had been relatively unaffected, apart from the government's directive to remain indoors and await further instructions. With most communication channels down and local news being sporadic, they hadn't heard from Emy and assumed her community college was hopefully spared. However, the reality was starkly different.

Emy's paternal lineage had a history of severe mental disorders, and it appeared that Emy was exhibiting symptoms similar to the "visions" experienced by her ancestors. Her father was relatively stable, unlike her grandfather and great-grandfather, who were both plagued by debilitating anxiety and diagnosed with Schizophrenia. These conditions led them to drift aimlessly and ultimately abandon their family. Ben and Melissa tried to support their daughter when she began showing the same early signs of mental illness; however, disagreements over medications and a lack of understanding on how to provide mutual support gradually drove them apart over the years. They found solace in Emy having a friend like James to confide in.

Now, virtually sitting next to James's parents, Judy and Mike Gray, the sight of their daughter and James in the center of an arena, with a colossal flying snake hovering above them, was an image that would be etched in their memories forever. The fear of soon losing their daughter lingered for a few moments before the entire stadium erupted in cheers for her, and just like that, it was over. Their daughter had become a hero. The world as they knew it had transformed. Overwhelmed with fear and emotion, Ben and Melissa looked at each other, wondering about their future, the fate of the world, and the fate of their daughter.

△△△

THE HANGAR

"Brr ba brr ba brr brr brr brr," Frank hummed, valiantly trying to mimic the royal trumpet from his mouth, but without much success, as the team returned to the Hangar's sanctuary.

"The Kings and Queens have returned!" Frank announced. "You all are absolute legends now!"

"I was a complete wreck watching that last round. I knew this was a competition, and the stakes were high, but I didn't anticipate it would be so nerve-wracking for me as a spectator. I nearly fainted twice," Trish admitted, embracing each team member.

"Four times," Frank corrected, offering everyone a fist bump. "And honestly, same here!"

"Excellent work, everyone," Williams said from the back of the room, allowing the team to bask in their camaraderie. "I'm proud of all of you. Once you've caught your breath and grabbed some food, meet in the strategy room."

"Understood, Coach," Frank responded, glancing back before turning his attention to the group again. "But first, Surge? Grace? How fitting are those names?" He then turned to Nadia. "I've been brainstorming a ton of options for you too!"

Nadia chuckled. "I'm curious to hear them, Frank, but I might already have a name picked out," Nadia responded, adding a wink.

"What?" Frank exclaimed, joined by Will. "Nadia, you can't leave us hanging. Spill the beans."

"I believe she'll reveal it when the time is right," Trish defended her friend. "What I'm really curious about are those new energy signal devices."

"Oh, you tech geek," Frank teased, flashing a quick grin. "I want to hear about the action! Which opponent was your favorite to face?" Before anyone could answer, he continued, "Will's sharpshooting with that bird? The not-so-tight Titans?" He paused for dramatic effect, clearly proud of his joke. "Or Emy's captivating fire-eagle display?"

"Wait, what eagle display?" Emy asked, puzzled.

"Your fiery eagle at the end?" Trish clarified, but Emy still seemed confused. "You're kidding, right?" Trish glanced at the others, who shared her confusion.

"Nex, can we, uh, replay it?"

"*It was absolutely epic!*" Nex agreed, sounding like they were trying out a new slang term. "*Take a look!*"

A video screen appeared in everyone's view, allowing the team to replay Emy's final performance. Emy's eyes widened as she saw herself in the center of the arena with giant wings of fire and smoke extending from her arms. "I did that?"

"You sure did," Will confirmed. "Once again, someone stole the spotlight with the final superhero move."

"This isn't going to become a trend, is it?" Emy asked, a hint of hope in her voice.

"*It's already a trend! You should check out your merchandise section,*" Nex suggested.

"Merchandise section?" Will asked in surprise.

"*Absolutely! It spans the entire Cosmos!*" Nex clarified. "*Everyone can instantly access digital art for a fair price, and physical items too, although they take a bit longer to deliver.*"

"Do we receive any royalties for our likeness?" Tuck questioned.

"*Not at all! At least, not until you turn professional. It's similar to the old rules for college athletes. Once you start accepting funds or revenue, you're no longer eligible. The System frowns upon that type of manipulation.*"

"That's a poor comparison. They revised that rule for a reason," Tuck retorted.

"*Oh, right.*" Nex seemed to reconsider and arrived at a simple conclusion. "*Well, rules are rules.*"

"Wait, can we just backtrack a bit? Emy, what the heck was the skill you used out there?" James halted the conversation in an attempt to understand what he had witnessed.

"I have to admit, this one was as much of a gut feeling as it was knowing what I was doing out there," Emy replied as she and the team reviewed the new skill:

Skill: Void Control
Allows the user the power to manipulate the void itself. In the absence of matter, there is only the void. The user can open, close, and connect breaches in the void. (R)

"Wicked…" Frank commented as he read the text in front of him.

"Very." James agreed and then shifted topics. "I must say, regardless of all the cool skills and gifts we got, I'm just happy to be out of that arena. Don't get me wrong, I adore you all, but that place will haunt my dreams for years."

"Agreed. And speaking of the arena, if it weren't for your destruction of our Castle, we might have made it to the top 25 in the Galaxy," Will responded, grinning broadly.

James started to return the comment to Will when Trish intervened, "Oh, Will. You know that was just as much your idea. Being in the top 7 worldwide is incredible. Any thoughts on who those AD guys might be?"

"I was planning to ask Coach about that when we had the chance. It seems a bit odd. Two of those teams from Earth even made it to the Galaxy top 25. I guess that means there's hope for us even if we don't win?... I'm not suggesting we stop trying. I'm just glad to see Earth getting some recognition," James added.

"Even though you all might not be on the Galaxy roster, completing the seventh round in under a minute must be a record. That's bound to leave everyone in awe!" Frank stated. "But could we please head to the Kitchen now? I'd rush off, but I've missed you all, and honestly, I'm starved."

"Dude, you just had something to eat," Trish retorted.

"How many times must I explain? Stress eating doesn't qualify as a proper meal," Frank shot back.

"It does when it's a whole turkey leg."

Aiming to defuse the situation, Nadia interjected before Frank could reply, "I believe we could all benefit from a good meal."

△△△

The team comfortably resumed their usual spots and conversations in the cafeteria, making life feel complete again. Trish and Frank had integrated into their lives, and their presence noticeably lifted everyone's spirits. Rest and camaraderie can mend even the deepest wounds.

"Okay, we need to decide on the cake for our ascension celebration. It's not every day that someone advances to D-Class!" Frank declared.

"I'm all for ice cream cake; remember, you still owe me," Nadia joked. "But perhaps our honoree should make the final call. What's your preference, Emy?"

Emy laughed. "Ice cream sounds delightful, but we don't have to do anything. Honestly, I don't feel much different…"

"That's not what your energy core is showing," James spoke. "I had to dial down some of your energy readings with Nex. You're practically radiating."

"Agreed. We could see your progress before, like everyone else's, but after you defeated that snake, it's like your core doubled in size," Nadia corroborated.

"That's accurate!" Nex added. *"While these levels and classes merely evaluate your abilities and determination, the leap to a higher Class is typically propelled by a significant shift in your energy core. Your victory in a battle against a late D-Class's willpower to control the void stretched and expanded your energy capacity. It wasn't so much the act of defeating the giant as the effort you put in to overcome it."*

"I should probably let Williams instruct you further, though!" Nex concluded.

"That sort of makes sense," Emy responded, "but these days, making sense seems to be a moving target." Emy smiled and glanced around the table at the nodding heads. "Should we open the last round's drop box and level prize before we head to the strategy room?"

"Uh. YES!" Trish exclaimed with excitement. "Let's see the stage prize first, please. I've been dying to see what that snake dropped."

Emy brought up the box and opened it in front of the team.

New Device Detected - Quantum Gateway
Legendary

This revolutionary device stands at the forefront of cosmic exploration. It employs an advanced process that uses void holes to create a link betweentwo locations using the user's Nexabot. This state-of-the-art system accurately identifies cosmic destinations, whether previously visited places, remotely observable sites, or locations pre-determined and shared through data transfer. Understanding the unique signature of space is crucial for the operation of this portal, ensuring a stable, secure, and exact voyage across the immense stretch of space-time.

As the group read the description, a hush fell over them. Shocked expressions, wide eyes, and open mouths were shared all around.

"I get to be a **SPACE TRAVELER**?" Frank blurted out, still clutching his hot turkey sandwich.

"*Will someone please ask me about this?*" Nex's voice carried urgency.

"Nex!" everyone shouted. "What have we told you!"

"*Oh, right. I can't quite find the words to express my excitement about this item! These devices are typically only found in central government facilities or transportation centers across the Cosmos. Only the greatest of heroes possess these personal devices—mostly because only a select few can manipulate the void!*" Nex explained.

"So, we can go anywhere?" Will asked.

"*It'll take some time for Emy to master it, but yes. That's the idea. Emy must hone her* **Void Control** *skill and establish a connection to the gateway itself. But soon, all of you should be able to travel anywhere.*"

CHAPTER FORTY-NINE

Life unfolds through choices—the ones you've made in the past and those awaiting you in the future." – E.B.

EARTH - QUILL CREEK

Penny surveyed the scene as parents swarmed the campus, frantically searching for their children. It had only been a few hours since she had parted ways with Will and his team, but it felt like a lifetime had passed. The reality of the situation was hard to grasp. One moment, she was in chemistry class, and the next, a young man pulled her out of her emotions and introduced her to a whole new world.

It felt as though a dormant energy within her had suddenly awakened. As Will's energy surged through her mind, her newfound abilities emerged potent and ready. The experience was transformative, particularly when she sensed her energy intertwining with Shelby's. It was as if her energy had realized its potential—a spark igniting within her. Witnessing Will risk his life for her fueled this ignition into a burning flame of capability and courage she hadn't known existed.

After replicating Will's **Flow Perception** skill on the other students impacted by the mental comatose, she knew she had to do more. Assisting these students was just the beginning. When Will asked her to gather the students, she was eager to help. She ushered the students back to the school and found herself amid madness. With the help of a few unaffected teachers, she did all she could, primarily working with the administration to contact the parents of those most affected. Most others fled, contacted their families, or took refuge in the dorms. That's when she heard about other incidents happening around the world. Quill Creek was just one of many places affected, and they were fortunate that Will and his team had arrived when they did. *Were there others like Will out there?*

"Are you Penny Duplaine?" a man she recognized, who had also been helping others during the crisis, asked.

"Yes?"

"Apologies. I'm the Athletic Director for the School, Mr. Reynold... Forget that. Just call me Steve."

"I'm familiar with you, Mr. Reynold. Your office is next to the school counselor's. I visited there quite often," Penny replied, then stopped, unsure why she had shared that information.

"Right. Well, once again, thank you for all your help here," Mr. Reynold said as he gestured around the room. "But if you don't mind me asking, Will Weiss stopped by my office earlier looking for you. He said he was looking for you to be his tutor?"

Steve paused, second-guessing if that was still the case. "You see, Will is very close to me. I knew... I mean... I know his family. Have you seen him at any point?"

"Yes... He saved me," her voice faltered. "He saved all of us—him and his friends."

"Saved us?" Mr. Reynold asked with a hopeful concern. "Is he okay? Do you know where he is?"

"Yes, he's okay," Penny began, noticing Mr. Reynold's relief. "At least, I think so. He and his friends went to the biodome after they saved us, and when we returned a bit later, we found..." Penny stopped, realizing what she was about to reveal. "Several students were there with Mrs. Wallen, but the rest of the intruders were killed."

"I have to believe that he's okay. It seemed like Will and his friends had a mission, and once it was completed, they were taken away," Penny said somberly.

"The loss of those students and Mrs. Wallen is the worst tragedy this school has ever seen. I will make sure they are all remembered," Mr. Reynold began. "I will choose to believe that about Will as well. We've heard rumors from students about 'heroes' appearing and disappearing in other locations too."

"Penny, I don't mean to be intrusive, but I don't see that you have any family here. What are you planning on doing next?" Mr. Reynold asked as they both found a moment of respite on a nearby bench. It was their first chance to sit since the news had circulated.

"My family situation is complicated. I'll make sure they know I'm okay," Penny replied. "As for what's next? I can't help but feel that this," Penny looked around, "is just the beginning and that I need to do more." Then, as if an idea had crystallized, her next step became clear. "If the rumors are true, Reno has been hit harder than here. Many of our students have family and friends in that area, and from what we've heard, those other heroes may not have been as successful."

"So, what's the plan?" Mr. Reynold asked.

"The plan is simple, sir... I'm going to Reno," Penny finished with a small smile.

Mr. Reynold heard Penny's determination as guilt and silence washed over him. He realized he should have done more already—more for Will and more for his students. After all, wasn't his identity intertwined with the support he provided to his loved ones? Finally, he returned, "Normally, as a member of the school's administration, I would discourage you from doing that."

"But?" Penny asked.

"But... I'm going to ask if I can give you a ride," Mr. Reynold replied, "If you'll let me."

△△△

THE HANGAR

"Okay," Will declared, "I think it's fair to say that the

previous prize was probably the best of the round, and perhaps we should temper our expectations for what awaits us in this next reward box." The group still buzzed with excitement over the prospect of cosmic travel.

Around the table, nods rippled slowly as each member emerged from their reverie. "Ready?" Will questioned, his eyes scanning the eager faces.

"Yes!" Trish exclaimed, hastily brushing her hand across her mouth. Just moments before, her hands had been clasped tightly over her face, her mouth wide open in shock.

New Items Detected - Revive Pills (1,000)
Common
When ingested, these pills replenish famished bodies by delivering essential calories, vitamins, and daily nutrients. Additionally, they alleviate muscle pain, cramps, and fatigue. Their adrenaline-boosting properties can even pull someone back from the brink of death, reinvigorating their entire system. Note: These pills are intended to stabilize those without talent and should not be used as a substitute for healing.

"I, for one, didn't expect this," Will mused aloud. "Nexy, don't make us ask twice."

Nexy's response was a sultry purr, her voice a velvet whisper, *"Oh, hun,"* she teased, *"I was going to speak, I promise,"* her words hung, tantalizing and suggestive. *"Based on my intelligence,"* she continued, drawing out each syllable, *"the System often bestows items—gifts, really—that aid the team and benefit those they encounter on their journey. Guidance reveals that these contributions spare the team from purchasing items that wouldn't truly impact their personal growth."*

Will smiled; he had made the right choice. The others listened to their Nexabot's standard communication voice, unaware of Nexy's potential.

Emy's voice broke into the team's smiles, her tone somber, "I think that means we should expect more of a local presence soon."

James attempted to inject optimism. "And we should be happy to know we can now help."

"Only if we can get there in time," Emy returned, soon sharing a look of remorse with Will.

CHAPTER FIFTY

"The initial shock arises from realizing that a void monster could strike your world at any moment. The subsequent clarity dawns when you recognize the multitude of ancient monsters lurking out there." – Trident, Former Champion.

THE HANGAR

After reconnecting and sharing a meal, the team reconvened in the strategy room. The main wall was still adorned with their updated Champion profiles, reflecting the progress made since the last round. It was a powerful moment for the team to acknowledge the significant improvements they had all achieved since the first intermission. Not just in levels but also in talents, skills, and abilities. Next to this wall was a new digital board labeled "Eagle Eye."

"Eagle Eye? Is this your handiwork, Nex?" James questioned.

"*Technically, everything in this room is my handiwork,*" Nex responded, "*but yes, it seems someone appreciated my earlier symbolism ideas!*"

"That was us," Trish interjected, speaking for herself and Frank. "It's an effective way to highlight strengths and areas for improvement. We must understand both observed and inherent feedback, but Coach is best suited to guide us through it."

"Well said, Trish," Coach Williams affirmed as he entered the room. "Reflection is key to shaping our future, especially while the feedback is fresh."

"I won't make everyone discuss this in a roundtable format again, but I expect active participation. Trish and Frank, this includes you both, given your close observation of the team."

"Let's start with the positives. What worked well in the Trials?"

A silence fell over the room, akin to the quiet after a presentation when questions were invited. But silence always prompts someone to break it.

Trish took the initiative. "Well-rounded skillsets," she began, earning an encouraging nod from Williams to continue. "Each stage was unique. New creatures, new challenges, new threats. Everyone brought a skillset that complemented each other, and when one of you was less effective, others excelled."

"Thank you for starting us off, Trish," Coach replied. "Yes, diversity is key. Identifying the strongest asset across your team for the task at hand and maximizing its potential," Williams concluded, writing "Diversity" on the board with a digital pen.

"What else?" Williams prompted.

"Shielding," Nadia offered. "We have three effective methods to block or limit opposing forces, not to mention James's restrictions."

"That's right. During the bird event, you all were able to adapt with Emy's **Disintegration**, Will's ice wall, and James's **Energy Blocking Field**." Williams wrote "Protection" on the board.

"We have some serious power hitters on the team," Frank added. "Those Titans didn't stand a chance."

Williams chuckled. "Yes, Frank. We agree there." Williams wrote "Damage Dealing" on the board.

"Let's finish with one last item," Williams encouraged the team.

"Healing," Will suggested, looking at Nadia, which prompted a confirming nod from Coach. "Yes, healing, but think bigger," Williams urged.

"Having a haven," Emy suggested, initially softly but more confidently with her follow-up. "With James and Nadia's talents combined, we can create a fortification—a fallback in case we get into trouble."

"Well said, Emy," Williams commended. "Yes, Nadia's talents are vital and allow the team to take considerable risks in combat, but combining all your skills can create an impenetrable stronghold." Williams concluded the section by writing "Haven" on the board and moving to the second area.

"Okay. Now let's discuss opportunities."

"Movement," Tuck announced, having waited for this moment. "We were out of options until those mist creatures fell for Will's loud mouth."

"Good start," Williams noted, jotting down the word while Will theatrically mimed a knife stab to his chest.

"Next?"

"Precision," Emy noted. "Besides James's bow, Will was the only one able to channel his power into precise targeting." Emy glanced at Will. "But I think he would agree that was also limited. Everyone else used brute force."

"Good. Good." Williams continued to write.

"Finishing move," Frank added and then continued, "Don't get me wrong; you guys are beasts, but without Emy's control of the void, I'm not sure you would have been able to take down He-Who-Must-Not-Be-Named's companion."

Williams nodded and wrote down "Finisher" on the board. "Now, let me add one last item to the board."

"Stubborn."

"You had no certainty that your plan would work. Let this serve as a stern warning. Never, ever, rely on the System to save you. Yes, Will, I admire your creativity, and yes, the System has saved some Champions, but the System has also allowed chaos to reign. Never entrust your life to chance."

Williams sighed, releasing a breath he had held in for a while, and continued, "Now, look at the board."

Strength	Weakness
Diversity	Movement
Protection	Precision
Damage Dealing	Finisher
Haven	Stubborn

"If you read any pointless business book, you might learn that the goal is not always to work on your weaknesses but to accelerate your strengths to compensate for your weaknesses. While some of that is now nonsense only applicable to business, it still holds for this exercise. You have two days to continue to work on yourselves. Yes, expand your skills, but also focus on maximizing your current capabilities."

"Tuck," Williams said as he gazed at the largest one in the room. "Who's to say that your **Electron Surge** skill couldn't one day be as good as the shifting of the Mistblades?" He paused. "Who's to say that your **Ion Storm** can't bring down that of a Singularity Serpent?" Pausing again. "I for damn sure am not going to say that. Will you?"

"No, sir," Tuck responded firmly.

"Remember, this isn't just about Tuck. It's about all of you. Grow, adapt, and thrive." Williams gave the room a moment to absorb his words.

"All right. Now that we've established that, let's change gears. I understand Nex has shared details about Emy's recent Class transition?"

Heads around the room nodded in agreement, so Williams continued, "So, how do you want to go about this? Do you have specific questions, or would you prefer an overview?"

"Coach, how does one build their willpower?" Will prompted a question, interrupting the chorus of murmurs.

"Ah, so it's questions then," Williams laughed lightly. "Okay. Let's begin with the basics. You all moved from F to E-

Class after the Games commenced. This is because the initial grade transition is about being able to exert some influence on your surroundings. Most of Earth's inhabitants will remain in F-Class, even if they can sense their environment. During the tutorial, you all demonstrated the ability to engage, and once you entered a realm bound by time, you validated that capability."

Williams shot a glance at Will, who seemed eager to interject again. "Patience, Will. I'm getting there... When you're in E-Class, you're accumulating potential and willpower. Even though you've just gained the ability to perceive energy, you might have noticed others around you developing power. Advancements in the E-Class are achieved either by learning and expanding skills OR increasing your willpower. Heroes can get stuck in E-Class with only one skill or insufficient willpower to impact the world. That's why we could postpone this discussion. Leveling up was simply a matter of testing and applying influence."

"Now, to answer Will's question. We all understand that interacting with our surroundings is known as 'building.' The higher the willpower, the better the builder, and vice versa."

Williams then asked Will, "So, Will. What happens when you exercise a new muscle group for the first time?"

"Uh. You feel more... sore?" Will replied, sounding unsure.

"True. But in essence, you've challenged your body in a new way. Muscles were torn, your body adapted, and as a result, you became stronger."

"Stretching your limits is crucial to strengthening your 'building' muscle. Emy pushed her 'building' muscle beyond the D-Class threshold," Williams concluded, looking at the group for another question.

"Coach. You've participated in numerous events and have a wealth of expertise, yet you appear to be in your 40s... is that because of your Class?" James asked.

"That's an excellent question," Williams said, now grinning. "Life takes a turn once you merge with the Cosmos. Access to superior healthcare, medicines, and cell regeneration allows an average F-Class citizen to triple their lifespan, and that's without substantial funding or obtaining aid from a healer," Williams continued, taking in the stunned expressions on everyone's faces.

"And that's just for F-Class." Williams paused for effect. "The moment you transitioned to E-Class, your lifespan increased tenfold, and even more if you have a healing talent," Williams said as he looked at Nadia. "Now imagine a hundredfold increase for the leap to D-Class," Williams added, relishing the astonished looks on everyone's faces.

"But while Emy's maximum age has now reached the 7,000-year mark, her life is fraught with increased danger and risk, much like any ordinary citizen of the Cosmos. Shift your focus from heart disease being the leading cause of death to a random void collapsing an entire city."

"So… how old are you?" Nadia spoke in a quiet but firm tone.

"Ah. Nadia. I'm old, but age doesn't apply to me anymore. I've participated in 460 Quantum Games Tournaments. Some lasting longer than others."

Williams looked around the room, acknowledging that he anticipated the next question. "I'm currently a late B-Class hero." Williams paused. "But I'd prefer if you thought of my talent as more Artisan than Champion."

"All right. That's enough for now. We should probably move on, and I must admit, I'm not looking forward to this next discussion," Williams stated, a hint of remorse flashing in his eyes.

"Coach?" James questioned the abrupt tone shift.

"I need to share the history of my planet," Williams answered, voice carrying sorrow.

CHAPTER FIFTY-ONE

"Change is born from defeat." – E.B.

THE HANGAR

"I was once a Champion," Williams began, the atmosphere in the room shifting with his words.

"When my universe merged with the System, we became participants in the 720th Quantum Games. I was an 18-year-old, just as clueless as you all about the vastness of the Cosmos."

Williams paused, sighing deeply. "I selected to be part of a team; though it was far less structured than it is today, I was able to team up with my closest friends. We were all at a bar, and before we knew it, the world 'popped,' and we found ourselves in the tutorial."

"Back then, we didn't have a coach or mentor. Just a system messenger guiding us on what we could and couldn't do. It would gauge our energy and present us with manuals and videos of other heroes demonstrating those abilities. We were left to our own devices, and honestly, it was a blast." A faint smile crossed Williams' face. "Just as you are now, young adults told you possess unknown superpowers that could potentially save the world. Who wouldn't be thrilled?"

The room remained silent, allowing Williams to continue at his own pace. "We were naive but performed well in the first two levels. Creativity, untested confidence, and friendship can take you a long way. When we reached the Trials, we encountered a series of tunnels, time trials with creatures, and tests along the way. We did so well that we ranked 75th in the Stellar Ascendancy."

"When we were placed in our city of residence at Level Four, the fun stopped. Our hometown was overrun by death, destruction, and decay, and four 18-year-olds were tasked with stopping it..."

"We succeeded, but at the cost of a friend..."

"After the mission's success, we were immediately sent back to the intermission for more training. There was no time to mourn our friend, no extension, no additional rewards for the sacrifice of one of our own. The expectation was to carry on. Our journey ended in that fourth level. We continued to push forward, but our passion was lost. It was at the Seventh Level that we decided to withdraw."

"What happened next? Where did you go?" Trish prodded Williams to continue.

"We were left on the same dilapidated streets we encountered in Level Four—no exit prize, no communication, no indication that we had accomplished anything. Only a week had passed since we had been there for the fourth level, and we returned to give our friend the proper burial he deserved. The remaining three of us split up, deciding to return to our families to protect them if we could."

"My world was devoid of a team capable of winning the Quantum Games, and knowing what I know now, had we chosen to proceed to the next level, we could have prevented the incursion that ultimately led to our planet's destruction."

"... Coach, I'm sorry. What did you do?" James asked softly.

"I lived through some of the longest years of my life. Being at the peak of D-Class then, I had ample time to witness my world's downfall. Let's refer to those as the dark years. It wasn't until the CNC decided to integrate with the remaining population that I got a chance to start over. That was my saving grace. I had long believed I would be the last person on my planet."

"I devoted my life to supporting others in the hope that they might achieve what I couldn't, by any means necessary. When you've seen the dark side of failure, you'll do whatever it takes to ensure your team's success." Williams paused, surveying everyone in the room.

"I'm not sharing this story to bond with you all. Yes, I value our connections, and you can rely on me to do what's necessary for the team, but that's not the point. The point is that my world is just one of many that have failed. Countless planets are currently living through their version of the dark years."

"What do you expect from us?" Emy challenged.

"Understand what's at stake. But also understand that when people are forced to endure those times, it can change you. I believe you all saw the Ascension boards?"

"Yes?" Everyone in the room looked at Williams, puzzled.

"And now you should know that AD stands for the Astral Dominion."

"As in another civilization? Those names were on Earth's leaderboard." James asked.

"Yes, they were. Many integrations ago, the Astral Dominion's world fell just like mine. A fraction of the once-thriving population survived. A culture deeply rooted in hatred for the System. The AD chose not to aid others but to retest their fate in other worlds. They raised their young and integrated the strongest into planets on the verge of integration."

"They risked their children?" Will asked, anger resonating in his voice.

"Not in their eyes. They pushed their future generations to find new planets to thrive on. The Champion or Champions of the Quantum Games have the power and ability to take over a planet. Kings and Queens of new planets capable of transplanting their own into the new world. While the System restricts tampering and foul play for higher classed heroes before the Games end, it can be bypassed with those of the younger generation matching the skills and capabilities of the planet."

"These future heroes succeeded many times over, creating one of the most expansive organizations in the known Cosmos. It's ingrained in their culture that all high-ranking warriors must prove their fate in the Games to be deemed worthy of the kingdom."

"So, these hostiles are looking to take over Earth?" Will asked again.

"I wouldn't call them hostile... yet. They must achieve mission success to be declared the victors of the Games, but once that is achieved, they will enslave those on Earth opposing their reign and turn it into another step in their path to astral domination."

"And we just so happen to have the number four AD Galaxy Ascender within our planet," Nadia concluded.

"Correct," Williams confirmed.

"Coach, why did you recruit Trent?" Emy asked, causing a shift in the room as the others began to grasp her intent.

Williams didn't seem taken aback by the question; instead, he appeared relieved that it was finally asked. "Trent, like all of you, was identified as possessing immense power potential. I brought him on board with the idea of integrating him into your team, but once he arrived, I began to harbor doubts about him."

"So, why did you bring him into your classroom?" Emy pressed on.

"Trent was never going to agree to join a team, and if Trent is affiliated with the Astral Dominion, I'd prefer him to be in the same region as you."

"Why is that?" Emy persisted.

"Because you all can stop him."

CHAPTER FIFTY-TWO

"Allow your journey to shape your destiny, but never permit your history to control your future." – Noble, Former Champion.

THE HANGAR

The team decided to take a break and start fresh after questioning Williams. Everyone had mixed feelings about his story and confession regarding the possibilities of Trent's background, so they needed some time to refocus. The situation was unusual for the team. Even though their newfound ability to control energy meant they could reduce their need for sleep, their bodies and brains still required rest after long days. Without the natural cues of sunlight to guide their sleep patterns, the team aimed to schedule two 4-hour periods for rest, considering the timing based on recaps, strategy discussions, and the physical and mental strain from the previous round.

Regardless of the varying timelines during their absence, Trish and Frank always synchronized their sleep schedules with the team, even if Trish often spent her time meditating or reading in bed while others slept. As the four-hour period came to an end, everyone was already awake. The sad stories of defeat and the realization that an unknown alien race was attempting to take over their planet were powerful motivators. So, when the timer went off, everyone promptly regrouped with their assigned partners for the intermission.

"James, I've got a couple of things on my mind,"

Frank started the conversation as they strolled towards a multipurpose room in the Hangar. "Firstly, what's the deal with Emy?" he questioned, acknowledging his emerging role as the team's primary gossiper.

"Why do I feel the second question will be more troubling than the first?" James retorted, grinning.

"Secondly, have you ever gone hunting?" Frank asked his follow-up as James was left puzzled by the line of questioning.

"Nope," James responded, answering the second question first. "My folks weren't into hunting, so it's not something I've been exposed to. I've never even fired a gun."

Frank's eyebrows shot up. "Even with your archery skills?"

James laughed, "Yep. Before the Games, the only targets I've ever aimed at were wooden boards with bullseyes and a few plastic deer dummies, just for kicks."

"Understood… now back to my first question," Frank shifted again, a broad smile spreading across his face.

"Emy and I are just friends. I know it's cliché—boy and girl, lifelong friends destined to be soulmates—but we're genuinely just friends. We've had our share of relationships with others over the years, none lasting too long, and our friendship has always remained unaffected. I want to keep it that way. My trust circle has expanded, but Emy is my rock."

"Interesting," Frank responded, smirking. "Honestly, the two questions are unrelated. I was just curious about both. It's like when you have two questions for a professor and are eager to know the answers to both. Do you raise your hand, get an answer, then wait a while before asking the other? Nah, you ask both."

"Frank, that analogy doesn't make sense. You seriously think you'd ask Coach Williams a molecular biology question and then follow it up with a question about his romantic life?" James challenged.

"Honestly, that's a valid point. I am curious about Coach's love life," Frank mused, appearing deep in thought.

"You're something else," James remarked as they entered the

room.

"So, no hunting experience. I'm guessing you've never been camping, and you're definitely not a Boy Scout?" Frank asked, hopeful.

"Well, I did take a wilderness survival class in case I ever got caught in an avalanche," James replied, hoping to impress Frank.

"I don't think that's going to be particularly useful. You can create a field that can withstand -90° Celsius, and you think snow survival skills are something to build on?"

James looked deflated. "Guess not."

"But that doesn't mean an Eagle Scout like me can't teach you," Frank said, having a sudden epiphany. "Hold on, have I been an Eagle all my life?"

"Welcome to the flock, Frank," James retorted, smirking as he extended his fist with his thumb out.

Frank's face lit up as he immediately locked thumbs with James.

"Fly as One."

"SUCCEED AS ONE!" Frank bellowed, causing both of them to burst into laughter.

"Thank you," Frank said, regaining his composure. "You have no idea how long I've wanted to do that."

"I had a hunch," James replied.

"But seriously, I have a bunch of ideas about all those prizes you won from the last level. There are tons of ways we can upgrade and use them, but first, I think you need to learn a few knots. It's the Boy Scout way."

△△△

Tuck & Emy

"Tuck, have we ever talked with just the two of us?" Emy asked as they made their way to the central arena.

"I don't think we have," Tuck acknowledged. "Why is that?"

"I don't know," Emy admitted.

"That's because if you two were ever alone, you'd both just sit there in silence," Will interjected as he and Williams headed for the strategy room.

"Go find a rock to kick, Will," Emy retorted, glancing back at Tuck. "He's probably right, though," she added in a softer tone, eliciting laughter from both of them.

"But I'd trust you with my life, you know?" Emy confessed.

"And I, you."

Emy and Tuck silently continued their walk to the arena's center. Coach Williams had assigned them to learn to scale their powers, amplifying and diminishing their abilities for greater adaptability.

"Tuck, before the tournament, was there ever a moment when you completely let your guard down?" Emy questioned. "You always seemed to have an air of reservation about you."

"What do you mean?"

"Have you ever found yourself alone somewhere and just screamed as loud as you possibly could?" Emy elaborated, quickly realizing that Tuck might not relate.

"Or maybe you heard your favorite song while driving and belted it out, not caring how silly you looked or how off-key you sounded?" Emy tried again, fearing she might have missed the mark again.

"I've wanted to," Tuck admitted softly, giving Emy hope that the conversation was progressing.

"Why didn't you?" Emy probed.

"I'm not sure you want to get into that," Tuck cautioned.

"Try me."

"Unrestrained behavior, wild antics, even losing yourself in laughter—it all signifies a loss of control," Tuck explained. "Surrendering to your emotions and letting them take over is a sign of weakness."

"But why?"

"It's what I was taught."

"Tuck, I'm making an effort here. You need to meet me

halfway," Emy urged.

"Look at me, Emy. I'm a large black man who grew up in a predominantly white town. My father, also a black man, was imprisoned for using excessive force in a bar fight and nearly killing someone. Growing up, I couldn't afford to let go. Letting go meant ostracism. Letting go meant incarceration. Letting go meant... expulsion from the team," Tuck confessed, his voice faltering towards the end.

"Tuck," Emy comforted, placing a hand on his back. "I'm sorry."

"Letting go is the only way to truly test your power. When you rushed the field to help Nadia, you let go. You might not have realized it, but your storm dominated the area. Rage drove you, but your power was unparalleled."

"So that leads me to a question: how do we get you to that state while maintaining self-control?" Emy finished her thought.

Tuck shook his head, still trying to regain his composure while thinking of his past.

"I think I have an idea," Emy proposed. "Tuck, what's your favorite song?"

"What?" Tuck looked up, surprised. "I-uh, don't have one."

"Perfect. I know just the one."

△△△

Emy, Frank & Tuck

"So, what did you want me to do again?" Frank asked Emy, his eyes now looking at the arena console.

"Circle of trust?" Emy asked Frank.

"Absolutely," Frank affirmed. "Always."

"We need to create a scenario for Tuck to go all out; he needs to be free to act on his own," Emy suggested.

"So, I want you to play this," Emy said as she input a song into the console. "Does the System have any repetitive workout scenarios?"

"Well, that's not a song I was expecting," Frank admitted with a broad grin. "I'm definitely staying. James is busy enough with his knots. As for the workout, we have countless scenarios. What about taking down a house-sized tree?"

"That sounds perfect," Emy agreed.

In the middle of the arena, Tuck watched as a massive tree began to sprout from the ground. It grew so large that Tuck had to retreat several meters to avoid being engulfed.

"Tuck, I don't care how you do it, but bring down that tree," Emy instructed before exiting the room and closing the door behind her. "This arena is soundproof, right?"

"Possibly..." Frank replied.

"Frank."

"Okay, okay. Yes, it is," Frank conceded.

"Great. Let's do this," Emy commanded as Frank pressed play on the console.

"Seriously?" Tuck's head shot up as the music began to play, his stern gaze meeting the eyes of the two observers outside the arena.

"Just go with it," Emy encouraged. "The fate of the world hangs in the balance."

With a sigh, Tuck relented. Emy was right. The world was actually on the line. Why not give it a shot?

Tuck eyed the towering redwood tree that now stood before him. He had seen pictures of cars driving through similar trees in California, but the one in front of him looked large enough to house a small dwelling. Tuck twirled his **Warhammer** and drew back, driving the spike directly into the tree. The spike's tip penetrated the tree and halted midway to the metal hammer.

"All right, here goes nothing," Tuck muttered, taking a deep breath before yanking out his weapon and striking the tree again. With each successive hit, Tuck chipped away at the tree's base. As his inner fire ignited, electricity surged over his weapon, sparking upon contact with the tree and charring the wood upon impact.

Tuck felt invigorated. A singular focus replaced his anxiety and fear. The mini arena was teeming with thunder and impact, with the music still blaring as Tuck continued his assault on the tree. At some point, Tuck flipped his **Warhammer** so that the hammer edge led into the tree. Despite the flat metal edge, the flat hammer still pierced into the tree, sending large chunks of wood flying.

"Keep going, Tuck," Emy said softly as she watched Tuck fully immerse himself in his strikes, quickly reaching his prior peak power.

The music and noise in the room ceased in Tuck's mind as he stood unbridled, his mind empty as he delivered blow after blow to the enormous tree. Unbeknownst to him, the clouds had darkened and billowed up. What was once a lightning storm had transformed into a monsoon of rage and fury, not through action, but through sheer will. As the storm clouds drew closer to Tuck, they morphed into a dense storm map. Tuck finally let his emotions go as a **Lightning Bolt** struck his **Warhammer**, delivering a final blow to the tree. The moment his **Warhammer** halted, the lightning continued, penetrating the tree's core as the gigantic redwood trembled and shifted.

Realizing the power of his strike, Tuck looked up to see the giant tree beginning to topple. Panting heavily, his arms trembling, Tuck watched as the tree disintegrated, leaving him alone in the room.

"DUDE!" Frank exclaimed.

"You did it," Emy said, approaching Tuck with a bright smile. "How do you feel?"

"Alive," Tuck responded softly, "... thank you."

CHAPTER FIFTY-THREE

"Ascending to power is equally about pioneering new ideas as it is about acquiring knowledge and honing skills." – Coach Williams.

THE HANGAR

Nadia & Trish

"Before anything else," Trish started, her voice shaky. "Frank and I kinda overheard your chat about nursing with Will. We felt a bit weird realizing we were eavesdropping. If we crossed a line, we're really sorry. We were just curious, thinking it might give us some useful insights for the team. But yeah, we get it. Maybe we should've stepped out," Trish shared, sounding like she'd rehearsed this as she and Nadia headed towards her lab.

"No, I was hoping you were listening. I don't think I can repeat that story too often, especially not in front of the entire team. I'm relieved it's out and glad I don't have to recount it," Nadia replied.

"Ah. That's a huge relief. I've been replaying this scenario for the past few days, and I half predicted you to get upset and storm off." Trish laughed lightly.

"Really?" Nadia joined in the laughter. "We've known each other for what, a week? And you think you can predict my reactions?" she retorted sarcastically.

"You never know!"

"Well, for future reference, I have pretty thick skin. Try growing up in a family that comments on your weight every holiday season," Nadia joked, pushing thoughts of her family to the back of her mind.

"Speaking of a thick shell..." Trish said as her eyes sparkled, "You couldn't have provided a better transition to our current project."

"But first... those knives or, uh, blades? Are they made of bone?" Trish questioned.

"Ha. Yeah, essentially bone or highly dense calcium compacts, but without all the nerves and tendons, so I don't feel anything."

"That's incredibly cool. Frank and I have been looking for ways to help you. You're the team's healer, but to be honest, you lack defense. Of course, in a team, you protect each other, but given your role, you often operate solo," Trish stated as she glanced at Nadia for confirmation. "And let's be real, you don't exactly give off damsel-in-distress vibes."

"It's like you're reading my mind," Nadia encouraged Trish.

"We discovered a liquid metal that can integrate with your body. It was originally used for joint and hip replacements," Trish started but noticed Nadia's confusion. "But! Imagine dynamic integration with one's body to improve malfunctioning body parts or simply strengthen existing ones... I may need to show you."

Regenium - 1 Point per Milliliter
Epic
This innovative liquid metal seamlessly integrates with living organisms, providing structural support and enhancement when needed. Its unique regenerative abilities are activated by a symbiotic connection with its biosphere, ensuring continuous reconstruction and fortification as long as a trace of the metal remains in the life form. The metal also has a high cooling rate, allowing it to solidify instantly when exposed to room temperature, providing immediate reinforcement in critical situations. The regeneration speed can vary based on the organism's body composition.

"Net, it's a bit of a gamble," Trish remarked as Nadia absorbed the information. "But with your talent and **Body Manipulation** skill, I believe this has a high chance of success."

"It's worth a try. One point per milliliter doesn't seem too steep," Nadia commented.

"Well, from what I've read, you need to start with a substantial quantity for your body to integrate fully. Otherwise, it's just a foreign object that your body tolerates or pushes out," Trish said, grimacing.

"How much are we talking about?"

"The estimate is 600 milliliters," Trish continued, her expression still pained.

"What?" Nadia cried out in surprise.

"And we won't know for sure until we begin the integration process," Trish added, maintaining her expression. "Okay, that's all the bad news. Promise."

Regaining her composure, Trish adopted a more assertive stance, "Look, would you hesitate to spend points if one of your teammates bought metal armor that could potentially save their life?"

"No," Nadia sighed.

"Then, if you think it will work, I'm making the decision to go for it," Trish smiled. "And did I mention that the metal is black?"

"Why the heck didn't you start with that?"

The pair immediately started their task, executing numerous iterations of metal infusion. With Trish meticulously synchronizing the metal to Nadia's inherent energy currents, they expended a collective sum of 653 points. This thorough process continued until they concluded that Nadia's internal chemical equilibrium was firmly established.

"Should we give it a try?" Trish proposed to Nadia.

"I believe so, but considering the number of points we've used, it should be something impressive, right?"

"Oh, I love that idea. Are you considering pulling a

Wolverine on us? I'd find that quite entertaining."

Nadia laughed. "That's definitely in the cards. But I was thinking more along the lines of a prank..."

"Yes! Do tell more!"

△△△

Will & Williams

"When do you plan to tell her?" Will asked immediately as he and Williams stepped into the strategy room, now away from prying ears.

"When the moment is appropriate," Williams responded, aware that Will had discovered his secret.

"I'm not sure if that's fair to her," Will challenged his former professor. "She deserves to know about your actions. I don't know the specifics, but I'm aware you played a role in all of us attending this school."

"I did."

"And after hearing Nadia's story and the hardships she endured at the hospital, not to mention her family afterward, it's not right. It doesn't matter if you believe you had the moral high ground."

"I agree."

"Do you have nothing to say, or do you simply acknowledge when you're in the wrong?"

"Will, I reflect on my past decisions daily. Not an hour passes without me contemplating my team's choice to abandon the Games, the young individuals I may have sent to die, or every instance I have deceived. Did you know that out of the 459 Games where I managed a team, only two have emerged as Champions?"

Williams sighed. "You listen to the things I tell you all. Right now, do you possess an ounce of quit in you?"

"No."

"458 other teams felt the same way at some point. That

accounts for many teams that never quit and didn't win," Williams continued. "My decisions resulted in the loss of thousands of promising young lives, and I live with that reality daily."

They remained silent for a long moment. "But you know what? I would do it all again. The haunting dreams and debilitating guilt are burdens I must bear to prevent innocent worlds from falling into ruin. Those thousands of lives saved trillions, perhaps not directly, but if there's even a slight chance that I can contribute to building a team capable of saving not just their world but future worlds, I will undoubtedly do it every time."

"As for Nadia, I'll tell her when I can, but I'm not in a hurry. My lie is meaningless if she dies. If I don't do everything within my power to push you seven to be the absolute best, that's worse than any lie I could ever tell."

Will was never resentful toward his Coach. He always understood, and his understanding deepened now. For Will, it was about deceit, trust, and Nadia knowing she wasn't at fault. He had to admit he was glad Coach did what he did. They needed Nadia, but Nadia deserved the truth.

"We're stronger than you realize," Will concluded, holding his eyes on Williams. "Don't judge our potential reactions based on past events. Trust and commitment form stronger bonds than lies and manipulation."

"Now, what did you have in mind for training?"

△△△

Full Team

"Hey Frank, has James earned any badges yet?" Will asked across the table as James sat down next to Nadia.

The team was enjoying their first lunch break following an intense morning of training, and the conversation naturally veered towards their progress.

"Absolutely, he's got at least five! My personal favorite is the bunny ears knot badge. After just three hours of knot practice, James can officially tie his shoes. I'd even venture to say he could tie anyone's shoes at this very table."

"Wow, James," Emy added, "I had no idea you were so skilled at knot tying."

"I know, right? I've been able to dive right in. It's almost as if the guidebook was designed for kids or something. I'll be a knot-tying expert by sundown." James decided to play along.

"What about you, Nadia? You've been rather quiet about yours and Trish's work this morning," James redirected the conversation.

"Ah, well," Trish interjected, "Nadia and I have been developing a new vanishing talent. We were waiting for lunch to end before showing off."

"Why wait? I want to see," James insisted. "I propose a working lunch."

"Alright, alright. But we'll need your archery skills to test it out."

The team finished their meals and gradually moved into the main room near the mini arena. They needed a larger space for James to use his bow and arrows.

"Hold on, you just want me to shoot at you? I'm not sure how I feel about that."

"Don't be a wimp, James," Trish retorted. "We've practiced at least ten times."

"Ten?"

"Oh, just do it already. Just make sure you aim for her chest," Trish instructed, with Nadia nodding in agreement at the end of the long corridor.

The group gathered around James as he drew his bow, aiming at Nadia, who stood still with a blank expression. "Last chance."

"Oh, just do it!" Nadia answered, prompting the arrow to fly through the air, hitting her squarely in the chest—**Tink**!

Nadia fell to the floor, screaming as the arrow pierced into her, shirt now soaked in blood.

"Nadia!" James cried out in terror as everyone rushed towards her in a panic.

Tuck quickly picked her up in his arms. "Hang in there, Nadia! Can we use those **Revive Pills**?"

"Nadia, can you hear us? Stay with us! Use your **Vitalize** skill!" Will placed his hands over Nadia's heart, trying to close the wound, while Trish and Frank burst into laughter.

"Why are you laughing?" James demanded, looking at Trish and Frank with revulsion.

"Because it's ketchup." Nadia opened her eyes and lifted her head from Tuck's arms.

"What?" Will looked at his hand, now covered in tomato sauce.

"Look closer," Trish said, grinning. "Nadia's got some new armor." It was then that Nadia pushed the **Regenium** into her forearm and rolled up her sleeve.

"Cool, right?" Nadia smirked at Tuck, who was still holding her.

"No. Not cool," Tuck responded flatly. "You know we're all on edge already."

"Oh, just let it go, Tuck," Frank said, now grinning widely with a slight wink. "Look how awesome that is."

"Wait, how did you even know?" Trish looked at Frank. "You weren't even in on it."

"Oh, ladies. You need to work on your acting skills. You grabbed a ketchup packet in the kitchen and ate a house salad."

"Oh." Trish looked at Nadia and laughed harder.

"Okay. I agree that's pretty cool, but can you also go full Wolverine?" Will immediately asked, with the rest of the group nodding in agreement.

CHAPTER FIFTY-FOUR

"Being accompanied by a coach during the Games is a significant advantage, particularly at the start. The challenging aspect is realizing that this coach isn't your buddy but someone designed to propel you to reach your utmost potential." – Quist, Former Champion.

THE HANGAR

"SPEECH!" bellowed Will from his spot at the table while Emy stood by the ice cream cake that had just been placed before her. Frank possessed a unique talent for telepathically communicating his desires to the cookless kitchen, which consistently delivered precisely what he envisioned, down to the last detail. In this instance, it was a cake adorned with typed lettering, beneath which a majestic eagle clutched a serpent in its talons.

'Fury'
'D-Class - SNAKE SLAYER'

"I'm not one to give speeches," Emy began hesitantly, only for Frank to interject enthusiastically, "Allow me to handle this one."

"Um, okay. Thank you?" Emy responded, a touch bewildered.

"Okay, glasses up, everyone," Frank started as he looked to be pulling up something prepared via Nex. "She was once isolated, but it looks like now she is our Queen. Who knew what swirling storm was inside her? Here's to never going back; the past is in the past. Let her storm rage on!"

"Why does that sound familiar?" Nadia remarked, raising her glass, while Tuck interjected, "Oh, it's just Frank being Frank."

"Isn't that right, Frank?" Tuck asked, giving Frank a meaningful glance as he raised his glass.

"Absolutely. It was a spur-of-the-moment creation!" Frank declared with a grin.

The team capitalized on the chance to celebrate their advancements over the last day and a half. Diving back into intense practice drills, they persistently stretched their capabilities and explored avenues for improvement. The occasion of Emy's ascendance to D-Class served as the perfect pretext for another team gathering.

Under Frank's mentorship, James honed his skills in diverse scenarios, including setting traps and tracking, enhancing the team's ability to fully utilize their new inventory. Concurrently, Frank lent his distinctive touch to these items, customizing them to seamlessly integrate with the team's tactical capabilities.

Tuck and Emy, occasionally joined by Will, diligently expanded their skill sets. Tuck honed his **Warhammer** techniques to enhance reach and force, while Emy concentrated on precise strikes, often utilizing James's targets that he had been using for archery. They soon realized that the challenge lay in diminishing the strikes' impact and preventing the flames' subsequent propagation.

This time, Will emulated Nadia's previous period of solitude and contemplation. However, instead of seeking isolation, Will remained close to his teammates, striving to attune himself to the ambient energies. He learned that Williams possessed a remarkable talent for discerning energies, intentions, and mindsets. Will recognized that his and Williams' abilities were closely aligned, with Williams' skills being particularly suited for identifying prospects, while Will focused on predicting and evaluating his surroundings.

Trish and Nadia developed a deep bond during this period, with Trish overseeing Nadia's biological development, growth, and maintenance of her new metallic integration. Trish devised methods to prompt Nadia to dynamically relocate her metallic elements from one body part to another, ranging from mock blade fights to blindfolding, attempting to enhance her predictive abilities based on the energy flows within the room. Their ultimate aim was to cultivate muscle memory for the metal's translocation, making it an instinctive reaction.

As the festivities neared their conclusion, Williams entered the kitchen.

"Congratulations, Emy," Williams greeted with a warm smile before turning to Nadia. "Please don't mind me, but Nadia, may I have a moment with you?"

The team exchanged knowing looks as Nadia rose from her seat. Although it wasn't unusual for Williams to engage in one-on-one sessions with them, this request seemed particularly intentional.

When Nadia stepped out of the kitchen with Williams, he guided her into the strategy room and gently shut the door behind them.

"Nadia," Williams exhaled deeply, a note of resignation in his voice, "it's become clear to me that keeping secrets from you all isn't right."

"I already know, Professor," Nadia spoke, her voice low yet assertive, catching Williams by surprise for the first time.

"You know?"

"Yes, I've had my suspicions, and the subtle clues you hinted about recruitment only solidified them. Ironically, I still find myself feeling responsible," Nadia confessed. "I understand your actions, and I'm not upset that you did what you did, but part of me can't help but wonder if there was a different path to get the same outcome."

Williams let Nadia's words hang for a moment. "I regret any distress this has caused you," Williams said, struggling to find the right words. "I took the path I believed was most likely to succeed. It was risky but ultimately brought you into this team."

"But how? How did you manage it?" Nadia questioned, her gaze now fixed on Williams.

"Potential coaches are spread across various regions of the worlds set for integration, but we aren't the only ones with our eyes on you all. I was fortunate to have the resources and the assistance of individuals adept in the art of deception. The man you administered the dose to was never in danger."

Taken aback and slightly relieved, Nadia wasn't sure how to react. "But out of all the people, why did you pick me?" Nadia asked, her gaze meeting his directly. "It's hard to believe there weren't others you could have chosen, yet you chose to uproot my life so profoundly."

"Interpreting energies is a subtle art," Williams clarified. "But the rationale is straightforward: when a single person, irrespective of their potential capabilities, exerts even the slightest pull over another, I will move heaven and earth to have them join my team. Those minute nuances can ultimately tip the scales towards our success."

"As for you," Williams collected his thoughts again, "when I came across your profile, I had to verify it personally. My sources identified you as someone with a high healing potential, which was one of the many gaps we had at that time, but that was just the start."

"Finding someone with healing potential is challenging as it's not a common trait in the Cosmos. On top of that, truly empathetic souls are rare. We encounter numerous Champions with a high healing rate due to a strong survival instinct. Still, you, Nadia, are motivated to assist others while acknowledging that you must take care of yourself first. That, coupled with a great deal of bravery, resilience, and an overwhelming sense of loyalty and dedication to those you hold dear."

"I now realize that I did not reciprocate the very loyalty

and dedication I recruited you for, and for that, I owe you an apology… Nadia, this isn't an excuse, but the past years have been challenging. Starting anew and shedding old preconceptions is tough, but it's a step I should take every time. This team means the world to me."

"I am not one to hold a grudge. I understand now why you took that path, but I can't help but feel vulnerable to deceit again," Nadia admitted, her thoughts swirling. Despite her current struggles with her family, Williams' decision ultimately changed her life for the better.

Though her words were brief, the energy between them confirmed that Williams had managed to salvage some of their bond, and for that, he was grateful.

"I didn't expect you to forgive me, but please know I am here for you and the team. My primary goal will always be your success. However, I now realize the importance of being more honest with all of you moving forward, and for that, you have my word." Williams understood that he had a long journey ahead with this team, but these students—no, these heroes—were unique. They had the potential to alter the destiny of the Cosmos, and he would do everything in his power not to stand in their way.

CHAPTER FIFTY-FIVE

*"No training will fully prepare you for
the devastations you will soon witness."
– Echo, Former Champion.*

THE HANGAR

The intermission hours were drawing to a close, and the team of seven savored their final moments before the next level of the Quantum Games. Coach's insight suggested that they would likely be transported to an Earth-based location—traditionally one where previous Champions had stumbled. This moment was bittersweet, especially after Coach had just recounted a story from Level Four, in which he lost a close teammate.

"You've got this!" Frank said confidently. You're already the greatest heroes I've ever met."

"Frank, we're the only heroes you've ever met," Tuck deadpanned.

"And that still proves my statement!" Frank argued. "Look, I'm trying to say that I believe in you guys, no matter what you might face."

"That makes two of us," Trish joined, matching Frank's smile.

"Three," Coach remarked from a distance as he approached the team. Usually, he let the team experience these moments without his presence, but this time, he was greeted by reassuring expressions as he decided to participate.

"Hey, Coach. I've been meaning to ask. What was the name

of your home planet?" Will asked out as Coach joined them.

"Galadra," Williams spoke softly with a slight smile.

"All right," Will started. "Everyone knows the drill. Hands in."

The team gathered around Will, each clasping the wrist of the person next to them. Trish and Frank also joined in, their faces brightening with enthusiasm. This was their first group huddle, but Coach hesitated.

"Waiting on you, Coach," Nadia gestured as the rest of the team looked at Coach, who then gratefully joined them all in unison.

"There's not a single place I'd rather be right now than standing next to all of you," Will declared. "Whatever the System throws our way, we'll be ready. Let whatever stands in our path know that we aren't leaving. Earth is our home, and we'll fight to protect it until the very end."

"Here's to Galadra and all the lost souls across the Cosmos who have fallen victim to chaos," Will added. "We stand together to fight for those who cannot. Let the ether soon know our names."

"Fly as One."

"Succeed as One."

△△△

Would you like to continue to Level Four of the Quantum Games?

"Yes"

Amidst the gray void, the team materialized onto a lonely road. Gone were the chaotic scenes and fervent crowds from their previous level; now, they stood alone, the only sound a gentle breeze whispering through their surroundings. As they glanced upward, they beheld a sign suspended over the once-bustling street:

"The Biggest Little City In The World"

They had arrived in Reno, Nevada, on the city's busiest road within the central downtown district, nestled along Virginia Street.

As her senses acclimated to the environment, Emy whispered a single word, "Home."

The team surveyed the sign and the surrounding buildings and observed powerful roots and vines winding around the blue and neon-lit arch suspended over the road. As sunset drew near, downtown clung to the fading remnants of natural light, withholding its usual illumination.

"Those vines seem to be growing," James called out.

Nadia agreed, "Look, they're even scaling the casino high-rises."

"Not upward. The roots are descending. Look at the energy signals. The most substantial energy readings originate from a few stories up and flow downward," Will remarked, recognizing that his energy training was already proving useful.

James asked the question that everyone was asking: "Is this the insurgent force—the plant itself?"

In response, the team consulted their mission log on their status screen, seeking answers for the scene before them.

Level Four Group Mission: Infiltration Scenario

A colossal, amorphous organism has infiltrated the city of Reno. Objectives: Neutralize the hostile entity and rescue a minimum of 50 hostages.

Hostages Rescued: 0

"Hostages?" Will's voice cracked as his mouth went dry. A rapid succession of barn-related images flashed through his mind.

< Alliance Re-Established - Cohort 8 – Limited communications are now available >

< Alliance Re-Established - Cohort 1 – Limited communications are now available >

Mere moments slipped by as Emy commandeered the communication channel. Her voice remained firm, yet it teetered on the precipice of rage. "Trent," she declared, "let this serve as a warning. We know your identity and are fully aware of your recent actions. Remove yourself from the City of Reno, or we will come for you."

The team stood in silence, absorbing Emy's words directed at Trent. He had reentered the range of their former alliance communications, but the line remained eerily quiet.

Then, breaking the stillness, a quick, mirthless laugh echoed through the channel. It was followed by a voice they all recognized too well, "Oh, Fury," the voice drawled, "you have no idea who I truly am."

< Alliance Severed - Cohort 1 – Limited communications are no longer available >

INTERMISSION HERO UPDATES #3

"Our heroes have experienced remarkable leaps in power during the previous level! Feel free to skip this part if you'd like!" – Nex.

Mighty Eagles (Cohort 13)

Total Team Points: **1575 Points**

Total Points Spent: **1413 Points**

Total Points Remaining: **162 Points**

Total Max Active Views: **1.3B**

Earth Rank: **113 of 37,191**

99.7th Percentile

......

Stellar Ascendancy - Earth - **7th Place - 7 / 99% / 0:53**

Stellar Ascendancy - Milky Way - **No Rank**

△△△

Fury (Emy)

Generalist
Level **10**
D-Class
Fire & Void Affinity

Primary Skill: Targeted Fusion (R) **(Level 8)**

Secondary Skills: Disintegration (T & R) **(Level 5)**; Pyroform (SELF) **(Level 6)**; Umbral Void Blaze (AOE) **(Level 2)**; Void Control (R) **(Level 2)**

Health: 100% Health + Natural Recovery Rate 10% each minute.

Shield: 100%: 90% Power based + 10% Gear based

Weapons: None

Augments: Level 5 Combat Training Module; Map Extension (Rare)

Gear:

Full Body: QuantumWeave (Uncommon) - 5% Shield Coverage

Head: None.

Upper Body: Mighty Eagles Letterman's Jacket (Unique) - 5% Shield Coverage

Lower Body: Leggings - No Modifications

Feet: Sneakers - No Modifications

Accessories: Engraved Fanny Pack (Uncommon); Soulpulse (x2) (Rare); Quantum Gateway (Legendary); Revive Pills (200) (Common)

△△△

Surge (Tuck)
Accelerator
Level **9**
E-Class
Electron Affinity

Primary Skill: Electron Surge (T) **(Level 6)**

Secondary Skills: Ion Storm (AOE) **(Level 7)**; Lightning Bolt (R + Metal) **(Level 3)**; Repulse (SELF) **(Level 2)**

Health: 100% Health + Natural Recovery Rate 8% each minute

Shield: 100%: 80% Power based + 20% Gear based

Weapons:

    Two-Handed Weapon: Celestium Spiked Warhammer (D-Class, Low) (Upgradeable)

Augments: Level 5 Combat Training Module; Level 5 Combat Weapons Training; Map Extension (Rare)

Gear:

    Full Body: QuantumWeave (Uncommon) - 10% Shield Coverage

    Head: None

Upper Body: Mighty Eagles Letterman's Jersey (Unique) - 10% Shield Coverage

Lower Body: Jeans - No Modifications

Feet: Sneakers - No Modifications

Accessories: Revive Pills (200) (Common)

△△△

Grace (James)
Catalyst
Level **9**
E-Class
No Affinity

Primary Skill: Empower (R, AOE) **(Level 5)**

Secondary Skills: Restrict (R, AOE) **(Level 4)**; Energy Blocking Field (T & R) **(Level 5)**

>(Resistance - Cold **(M)**, Heat **(M)**, Electric **(M)**, Blunt **(M)**, Piercing **(M)**, Toxic **(L)**
>Duration - 2:30 Mins, Reactivation - 5 Min)

Health: 100% Health + Natural Recovery Rate 8% each minute

Shield: 60%: 40% Power based + 20% Gear based

Weapons:

>**Bow:** Novaflight (E-Class, High)
>
>**Arrows:** Back Quiver with Statis Alchemarrows (E-Class, High) (∞) (Fireball, Neurofluxine, Crimson Cascade, Piercing, Ice, Fire)

Augments: Level 5 Combat Training Module; Map Extension (Rare)

Gear:

>**Full Body:** QuantumWeave (Uncommon) - 10% Shield Coverage
>
>**Head:** None
>
>**Upper Body:** Mighty Eagles Letterman's Jacket (Unique) - 10% Shield Coverage
>
>**Hands:** Stonebreaker Gloves (Epic)
>
>**Lower Body:** Jeans - No Modifications
>
>**Feet:** Sneakers - No Modifications
>
>**Accessories:** Revive Pills (200) (Common); Neurablocker (21) (Uncommon); Skyward Whistle (Rare); Energy Trigger (19) (Rare); Rootbound Seedling (20) (Uncommon); Cosmic

Glue (Common); Sonic Conduit (Uncommon); Tactical Sling (Uncommon)

△△△

Nadia
Cellulator
Level **7**
E-Class
Physiology Affinity

Primary Skill: Vitalize (T, AOE) **(Level 7)** 20% Recovery Rate each minute (Individual); 10% Recovery Rate each minute (Group)

Secondary Skills: Affliction Surge (T, AOE) **(Level 5)**; Body Manipulation (SELF) **(Level 3)**

Health: 98% Health + Natural Recovery Rate 20% each minute

Minor Inflictions: Neurofluxine (1%); Crimson Cascade (1%)

Body Chemistry: Regenium Metal (Epic) - 613 ml

Shield: 50%: 30% Power based + 20% Gear based

Weapons: None

Augments: Level 5 Combat Training Module; Map Extension (Rare)

Gear:

    Full Body: QuantumWeave (Uncommon) - 10% Shield Coverage

    Head: None

    Upper Body: Mighty Eagles Letterman's Jacket (Unique) - 10% Shield Coverage

    Lower Body: Jeans - No Modifications

    Feet: Ghostwalkers (Rare) - Flight (20 ft.), Duration 2 mins, 3x per day

    Accessories: Phantom Veil (Rare); Revive Pills (200) (Common)

△△△

Brick (Will)
Condenser
Level **9**
E-Class
Water Affinity

Primary Skill: Condense (T & R) **(Level 7)**

Secondary Skills: Cryostrike (R) **(Level 8)**; Flow Perception (T) **(Level 7)**; Permafrost (SELF) **(Level 6)**

Health: 100% Health + Natural Recovery Rate 6% each minute

Shield: 100%: 80% Power based + 20% Gear based

Weapons: None

Augments: Level 5 Combat Training Module; Map Extension (Rare)

Gear:

    Full Body: QuantumWeave (Uncommon) - 10% Shield Coverage

    Head: None

    Upper Body: Mighty Eagles Letterman's Jacket (Unique) -

10% Shield Coverage

Lower Body: Jeans - No Modifications

Feet: Sneakers - No Modifications

Accessories: Revive Pills (200) (Common)

Legend:
(T) = Touching, (R) = Ranged, (AOE) = Area of Effect
(L) = Low Skill, (M) = Moderate Skill, (H) = High Skill

△△△

Trish
Manipulator
Level **8**
E-Class
No Affinity

△△△

Frank
Creator
Level **7**
E-Class
Metallurgy Affinity

CHAPTER FIFTY-SIX

*"The worst plan is no plan. Start with something
—you can always adjust." – Coach Williams.*

LEVEL FOUR

"Michele, Darya, it's great to have you both back," James conveyed on behalf of the team. "We never got the chance to reach out, but we are genuinely sorry for your loss. Tabitha was awesome."

"It was a rough go, and it still is," Michele told the larger team. "I gave that traitor a piece of my mind before he abruptly disconnected. I'll add cowardice to the list of reasons we despise him."

"Emy might have contributed to his disconnection, too," Will reflected jokingly.

"Good on you, Emy. We always knew you were one of us," Michele praised before Darya interjected, "We're thrilled to hear you all again. Is everyone okay on your side?"

Before James or the team could respond, Michele added, "Wait, Mighty Eagles? As in the Eagles who took seventh place in the Stellar Ascendancy? I was making fun of that team name to Darya during intermission!"

James laughed. "That's us. The name was Emy's idea," James said, earning a look from Emy. "But to answer your question, we're physically intact and mentally persevering. We're positioned in front of the downtown Arch. How are you managing?"

"We're near the baseball stadium on Evan's Street. We're all right, despite losing our best friend..." she answered. "We're pressing on because we know she would have wanted that." Darya then questioned, "Do you see anyone around you? Our area is deserted, and we notice roots and vines in odd places."

"Same here. No one in sight, and confirming that those vines only intensify once you reach downtown. They seem to be most prominent near some of the larger casinos. Recon and report findings like before?" James proposed, then looked to his team, receiving nods of agreement.

"That sounds like a plan. Darya is still speedy, but after our loss, we'd prefer not to separate for too long," Michele said grimly.

"We get it. Do what you can. We're going to examine these creepy vines more closely and will update you both shortly," James said, ending the communication with Michele and Darya.

"I was wondering when someone would mention how eerie these vines are," Will commented. "Chances are there's more to these vines. That said, I propose Tuck be the first to cut a vine," Will suggested with a grin.

"Seconded," James concurred, "but only because... you know... you have a giant stick with a spike."

"All right," Tuck conceded with a sigh, "but for the record, I don't think this is a wise move."

Nadia added, "Agreed, but it's necessary. Let's move first to the Eldorado entrance and not stay in the middle of a street. Tuck, retreat to us if you spot anything. I think we should avoid fighting anything at this point."

As the group cautiously approached the double doors of the Eldorado Casino, they peered inside to find an empty casino building, lacking the usual hum and noises of slot machines filling the space, awaiting the next player. Inside, more vines, interconnected across the entire space, entwined around the slots.

"Tuck, hold off for a second. Let me do a quick sweep of the casino floor, just in case," Emy suggested before looking back at the others, "Unless Will or James wants to take the lead?"

It wasn't that the two were apprehensive about confronting a creature; the city just had an unnerving vibe, with the absence of people and creeping vines. The unknown was more daunting than any battle the team could knowingly confront.

"Here's the thing, Emy. I'm not 21 yet, so technically, I'm not allowed to be too close to slot machines…" Will smirked, and James shrugged in agreement.

Emy raised an eyebrow, turned, and pushed open the second set of doors. The air grew thick with moisture and heavy silence, punctuated only by the distant rub of roots expanding around the floor. Her senses were on high alert, every nerve attuned to any lingering presence.

Step by cautious step, Emy ventured deeper into the space. The once lively carpeted walkway now lay deserted, its signs faded, and its neon lights extinguished. Once a hub of laughter and clinking glasses, the casino bar and grill stood empty—a ghostly reminder of better days.

Emy's gaze swept the room, searching for any sign of danger. No other signatures revealed themselves. She had seen enough. With a determined nod, she retraced her steps, slipping back through the inside doors to rejoin her team.

"Still as unsettling as ever, but no signs other than those roots," Emy reported to the team. "Tuck, it's your turn."

"Roger that."

Tuck surveyed the roots twisting around the arch and selected a vine towards the arch's base connected to the sidewalk. The vines seemed to feel further down the pathway, growing slightly. Tuck took another breath, hoisted his **Warhammer** over his shoulder, and drove his spike down on the unlucky vine.

As soon as the spike penetrated the vine, it reacted like a snake had been struck. The severed end slowly deteriorated and lost its girth, shriveling, but the end connected to the still ascending roots squirmed as if under attack. That's when a loud siren-like scream emanated from the building next to the

Arch. Tuck's instincts screamed at him to flee as he hurried back to the Eldorado, quickly slipping through the doors.

"What happened?" Will asked as Tuck joined.

"Quiet. Look. Something's coming," Tuck warned his friends.

The grand doors of the neighboring casino beneath the archway swung open, and a creature made its entrance. It was a quadruped, a crawling entity woven from intertwining vines. Trailing not far behind was another being, this one bipedal, standing tall and composed entirely of the same gnarled roots. However, it bore an additional characteristic —its entire form was adorned with a menacing array of spores and thorns. Both creatures cast their gaze downwards, communicating with the rooting vines beneath them. Then, with an air of sentient curiosity, they scanned their surroundings as if sensing the presence of others.

Verdant Guardian: Level 8

A formidable creature composed entirely of entwined vines, leafy plants, and menacing thorns, the guardians' bodies bloom with blood-red flowers, creating a captivating appearance. These guardians exhibit various forms, ranging from bipedal to quadrupedal variations, each possessing unique plant-based attacks. Remarkably, despite their lack of sight, they perceive their surroundings through an intricate connection to their ecosystem.

James sent a silent communication to warn Michele and Darya. "Do not engage the rooted lifeform," he transmitted. "It seems capable of alerting more agile plant-based beings." He then shared the creature's description with the extended team.

"This is a tough one, guys," he admitted. "Our usual plans won't cut it. I've got an idea, but I'm not thrilled about it. Let's explore alternatives first."

Sensing James's unspoken suggestion, Nadia addressed the coming proposal, "You think we need to split up, don't you?"

His nod confirmed her suspicion.

Will, ever the skeptic, voiced his frustration, "I won't even make a cliché joke about it. We're approaching sunset, clueless about the city's danger zones and facing literal monsters with unknown capabilities."

James reiterated, "I'm actively seeking alternatives."

"But if you and Nadia are already on board," Will countered, "we're stuck with the worst option—just like in every horror movie."

Tuck interjected, "So, you're mad at James and Nadia for suggesting the best-worst option?"

Will sighed. "Fine, I'm in. James, what's your idea?"

"It's as much an idea as a contingency plan," James explained. "We're dealing with the unknown. Who'll save us if we all stick together and encounter something new? Darya and Michele are here, but they're just two people, and I don't think we can trust Michele's interests right now with Trent roaming around."

Will raised an eyebrow. "So, your plan is to have more people to save us when we fail?"

"Exactly."

"All right," Will said as his face moved into a grin, "so, who's on team Brick?"

CHAPTER FIFTY-SEVEN

"Fear is a complex emotion. Acknowledging its presence is not inherently negative, but allowing it to cloud your judgment can be detrimental." – Boost, Former Champion.

LEVEL FOUR

James ignored the remark about the team name and continued, "Our optimal strategy is to split into two groups. I'd prefer if no one ventured out solo for now, at least until we better understand what we're dealing with." James glanced at Nadia, who signaled her agreement.

James went on, "Given the limited information we have, there are two things we can be certain of. First, we need more information."

"Dude," Emy cut in.

"I know," James responded, "I'm just saying that we need a team dedicated to gathering more intel. Let's refer to it as the 'Infiltration' team, and I believe our best path is with Nadia, Will, and Tuck." James turned to Emy, seeking her approval. "Secondly, we need to level the playing field a bit. So, the second team, including Emy and myself, will be known as the 'Big Boom' team."

"James, I have two points to make," Will began but was interrupted by James, "You haven't been chatting with Frank, have you?"

"What?" Will was taken aback. "No, why?"

"Carry on then," James chuckled, remembering his earlier

conversation with Frank about Coach's personal life during the intermission.

"Okay? But first off, 'Big Boom?' That's obviously the more exciting assignment. And secondly, how on earth are you planning to include this guy," Will gestured broadly towards Tuck, "in an infiltration squad?"

"Didn't you read the descriptions of those things?" Emy questioned.

"Of course I did. But I'm objecting because there's no way this guy can be stealthy, even if those things can't see," Will gestured again.

"I can be quiet when necessary," Tuck defended himself.

"Tuck, you announce your presence by the sound of your car door slamming. That and you're now basically a walking strobe light of energy."

"Okay, I get your point. Would it help to refer to it as the 'Infiltration and Surveillance' team?" James suggested.

"Yes, that would be better. Thanks for considering my input," Will said, grinning, which drew a round of glances from the team.

"All right," James resumed, "when it comes to our planning, I will venture to say that the largest casinos in the vicinity are our best guesses for hot spots. Our entire map is lit up with red because of these vines, but those casinos are even more red. Based on the root formations, the areas of greatest influence seem to be around the third floors, making them likely bases of some kind."

"So, considering Reno, we have a few major casinos to target: Eldorado, Silver Legacy, Harrah's, Circus Circus, and, oddly enough, the bowling arena. Our maps show that place differently, and it seems like a spot where monsters hide."

"Honestly," Emy reflected, "that checks out. It is famous for being a well-known national tournament location, but I've never actually bowled there."

James smiled and continued, "Emy and I will head to the Silver Legacy. It's a good spot to start scouting for a suitable location for our 'Big Boom.' Our Infiltration and Surveillance team should begin here at Eldorado, then move to Harrah's, the haunted alleys, and possibly south toward the river. There are bound to be people around there."

"It's called the National Bowling Stadium," Tuck interjected, "And honestly, I don't find it scary. As a kid, I loved going there to watch."

"That's where you draw the line on jokes?" Will jested. "Of all the remarks thrown your way, you defend a sport that peaked in the 1800s?"

"Yes."

"All right," Will conceded. "No more bowling jokes, everyone."

"I have one more question, not about bowling," Will said. "Isn't the Harrah's building currently shut down? Do we think that matters?"

"I'll go out on a limb and say the vine creature doesn't care," Nadia replied, eliciting smiles from the group.

"Any other questions?" James remarked

"Nope," Will gestured, "I'm just thankful Circus Circus isn't on our path."

"Oh, that reminds me," James said, remembering the one last item for Michele and Darya.

△△△

Infiltration and Surveillance Team

"No way did you just happen to give Darya and me Circus Circus," Michele's voice rang over the communication channel as Will, Tuck, and Nadia moved silently back into the vine-ridden casino floor.

"Which of you all is afraid of clowns?" the team could hear Michele continue asking James. Will quickly communicated, "Nexy, mute conversations for now, please."

With Will's sly smile gone, the team moved deeper into the

Eldorado Casino. As the energy in the room heightened, Will began to activate his **Condense** skill on the surrounding water vapor. However, Nadia's urgent voice stopped him: "No, don't! We don't know what these vines can sense. Let's not risk anything until we have to. Who knows how they'll react to temperature changes?"

"Sorry. Good call," Will acknowledged, releasing the pent-up energy. The team continued to follow Nadia, their footsteps muffled by the once-luxurious carpeting. In most larger casinos, these pathways were designed to disorient visitors, leading them deeper into the labyrinthine maze and enticing them to spend more money. Now, they resembled what once was—a fading memory of luxury and indulgence, overrun by the Organism's relentless advance.

In their wild defiance of logic, the vines ripped through table games, slots, and bar tops. Emerging from ceiling vents and breaking through walls, their origins remained a mystery due to their chaotic growth patterns. Undeterred, the team continued their upward journey, guided by Nadia's soundless footsteps.

Ascending to the hotel area, they encountered a surreal scene. The former bustling hub for check-ins, clubs, and restaurants now lay abandoned. Vines snaked across the marble floors, their tendrils wrapping around chandeliers and decorative columns. The mirrored surfaces reflected twisted forms—distorted versions of themselves.

After passing the nightclubs and late-night buffets, they arrived at the heart of the casino—the Fountain of Fortune. Once a double fountain flanked by dual escalators, it now stood transformed. Thick vines erupted from the fountains, their tendrils pulsating with an ethereal energy. Creatures—part vine, animal, and monster—clung to the stems. Their bodies glowed with an unsettling luminescence as they drew sustenance from the vines.

"Hub," Nadia whispered over the comms. "I can't even see the floor or the escalators. It's like the vines are conduits for power for the other creatures."

"Our map looks like it's pulsing with red now. Do we do anything?" Tuck's voice wavered as the team stood frozen, caught between awe and dread. The nascent creatures wriggled, their forms still evolving.

"I don't think we should. We might trigger something we aren't prepared for, and we need to know how big this thing is first. I vote that we double back and report our findings." Nods of approval prompted the team to head back down the stairs and out the doors to the street. The light continued to fade as nightfall approached.

"That was crazy. How do you even fight something like that?" Will said as they stepped outside.

"I don't like that we still haven't seen anyone. Our mission states that at least 50 hostages are out here, but we haven't seen any signs of life," Nadia commented.

"Agreed. We have to be missing something," Tuck added.

The team relayed the update to the extended squad. "All right, we will now make our way over to the…" Will spoke and glanced at Tuck, "super cool and super fun bowling alley."

"Roger that. Be safe," James confirmed.

"I know what you did there." Tuck looked down at Will.

"Did what? Where?" Will gestured, looking around in an exaggerated manner.

"Oh, come on, both of you," Nadia exclaimed as they headed towards their original location.

"Is it just me, or have those vines grown exponentially since we were last here just 30 minutes ago?" Will asked as the team now passed the Biggest Little City Arch.

"It's not just you. I see no signs of Tuck's work earlier. It must have regenerated," Nadia offered.

"If these little vines are growing that much, I can't imagine we have too much time to wait before we attempt to destroy that fountain," Will finished as they rounded the corner on Commercial Row, now only getting a first glance at the old Harrah's building.

"And you think the bowling alley is creepy?" Tuck asked as they all took in Harrah's covered pathway entrance. Once filled with lights, screens, and bright red beams, it was now half-covered in darkness and filled with moving vines. The doorway read "no," with the first four letters of the "casino" sign removed.

"You're right. This makes me want to go back and face the clowns," Will returned.

"Guys, stop," Nadia suddenly returned.

"We are just joking around, Nadia," Will said as he turned to look back at her, halting immediately when he saw her face.

"No. Look at your maps. I see multiple dots approaching," Nadia said with confusion, "and all four of them are… blue?"

"Allies?" Will questioned.

CHAPTER FIFTY-EIGHT

"You never know when you'll meet someone who will stay with you for the rest of your life." – Boost, Former Champion.

LEVEL FOUR

Big Boom Team

"Big Boom, huh?" Emy began. "I think all that time with Frank during intermission has changed you."

James chuckled. "Maybe. I think it just shifted my perspective. Our plans have always been about reacting to hits and improvising. They've worked, but now we have the means to strike first and the materials to pull it off."

"I'm not complaining," Emy teased, "but you've changed. You're no longer the 13-year-old terrified of disappointing your parents with a dirty house."

"Nah," James said, laughing. "That still terrifies me. Looking back, it was more likely to be OCD. My parents didn't care." He glanced at Emy. "Ready to move?"

"Yes, your Grace," Emy remarked with a quick smile as they left the Eldorado and walked along an empty Virginia street.

Emy always found it unsettling that beyond the row of casinos, there were dead zones around Reno. While downtown, you were mainly inside the interconnected casinos, but stepping outside revealed how empty some streets were. Moving away from the Arch, they passed a parking garage, older buildings, and a few small streets heading towards the local Aces baseball stadium where Darya and

Michele had arrived. Outside Eldorado and down the street, the casino stretched for two entire blocks until they reached Fourth Street, showcasing the sheer size of these buildings.

Turning west, they approached the overpass connecting the two casinos: Eldorado and Silver Legacy. The Arch and casino vines were one thing, but the massive vines, as thick as tree trunks, weaving in and out of the overpass were nearly unimaginable. These had to be the foundational structures of the Organism, and the team was still unsure of the direction they were coming from. Both buildings had growths extending across to the other side, creating a bizarre sight before them.

"Dare we continue?" Emy asked James. They planned to proceed down Fourth to Center Street, parallel to Virginia Street.

"I have the big bad Emy with me," James quipped. "We're basically invincible." They pressed forward, noticing vines dangling from the ceiling, searching for room to expand on the ground. The path ahead might not allow passage much longer, at least without having to burn their way through.

"Assuming you want me to go first?" Emy asked.

"Ah, royalty always has a tester," James smiled.

"Whatever," Emy declared as she ventured underneath the overpass, now shrouded in darkness due to the setting sun and the lack of working lights within the area. It almost seemed like the roots were thriving even more in this darkness, as if they preferred cool, dimly lit spaces. Still, Emy pressed forward. The air grew moist, and humidity replaced the dry Nevada air—a sensation she had never experienced. As she continued, the air around her began to thicken, transforming into a viscous substance that made each breath feel like she was inhaling liquid. The atmosphere grew denser with every step, and soon, her movements became labored. Two more steps, and she felt an eerie sensation of weightlessness as if her body was now hovering off the ground. Her throat constricted painfully, and her lungs fought desperately for oxygen, each breath a struggle against the suffocating environment.

With one final, determined step, an unseen force seized her from beneath, a cold hand grasping her lower back and lifting her effortlessly off the ground. She felt herself being pulled away from the tangible world, her vision fading as she was plunged into an abyss of darkness.

△△△

Penny & Mr. Reynold

Penny and Mr. Reynold found themselves amidst a crowd on South Virginia Street stretching across the river, dividing the traditional downtown area from mid-town. The scene was chaotic: a few patrol cars remained, and frantic civilians clamored for entry to search for their missing loved ones. Flashing lights and road barriers heightened the tension, and Penny sensed that the patrolling officers were growing restless, eager to reunite with their own families.

"Come on," Penny urged, grabbing Mr.Reynold's arm as they moved eastward toward Center Street. A less crowded bridge was patrolled by a single officer on duty there.

"We need to get through. I know Will is in there," Penny whispered to Mr. Reynold.

Mr. Reynold stepped forward, his demeanor calm and collected. "I have an idea. Be ready to move," he instructed, approaching the officer.

"Hello there! I'm from the state offices, off duty, of course. I have a few questions for you," Mr. Reynold began.

The officer looked bewildered, uncertain of how to respond. His hand hovered over his radio.

"Let me get straight to the point," Mr. Reynold continued. "What would happen if one of these citizens attempted to cross the street? What are our orders?"

"Sir, please step back. I haven't received any backup," the cop stammered, "or heard anything, really. But we've been instructed to prevent anyone from entering without using physical force."

"Thank you, officer. I appreciate your commitment to following orders," Mr. Reynold acknowledged as he slowly turned back to face Penny.

"NOW, PENNY, RUN!" Mr. Reynold suddenly leaped away from the officer and sprinted down the bridge pathway toward downtown. Penny followed suit, the cop now shouting for them to stop.

Mr. Reynold knew that no one, not even an eager young officer, would risk endangering the larger population by chasing down two random citizens fleeing from them.

"I thought you said you had a plan?" Penny shouted as they ran.

"That was my plan!" Mr. Reynold replied. "Nobody wants to break protocol, especially during a crisis!"

"Look!" Penny exclaimed. "I see people over by Harrah's! Let's go." She darted forward before Mr. Reynold could caution her.

△△△

Michele & Darya

"Who do you think was afraid of clowns?" Michele questioned Darya after James updated them on their task.

"We both know it's Will," Darya answered. "But I like clowns, so I'm okay with it. Plus, I used to go to that arcade when I was a kid."

"You know, it's okay to be negative for once. I promise it's a good way of coping." Michele glanced at Darya.

"I know. Don't worry." Darya smiled. "I have my ways to cope."

"Seriously though, those guys got past the seventh stage of the Trials," Michele remarked, shifting the conversation. "We can't let them know that those nasty Sprites took down our Castle."

"I just wish we could have watched them in action," Darya added.

"Agreed. Emy seems like a caged monster. I'd love to see her when she's angry," Michele said with a small smile as the two continued their journey.

After a moment of silence, Michele turned to Darya, her expression serious. "Darya, we haven't talked about this yet, but after seeing them and that leaderboard, I'm not sure if we're going to make it to the end."

"I know," Darya said, keeping her smile.

"But I'd like to do everything in our power to support a team that can make it all the way," Michele said. "And I hope you're all in with me."

"Always."

CHAPTER FIFTY-NINE

"Never place your faith in luck. Believe in yourself and your ability to find solutions." – Coach Williams.

LEVEL FOUR

Big Boom Team

"Emy!" James jostled Emy, who was now lying beside him in the middle of what was once a bustling Sierra Street. James had managed to activate his **Energy Blocking Field** and grab Emy before the vines enclosed on her. She was unconscious, but she was still breathing, her body battling the poison effectively. He had refrained from calling Nadia or anyone else for backup, knowing that they were short on time and it wasn't feasible for anyone to abandon their tasks unless it was critical.

Kneeling beside Emy, James implored her to regain consciousness, assuring himself that he had made the right decision when he realized he still had one more option.

< Emy is boosted by 30% >

James's last resort was to use his **Empower** skill on Emy, hoping his boost would push her body's natural healing abilities. Although she was still lying on her back, her chest seemed to rise and fall more frequently, indicating her steady recovery.

As dusk fell over downtown Reno, James thought he saw fleeting movements in his peripheral vision, but he couldn't confirm anything. The darker it got, the more he thought he saw.

"Get a grip, James," he muttered. "Nex, reassure me she's all right."

"*She's going to be fine! She inhaled a potent poison. You managed to get her out just in time. My readings show that the toxin was probably not meant to be lethal. Her Nexabot indicates that her body is just gradually activating again.*"

"How much time do we have?" James asked Nex.

"*According to the readings, she should wake up in about 20 minutes. The good news is that her body has mostly healed!*"

"We don't have that luxury of time," James responded, scanning his surroundings for options as an idea struck him. "Nex, can you relay a message to Emy as soon as she wakes up?"

"*Certainly,*" Nex replied. "*What message should I convey?*"

"Tell her, 'Don't panic,'" James said, smirking at the thought of Emy waking up to the situation he was about to create.

"That's it?" Nex questioned.

"All right, also put 'From James.'"

Activating his **Stonebreaker Gloves**, James began to stack large planter vases, bricks, cement blocks, and other hefty items he could find. He then hoisted Emy over his shoulder.

He had built a temporary staircase leading to the valet area's rooftop on the Eldorado's Sierra Street side. Despite the challenging steepness of the "steps," he managed to climb, all the while ensuring Emy's safety. A feat that would have been unthinkable before, he could now quickly ascend the piled-up items and reach the top of the overhang, even with Emy's limp form draped over his shoulder. Upon reaching their destination, he carefully set Emy down and immediately tidied up the grounds below, removing the steps to prevent any noticeable traces of their presence.

Reaching into his **Tactical Sling**, a last-minute gift from Frank to store his equipment, James was once again struck by the impressive storage potential of his new preferred accessory.

Item Detected – Tactical Sling

Uncommon

This is the ultimate storage solution for the modern adventurer. Much like a versatile tool belt, it's designed to provide quick access and organization for your gear. It features ten slots of void-based storage, a revolutionary technology that allows for compact yet spacious storage.

Moving on, James found the **Cosmic Glue** and **Rootbound Seedlings**. James did a quick status check to ensure he was using the glue correctly:

Item Detected – Cosmic Glue

Common

The universal adhesive of the Cosmos. A substance that binds the universe together. Much like duct tape, it's versatile and omnipresent, providing extra support and stability wherever needed. This unseen force holds galaxies together, keeps stars in their orbits, and ensures the cosmic order.

Despite the description being as vague as possible, he eventually placed his trust in Frank and hoisted Emy to a hidden spot on the side wall, higher up the building, with fewer vines and less visibility. With a gentle nudge, James positioned Emy and promptly secured her with the **Cosmic Glue** and the **Rootbound Seedlings**. Frank had assumed that the seeds would work anywhere but made a note to ensure James also had the **Cosmic Glue**, as its need could arise anytime. Once in position, the roots grew, anchoring her in place. Even though the roots had a slightly unusual color, they blended in naturally, leading James to question the original purpose the System had for these seeds, especially considering they were up against a massive root creature this level.

With Emy now relatively safe, James reached the top of the second-story walkway connecting the Eldorado and the parking garage. He traversed the pathway and promptly began setting his traps across the entire 3rd floor. James felt a sense of ease as he moved across the garage, internally thanking Frank for the training and the confidence to execute this plan.

Finally, James put on his **Stonebreaker Gloves** again and gathered all the stone blocks, guard rails, construction pillars, and other objects to create a small room against a sturdy corner wall. He quickly set up the **Skyward Whistle** and **Sonic Conduit** that Frank had also procured for him to work in tandem with the whistle.

Item Detected – Sonic Conduit
Uncommon
This item is a remarkable sound enhancer. It holds the distinctive capability to escalate any sound to new heights. Just assign the sound you desire to intensify, and its integrated AI will acknowledge and adapt, paving the way for the sound to reach its maximum potential.

After ensuring the objects were correctly arranged, James exited the small area and sealed the space with more sturdy objects. Looking around, he was ready.

"James?" James heard Emy's voice-over communication.

"Emy—thank goodness. Stay put. I'll be right there."

"Where are you?" Emy asked.

"I'm doing the heavy lifting while you enjoy a power nap," James replied, pausing for effect. "You know, business as usual."

△△△

Penny & Mr. Reynold

"Hold on, Penny!" Mr. Reynold urged as Penny continued to stride towards the unfamiliar figures now positioned in the center of University Street, east of Virginia Street.

"Hello there!" Penny shouted, causing the two figures to pivot and gaze at Penny with bewilderment. The duo was garbed in identical orange jumpsuits resembling full-body athletic gear. They both wore long white socks and black sports shoes. As Penny neared, she noticed that one man was significantly larger than the other, with the smaller one roughly her height.

"Um, hi?" the more prominent man responded, puzzled. "Are you a civilian?"

Penny replied as Mr. Reynold caught up, "No, well, yes. We're not superheroes if that's what you're implying, but we're here to assist."

The same man glanced at his companion and then back at Penny. "It's not safe out here. It would be best if you headed back to the river. We'll try and handle things here."

"So, you're superheroes, too! Have you met someone named Will?" Penny asked, realizing she might need to provide more context. "Will and his team are from our school. They protected us during a previous mission, and we're trying to lend a hand in any way we can. I have a few minor skills, but I assure you, I'm a fast learner."

"We can search for Will on your behalf, but I still believe it's unwise. Listen, my name is Luck, and this is Tech. We promise…"

"Please," Mr. Reynold said as he entered the conversation. "We'll keep a low profile. Allow us to serve as your scouts. You must need a method to navigate and comprehend the area… here." Mr. Reynold handed Luck one of his radios. "Guide us to a vantage point, and we can keep watch for you."

In that instant, Tech seized the radio from Luck's hand, tinkering with it while muttering to himself. "We can't guarantee your safety, but Tech seems okay with the risk…" Luck began, and the realization dawned on him that this could be beneficial. "We can guide you both to the nearest building. We're hoping to get the lights back on. There's a rumor that…"

Before he could finish, Penny interjected, "The creatures come out at night, right? We've heard that too… That's a solid plan. I'm Penny, and this is Mr. Reynold. He seems to have some expertise in emergency preparedness and might be able to assist!" Penny gave Mr. Reynold a playful wink as she glanced at him.

"That could prove useful. But who is this Will?" Luck then asked.

"He's similar to you. He also has a team. An ice specialist, I believe. I'm still not quite familiar with the terminology."

"Ice is handy. I'm essentially a power bank with voltage, and Tech over there has a knack for everything electronic. Honestly, I'm not sure if he likes me for me or if he's just after my electrifying personality."

Penny and Mr. Reynold remained silent at the large man's comment.

"It was a joke... Never mind. Let's head north. It's starting to get dark," Luck said.

CHAPTER SIXTY

"Our hero population comes from a unique set of backgrounds. Remember, it's not the past that defines the person; it's their future! Can you imagine if we didn't have the likes of Inferno in the Games just because of his dark past?" – Tournament Director to the media outlets.

LEVEL FOUR

Infiltration and Surveillance Team

"It can't be Michele and Darya," Nadia murmured, her gaze fixed on the intersecting blue dots moving north on University Street. "They should be at Circus Circus by now."

"We don't have any other allies... and Trent is out of the question. That alliance dissolved long ago, so I guess he would be yellow or red?" Will speculated. "Definitely red on Emy's map."

"So, what's the plan? Do we confront them?" Tuck asked, deferring matters of people to those best equipped.

"Nadia," Will said, looking at her. "I think you go undercover and scout for us? Tuck and I will hang back."

"Sounds like the best path," Nadia agreed as she immediately activated her **Phantom Veil** while regulating her energy output, setting off to intersect.

As Nadia rounded the corner, she spotted a group of four individuals briskly walking beneath the Harrah's overpass to the garage. She recognized a few faces, and her eyes widened in surprise. Penny was there, accompanied by Mr. Reynold?

She hadn't interacted with Mr. Reynold, but Quill Creek wasn't a large school, so the connection was easy. The real intrigue lay in the two men in orange leading the group. Could they be other heroes? Or civilians? She guessed heroes, given their matching outfits, and suggested a System-based design.

Rushing back, Nadia rejoined Tuck and Will. "Will, your girl is here."

"My girl?" Will looked at Nadia, puzzled.

"Penny."

"Here?" Will blurted out, his gaze darting back towards University Street. Before he knew it, he sprinted down the block, hearing the other's voices behind him. "Will, wait! We don't know who the other two are." But Will didn't care. Penny was there, and he had to see her.

As he rounded the same corner, Will skidded to a halt as he saw the group of four, now adopting defensive stances to the unexpected person who crossed their path.

"Easy there, buddy. We're all friendly here."

"**WILL!**" Penny yelled from the back as she threw herself at him.

"It's you," Will said, smiling broadly. "What are you doing here?" But just as he finished the question, Penny wrapped him in a hug and planted a kiss on his cheek.

Realizing what she had done, she pulled away from Will, her face turning red as he stood stunned. His mind went blank for the first time, overwhelmed by emotions.

"Will," another voice said. This time, Mr. Reynold returned Will to reality, "It's great to see you."

"Steve?" Will looked at him. "What's... happening?" He felt another wave of emotion wash over him.

"We couldn't just stand by. We had a hunch you would be here and, well, mostly thanks to Penny, we're here to help," Mr. Reynold said, questioning his response but standing by his actions.

Will was at a loss for words. These two had come for him. They had risked their safety by entering another incursion site. "I... I don't know what to say," Will spoke with newfound emotion as he looked at his friends. "Thank you."

"Will, this is..." Penny began, pointing towards the other two when another voice sounded behind Will.

"Dad?" Tuck stood frozen behind Will with Nadia at his side.

"Tuck..." Luck responded, his words choked with emotion, "You're here."

As moments slipped by, the group struggled to process the unexpected reunions that had just taken place. It wasn't until Nadia broke the silence that the team returned to their current predicament. "I don't usually speak up like this, but we need to get moving," she urged. "Your voices have stirred up some activity. We need to find a safe place."

"We were heading to the top of the garage. Will you join us?" Luck suggested, looking first at his son and then the others.

"Let's go," Tuck spoke tersely, wrestling with his emotions as the larger team took off toward the parking garage across from the Eldorado in the heart of downtown.

△△△

"All right, I may have been a bit out of sorts before, but did I hear Tuck say 'dad?'" Will addressed the now larger group as they stood atop the parking garage. The team was overlooking western downtown towards Eldorado and the Sierra Nevada Mountains in the distance.

Tuck looked at Will and then back at Luck. "How'd you guys get here? Shouldn't you be in prison?" Tuck spoke, able to hide all his mixed feelings except bitterness.

"Prison?" Penny now spoke up, looking towards the man she had once sprinted towards. "I thought you were heroes?"

Luck glanced at the still-silent Tech and spoke to the group more quietly than usual, "It seems like the System didn't care much about current situations on Earth when it announced the Games."

"Tech, myself, and another inmate were merged into a team to start the tutorial and first level. We were part of the good behavior program at the prison and had a maintenance team. The three of us would go around maintaining the prison, repairing equipment, handling minor fixes, and assisting with routine inspections. Tech was the team's real star, but I had a knack for electrical work—I was never one to back away from a live line or two."

Luck continued, picking up his pace: "After the first level, which was held in prison, our third team member bailed when asked if he wanted to continue to Level Two. If at least one of you says 'continue,' the team stays in the running, but the other person will be removed from the Games. We imagine he's running off somewhere to be with his family."

"Nex, I thought there was an age limit to the Games?" Tuck looked at his dad, who mockingly expressed disgust at being called old.

"It was stated that there isn't a rule about who can and cannot enter the Games, except that the user must possess some talent. Many people over the age of 30 wouldn't have the energy awareness to grow into heroes. However, that's not to say there are no exceptions," Nex stated flatly, recognizing the energy in the moment.

"I don't remember 35 being that old," Luck said, laughing, attempting to relieve some pressure. "Tech here may look older, but he's only 24."

"Tuck, would you mind if we talked privately for a minute?" Luck asked, looking up at his son.

"I don't think we have time," Tuck responded dryly.

"Tuck..." Nadia spoke but was interrupted by James over the communications.

"Team, we are ready for phase one of the 'Big Boom' at the western parking garage. Is everyone safe for the time being?"

"James, we have some new... alliances? I'll explain later. Give us 2 minutes to update the new team," Nadia spoke directly to James as the others looked at her blankly.

< Alliance Established - Jail Birds - Limited communications are now available >

"Jail Birds?" Will spoke out loud. "What the heck is the System's fascination with winged creatures?"

"Nexy, can we add Penny and Mr. Reynold to the team communications?" Will spoke out loud, getting a few more strange looks from the team for differing reasons, as the Nexabots responded across the active group members.

"Why yes, hunny. But only Penny for now, as she was integrated with a Nexabot around when you were. It looks like she may have chosen not to participate in the Games. The good news is that any other Nexabot can awaken her Nexabot through an energy connection. Simply touch her hand. Don't be shy," Nexy spoke directly to Will as the others heard similar responses.

"Penny, may I grab your hand?" Will spoke directly to Penny, who was thrown off by the sudden request. Not having heard any other interactions, she held out her hand to grab Will's outstretched arm for the second time.

A resounding presence was awakened within Penny as if a mini-spark of energy ignited.

"Penny, let me introduce you to Nexy... er, Nex!" Will announced.

"Hello, Penny. It's wonderful to finally meet you after all these years," a voice immediately projected across the team as Penny's eyes widened in realization.

"Mr. Reynold, we may need to find other means of communication for you soon. For now, we can use Penny's Nex to talk with the teams," Will concluded.

< Connection Established - Penny - Communications are now available >

< Penny has now joined your extended team communications channel >

"Once again, I promise this is not like me, but our teammate is set to blow up an entire building. We need to get into place," Nadia spoke, squirming as she knew she had pressed the moment again.

"Blow up?" Luck questioned.

"Our team wanted to take the offensive for once. You might want to plug your ears, although I am not sure what to expect for this first part," Will said aloud as the team huddled next to the western wall, eyeing the targeted structure.

CHAPTER SIXTY-ONE

"Despite any doubts you may harbor, your position within the Stellar Ascendancy inherently designates you all as team leaders. Harness this authority, but cultivate trust among your teammates." – Coach Williams.

LEVEL FOUR

Big Boom Team

"Cohort 8, Operation 'Big Boom' is underway. Please confirm your safety," James relayed over the comms.

"First, I confirm. Second, we need a new team name. Everyone except Will is welcome to suggest a name," Michele responded.

"Squawking Pigeons!" Will blurted out instantly over the comms.

"Cover your ears, everyone. This is the first time we have used these devices. Keep your eyes peeled on the surroundings," James advised.

Emy and James had stationed themselves on the rooftop of the Eldorado, nestling into a corner of the foundational structure that transitioned to the hotel section of the casino. They maintained visual contact with the garage to ensure their strategy unfolded as planned.

"3. 2. 1... Activating *Skyward Whistle*."

The *Skyward Whistle* was equipped with several features, including a traditional blow function and a remote mode that Frank had also helped set up for James. In addition to this remote mode, Frank had installed a **Sonic Conduit** attachment for scenarios where the team needed to cover an expansive area. Frank was vague about what constituted a "larger area," but James saw no harm in activating the downtown district.

Instantly, a shrill scream emanated from the garage, spreading outwards toward the wider downtown region. James promptly erected a protective barrier as the sonic shockwave from the noise assaulted his and Emy's senses, resulting in muffled hearing and a sharp pain coursing through their bodies as they collapsed to their knees.

James and Emy switched to Nex to coordinate their subsequent actions as they struggled to regain their footing and assess the aftermath of their plan.

"Damn. That's deafening, and that's not even the explosive part," Will remarked from his team's location.

"No activity detected yet," Nadia reported as all teams scoured for signs of the **Skyward Whistle** luring out the city's creatures.

This rapidly changed as the casino doors were violently thrust open, unleashing a flood of vine-like entities. The continuous surges validated the extensive proliferation of these distinctive beings across the downtown region, previously hidden within the secluded depths of each casino. As the sun descended behind the mountainous horizon, the area was cloaked in darkness, diminishing the once discernible creatures to silhouettes resembling a synchronized march of ants swarming dropped food.

"James, expect visitors soon," Will warned.

"Lots and lots of visitors," Michele confirmed from their observation point.

James and Emy watched as the nearest creatures inside the Eldorado began to infiltrate the parking garage, drawn by the sound.

"We might be getting more than we bargained for," James said directly to Emy.

"We just need to round up as many as we can, then we need

to get out of here," Emy concurred as they spotted a towering creature now positioned between the casino doors and the parking garage, observing as the other creatures gravitated towards the sound.

Verdant Arbiter: Level 15

Standing tall, its twisted form reaching skyward like a gnarled tree, this enigmatic being commands attention. Its thick, rooted skin bears etchings of cosmic symbols pulsating with a golden hue. Blood-red blossoms cascade from its shoulders, each petal harboring latent power waiting to be unleashed. And its eyes—clusters of luminescent moss—survey their domain with eerie intelligence.

"Gang, we've made contact with a Mid D-Class lifeform. I'm unsure whether it possesses visual capabilities, but its appearance suggests it," James declared as he relayed the description through Nex.

△△△

Infiltration and Surveillance Team

Nadia, Will, and Tuck surveyed the scene at the old Harrah's Casino, watching a steady stream of creatures emerge.

"Our best shot is now," Nadia declared, her friends quickly grasping her plan.

"Over my dead body. You are not going in there alone," Will shot back.

"I thought as much, but it's now or never. We either move or expect to fight through hordes to rescue civilians. James doesn't have the firepower to eliminate them all."

"Agreed," the other two spoke in unison, but Tuck seemed to contemplate something.

Nadia and Will caught on instantly, but Nadia spoke first, "Yes, stay with your father and Tech. We will need a wide range of support on this one."

Tuck appeared to want to add something, but instead, he sighed, nodded in gratitude, and listened as Will addressed the larger group, "Change of plans, everyone. Nadia and I will infiltrate Harrah's while the creatures are distracted. Tuck will stay with Luck and Tech to locate a power line and restore the city's power. Regardless of the outcome, maintain contact. Safety first. We're all heroes here, but don't play the hero. Penny and Mr. Reynold, you're on comms. Report any changes in the creatures' behavior. We trust your judgment. No questions asked."

The group nodded in agreement. Will fist-bumped Tuck, then extended his thumb. As they locked, Tuck said in a firm yet gentle voice, "I'll come running at the first sound of danger. Stay safe."

"You too..." Will responded to Tuck.

"Ready?" Will asked as Nadia hugged Tuck tightly and gave Penny and Mr. Reynold a thumbs-up. Will followed her lead, and they both headed down the stairs.

"Did you just give Penny a thumbs-up with me?" Nadia teased Will on the staircase.

"Was it that bad?"

"Definitely. But I don't think it matters at this point. Let's get back to them soon so you can have a do-over, okay?" Nadia winked at Will, suddenly realizing she was acting more like Will than he was.

They descended the stairs and exited the building, noticing the flow of creatures from Harrah's was slowing. "As tempting as that red tunnel up front is, I think we should use the back entrance," Will suggested.

With a nod and a burst of speed, they crossed the street to the entrance and cautiously opened the door. The scene inside the abandoned casino was as unnerving as one might expect. Sparse slot machines and dim moonlight cast long shadows over the area as vines covered the entire building.

"If this is anything like the Eldorado, the people are probably near the largest growth areas upstairs," Will communicated quietly.

With no time to waste, they followed their instincts and ascended the stairs. As they climbed, the vines thickened and seemed to originate from the top of the shut-down escalator.

"We're close," Nadia said, invoking her **Phantom Veil** as they reached the top of the stairs. The buffet area was now a mass of sprawling vines resembling the roots of a giant tree. But as Will joined Nadia, a creature detached from a vine and lunged at them. Without hesitation, Will downed the creature with an ice pellet, just as he had done with the larger black birds during their Trials.

"They call me Quick Draw..." Will began but was cut off as the vines in the area started to thrash wildly.

"We need to find them!" Nadia urged, and they both sprinted deeper into the swarm.

"I don't see anyone," Will said, his voice tinged with confusion as he stared at the tangled maze of vines. "This doesn't make sense."

"They have to be here," Nadia insisted, her gaze falling on a foot protruding beneath the vines. "They're under the roots! We need to clear them, fast!"

"Teams, brace yourselves—phase two of 'Big Boom' in two minutes. We can't hold off any longer," James warned over the comms.

"I can't freeze them," Will admitted. Just as he spoke, Nadia released her **Affliction Surge** skill. It radiated out from her, targeting the minor lacerations on the vines. The afflictions acted like a blight, spreading rapidly and consuming everything in their path. The once vibrant vines on the floor withered and died, revealing masses of prone civilians beneath.

< Level up! Nadia is now a Level 8 Cellulator >

"Yep, that works much better," Will muttered to himself as the **Skyward Whistle** ceased. Immediately after, the building rocked from the distant explosion. Nadia and Will exchanged a glance, realizing their time was running out.

CHAPTER SIXTY-TWO

"Understand the energy in others. Sharpen it and uncover hidden potential." – Coach Williams.

LEVEL FOUR

Big Boom Team

James and Emy found themselves poised on the rooftop moments after issuing the final alert to their team about the imminent deployment of the bombs.

The area was now besieged by thousands of creatures, with hundreds pouring out of each casino and more still showing up. The situation was dire for James and Emy; they were trapped as a horde of creatures, exhibiting a myriad of vine-like shapes and patterns, flooded the streets from all sides. The creatures had discovered James's makeshift room in the parking garage, where he had hidden the **Skyward Whistle** and several bombs primed to explode at the touch of his manual **Energy Trigger**. It was only a matter of time before the creatures breached the room and set off a series of minor explosions that could jeopardize their larger scheme.

James glanced at Emy, ensuring his **Energy Blocking Field** was operational. Emy braced inside the barrier and was ready to deploy an additional **Disintegration** shield to intercept any debris. Realizing they had another opportunity, James tossed a pair of **Rootbound Seedlings** at their feet, allowing the vines to provide extra reinforcement.

James retrieved a receiver from his **Tactical Sling** and activated the device. He could have connected it to his Nex, but

Frank had insisted that a button was far cooler. As the button illuminated, James took one last look at the garage and pressed down. In an instant, the world plunged into a maelstrom of energy and noise. The detonations were ear-splitting, each explosion a sonic boom that assaulted the senses. The air seemed to tremble, pulsating with the raw, unbridled energy of the blasts. Bright, blinding flashes bathed the world in harsh, stark light, casting elongated, dancing shadows as vines and creatures were torn apart. The ground beneath them shook violently, a jarring tremor that rattled their bones. Yet, amidst the bedlam, James felt an odd sense of detachment, observing the spectacle from within his *Energy Blocking Field*. A scorching wave of heat swept over them, but it was a remote sensation, muted by the protective shield and the encircling vines that held him and Emy securely.

PRUNED! 133 POINTS!

The acrid scent of smoke and scorched earth filled the air, a grim outcome of the destructive force they had just unleashed. James extricated himself and Emy from the *Rootbound Seedlings* holding them. They promptly surveyed a scene of devastation, with creatures' remains strewn about in the darkness. Their plan had worked; they had prevailed.

At that moment, a savage shriek echoed throughout the city. It was not a cry articulated in words but a wave of loathing, signaling the immense loss of its spawn. The piercing wail reverberated as the dispersed creatures started to rouse, distancing themselves from their fallen brethren caught in the explosion. A significant number lingered, and an even larger horde continued to swarm toward the building, searching for any indication of life.

"*I understand that this might not be the most opportune moment, but holy moly, your viewership skyrocketed. There were 4.3 billion active viewers tuned in to that,*" Nex communicated.

"Should we make a run for it?" James asked Emy in a hushed tone, ignoring Nex's comment.

"And head where? We can't lead them straight to our team," Emy responded, contemplating their next move as the groups of creatures began to disperse in various directions.

"Team, Operation 'Big Boom' was successful, but we still have a significant number of stragglers in the area. Some are returning to their previous locations, while others are branching out. I fear we may have stirred up something bigger," James informed the team.

"Roger that, James. Will and I are currently working on evacuating Harrah's. The hostages are being used as energy sources for this entity," Nadia updated the team.

"Will, Nadia, expect company soon. I've spotted at least 20 creatures and a D-Class headed back toward the doors. Estimated arrival in 3 minutes," Penny reported from her vantage point on the rooftop.

"Oh yes, it's confirmed. These creatures sure are agitated. Many are returning to the doors, but we see a large amount heading out into the broader city," Darya added.

"It's the darkness," Penny spoke as she realized. "They must emerge at night in search of life. The locals by the riverfront reported that the creatures had abducted their family and friends at night. They must be out to feed."

"… and we just triggered an early feeding frenzy by releasing all the creatures," James voiced his realization.

"We're on it," a new voice belonging to Luck answered. "Mr. Reynold mentioned that the power lines in Reno are underground, so we're heading there to see if we can turn back on the lights."

△△△

Tuck, Luck & Tech

"Are we sure Tech can repair it, if we can even find it?" Tuck asked his father as they descended from the rooftop.

Upon hearing this, Tech grunted in annoyance, but Luck responded, "Tech can fix anything. Before he discovered his talent, I had never encountered a gadget that Tech couldn't repair."

The trio and Mr. Reynold reasoned that Reno likely had subterranean power lines accessible via maintenance entry points or utility tunnels. They hypothesized that the lines entered from the east and ran down the city's core. Therefore, they ventured north towards Fourth Street, estimating that the lines ran beneath the street, extending east and west through the longest major intersection. As they proceeded down University Street, they passed the Bowling Stadium.

"Do you remember when I brought you here as a child?" Luck questioned as they slipped by. "How the times have changed."

Tuck merely nodded at his father, unable to engage in much conversation as they kept their eyes peeled for signs of access points. They arrived at Fourth Street with no creatures in sight apart from the vines sprawling in all directions.

"What do you think, Tech?" Luck asked as they arrived at the crossroads. "Left or right?"

"I'm a fixer. Decisions based on luck are your domain," Tech responded.

"All right, what about you?" Luck turned to Tuck, who shook his head in response. "All right, then. It would be foolish to suggest splitting up, but I suspect they might need a primary powerline closer to the casinos. Let's head west. If we don't find anything on this block, we can retrace our steps towards the bus station heading east from here. Chances are there's something between here and there."

With no further discussion, much to Luck's disappointment, as he now had two reticent conversationalists, the trio silently made their way towards downtown. They soon spotted the overpass that had ensnared Emy less than an hour earlier.

"Found it," Tech announced as the team stopped, facing Virginia Street's main road. However, Tech was focused on a circuit system just below the streetlights on the road's eastern side. "It seems Lady Luck is on our side."

Try telling that to my son, Luck mused as he approached the circuit and the underground maintenance holes beneath it, now encased in large protruding veins.

"What do you need, Tech?" Tuck asked the man who was now inspecting the lines.

"A bit of muscle, followed by a bit of patience," Tech gestured at the locks barring entry to the devices. Tuck approached, placed his hand on the lock, and with a surge of energy and strength, the locks popped off. Luck then assisted by removing the maintenance hole covers and revealing a small underground access point large enough for just one person.

"Now we just need time," Tech stated as he lifted the hinges, avoiding any root interference for the time being.

Luck and Tuck stood guard over the man, having heard about the approaching creatures from James. They were somewhat out of the way but soon had to confront these beasts.

"I didn't mean to, you understand, right?" Luck glanced sideways at his son, hoping to take advantage of their limited time. "Yes, I wanted to hurt that man, but not in the way it happened... There wasn't a moment in prison when I didn't think about you and your mom and how I messed everything up."

"Whether you want to hear more or not, I am sorry," Luck concluded, looking back over the streets.

Tuck listened. He knew this. He knew now more than ever that his father carried the same burdens as him. Who knows where Tuck would be if he hadn't had football. But it was more than that. He chose to go out that night. He chose to let go of his emotions. He chose to leave him and his mom alone all these years.

"You had a choice and made the wrong one," Tuck began.

"You chose your pride over your family, regardless of the outcome or intent."

Luck looked at his son but remained silent.

"You abandoned us... You left us alone to fend for ourselves, but not just that, you left me to constantly fight for my acceptance, to prove that I won't just snap and kill someone when my anger gets the better of me."

"Tuck..." Luck began, but Tuck interrupted him, "We have incoming."

Luck gazed at his son for a moment longer, overwhelmed by emotions and guilt. He was right; he had done this, but he would prove he was more than just prideful. He had been given a second chance at life and was determined not to waste it. Energy filled him more now than ever, realizing he had another opportunity to make things right with his son. He looked towards the streets and saw what Tuck was pointing out. Swarms of creatures were slowly making their way through the overpass directly ahead, and even more were funneling in from the south from the Arch. They had only moments before things would turn chaotic.

"Tech, how much time do we need?" Luck yelled back to Tech.

"A few minutes, but we need to detach these vines," Tech responded as Tuck looked at his father, knowing what would happen once they made that move.

"There's no time like the present," Tuck stated. "They're closing in anyways."

Raising his **Warhammer**, Tuck identified the most prominent veins feeding into the power lines. He glanced back at his father and, upon receiving confirmation, stabbed down on the vines, causing a distant bellow and a pulsing vine to retract from the incision point. Tuck didn't waste any time and followed up the strike with three more. He then used his hands to remove the remaining vines from the box and the power lines.

"Two minutes," Tech's eyes lit up as he saw the problem—

several power lines were mangled.

"I'm not sure we have that much time," Tuck said as he saw the creatures sprinting in their direction.

CHAPTER SIXTY-THREE

"You can't save them all." – Echo, Former Champion.

LEVEL FOUR

Will and Nadia

Nadia channeled her energy and **Affliction Surge** through the sprawling vines that blanketed the floor. The vines writhed and disintegrated as their roots yielded to the floor, revealing hostages on the brink of death. Will soon followed, administering **Revive Pills** to each body he found beneath the vines. He forced the medication into their mouths, where it promptly dissolved on contact, immediately initiating the processing of the necessary nutrients.

A total of twenty-two bodies were entangled within the vine labyrinth, each life beginning to stir from dehydration and mental stupor. Nadia and Will tirelessly assisted those regaining consciousness, helping them to their feet and guiding them towards the rear escalator and onto University Street. The sheer number of people and the confusion on every face led to a frantic scene. Will took the lead, ushering people away from the former restaurant, while Nadia focused her **Vitalize** skill on those still struggling to rise.

It was only after half the hostages had been evacuated that they heard Penny's warning and a loud commotion from the ground level.

Will glanced at Nadia, who was ushering more hostages towards the back exit, before ascending to the top of the escalators. He concentrated his energy, creating an ice wall in the center of the escalators, separating the casino's lower and upper floors.

"That won't hold for long," he told Nadia. "Get as many people out as you can. I'll try to hold off the creatures."

"No, you get the people out. I'll hold them off as long as I can. My talent is better suited against these... things," Nadia countered. Will looked ready to argue, but time was not on their side, and he quickly returned to the room.

"Move! Move! Move!" Will shouted at the hostages. "Help is coming, but we need you all out of here now!"

Will's voice continued to spur the remaining stragglers as he clung to the last few victims, holding them close to his body.

BOOM! The ice wall shuddered and cracked as Nadia fortified her *Affliction Surge* aura at the top of the stairs.

"Nadia, we need to move now!"

"Trust me, Will. GO!" Nadia's voice was resolute as Will hoisted the last hostages over his shoulder.

"I'll be back... Promise," Will called out as he carried three other hostages through the door.

CRACK! The ice wall shattered as a wave of vines and talons surged through the ice, and a horde of creatures rushed forward.

Nadia released her energy towards the oncoming creatures, none of which could resist the destructive power of Trish's *Crimson Cascade*, now amplified by her greater knowledge of her *Affliction Surge* aura skill. Decaying and disintegrating roots began to accumulate around her.

A new form slowly ascended the stairs, watching the scene with disgust as the rest of the hoard soon gave way. The D-Class Arbiter had returned and was now just a meter from breaching Nadia's destructive aura. The three-meter-tall root creature extended its arm-like roots as if to touch the barrier preventing its creatures from advancing further into their hive.

With another inch, the aura washed over the Arbiter's hand and immediately began integrating with the beast's chemical structure. But as quickly as it advanced, healing energy emanated from the creature as the damaged roots restructured and reformed, and the Arbiter progressed further.

Nadia had feared this moment. The creatures possessed self-healing abilities, but their source and mechanism were still a mystery to the team. These Arbiters seemed to mimic the regenerative effects of the single Organism. Nadia remained resolute, channeling ever-increasing amounts of penetrating energy into the monstrosity. Creation and destruction were now locked in a fierce battle, with creation gaining ground as a vine wrapped around Nadia's ankle, only to dissolve when she directed her *Affliction Surge* skill on herself.

The initial grab was just a test, but soon, multiple vines shot forward, targeting every part of Nadia's form and lifting her off the ground. A surge of new energy and emotion overwhelmed Nadia's body as the hive sought to assimilate her into its ecosystem. Overwhelmed and out of control, Nadia sent one last message to Will, who was now sprinting back up the stairs, as she became fully entangled in the regenerating vines.

"Hold... Trust."

△△△

Penny & Mr. Reynold

"I feel so helpless up here," Penny confessed to Mr. Reynold. "Creatures are swarming our friends, and all we can do is stand by and watch."

"We each have our roles to play. Any further intervention on our part would only endanger us and them," the former athletic advisor reasoned.

"I understand that, but ever since Will taught me how to harness energy, I've felt this urge to be capable of more." Penny sighed, watching as the front doors of Harrah's collapsed and more beasts poured in, heading straight for Will and Nadia. "I just need to learn."

Just then, Penny spotted Will and a large crowd emerging onto University Street from one of the backdoors of Harrah's. "I see him!" Penny cried out. "He needs our help."

"No, they need you to stay here and keep watch. I'll go and make sure they get back to the river," Mr. Reynold reassured her, handing her the radio that Tech had set up to maintain communication between them. "They need someone to keep an eye out right now. We'll have our chance to do more, I promise you. This is just the start." Mr. Reynold took off down the stairs and towards the gathering of released hostages.

△△△

James & Emy

James and Emy gazed upon the swarm of creatures that had taken over the deserted streets of Reno. The distant screams grew louder, a chilling testament to the creatures finding fresh victims.

"Can't we do something?" James asked Emy, his voice heavy with the knowledge of their grim reality.

"We need to have faith in our team. Us wandering through Reno's streets won't help anyone, especially with these creatures multiplying," Emy replied, her voice also strained as she thought of the people she could have helped.

Emy's gaze shifted to the walkway that bridged Center Street, connecting the remnants of a parking garage to the second floor of the Eldorado. "We now know people are likely trapped beneath the vines around the water fountain. I think it's time to see if we can help them."

They traversed the rooftop swiftly and made their way over the walkway's roof. They were grateful that most of the glass that once enclosed the path had been shattered earlier, providing an unobstructed entry into the building. But before descending, they checked their mission status.

Hostages Rescued: 22

A fleeting exchange of smiles acknowledged Will and Nadia's successful rescue, instilling renewed confidence in them.

"I think it's our turn," Emy declared, winking at James. Then, nimbly, she leaped over the edge, landing on the carpeted path leading back into the casino.

"Always the show-off," James muttered before following suit and dropping next to Emy.

CHAPTER SIXTY-FOUR

"Your energy signature is an integral part of your being, akin to your physical body." – Coach Williams.

LEVEL FOUR

Tuck, Luck & Tech

The air thickened with moisture as Tuck and Luck stood side by side, watching the oncoming vine creature army. Tuck's grip remained unyielding on his formidable **Warhammer**, the metal humming with latent energy. Waiting until the last possible moment, he surged forward and swung the spike into the oncoming masses. The resulting wave of power rippled outward, casting a radiant force that extended beyond the primary spike, forming an additional energy-based blow. The collision sent the horde's frontlines staggering backward, their vines ripping to shreds. Suddenly, the dark Reno streets blazed with dazzling white light, revealing more twisted forms of vine-based creatures headed toward them.

Despite his more diminutive stature compared to his son, Luck was no less intimidating. He moved with the grace of a ballet dancer, his hands and feet ablaze with electric energy. Each hit he delivered sent shockwaves through the vine monsters, their forms shuddering under the impact. His actions were a tempest of strength and accuracy, keeping the creatures at a distance. Together, Luck and Tuck created an unbreakable barrier, protecting Tech as he tirelessly worked to restore the power grid.

The initial victory faltered as Will's panicked voice came

over the comms. "It took her..." his voice wavered as he forced the words out. "It has Nadia in its vines. She told me to stay away... I don't know what to do."

Upon hearing the news, Tuck was soon engulfed by madness. He hurled another cluster of creatures back into the darkness and responded. "I'm coming," Tuck engaged over the comms, his emotions causing a stir, while Luck observed his son grappling with the news of their friend's capture.

"Stay put, Tuck," Will tried to calm him. "I won't let this thing have her. She must have a reason. I promise I'll be ready."

"No. This is Nadia we're talking about. We need to get in there now," Tuck snapped, his voice filled with determination and lethal energy as he slammed the **Warhammer** on more creatures, sending vines erupting in all directions.

"Tuck..." Luck softly urged, "Listen to him."

"Keep out of this!" Tuck yelled back to Luck, his father observing with concern as his son's emotions began to spiral.

"30 seconds," Tech announced from behind them, still thoroughly engrossed in his task.

"Manage what's within your control and trust in your team... Don't let the anger take you," Luck spoke to Tuck directly. "Be better than me."

Luck's last words seemed to draw Tuck back from his fury, his head shaking as he tried to regain his composure.

"Nadia, we will get you. Stay strong," Tuck declared, not knowing if Nadia could hear them but having his emotions channel a display of raw confidence and strength, leaving no room for doubt.

Then, a voice that sounded eerily like Nadia's came over the comms, "Three..." and abruptly cut off.

"Nadia, are you okay? I'm coming in," Will responded instantly.

"No..." Nadia's distorted voice spoke again as a tidal wave of creatures closed in on Tuck, unaware of anything but Nadia's unnatural voice.

Seeing his son's mind in turmoil, anxiously awaiting their

friend's response, Luck hurled himself at the encroaching creatures near Tuck. Throwing multiple punches, he soon realized they were quickly being enclosed. With no other path, Luck used his last skill, his body morphing into a weapon. A flash of light erupted from his chest, followed by a mighty explosion of energy. An electric burst shot forth, hurling the creatures in all directions. Luck crumpled to the ground, his body reeling from the intense energy discharge.

Snapping back to reality, Tuck saw his father bent over, fists planted firmly on the ground as he tried to recover from the internal blast that had burst from within him.

"I'm done here, but we need power. We need to re-energize the cables," Tech announced, glancing at the battered pair in the middle of the street.

In a heartbeat's span, Tuck slipped past his father, launching himself at the surrounding beasts. A raw, electric rush of energy erupted from him as he used his **Repulse** skill in the surrounding area, pushing back the creatures coming near his father. It was a release of pent-up fury, worry for Nadia, and newfound feelings for his father. His **Warhammer**, now pulsing with renewed vigor, met the oncoming tide of creatures. The weapon's spike sliced through the horde, a secondary **Lightning Bolt** branching from its edge like a tree. Electrical surges radiated toward the beasts, igniting their forms with electric might. Their bodies illuminated the darkness as the street returned to its deserted state.

< Level Up! Tuck is now a Level 10 Accelerator >

< Tuck has Ascended to D Class >

Tuck dashed back to Tech, his gaze falling on the powerlines that Tech had just revitalized. Grasping the hefty wires in his hands, he channeled his newfound energy into them, causing the gears and boxes to illuminate with power.

"Needs more," Tech murmured beside him as the lines went dark again. Tuck once again surrendered to his power, infusing his body with a storm of energy into the previously dormant power source. In that instant, a lightning strike struck Tuck, adding to his power and filling his body with a moonlit glow. This time, the line shimmered with Tuck's energy, and the surge coursed through the system. Light began to permeate the city. Red, yellow, green, and blue neon lights burst across the once-dark sky, the downtown area of Reno now aglow with the warmth of city lights.

"Success!" Penny voiced over the comms to Tuck and the entire team. "I see creatures retreating into the casinos! James, Emy, be on alert over there."

Tuck sensed a hand on his back and an arm reaching out to assist him from the crevice. "Thanks, Tuck. It's time to find Nadia," his father's voice came, soft yet resolute, as Nadia's ethereal voice resonated once more.

"Three... hubs," Nadia voiced again to the team.

"Three... voids."

△△△

Nadia

Nadia was in a desperate struggle for survival, ensnared by the massive vine entity. The creature was draining her vitality and energy, but she was determined not to succumb. As she valiantly battled to remain conscious and alive, the relentless energy coursing through her body attacked every part of her as she was dragged across the upper casino floor. The vines constricted her, their grip tightening until they completely enveloped her, obscuring her vision of everything around her.

"Keep your focus, Nadia," she whispered to herself, trying to transmit vital information to Will and the rest of the squad. Nadia was engaged in a fierce battle, compelling her body to resist the creature and recover what had been taken. Her energy was slowly being constricted, but she was learning. She strained every muscle and stretched her mental faculties to their limits, preventing the entity from fusing with her mind and spirit. She had to maintain her sense of self; she couldn't let this creature triumph, as defeat meant death and catastrophic losses for humanity. She wouldn't be defeated. With a burst of energy, Nadia's core pushed back against the intruding forces within, her ***Vitalize*** skill shattering the chains that sought to control her.

< Level Up! Nadia is now a Level 9 Cellulator >

Feeling the growth in Nadia's power, the creature intensified its attack. A standoff unfolded as Nadia retaliated. Yet, Nadia understood that the impasse was not to her advantage. Considering the entity's colossal size and unending energy source from those trapped beneath the vines, she needed a strategy.

Every entity that has power is interconnected in some way. If she was to win against this creature, she needed to delve deeper into its realm. This body was not so different from hers, just... larger.

Nadia had a sudden idea and dropped her defenses, allowing the alien energy to flood her body. Instead of resisting or letting it take over, she intertwined her essence with the Singularity. Using her ***Body Manipulation*** skill, she extended her existence, making the Singularity a part of her. She mentally explored every part of the creature, pushing waves of her energy through it and taking control as she wove her way through the monstrosity, exploring every limb, every connection, every... thought. This was now her body; she was in control.

She focused on the creature's energy center, drawing herself into its heart and soul. As she followed the most vital energy paths, she watched the source and its vines grow larger and larger. The journey took her deeper into the creature's very essence, navigating through its intricate network of pulsating energy. When she expected to find the creature's core, she was suddenly transported across an empty void to a new location.

It was as if the being existed in another world, a place she couldn't navigate to just yet. Nadia realized that the entity wasn't truly on Earth; it was using these voids to expand and construct across the city, each void establishing a hub of creation. *Just how giant is this creature?* There were already three such voids, with more imminent. She needed to alert the team, but at that moment, Nadia and the entity were one. Finding her body, she sent a mental command through her Nex, transmitting a brief message while maintaining her new sense of self.

Now, she needed to halt this creature. She projected herself once more, discovering new connection points. Future hubs, energy bases, and hostages for the Singularity... Sensing the newfound energies, she extended her mind across the tendrils, locating the new fuel sources. Realizing she was now controlling a new hub, Nadia issued a command.

Leave.

Vines and tendrils scattered as Nadia exerted her mental energy to overpower the entity and withdraw from the site, shifting it back to the previous hubs.

Nadia was far from finished, but she now realized that the entity was alarmed by the sudden shift in its formations. At that moment, she decided it was time to change tactics and focus on... destruction. Spreading her energies even further, she unleashed a wave of death from her **Affliction Surge** skill. This deadly energy radiated from her body at the Harrah's base, spreading to the surrounding areas, stunting growth and restricting access to energy. The Singularity reached out mentally to the unknown energy source, now disseminating devastation within it.

"*Whoo aree you?*" a thunderous rumble of mental communication assaulted her.

Unyielding in her onslaught against the monster, Nadia then voiced her identity:

"I am death..."

She pushed all her energy out as the creature sought to expel her energies with force. But Nadia held on, continuing to flood the entity with her power.

"... I am the Kamatayan."

< Level Up! Nadia is now a Level 10 Cellulator >

< Nadia has Ascended to D Class >

Triggered by her newfound awareness, the guttural sound once again echoed through her, "Killl-hher." Nadia felt her physical body shifting as she retracted her energy from the entity. She rushed to pull in her presence and energies, re-emerging within her body. With a swift mental command, she sent an urgent alert to Will and the team.

"Help."

CHAPTER SIXTY-FIVE

*"Understanding the enemy's mind is not
about predicting their next move, but
about comprehending their perspective."
– Quist, Former Champion.*

LEVEL FOUR

Michele & Darya

"Uh, team... There are people casually exiting the Circus Circus," Michele alerted over comms as she and Darya rushed to assist. The once dark and deserted casino was now a spectacle of lights, sounds, and chimes. The recently liberated hostages were still in a daze, their movements reminiscent of the early morning downtown crowd before integration.

"Darya is moving to usher them out, but we might need additional hands to protect them on the street," Michele appealed to the larger team.

"Mr. Reynold is coming to your location. He's equipped with **Revive Pills** and will help get them to the river base. Tuck and Luck are already charting a course through University Street."

"Copy that, Penny. Much appreciated," Michele responded. "Circus Circus appears to have been spared the worst of it. I'll clear out the remaining creatures as Darya handles the evacuation, and then we'll head to the Silver Legacy."

"Stay safe. Emy and James are currently the nearest to your location. Expect a heavy population of creatures."

"Has anyone spotted Trent yet?" Michele asked.

"Negative," Penny responded over the comms, having

received a brief update about Trent from Will earlier.

After assisting the last hostage towards the exit, Michele and Darya reviewed their mission log.

Hostages Rescued: 32

A smile spread across Michele's face at the increase in the numbers as she channeled her energy mass into her hands, forming fists and now glaring at the remaining creatures in the building. Her abilities might not be the most effective against these vine creatures, but crushing them was undeniably satisfying.

△△△

Nadia
Nadia stirred, her senses returning to a world of pain and disarray. The massive, vined Arbiter thrashed against the once-constricting vines. Her body, still adjusting, strained to assess her situation. She felt like a trapped fly in a web, the blood-red blossoms of the D-Class beast inching closer. Thorn-like talons embedded in the now eroded vines swept across her as the first blow struck her abdomen. Nadia's quick reflexes and training with Trish allowed her to shift her **Regenium** metal, blocking the thorn strike from piercing her body.

The victory was short-lived. Four more sharp thorns immediately stabbed into her, her left arm losing function. Her shoulder now bore the jagged stem of the monster while three other blows pierced across her body. One thorn penetrated her lungs, causing the air to evacuate in a desperate gasp.

< Nadia's health is at 37% >

The vine creature wasted no time as Nadia braced herself for more strikes. She strained her muscles, pulling the vines to curl her body into a protective ball, determined to survive longer. But the expected blow never came. Instead, an icy chill enveloped the room.

"Will," she coughed out, fighting off the poison of the thorns now seeping into her body. The tendril thorns in front of her were covered in ice, frozen to the creature's body. But the ice began to crack as the colossal beast thrashed about.

In a burst of determination, Will charged into the scene. **Permafrost** engulfed him as he threw himself at the creature, his ice blades extended. He sliced and pushed the beast back, driving it toward the rear of the restaurant. Nadia watched, heart pounding, as Will stood at the heart of the tangled vine grove. Ice and thorns connected, both seeking to penetrate the thick shield guarding each other. Blow for blow, they clashed. Will's ice slowed down the lifeform, but it continued to expand, growing new life even as it attempted to break through the barriers of ice restricting it.

Will pushed away from the creature, assaulting it from afar with **Cryostrikes** soaring through the air. The creature morphed into the ground, shifting its blackened, rotting vines across the café flooring. Lightning sparked behind him, but Will paid no heed. Locked in battle, his opponent had just made a costly move. The air thickened with frost as he pushed the condensation to the ground, immediately triggering thin, piercing ice spikes to spring up from the floor, impaling the creature from all sides. Now thrashing, the creature realized that regrowth was futile against the relentless assault as Will drove another huge ice spike through its remaining core.

DETHORNED! 103 POINTS!

< Level up! Will is now a Level 10 Condenser >

< Will has Ascended to D Class >

Shifting his attention back to the room, Will caught sight of Tuck, consumed by vehemence, hurling the last remnants of the vine creatures across the space. Lightning strikes scorched the vines all around, leaving charred remains in their wake.

"Nadia!" Will called out, regrouping. "Where is she?"

"She's here. She's fine," Luck's voice came from behind Tuck. The man helped Nadia up from the ground where he had been protecting her. "She recovered remarkably fast."

With a smile creeping onto his face, having seen Nadia, Will moved towards her with Tuck close behind. "Didn't you pick up anything from my hostage situation? Did you have to copy my move?"

"It was all a part of my plan to ascend before you," Nadia joked, another cough interrupting her as she continued to trigger her *Vitalize* skill.

"Could you..." Tuck gasped, catching his breath, "please explain what we missed here." He managed to say between labored breaths, having just sprinted nearly 300 meters before transitioning into battle once again.

"Nadia here decided to borrow my move; that's what happened," Will responded promptly. "I explicitly told everyone NOT to play the hero, and she just went ahead and ignored me."

Will's eyes lit up as he noticed a change in the team status section: "And you have a new hero name? Kama? Were you not going to run this by me?"

"Do you want to hear what I discovered, or would you prefer to keep talking?" Nadia shot back at Will, who immediately fell silent and put on his best "please proceed" expression.

This time, Nadia addressed the entire group, "Team, we're up against three main activity hubs, but there are additional sites throughout the city. Each base has a void space linking this massive entity to our world. If we close these voids, we can eliminate the threat." Nadia paused, scanning her surroundings. "One or two Arbiters control each site and have hostages whose energies are being drained to accelerate the creature's expansion. We must seal the voids and neutralize the secondary bases before they can establish another void connection."

"Hold on, there's a void space in this room?" Will cast a skeptical glance at Nadia.

"Go look over at the serving station," Nadia suggested, gesturing towards the back of the room where prime rib used to be served. She then turned her attention back to comms. "James, Emy, are you both good with the details? We may need Emy's new skill to close the portals."

"Understood," James responded. "Emy and I are currently looking at the Eldorado hub. Can you confirm that it's a main hub?"

"Confirmed, James. Stay safe. Michele, Darya, target three is at the Silver Legacy. We will be joining you shortly," Nadia replied, allowing James and Emy to concentrate on their mission. She then turned her attention back to her team inside Harrah's but continued to communicate over the comms, "I located two other hostage points across the city with less growth: at the National Bowling Stadium and the Whitney Peak hotel."

"Given our skill levels, Tech and I can handle the two secondary bases," Luck said from the back of the room. He glanced at Tech, who nodded in agreement. "I'm confident we can manage while you assist the Hummingbirds."

"Hummingbirds, huh?" Michele questioned over comms, intrigued by the team name suggestion from an unexpected source.

"Speed and resilience," Luck replied with a smile. "I heard you were in search of a new name."

"I think we might have a front-runner," Michele responded. "Kudos to the new guys."

"Hold on, let's not rush into anything," Will interjected. "Have you considered the Long-Wattled Umbrellabirds or the Naked Neck Chickens?"

"Voting's closed," Darya voiced on the comms. "Sorry, Will."

< *Alliance Name Change - Cohort 8* > *Hummingbirds* >

"Let me get this straight: we've had two name changes in the span of, what, like five minutes? And I wasn't included in either decision?" Will voiced, feigning indignation.

"Kama is an abbreviation for Kamatayan. It's a Filipino term that you might equate with the Grim Reaper or death. But for me, it signifies death and rebirth," Nadia clarified to Will.

"All right, I retract my previous statement. I'm backing Nadia's choice for Kama. We still need to settle on Hummingbirds, though," Will said, grinning.

"You know, Will, your nickname is becoming more fitting every day. Talking to you is like talking to a brick wall," Michele retorted over the communication line.

CHAPTER SIXTY-SIX

"The void whispers secrets to the chosen few. AIs analyze data, foreseeing outcomes, yet the enigma of the void eludes all comprehension." – CNC Lead Scientist.

THE HANGAR (LEVEL FOUR)

Frank & Trish

"That **Regenium** metal is incredible, Trish. I think it just saved Nadia's life, or at least bought her some time for Will to kick some plant ass," Frank said as they headed back to their workstations after watching another broadcast of the team.

"Yeah, it was painstaking, but the result was amazing. Sometimes, I wonder if everyone with a talent like mine enjoys overly tactical work. I have so many ideas, but everything takes so long. It's like every application is a thousand-piece puzzle of a blue sky, and I hate puzzles."

"Oh man, I love puzzles!" Frank exclaimed, then quickly toned down his excitement. "Sorry, I mean, I get it. I love what we're doing here but feel forced into a path that takes the fun out of my craft."

"Maybe we're thinking about this wrong?" Trish stated while in mid-thought. "Williams always told us to follow our gut. I'm now finding that 'gut' just means our energy urging us to do something," Trish reasoned.

"But how? We can't just stop what we're doing. I wish we had more time to learn on our own," Frank sighed. "I know that may seem selfish, but—" Frank continued, but Trish cut him off.

"That's exactly what we need! It's not selfish. It's about being the best version of yourself to create better things for our team."

"Oh yeah," Frank agreed, though internally, he struggled with how his desire to swing an anvil benefited the team. "Totally."

With the extra time at this level and the emotional toll of watching their team, they channeled their frustrations into learning everything they could to improve themselves. Watching their team risk their lives led to a hyperfocus on advancements. Trish vowed to let her gut guide her. As the team worked on the newest item, Trish performed her usual weaving but felt a nagging pulse towards something else in the room. Stopping, she tried to sense where her energy was pushing her.

"What are you doing?" Frank asked, watching Trish's flustered face move away from the item they were building together.

"Hush, I'm onto something," Trish said to a now grumbling Frank as she followed her pull. *What could it be?*

Moving away from the object, she felt her body gravitate towards... Frank? No, not Frank—the computer he was using! Pushing past the gasping Frank, Trish followed her instincts and looked at the computer connected to the mechanical smithing machine.

"Frank, I think I found it," Trish said, not bothering to look at him.

"Who are you, and what have you done to my Trish? You're walking around like a zombie!" Frank blurted out.

"Oh, stop. I think I can bond with the computer. Is it really that different from the metals I've been working on?"

"Uh, yeah. It's an advanced AI tied to a motherboard with access to quantum formulas for precise smithing," Frank said as if reciting from a book.

"So what?"

"So... it's different?" Frank answered, still bewildered.

"No... I think it's my path forward," Trish said, a wicked smile spreading across her face.

△△△

LEVEL FOUR

Emy & James

"You ready?" James asked, his gaze shifting towards Emy while he pulled his bow into position, an **Alchemarrow** at the ready, awaiting her go-ahead. They were looking at a scenario that mirrored the one their team had briefed them on earlier in the mission. Until now, Emy and James had successfully evaded detection, deftly navigating around the creatures flooding into the building through the remnants of the garage and the main entrance. James was ready to activate his shield wall at a moment's notice but had managed to hold off due to the frantic dash back towards the central hub. With Nadia's affirmation, their mission objective was crystal clear: eliminate the vine creatures while ensuring the safety of the hostages, who were known to be helplessly trapped beneath the vine-infested floor.

The knowledge that this entity existed in multiple locations across the Cosmos was indeed peculiar. Still, their most pressing challenge was preserving their stealth as they approached the hub. They could now spot not one but two Arbiters on patrol in the area, but their ability to sense within the space remained a mystery.

"Born ready," Emy silently declared back to James, rising to her feet and revealing her presence to the creatures.

"Hello," she announced, internally cursing herself for not thinking of something cooler to say. Despite her simple greeting, the new voice caused the creatures scattered across the vine enclosure to reorient their bodies toward the sudden, unfamiliar sound. Both Arbiters pivoted and advanced in sync, their heads turning directly towards Emy as she distanced herself from the still-hidden James and ventured into the open space before the creatures.

"You may not understand my words, but I will say them anyway. **This** is **OUR** city, and those..." she gestured towards the vine path, estimating the locations of the hostages, "are **OUR** people... Either retract your vines through the portals you emerged from or face death by **MY** fire," Emy's words were filled with resolve as she ignited her hands, stepping into an open space and standing resolutely.

Having detached from the core vines, the creatures edged towards Emy, awaiting a signal to attack. She maintained her stern gaze between the two towering Arbiters commanding the group as an unexpected, groaning voice echoed from the vines, "Wee can coexist. Support our grrowth and we shalll allow yourr people to livve."

"You almost had me until you used a certain word," Emy said, chuckling. "Care to guess which one?"

Emy observed as the creatures stared blankly at her, oblivious to her intentions. "Just as I thought... No one will ever 'allow' us to live... Earth will always make that choice for itself," Emy smiled as two fireballs soared through the air and struck the two D-Class beasts, triggering screams across the field. In a swift motion, all the monsters abandoned their base and charged in unison towards Emy, who remained still.

While Emy engaged the creatures, distracting them, James strategically moved out of immediate danger. He unleashed a flurry of *Alchemarrows* at the encroaching vines, leveraging Trish's *Crimson Cascade* concoction mixed with Nadia's *Affliction Surge* energy, held in stasis within his *Alchemarrows*. As soon as the arrows hit, they caused the vines to wither, clearing a path to the hostages. As the aggressive plant growth receded, numerous previously obscured humans were revealed lying collapsed across the area.

Ignoring James's arrows, the creatures continued their

onslaught toward the smaller human, who remained unprovoked. They anticipated a quick slaughter of the audacious being standing before them. However, as the humanoid creatures closed the gap to just a meter from Emy, a wall of energy was generated between them. Unfazed by the unknown creation, the creatures remained undeterred in their attack as one after another launched themselves at the wall, only to see their bodies disintegrate as their momentum carried them across the threshold.

Unable to halt, hordes of creatures continued to rush through, dissolving into mist before a shriek from one of the Arbiters brought them to a halt. With the hysteria now under control, Emy remained in the same stance as before, smirking at the two beasts now taking her presence seriously. Unwilling to let the creatures return to the fountains, Emy persisted with her provocation.

"I don't choose my words lightly," Emy declared to the creatures. This time, she unleashed the **Umbral Void Blaze** skill across the area. Flames of darkness spread, eclipsing various vine forms as pieces of the creatures caught fire and disintegrated inward toward the center of the flames, leaving no trace of their existence.

The two leaders attempted to shift their vine forms as the mini-void blazes targeted them. Seeing this, Emy transformed into her final form by activating her **Pyroform**, advancing through the smaller creatures. Her hands ignited, spreading flames as she reached for the creatures, adding to the area's destruction. One of the Arbiters chose to flee toward their base, heading toward James, who was now distributing medication to the uncovered hostages.

"James!" Emy called out, unconcerned about the remaining creatures hearing her voice. Many joined the lead Arbiter's assault back to the void space and human energy sources. This time, the Arbiter demonstrated its skills by sending swarms of thorns flying towards James and the others. Without much thought, James assembled a large **Energy Blocking Field** covering the entire area, stopping the thorns and allowing him to continue his path toward reviving more civilians. Emy exhaled as she regained her focus amidst the torrents of creatures, leaving a trail of dust and death.

Upon the second Arbiter, Emy stood stoic as the creature twisted its form, and a mist formed in the area. The creature had learned and recreated its earlier feat of knockout gases, now surrounding Emy. Emy, in turn, merely smiled at the beast. "Don't think I learn?" Emy then looked inward, countering with an immunity now created in partnership with Nex from the samples of the prior event. Reactions were blocked through energy surges across her body, partnering with her natural healing paths.

< Level Up! Emy is now a level 11 Generalist >

Without hesitation, Emy charged toward the entity, intent on obliterating the monstrosity. The elements of her **Umbral Void Blaze** wreaked havoc on the area as the black cores continued to grow. Emy's willpower was now on full display as she pushed to end the battle. As the victims of her wrath vanished into mist, Emy flung herself at the Arbiter, striking the eroding creature with a fiery fist aimed at its core. As it disintegrated before her, she moved to the second beast that had attempted to target James. In a flash, Emy bridged the distance to James's **Energy Blocking Field** and thrust a pulsating hand of fire through the remaining Arbiter, heedless of the looming attack. This action elicited a final cry of distress as Emy unleashed a barrage of fireballs, causing explosions that consumed the remaining creatures, effectively wiping out all the enemies in the vicinity.

INCINERATION! 147 POINTS!

James's shield fell as Emy joined him, aiding the former hostages in gathering their bearings and moving to evacuate the area. "Penny, we are going to need another hostage escort," James said into the comms as he continued to assist the remaining hostages.

"On it, James. Mr. Reynold will be waiting outside by the Virginia exit. We should have a clearing by then. Move them to the lower floor, and we will grab them."

Suddenly, a desperate voice resounded through the team communication, "He has her!" Darya gasped, her voice trembling. "Trent has Michele at the last void. He's going to kill her!"

Emy halted her descent to the lower floor and looked back to the fountains where the second void remained. James grasped her arm, concern etched on his face. "Emy, we don't know if that plan will work. You can't go alone."

Ignoring doubt, Emy charged toward the void, its dark maw marking the entrance to the Eldorado Hub inside the large fountain base. "Nex," she muttered, "you'd better make this work." With James's shouts fading behind her, Emy activated her **Void Control** with her **Quantum Gateway** and stepped into the open void, swallowed by darkness and silence as the void breach closed behind her.

CHAPTER SIXTY-SEVEN

"It's a humbling realization to acknowledge that your planet lags millions of years behind in technological progress compared to others, yet the mysteries of the Cosmos remain just as abundant and elusive." – Radan, Former Champion.

INTO THE UNKNOWN

Emy

In the heart of the void, where shadows clung like desperate memories, Emy materialized. Her form flickered—a mere wisp against the vast emptiness. The void stirred, tendrils of darkness coiling around her ankles, testing her presence. It was a place beyond time where reality frayed and sanity unraveled.

And then it came—an unknown entity—a being woven from the very fabric of the void, its contours shifting like smoke. Its eyes—no, not eyes, but voids within the emptiness—focused on her. It analyzed her with a transcended hunger, a curiosity that defied reason. The girl's essence pulsed like a distant star, and the entity hungered for her light.

"*Intriguing,*" it whispered, its voice a dissonant hum that resonated through her bones. "*You, little wanderer, defy the boundaries of existence. Your skills—unmatched. Your potential—limitless,*" The words slithered, insinuating themselves into her mind. "*What secrets do you harbor? What future realities have you stitched together?*"

Emy stood on the precipice of fear and fascination, caught

between the unknown origins of her arrival and the uncertain path of her departure. The void being hungered the very essence of Emy, its palpable desire clawing at her senses, yet its curiosity was equally compelling—a magnetic pull that tugged at her energy core. She had glimpsed its proper form—an ever-shifting mosaic of lost souls, each fragment whispering forgotten truths. Within that fractured tapestry of energy, she sensed a shared purpose, a thread connecting her fate to this enigmatic entity.

"I seek a path," she replied, her voice steady. "To mend what's broken and fight for those lost."

The entity pulsed, tendrils of darkness reaching for her. *"And what will you sacrifice?"* it asked. *"Your memories? Your sanity? Your very existence?"*

Emy frowned, her resolve settling as she thought of the newfound chaos across her galaxy. *"Everything,"* she whispered.

With that, she pushed away from the void being and back into fractured light as the entity watched her go, its hunger undiminished. For in her, it glimpsed a chance—a fragile hope.

△△△

LEVEL FOUR

James

"She gone!" James exclaimed to the broader group over the comms. "She entered the void. I think she's headed for Trent." With a sense of urgency, James darted past the sealed void, ascending the once vine-ridden escalators.

"I'm heading to the Silver Legacy!" James gasped, now sprinting towards the pathway between the two buildings.

"We're right behind you," Will responded, his voice rushed as they headed down Virginia Street. Nadia and Tuck were hot on his heels, the Eldorado Casino a blur in their peripheral vision as they made their way toward the grand entrance of the Silver Legacy.

△△△

Emy

"*Yikes!*" Nex's voice spoke as a glimmer of light danced in the distance, and Emy found herself again facing an endless horizon. "*We veered off course for a moment, but it looks like we've rediscovered our route. Brace yourself, Emy.*"

Emy tried to steady her fluctuating emotions, having just oscillated between the abyss and reality. "*What was that thing?*" she asked Nex as they neared the radiant source.

"*Thing?*" Nex's confusion was shared as Emy attempted to transmit a mental image of the creature she had just witnessed, but Nex remained silent.

"*Emy, irrespective of the events that transpired, we should have experienced no time lapse. Your entry and exit from this realm should be instantaneous. We are transitioning back in 3… 2,*" Nex began the countdown as Emy refocused, allowing her anger to resurface. Michele was in danger, and Trent was responsible. She was ready.

"*…1,*" Nex concluded as a brilliant white flash filled the space, and then a burst of color painted a cloudy sky within an indoor dome. The renowned faux mining rig encircled the central elevators. A quick scan of the surroundings revealed Trent standing arrogantly beneath the main escalator leading to the casino spaces' upper floors. Beside him was what appeared to be a large metallic crate… and Michele.

Michele remained upright, her form adorned with splatters of blood. Her arms dangled lifelessly by her side, her face marred by an expression of agony. Circling her was what looked to be metallic dust similar to a spider's web ensnaring its next victim.

"Release her," Emy demanded, momentarily catching Trent

off guard.

Without fully turning around, Trent responded to Emy with disdain, "I thought this might provoke you..." Trent chuckled. "It's quite impressive that you navigated a void hole solo. Did your coach teach you that?"

Emy was puzzled about why Trent would mention Mr. Williams, but she persisted, "Astral Dominion, right?" Emy began to circle Trent, hoping to slowly inch closer to Michele. "Attempting to validate your worth against a lowly planet like this?"

A spark of anger flickered across Trent's face. "I've been deserving since I first stepped into the realm of princehood... This?" Trent gestured to the vines strewn across the area. "This is merely a game for me."

"Suppose you were to lose this game. What do you think would happen?" Emy challenged, trying to provoke a reaction.

"The concept of losing doesn't exist in my mind. Especially when I can have you all complete the missions on my behalf," Trent responded with a smirk. "52 hostages rescued, even without counting the ones squirming beneath my feet. Nice work. I would have been fine waiting until this one provoked me."

Emy suppressed a shudder at the veiled threat in his words. The mission was successful; there was no need for Trent to save anyone else. She needed to buy time; she needed her team. "I assume you've dealt with the last Arbiter?"

"Ah, yes." Trent glanced at the metal enclosure. "That was taken care of promptly." Trent made a gesture as if releasing something, and the box sank into itself. A wailing voice soon rang out and faded as the box completely compressed along with the last Arbiter inside.

"However, I believe it's time to conclude this amusement. Be sure to inform your friends that Prince Morgrax was here, and he wishes them peace and prosperity."

Raising his hand, Trent's form began to change. Black metals and darkness still surrounded him, his blade extended.

His face morphed into a somewhat human-like oval shape, with wide, discerning eyes that glowed with an eerie light. His sharp ears tapered to fine points, giving him an almost elfin appearance. His short hair now sprouted from the center of his head, forming a crest that ran down to the nape of his neck. His skin turned a sickly white color, with veins of dark energy pulsing beneath the surface. A smug expression settled on his features, his thin lips curling into a sneer. His fingers elongated, ending in sharp, claw-like nails. "I regret that Michele won't experience the same tranquility," he sneered, his voice dripping with malice.

With a snap of his fingers, a dust implosion occurred, eerily similar to the scene in the dome when Tabitha and Mrs. Wallen's former bodies were consumed. But this time, Emy was prepared. A **Disintegration** shield formed a dome-like barrier around Michele's head, protecting her from the initial blast. Emy then lunged towards Michele as the metallic dust engulfed them both. Trying to repel as much energy from her body, Emy generated a wave of disruption between them as she tightly embraced Michele. Simultaneously, Michele focused her primary mass into her torso, striving to safeguard her vital organs.

It wasn't sufficient. Metal dust hit them both, feeling like thousands of tiny bullets piercing their bodies as they crashed to the ground, writhing in an attempt to survive the onslaught.

"Foolish," Prince Morgrax observed as he conjured another wave of metal, now swirling and gathering as if a tornado was forming in the atmosphere around the two, blood pooling around them.

"Now, I must kill you both." The metal dust charged at them again as Emy and Michele watched in terror. Michele gazed at Emy as if to offer an apology. Both were calm, accepting their fate and closing their eyes. Yet, moments later, the pain didn't come. Instead, a notification rang in their vision.

< Level Up! James is now a Level 10 Catalyst >

< James has Ascended to D Class >

James was now just meters away as a dome was erected. The **Energy Blocking Field** was now shielding the prone forms of Emy and Michele. Within the dome, James stood defiant against the relentless onslaught of fine metal that sought to breach his defenses. As the battle raged around them, a comforting wave of warmth enveloped them. Emy soon felt a reassuring hand on her back as a figure hovered over the two within the dome. "Nadia…"

Morgrax was taken aback, now recognizing that help had come, as he triggered a storm of metals to burst forth in all directions. Those metals soon brushed against electricity as a **Lightning Bolt** took shape beneath the domed vault, weaving in and out of the most significant metal shards in the sky. The strikes didn't stop as the entire area was soon engulfed with power, and Tuck's **Ion Storm** skill was activated. Now brandishing his **Warhammer**, Tuck dashed in from the casino floor with Will on his heels, **Permafrost** covering his body and hurling a barrage of **Cryostrikes** through the air. Still reeling from the bombardment, the Prince promptly triggered pulsating metallic shields, saving himself from the havoc.

"**STOP!**" Morgrax roared, only to be silenced by a sudden bout of coughing as if an unseen force had struck him. As he caught his breath and wiped the blood off his mouth, his eyes gleamed with unadulterated insanity. He turned to face a smirking Darya, who had just landed the knife blow to his ribcage. In an instant, the metals in the room shuddered in response, breaking free from their structures and plunging the casino floor into chaos once more. Prince Morgrax now floated half a meter above the ground, blood now showing on his clothes, when a voice once again spoke. A blood-soaked Emy walked towards the hovering Prince, calm in the face of madness.

"Make sure you tell your other Dominion friends that the Mighty Eagles are here to stay," Emy voiced, tone filled with rage as a barrage of fire, ice, arrows, and lightning surrounded their former classmate. Just as this fierce assault occurred, the room's metal began to compress, moving the team to quickly take cover. When they finally looked up, they found that Prince Morgrax had vanished, nowhere to be seen.

CHAPTER SIXTY-EIGHT

"Thrown into the Games, you're compelled to respond quickly, adapting to the Games as your new reality. However, for those outside the Games, change is a gradual process. Your world will respond in isolated instances, denying this new reality until it becomes unavoidable." – Noble, Former Champion.

EARTH - SECRET BUNKER

"How did they find us?" the President of the United States questioned, his gaze sweeping across the room as the Secret Service reported a security breach. "This place is classified and a considerable distance from the White House."

The room fell into a hush as the Secretary of State and the National Security Advisor tirelessly sifted through every intelligence source but to no avail. The Vice President then broke the silence, "Any news on the civilians, I mean, heroes spotted going into the White House?"

The National Security Advisor responded grimly, "Regrettably, no. Our intelligence report suggests that we've lost all visibility with these teams regarding their advancement into the building."

"That doesn't necessarily imply they're dead, does it?" she probed further, only to receive a slight shake of the Advisor's head, indicating the likely failure of the mission.

"Is there any insight into what 'they' might be? Any shred of information at all? Surely, there must be some understanding by the Air Force?" The President's voice conveyed a hint of emotion, but he consciously tried to remain composed before his team. "We've received reports of sea creatures in Seattle and insect infestations in Italy, yet we remain in the dark about the very place I called home just yesterday?"

"Any equipment that approaches the area is instantly neutralized. Our only source of information is the accounts of those who managed to escape. We believe they are robotic, highly adaptable to technology, and capable of impersonating humans when necessary."

"A staggering two hundred billion dollars expended on our military and not a thing to show for it," the President spluttered. "Impersonate humans, you say? So, we're up against extraterrestrial robots with superior intelligence?"

"Yes."

"**DAMN, IT!**" the President's frustration was now overwhelming. "Do we know any damned thing that could help us?"

"Based on the limited information we've gathered primarily through radio broadcasts, we know there have been victories in Sydney, Oxford, Paris, and Reno."

"Reno, Nevada?" The President looked perplexed.

"Yes, sir. But we expect to hear from other locations soon. All other intelligence is sourced from our last contact with the United Nations."

"Right, right." The President sighed. "The Trials, which were utterly nonsensical, and a listing of hero names that offer no insight."

"We have to remain hopeful," the Vice President interjected, "If the rumors hold any truth, civilians witnessed those Games and saw the potential of humanity. That's not insignificant, sir."

"Yet it does nothing to stop those robotic aliens from breaching that wall in the next few hours," the President's voice held a note of despair as he gazed at their final line of defense.

△△△

LEVEL FOUR

Full Team

Emy surveyed the wreckage that now surrounded the inside of the Silver Legacy. The once towering mining rig that stretched towards the domed sky was now a memory, as large metal components were strewn across the casino floor, resting atop the gaming tables and slot machines. Emy silently wondered if this casino would ever be normal again as a noise snapped her attention back to her team.

"Thank you," Michele's voice was softer than usual, tinged with regret and disappointment, "I made a mistake. I put all of you in danger, yet you still showed up."

"We showed up," Emy affirmed, her smile encompassing her team and Darya, who were now huddled together. "And honestly, I'd like to think I would have avoided that situation, but I…"

"Would have done exactly the same thing," James interjected, his laughter punctuating the sentence.

"Did anyone see where Trent… I mean, Morgrax went?" Nadia questioned as they all slowly scanned the area.

"No, but there's not much red left on this map. I think he might be done with us for this mission," James speculated as Tuck's voice sounded behind them.

"Is anyone going to help me get these people out of here?"

"Absolutely. We certainly didn't forget about the hostages trapped under the vines," Will responded promptly, the team now scattering and rushing to assist Tuck.

They found thirty-three more people entangled within the vines of the Silver Legacy. Together, they used their **Revive Pills** and combined efforts to transport all the remaining people to the street. Outside, they were met by Penny and Mr. Reynold.

"Team, I'm going to help this shuttle to the river. Report if you need anything?" Will announced, receiving nods from the team and a playful wink from Nadia.

But before he could leave, Michele interjected, holding up a large, dull white egg, "Wait! I found this near Morgrax. It might be a drop from one of the last Arbiters."

"An egg?" Will blurted out.

"Yeah," Michele confirmed. "Check the description. I believe it was meant for you all."

New Entity Detected - Mighty Eagle Egg
Unique
Handle this egg with utmost reverence, for in due time, it shall hatch into a cosmic entity that strikes fear across the galaxies. Unlike the beasts you fight, these creatures forge unbreakable bonds with Champions they deem worthy. And like fledgling heroes, this enigmatic creature will require nurturing to evolve alongside you.

Michele handed the egg to Emy, who hesitated before grabbing it. Soon, she sensed the energy within repulsing away from her, targeting someone else.

"James, I think it wants you," Emy said, relieved she wouldn't be tasked with caring for another creature when she could barely hold herself together.

"You sure, Michele?" James asked, taking the egg from Emy.

"Not a doubt in my mind," Michele replied with a smile.

"And James, just be careful; we all remember what you did to those Castle walls," Will added.

Nadia cautioned, "Will…"

"What? I'm just warning him that eggs break, too!" Will grinned, giving James a gentle shove as he departed from the group, accompanied by Penny, Mr. Reynold, and the other former hostages.

"I think Darya and I will do a quick scan around the downtown district to make sure no stray beasts are still roaming around Reno," Michele voiced, her tone still softer than usual.

"Appreciate it, both of you. Use the comm if you need anything," James replied as two more members departed.

"That's the largest group of hostages we've found so far," James then said as the other three left, now glancing at the mission log, which included both Eldorado and Harrah's hostages, plus another group from Whitney Peak, recently visited by Luck and Tech.

Hostages Rescued: 92

"Emy, James, how about the three of us head back to Harrah's to seal that void? Maybe Tuck can assist Luck and Tech at their last location?"

"The National Bowling Stadium?" James questioned, to which Emy stepped in, "That sounds like a great plan, Nadia."

"I see what you guys are up to," Tuck replied flatly, sighing, "but I appreciate it." With that, Tuck departed the group with a soft smile towards Nadia.

As the remaining trio left the casino, they savored the tranquility, giving the other two ample time to reconnect with their friends and family. It was then that James remembered the question he intended to ask. He turned to Emy, "So, how was going through the void?"

"It's... a story for another day," Emy responded, causing confusion to flicker across James and Nadia's faces until Emy discreetly shared the active views counter.

"*13.1 billion active views, but you should have seen the number when Morgrax was here! Do you want to know that number?*" Nex exclaimed.

"Uh, sure?" James replied.

"*27.3 billion! That might be a record for just the fourth level! I'll have to verify when we return to the intermission.*"

CHAPTER SIXTY-NINE

"Among all the abilities and gifts in the Cosmos, the most potent is foresight. It requires understanding the past, present, and future to initiate alterations and shape results." – E.B.

LEVEL FOUR

Tuck, Luck & Tech

A communication was shared that Tuck would join Luck and Tech, so the two waited outside the Bowling Stadium for Tuck's arrival.

"Impeccable timing," Luck hailed as his son approached the two of them, leaning against a tree outside the building's entrance. "You're about to witness the magic of being part of Tech's team."

Tuck glanced at his father and then at the younger, slender man with a buzz cut and a perpetually disgusted expression, grunting in response to Luck's words. "Come on, Tech. How about we showcase some of your real talents?" Luck goaded, patting the man's back heartily as they headed towards the building's front desk. Tech immediately veered off into a hidden power room in a secluded corner of the entrance. The remnants of a few former vein creatures were strewn across the floor, likely due to a previous encounter with the pair, with Luck probably breaking through the lines to enable Tech's skills.

"Should we take our old seats?" Luck suggested with a smile, receiving a nod from Tuck and a grunt of approval from Tech, who was more at ease with power lines and motherboards than with people.

"Do you remember what they used to call this place?" Luck asked his son as they entered the central bowling alley of the facility. "The Taj Mahal of Tenpins," Tuck responded and chuckled briefly, falling silent as they navigated past several large structures and ascended into the stadium's stands. They looked down at the 80-lane viewpoint filled with vine-infested monitors, lane scoring, ball retrievals, and banners and flags in the background. The major growth areas were around the middle lanes, where a large vine and a mass of creatures clung to their base.

"Did you know that the first time I brought you here was somewhat of a mistake?" Luck's voice was softer now, but they were pretty far up in the stadium seating.

"No?"

"Yes, your mother and I had a bit of a fight, probably my fault. But she insisted that I take you with me when she kicked me out," Luck confessed. Tuck looked at his father with a hint of awe; he had never really heard his father talk like this, usually not allowing others to believe he was in the wrong.

"I drove downtown, clueless about what I was doing. We didn't have much money, and I wasn't about to ruin an opportunity by showing you how little money I had at the Circus Circus. So, I parked the truck and tried to wing it," Luck reminisced with a self-deprecating smile. "I got lucky. Honestly, I always found the stadium a bit creepy, and I never really understood why."

"Wait, you thought this place was creepy too?" Tuck interjected, shaking his head with a laugh.

"You don't?" Luck retorted with a smile, then continued, "I saw a sign on the wall saying USBC Open Championships and decided right then and there that I would make you believe this was the plan all along."

"To my luck, it remains one of the best days of my life. The joy on your face that day has been ingrained in my mind. That face got me through many tough times."

Tuck was still taken aback by his father. He didn't quite know what to say or how to connect that the man before him was the same man he remembered—the smile, the joy, the humble and candid conversation.

"All right, are you ready for the big reveal?" Luck asked. "This is my favorite part." He then gave Tuck a subtle wink.

"Ready, Tech. It's on you," Luck communicated directly over comms to Tech, who was still in the cable room.

Three seconds ticked by, and a light flashed. Another second, another light, and suddenly sparks flew, and all the monitors across the entire space began to spark as flames and eruptions filled their whole viewpoint. With the creatures awakened, the ball retrievals started to light up as the location around the large mass of creatures exploded, vines spewing across the lanes and up into the stands as the masses below looked perplexed at the unfolding destruction.

"Tech is a bit of a pyrotechnic... Care to help me take out the stragglers?" Luck asked Tuck as the two went down to the bowling floor. With efficient work, they were able to take down the remaining vine creatures and, with some physical effort, pulled the vines away from the flooring to reveal the last of the hostages around the city. Seven were given **Revive Pills** and taken to the street to be ushered to the river with the rest of the civilians.

Only after the last of them had left did Tuck and Luck return to the same chairs now overlooking the empty alleys.

"Tuck... Tech and I will go through this next intermission and then opt out of moving to Level Five," Luck announced without a hint of regret about quitting, leaving Tuck stunned.

"Not a day goes by that I don't think about your mom. I need to find her and make sure she's safe. Tech and I are good in planning, but we can't stack up like you and your friends," Luck continued, leaving Tuck staring at his father with newfound pride, emotions overwhelming him.

"Tuck, you might not have realized it yet, but you and your

friends are Earth's best hope. Tech and I will always be here if you need anything, and I mean that sincerely. We don't have a role in the upcoming Games; our place is here, supporting from the sidelines. Let me ease your burden. Trust me to find your mother... Trust me to set things right."

Tuck allowed his emotions to show as he lifted an arm and wiped a tear from his face. "Thank you... Dad. But I do need something else."

"Anything," Luck assured him.

"These friends are my family now, and they need support too. Don't stop with Mom; stop when you find every last person who means something to my new family."

No sooner had the question been asked than Luck responded, "Done," his voice brimming with determination. He and Tuck shared a heartfelt hug, tears dripping down their faces as they sat in silence, cherishing the precious moments of togetherness, uncertain when they would see each other again as Luck asked one more question.

"So, about this Nadia girl?"

△△△

Will, Penny & Mr. Reynold

"I still can't believe you both decided to just plunge into this madness," Will voiced, striding alongside Mr. Reynold and Penny. They were behind the group of hostages recently rescued from the Silver Legacy. The group was physically unscathed, but their minds were clouded, and their social skills dulled, allowing the trio to talk more openly.

"Frankly, it might be the best decision I've ever made," Mr. Reynold retorted to Will's remark. "Can you picture the onslaught of angry parent calls I'd be fielding in the coming weeks? I swear, dealing with disgruntled empty nesters with abundant alone time constituted 90% of my job."

"So, not the part about saving me or the chance to, perhaps, save the world?" Will questioned, a smile playing on his lips.

"Absolutely not. Who'd want that? Well, maybe Penny here. I'm just thrilled to be rid of my office phone." Mr. Reynold chuckled softly.

"I'm not so sure about that. You should see Mr. Reynold's people skills... he convinced a cop to let us into the city single-handedly."

"Really?" Will's question caught on to Penny's hint of sarcasm.

"Yes. Well, if you consider yelling 'run' after asking the man if he'd stop us."

"I was... inventive," Mr. Reynold countered, and the trio fell into laughter.

"So, what's next for the team?" Penny questioned Will as they were now a block away from the river.

"I think we have to keep going," Will said after a moment of silence. "You've seen what's happening and what will continue to happen. What you probably don't know is what would happen if Earth fails. Our Coach, Williams..."

"Wait, Professor Williams?"

"Ha, yeah. The same one. Turns out he's somewhat of an alien," Will chuckled at the comment, noting Mr. Reynold's expression.

"Well, I'll be damned," Mr. Reynold exclaimed, instantly revisiting all his interactions with the former girls' soccer coach. "I guess he was a bit overzealous?"

"Yeah, well, he... shared some stories with us. Earth isn't alone in this challenge. Not now and not in the past. I'll leave it at that, but let's say we plan to avoid his fate."

"What are you both planning on doing?" Will asked, looking back to the two after remembering Williams' home planet again.

"I'm this one's chauffeur. Wherever she tells me to go, I'll be there," Mr. Reynold said, smiling at Penny.

"...I think we need to give Earth hope," Penny declared, almost surprised at her lofty goal, but it was met with smiles from the other two.

Their reactions now building her confidence, she continued, "Will... I've been meaning to ask you. I was able to replicate your skill back on campus, and I think I can learn more from it. Would you mind showing me another skill and letting me feel it?"

"Uh, yeah," Will blushed instantly at Penny's statement, and Penny's face turned to one of horror. "Your energy, of course!"

"I, uh, am going to take these people over the bridge. Will, you might not want to join much further. There's much joy but equal parts of fear and confusion. Let me take this from you. I'll let you two catch up more."

"Thanks, Steve," Will said, embracing Mr. Reynold warmly before Mr. Reynold hurried to catch up with the former hostages as they approached the bridge line. "Maybe we can head to the river path away from the crowd?" Penny suggested.

"I'd like that," Will agreed as the two veered off the path and strolled the walkway. Penny delved deeper into the Games and previous events, trying to learn as much as possible during Will's remaining time. Penny pushed her bothered emotions to the back of her mind as she tried to support Will, knowing that she didn't want to add anything else for him to worry about as they made their way to a spot by the river.

"It might be good to start here?" Will suggested as he walked closer to the flowing river. "May I?" Will extended his hand to Penny, who eagerly took it. Their energies synchronized once more, and Penny was able to map Will's energy flows with her own as he began using his **Condense** skill on the rushing water near the path. Slowly at first, then more and more, the pressure against the water continued, and a thick sheet of ice began to form along the river top.

"Feel it?" Will asked, now looking at Penny, who had her eyes closed and was trying to mimic his form. Will wasn't able to intermingle his energy like Penny. Still, he could see and feel her subtle shift in energy signature across her body, moving a portion of her internal energy outward as she then looked to allow that energy to condense the elements around her. A second later, the water shifted into a thin sheet of ice before the heavy flow of the Truckee River pushed it away.

"You did it," Will smiled as Penny opened her eyes wide in excitement. She threw herself at Will and, without thinking, kissed him. Realizing again how socially inept she was, she pulled back only to be caught by Will, who pulled her in again and kissed her once more.

The moment was brief, but it was the first time Will felt true happiness since the beginning of the Games, since the death of his former teacher and friend, and since the unease and pressure of winning and leading Earth to success. He was just there, with a friend, enjoying himself, when a new idea rushed to him.

"Hey, Nexy, can you share energy signatures and visualization through Nexabot connections?" Will spoke aloud to let Penny hear his idea.

"*Oh, darling. Of course. Especially for this sweet angel here. Send me a mental idea of the scenario, and I can share it through touch.*"

Will and Penny exchanged smiles, recognizing the potential for Penny's talent to flourish. Will maintained his touch on Penny's hand, imparting images and ideas of his team and all the other heroes they had encountered. He offered every detail he could to enable Penny to analyze and emulate. A gentle smile graced Will's face as Will wondered if this had been Mr. Williams' underlying intention during the last intermission and his urge for Will to comprehend energy signatures more deeply.

Penny's heart was beating faster than ever over the moment she shared with Will and the surge of visions now entering her head. Thankfully, Nex would store and replay these for her later, but she couldn't wait to start studying.

"Thank you," Penny smiled as a voice broke through team communications.

"Team, we are now near the last void. We are feeling quite a bit of energy on the other side. It's best if we close this down in the next five minutes," James stated, intent on allowing everyone to say their goodbyes.

"Penny, can I ask you a favor?" Will asked before they had to go.

"Of course," Penny answered, immediately shifting all focus back to Will.

"My Mom and brother... I haven't heard anything from them since the start of these Games."

"Yes," Penny responded without letting Will finish his question.

Will let out a short chuckle and smile. "I figured you would say that. Luck and Tech have already agreed to it, but I was hoping to have you and Mr. Reynold join them. I trust Luck, but having you with them would make me feel better."

"How would you feel about joining a new hero team?"

△△△

MISSION ACCOMPLISHED!

The Organism has been effectively removed from the City of Reno, with all three void entrances securely closed and the minimum rescue quota for hostages achieved.

Total Hostages Rescued: 99

△△△

Mighty Eagles (Cohort 13)

Level Four Results:

Total Team Points: **903**

Total Max Active Views: **27.3B**

Earth Rank: **34 of 14,876**

99.8th Percentile

EPILOGUE
SYSTEM GAMES HEADQUARTERS

"Shukar, reassure me that the situation is more promising than the uproar I'm hearing from the committee. I've received more calls about Earth than all other planets in the galaxy combined."

"I'm sorry, sir, but it's not. It has come to light that Morgrax is the legitimate successor to the Astral Dominion. His claim that this was all in good fun was accurate. Rumor has it that this wasn't a test but an expectancy, and failure jeopardizes the future of the Dominion itself."

"So, in addition to the calls questioning why the CNC didn't prevent this rebel group from actively participating in the Games, we now have to be concerned about the Dominion taking unauthorized actions against the Games themselves."

"It appears so. I see no deceleration in Fury's growth, although she's still significantly behind Morgrax. It seems the Prince will be able to establish contact with other Dominion members soon, setting the stage for a showdown of immense power."

"It appears destiny has thrust power together. In my tenure, I've never witnessed a planet combat both insurgent life and a hostile takeover in the same Games."

Viggo continued, "Do we have additional information on their coach?"

"With the System's restrictions on intermission visibility, our knowledge is limited to what the hero, Brick, has disclosed. He has been supporting the Games for numerous seasons, but his backstory and power level remain enigmatic within our systems. His coaching history has had mixed results but with a few unexpected teams."

"Unexpected?" Viggo scoffed. "At this point, I think I'm ready for anything. Please elaborate."

"Well, under the tutelage of Coach Williams, two teams have seen victory in the Quantum Games."

"Yes, those are long odds, but how is that unexpected at this stage?"

"I'm unsure how to phrase this, but both teams have now lost contact with the CNC."

"Do you mean they chose not to participate in the Celestial Ascendency? That's not unprecedented..." Viggo questioned his assistant.

"No, sir... both teams have vanished from existence."

ΔΔΔ

EARTH - POST - LEVEL FOUR

"Are you certain this will work?" Penny questioned Luck as she and Mr. Reynold occupied a deserted news station outside downtown Reno.

"If we're to work as a team, you must understand that Tech always speaks the absolute truth. Never ask him if your outfit looks good or if your hair is okay. He'll deliver the hard news. In this instance, when Tech says he can build an outbound radio channel, he'll make it happen."

"Standby. We're close," Tech declared from behind a maze of wires and connections spanning various systems. The three other new teammates exchanged glances, but Mr. Reynold and Luck seemed to communicate more effectively through mere eye contact.

"Penny, this is your moment," Luck asserted, receiving a confirming nod from Mr. Reynold.

"What?" Penny retorted. "I can't do this. You both are far

more qualified."

Luck chuckled. "Wait, you mean a felon and a junior college guidance counselor?"

"Athletic director... wait, never mind that. What's important is that this needs to be you, Penny. If you can't see that yet, take our word for it."

"But..." Penny began, only to be cut off by Luck.

"No buts. Do you want Tech over there to do it, or you? Embrace it, have faith in yourself, and let your voice be heard."

Penny remained silent but gradually agreed to do it. She slowly approached the anchor desk, where Tech had positioned a single microphone. Tech could set up a video feed, but the challenge wasn't in the outbound success but the scarcity of receivers capable of disseminating this message worldwide. It had to be voice—voice over a radio—Penny's voice.

Seated at the desk, she waited for Tech to signal that he was ready for her speech. Yes, she had crafted it with Will's input but hadn't anticipated delivering it until now. It didn't matter; she was there and wouldn't allow herself to be the source of failure in her team's ambitious goals.

"Standby on three," Tech announced as a blinking red light flashed on the microphone. One blink, two blinks, three blinks, and the light turned green. She was now live, her voice broadcasting across millions of devices globally.

"Hello," Penny began in a soft voice, but Luck's loud cough adjusted her posture.

> This is Penny Duplaine, broadcasting from Reno and sending a message to all willing to listen.
>
> Earth has transformed. Our world will never be the same. The sooner you accept this reality, the more likely Earth will prevail.
>
> Days ago, a barrier around our planet burst, enabling

quantum shifts in its molecular composition. Many people across our planet will now possess talents—talents that allow us to interact with the world in profound ways. This new talent is called 'building,' but how someone builds is based on their unique energy signature.

I am sharing this with you all because, with this integration, our world now faces unprecedented threats across our societies. Just as humans of our Earth have the power to interact at an atomic level, so do extraterrestrial powers across the known Cosmos. Yes, aliens are real. Life is abundant across space, and we are lagging. Behind in technology and talent to shift and protect our world.

We do have hope. Many of our most talented heroes have chosen to participate in the Quantum Games tournament. These Games are ten distinct levels in which our heroes are tested for the right to be named a Champion within the Galaxy. Many of you may have seen or met these heroes just as I have. They are often sent back to our planet to help known incursions to test themselves, both in protecting our home and gaining strength in 'building.'

The purpose of my messages is simple. There is hope. There are heroes, but Earth is not safe. For those in the Reno area, downtown Reno is cleared of all hostiles and will be known as a secure point for those in need. This will be the first of many as we look to rebuild our world from the chaos that reigns today.

I will be broadcasting on this frequency daily until we have a better communication path. It is in our best interest to share and spread information to help others. Should you have the talent to build and defend our world... do it.

Once again, this is Penny Duplaine, an extended team member of the Mighty Eagles, reporting from the Crow's Nest.

Stay informed and stay safe.

POST AUTHOR NOTE

Thank you for reading book one of The Quantum Games! I hope you had as much fun reading it as I had writing it for you all! The Quantum Games will continue with book two, targeting the New Year 2025! To keep up to date on my progress, please follow me on the sites below. Lastly, if you enjoyed this book, please review it and share it with your community or someone you believe would enjoy it. The LitRPG community is small but growing! Help build and support fellow new authors in the genre like myself.

Robably.com

Patreon

https://www.patreon.com/TheQuantumGames

RoyalRoad

https://www.royalroad.com/fiction/83369/the-quantum-games

Instagram

https://www.instagram.com/robablywriting/

Finally, if you're looking to join a vibrant community of LitRPG and Progression Fantasy enthusiasts, I highly recommend checking out the following Facebook groups.

Facebook Groups:

LitRPG Books (https://www.facebook.com/groups/LitRPG.books)

LitRPG (https://www.facebook.com/groups/litrpgs)

Progression Fiction Addicts (Fantasy/Sci-Fi/Gamelit/litRPG/Cultivation) (https://www.facebook.com/groups/progressionfictionaddicts)

LitRPG Forum (https://www.facebook.com/groups/litrpgforum)

ACKNOWLEDGEMENT

To Linda Valerius, my mom,

Thank you for always being my very first reader! Your enthusiasm and support, though biased, have been invaluable. I love having a fellow LitRPG lover in the family.

To Matt and Erik Edgington,

Thank you for our book club, "Book Nerds." Without your passion and energy for the progression and LitRPG genre, The Quantum Games would have never seen the light of day.

To Terry Rudd Smith,

Thank you for your wonderful editing and for being a first reader. I truly appreciate your willingness to jump right in and provide candid feedback!

To Annie Neudorfer and her sons, Drew and Caleb,

Thank you for your incredible support and editing throughout the process. I truly appreciate your dedication and look forward to future editing sessions with the family!

To Tarvis K'mara and others on RoyalRoad,

Thank you for supporting every unedited chapter I've written. Your positive encouragement and love for the book and its characters really pushed me to continue writing.

ABOUT THE AUTHOR

Rob Valerius (Robably)

Hailing from Carson City, Nevada, my journey has led me to the lively city of Reno. Here, my incredible wife and two wonderful daughters support my part-time writing pursuits, which I dive into after tucking the girls into bed. I am deeply moved by books that evoke strong emotions, and recently, I've developed a passion for LitRPG and progression fantasy novels.

When I'm not immersed in writing or being a dad, I enjoy being a Dungeon Master in Dungeons & Dragons sessions. Guiding my heroes through treacherous adventures and watching their inventive solutions brings me immense joy. Writing fiction allows me to share stories exactly as I envision them—a stark contrast to D&D, where my players often creatively dismantle my meticulously planned campaigns.

△△△

Congratulations, true fan! If you've made it this far, you now have the exclusive opportunity to contribute to future books! If you enjoyed the puns in this book and have some creative ideas of your own, I'd love to hear them. Your submissions can be based on hero names, scenarios, or any themes related to the book. If I select your pun, it will be featured in a future book with a special dedication to you!

You can submit your ideas through any of my platforms: Robably.com, Instagram DM (make sure to follow first!), Patreon, Royal Road, or via good old-fashioned email at support@robably.com.

Thanks,

Robably Out.

Made in the USA
Middletown, DE
03 December 2024